Enjoy

July '09

# Dart

Phil Rustad

authorHOUSE®

AuthorHouse™
1663 Liberty Drive
Bloomington, IN 47403
www.authorhouse.com
Phone: 1-800-839-8640

First published by AuthorHouse 5/19/2009

ISBN: 978-1-4389-5436-3 (sc)
ISBN: 978-1-4389-5437-0 (hc)

Library of Congress Control Number: 2009904760

Printed in the United States of America
Bloomington, Indiana

This book is printed on acid-free paper.

# Prologue
**Boom! Boom! Boom!**

The sound of gunshots indoors is startling, even for someone familiar with the sound—much sharper, louder, and more immobilizing than portrayed on TV. The shots were coming from the branch bank in the front lobby of the big-box grocery store. Ben Harris was in the back of the store, picking up a forgotten loaf of bread when he heard the rapid gunfire. Like the warriors he'd worked with for much of his career, he rushed toward the sound of fire—the front of the store where he'd left his wife in the checkout line. As he ran he heard many more shots. He ran back to the checkout lane where Anne was standing in line. He got there in time to see her slumping to the floor, her back against the magazine rack. He looked up in time to see the two hooded figures running from the bank branch office in the front of the store. He only saw their backs as they fled the building.

Turning back to his wife, he looked into her eyes and felt her confusion, pain, and fear. Her grip on his hand softened—as her life quickly faded.

# Chapter 1

## Eighteen Months Later, Mid-April
## Hennepin County Government Center, Minneapolis

Like most Midwestern cities, Minneapolis is home to its own blend of eclectic and architecturally unique buildings. The downtown is littered with mid-twentieth-century skyscrapers mixed into the older stone department stores and office buildings. Toward the end of the century, the designers began forsaking chrome and glass and started drifting back to natural materials. The Hennepin County Government Center on South Sixth Street was one of these. It's set across a street and plaza from the old city hall building, which still holds the city government and the Minneapolis Police Department. The older building was put up in the early 1890s and is made from roughly hewn, rust-colored granite that had been hauled in by horse-drawn wagons from western Minnesota. There is a stark contrast between the city building and the county building. The newer one was constructed from the same stone, but the stone is cut flat and square. The glass is minimal, with only a few narrow windows. The building also has the dubious distinction of having had to glass off its interior balconies to stop the frequent suicides that were occurring. From the ends, the window pattern makes it look like a big H.

There is a plaza between the north side of the Hennepin County Government Center and the older city hall building, which looks very out of place sitting across from light-rail tracks that run down Fifth Street. About half a city block in area, the plaza acts as a buffer between the old and new. It has old-London-style street lights ringing a circular fountain in the center. The lights, which recall a Dickens novel, have modern features—round white globes with modern supports—a lighted bridge between the old and new. Ben Harris walked out through the revolving doors from the Government Center into this plaza.

He was dazed and disillusioned. After 15 months waiting for the trial to begin and three and a half months of the trial, it was over. And the verdict was stunning. He had left the sixth-floor courtroom and walked down the hall to the elevators. The press that had been allowed into the courtroom for the verdict pronouncement had the Midwestern courtesy to leave him alone, at least until he got downstairs. He rode the elevator down, grateful to have grabbed an empty one. On ground floor he walked out past the security point into the spotlights. The media had regrouped here, at the border of courtesy.

The talking heads and cameramen had received the verdict by cell phone from their counterparts upstairs and were swarming with questions:

"Mr. Harris—what's your response to the verdict?"

"Do you think justice was served?"

"How do you feel about the verdict?—Ben—Ben!"

He didn't hear them. His senses were overloaded and it was all he could do to walk away. "How could this have happened," he thought over and over, "This is America—this is Minnesota—not some third-world country where you couldn't trust the system. This wasn't even California, where you could get away with murder if you had enough money and an incompetent DA's office. How could this happen here?" He walked away in a daze, oblivious to the chattering of the flock of vultures, who were circling to scavenge the nine seconds of misery video that would lead the evening news. He strode across the indoor courtyard and walked the escalator down to the ground floor.

He walked out of the Hennepin County Courthouse, out the entrance flanked by three-foot-high planters full of green plants. Ben Harris looked skyward, squinting in the strong April sun. He was witnessing spring in full force—returning the city to its green summer glory—but his mental focus was blurred. He was still in shock over the verdict. *Both* of the accused bank robbers had been acquitted on *all* charges!

Ben groped for some intellectual—logical—sense in the outcome: The famous defense attorney had turned the trial into a circus—for some reason the judge had denied the prosecution's attempts to introduce important evidence—and the publicity had turned the defendants into celebrities.

The reading of the verdict had been greeted with both boos and cheers—representing varying views of social justice and personal responsibility. As he walked across the plaza, Ben allowed disillusionment to settle in. He had always believed in the American justice system. He knew, in a subliminal way, that the guilty occasionally got off and that was to make sure that the innocent were not convicted. He'd seen the news stories all of his life and knew that the system was usually the best on the planet.

But in recent time it seemed to Ben as if, especially for the rich and famous, the balance of justice had tipped toward impunity for the obviously guilty. He fumed at how they sometimes even made money off it afterward. Celebrities did it all the time. And non-celebrities occasionally did too, if they had a worthy cause or the right connections. It seemed to Ben that only the common, run-of-the-mill perpetrator was likely to be convicted.

He looked skyward in search of an answer, as if asking for some kind of guidance. But he knew in his heart that any almighty guidance wouldn't be the message he wanted to hear. His heart and soul burned for revenge. If Anne was to get any justice—he would have to find it for her. The system had let her down—for all the wrong reasons. It had failed due to greed, selfishness, pride, lust for power and fame, and incompetence. The people he'd trusted to provide an answer for his pain and her loss had failed. Now he'd have to place the responsibility.

"But who should I hold responsible?—that would take some thought. And what is justice?—that would take some thought too," he reasoned. He would take his time—he would find the answers. A light-rail train rolled through the station on Fifth Street. It had a full-body billboard graphic advertising that depicted a blue sky and cool green waters at some beach, enticing the reader to "Take a Vacation on Northwest Airlines."

"A vacation—that sounds like a good idea," Ben thought.

# Chapter 2

The air was as dark and thick as it could be. The remnants of the early evening's thunderstorms lingered on a moonless Minneapolis night. Despite the the weather, there was a party going late this evening. As the rain stopped the revelers had spilled out onto the front lawn of the house on North Hamilton Avenue and they paid no attention as the dark sedan rolled up the street. Tyrone Hill, one of the two suspects from the bank robbery, was celebrating, as he had on many nights since the acquittal. Life was good for Tyrone.

He was 20 years old and determined to not waste any time on his youth. Born to activist parents in Minneapolis, somehow he'd missed their noble dedication to the 1960s causes of the Civil Rights Movement, advocating for the poor and the more recent neighborhood-based initiatives. Of course, his parents' involvement in those causes didn't necessarily mean that Tyrone grew up poor. They had college degrees and were self supported throughout their careers as social activists. Tyrone was raised by well-meaning parents in an un-well community. As a result, he wound up involved in gangs, entranced by the dark side of hip-hop culture. When it came time to find his own way in the world, he chose the easy road of living off friends, dealing drugs, and murderous armed robbery.

His brush with criminal justice hadn't slowed him down. His parent's friends came to the rescue. He and his co-perpetrator had the most effective defense that money could buy. He was released on bail, showed up for the court dates, and eventually walked. Now he had time to celebrate his freedom and think about what was next. For tonight, anyway, he hoped that next was the 17-year-old girl he was talking to. She was awed by his celebrity and was showing all the signs of willingness to take personal responsibility for his pleasure. The only questions left were when and where.

They slipped around the back of the house where she quickly satisfied his physical need. As he walked back to the front of the house, he was feeling the high of a male in his prime—strong, invulnerable, and in control. Nothing could change that. He was the ruler of all he surveyed, even if it was just one block of North Minneapolis.

The Shooter saw Tyrone as he returned to the front yard and took his foot off the brake. The car had been rigged with a switch hidden under the dash that allowed the driver to turn off the brake lights so they wouldn't show while he sat waiting. He rolled the car down the street and prepared for the work at hand. He had an AR-15-type rifle, basically the same rifle used by the U.S. military since the 1960s, but a civilian model that wouldn't fire full automatic. That didn't matter to the Shooter—he was an expert. He could fire nearly as fast as the full auto version and, even more importantly tonight, he hit what he aimed at. The AR has a big following among shooters of all types. There are enough after-market accessories available to fill a van. This particular rifle had a lot of custom features, including a cushioned grip and Picatinny rail fore-stock, a 1,400-dollar scope and laser optics system, and a tuned-up trigger set. The Shooter could place three rounds in a space that you could cover with a nickel at 300 yards from a bench rest, but this shot wouldn't be stationary. He'd need the rifle's features and all of his skills for this shot.

The passenger-side window was open as the car approached. The Shooter had his earplugs in, prepared for the man-made thunder that was to come. He raised the rifle with is right hand on the fore-stock just ahead of the magazine and slowed the car as it approached the party. One house away, he took his left hand off the wheel, switching it to the pistol grip of the rifle, and let the car roll down the center of the street. He looked through the scope as he squeezed a pressure switch on the grip. A small red dot appeared on Tyrone's chest. Tyrone seemed to sense the dot and looked down at it in wonderment. He had just enough time to utter "what the—" before there were three loud closely spaced reports. Tyrone fell—dead.

# Chapter 3

**Monday, June 16th**
**Robbinsdale, a Suburb of Minneapolis**

"God!—how can the floor be so cold in the middle of the summer?" It was 5 a.m. and I was on the way to the bathroom. This mid-life thing is getting old in a hurry. It's common and normal, except for maybe all the guys talking about it—that's a symptom of the more open and sensitive Dr. Phil and Oprah age we're living in. I'll tell you—things are already as open and sensitive as I ever want to see them.

I was just drifting back off when the phone rang.

"Dan Neumann," I answered.

"Wake up, Danny boy."

"This better not be you Olson."

"Of course it's me. Who else has this number and would dare call you at this time of night—or morning, as it were?"

"I can't wait to ring your scrawny neck."

"Well, you're going to get the chance. I'm on my way to pick you up right now."

"This can't be that big a deal if you got the call," I said.

"It's just your everyday drive-by, except for one thing—the shooter, or shooters, we're not sure how many there were—used frangible ammunition. And the Chief said to wake you up and get you on it."

"You're sure?" Frangible ammo is special ammo used by SWAT teams and air marshals for situations where there is a concern about what's behind the target—things like other people and airplane windows. It's designed to stop at the first thing it hits.

"That's pretty out of character for gang bangers—they aren't going to spend any extra money just to protect bystanders from their bad aim," I yawned.

"You got that right, only this shooter doesn't have bad aim. Three hits right in the 10 ring—right on the number 10. That's why they're hoping you'll take an interest. It seems that you are the local expert on frangible. The guys upstairs want to know why someone would use it for this and where they'd get it."

"That's what I get for writing a book"—but *now* I was awake. A few years ago I wrote a book on ballistics and forensic ballistic investigation technique that has sort of become the bible for shooting investigation. The book wasn't a big money maker, but now I get to do seminars and consult on TV drama shows—basically vetting their scripts for what is plausible and what is just drama. They usually just go ahead and do what looks best on TV but it pays pretty well. So I'm retired, sort of. The MPD keeps me on the employment roll so I can still carry a shield and a gun nationally. I still do consulting work for police departments, especially locally, but I charge for it. I'd already answered all the late-night calls I wanted and was now only interested if it was something unusual.

I was already mulling it over—I had a pretty good idea why someone would use frangible. But that led to a lot of other questions—questions I didn't want to have to ask at five o'clock on an otherwise-lovely summer morning.

# Chapter 4

Detective Robert "don't-call-me-Bob" Olson picked me up at my home in Robbinsdale and we headed east to North Minneapolis. The address was in a neighborhood where the long-time residents are fighting to keep the 'hoods under control. There is a community watch group, but it's mostly older people and they don't stay up all night. A local radio personality and philosopher once said that nothing good happens between one and five o'clock in the morning, and he's right. Just listen to your local news and you'll find that's when the bad guys are out.

Olson and I rolled into the crime scene while the MPD Crime Lab guys were still there. The sun was already up at 5:45 a.m. on a wonderful mid-June morning. The forecast was for heat, humidity, and threatening weather, but for now it was superb—temp in the mid-70s and dry. It almost made the early phone call worth it, but not quite.

The front yard of the house looked like a thousand others in North Minneapolis, except for the crime scene tape and the crowd of vehicles with flashing lights. There were wilted hostas around the foundation, indicating that someone had once cared for the home. The tough little perennials—the unofficial state perennial—could stand almost any lack of care, but these were showing it. The yard showed a need for watering, in spite of the recent rain, though the dandelions were thriving. In the back yard I saw rhubarb gone wild from lack of harvesting. Apparently the current tenants didn't make jam or pies.

The body had been hauled off by the coroner and I knew her office would be our next stop, but I wanted to see the crime scene myself. I believe that you can pick up little details and insights that would invariably be left out of the reports. The crime scene will talk to you if you open yourself to it. It's a sense that you can only get by being there. Photos and diagrams just won't cut it. My first rule in criminal investigation is the same as the first rule of life—Show up.

I asked the responding officers for a quick rundown on what happened. They told me that the witnesses had been processed and released. Typical of these incidents, no one knew anything, no one had seen anything, and no one knew why anyone would like to pop poor Tyrone. He was a good kid and a good neighbor. It figures. I've been to crime scenes where it turned out that the guy was growing half an acre of grass in the basement and garage, was hauling in dirt and fertilizer by the truck load, was almost never there except to meet other people, and was using so much electricity that the transformer on the pole in the back yard glowed at night and the neighbors still hadn't noticed anything out of the ordinary.

Anyway, I returned to the front of the house to where the body had been. There hadn't been much blood, indicating Tyrone had checked out quick. The grass was trampled and in need of cutting and fertilizer. Olson guided me over to the techs that were still on scene.

"What do you have so far?" I asked.

"Actually, not much," a tech replied. "As far as trace, there's nothing here except the vic and the other party goers. There's nothing in the street in terms of tire tracks and no shell casings."

"So you think the gun was inside the car."

"Must have been—we know it was a .223 caliber or 5.56 mm and that means semi-auto or automatic rifle fire."

"Please don't tell me full auto. I really don't need that."

"Well, I don't know, but the witnesses said the shots came pretty fast. Either full auto or someone who knew what they were doing."

Olson chimed in "They knew what they were doing all right. I saw the body and you could cover all three hits with a quarter."

"Great," I said with as much sarcasm as I could muster, "a drive-by sniper. This is what I live for. Olson, you're going to pay for this." I was already thinking that this shooter knew his stuff. It was only about thirty yards, but from a moving car. "Okay—this was someone who knew how to shoot. He was even better than good if he was alone and doing the driving." I had gone into thinking-out-loud mode—it happens a lot. "No, that couldn't be, there had to be two people in the car."

"Well it won't be me paying for it, but I figured you'd take the bait," Olson said.

I had one more thought. "Which way was the car going?"

Olson didn't know. We hunted down one of the officers who had been taking statements. He didn't know either. A quick round of the other officers finally produced an answer.

"Yeah, I kind of thought you'd want to know about that. One witness, a Shirley Jones," he said consulting his notes, "a guest at the party, said she was sure that she saw the car come from the north, slow, the shots came and the car rolled off to the south. She said that it didn't speed away or anything—just sped up a little after the shots and went away."

"Is she still here?" I asked.

The cop looked around and saw her over by the cars. "Yeah, that's her right over there."

I walked over and introduced myself. "Shirley, you told the other officer that you saw the car the shots came from, right?"

"Yeah, I did. Dude rolled right down the street to 'bout here." We walked over to a point in the street. "Right here, this is where they shot Tyrone."

Actually, this was where the shots came from, not where Tyrone was shot, but I knew what she meant. "You said *they*—was there more than one person in the car?"

"There musta been. The gun was shootin' right out the window at Tyrone."

I looked at the street. The car would have been coming with the passenger side to the party house. "Did you notice whether the shots came from the front seat or the back?"

"They come out the front window, just like I told that cop."

That was good news. In order to come from the front, the shooter, who would have been the front seat passenger, must have stuck the rifle out the window. There would be shell casings. I looked at the cop with me and asked, "What about shell casings—anyone find any?"

"No, and we really looked. There were three rounds fired and no cartridge casings."

That didn't square. There was only one way a rifle could have been fired from the front seat of that car and not eject the shell casings out onto the street. That was if the driver had been the shooter. That took a difficult shot to the expert level. Good-freaking-grief! "Shirley, could you see the gun—was it sticking out the window?"

"No, when the gun went off the whole inside of the car lit up, you know, like someone turned the lights on."

"Did you get a look at the driver?"

"Yeah, he was real dark, like he had a hat on and gloves and stuff—pretty stupid for the middle of summer."

Right, stupid unless you don't want to be seen. "Anything else you can remember—was it a man or a woman, black or white, anything like that?"

"No, he was dark and when the gun went off it was just like a flash. I couldn't tell, but I think it was one of those punks from east Lyndale. They always be after Tyrone. Anyway, it coulda been one of their cars."

"Why do you say that?"

"They're always driving big cars like that. I don't know what kind it was, a Gran Vic or a Caddy—or something. Anyway, who else would want to do poor Tyrone?"

Good question. On the other hand, if the driver had been the shooter and had shot through the passenger window from the driver's seat, that tells me something very special about him. I thanked Shirley and she returned to the impaired party-goers who were lingering in shock.

Olson nodded and said, "Oh, and you can rule out the most likely suspect."

"Yeah, who's that?"

"You don't know who the dead guy was, do you?"

"The name kind of rings a bell, but—no."

"He was one of the two guys tried for the Plymouth grocery-store bank shooting—the two guys who were acquitted in April. I already checked and the husband of the woman who was killed, Ben Harris, was in Fargo last night."

"I don't recall from the coverage that he had any military background or was a big time hunter or anything, was he?"

"No, but you've got to look at the obvious to eliminate them," Olson chided.

"Yeah, I seem to recall that from crime investigation 101."

Before we could get out of there, the press cornered us. I know most of these people and they are usually reasonable. Today it was the standard questions on who, what, where, when, and why. Jane Vanderloo was a reporter with the Minneapolis paper and had been both a good reporter and occasionally a good source for me in the past. I slid away from the others to talk to her alone.

Jane smiled and nodded, "So—typical drive-by?"

"I'm not sure yet," I carefully answered, "could be nothing, but I'm going to have to look at some other possibilities."

That wasn't the answer she expected. Jane was interested. "What else is there to look at?" she asked, while batting her eyes at me. This was distracting but moderately effective. We had had a steamy relationship about ten years back. She was arguably in the top three on my list of best lovers on the planet. But that was long over and well done with. I'm amazed at how objective you can get when dealing with someone you'd had great sex with—who then dumped you.

"You know who this kid was and who his parents are. Don't tell me you haven't already started putting together some kind of human interest twist on this?"

"I don't know what you're talking about. All I have is one dead guy, whose parents happen to be neighborhood activists, and that doesn't really add much to the story. Maybe it's a human tragedy angle—how his parents worked so hard in the community and their only son winds up dead in a gang-related shooting."

I asked about the gang angle, "You think it's a gang deal?"

"Sure, unless it has something to do with that grocery store bank holdup that went wrong."

I'm not exactly sure how a bank holdup goes right, at least from my point of view. "There is that. But Olson says that the dead lady's husband was in Fargo last night, so he's out."

"You have any other person of interest?"

This kills me. "Person of Interest" is a term made up by the press to describe someone the cops like for a crime, but haven't arrested yet. To cops, after a crime, there are only three kinds of people: victims, witnesses, and suspects. It's pretty clear who the victims are and somewhat clear who the witnesses are. Everyone else is a suspect. And some people fall into more than one category.

"No other person of interest at this time," I replied. She said thanks and headed off to find someone more interesting to talk to. At least with her, you don't have the cameras in your face looking for a nine-second moment.

"So," I asked Olson, "What do we have?"

"Before I tell you what we have, I'll tell you what we don't have. We've got virtually no trace—no blood other than the victim's—no shell casings, even though the shooter should have had to stick the rifle out the window—no other trace from the shooter—he was in the car—no tire tracks—five different descriptions of a car that fits half the cars in the state—a flock of witnesses who say that anywhere from one to ten shots were fired—and no physical contact with the perp that would leave anything like fibers, hairs, or anything else that would yield DNA. What we *have* got is one dead guy with three rounds expended. The most probable doer was 200 miles away last night and we don't know anything about him other than he might have a motive."

There was one more thing that Olson didn't list—I thought, "The shooter must be left handed."

# Chapter 5

We got into Olson's standard, black Ford POS, which is cop for "Police Officer Special" or "Piece of Shit," depending upon your point of view, and headed for the morgue. I asked him if he thought the Twins had a shot this year.

"Actually, better than most years. I don't know how they do it, but they keep coming up with young talent. If they had any middle relief, they'd be leading the division."

"You're right about that bullpen. Neshek goes down and it's a scramble. If they can get seven innings out of a starter and go to the eighth with a lead, they have a pretty good chance to win," I agreed.

Olson followed up with the usual statistics. He's a fountain of Twins information once you get him started, which I do to take my mind off of a case sometimes.

"You know that Nathan has the best record as a closer for the last three years and the second-highest lifetime save percentage for any closer with more than 200 opportunities?"

"I knew he was good, but not that good."

"That's why I always take him in my fantasy league. Everyone wants Rivera or Issringhausen but Nathan's better."

As we closed in on the morgue, I reviewed everything out loud.

"So, what we have is a dead guy who was just sprung on a bank robbery and murder charge. He has any other enemies?"

"Not that we know of," Olson replied. "But these guys all have some history. Maybe gang related, maybe drugs, maybe a pissed-off girlfriend, maybe a pissed-off girlfriend's new boyfriend or brother—who knows? Personally, I'm going with the gang thing."

"Besides what Shirley said," I asked, "why gangs?"

"He has the history. Of course, during the trial the defense stressed his disengagement from the gangs as part of why he was such an upstanding individual. But I think he was still in."

"That's right—you were on that investigation weren't you?"

"Just the Minneapolis part—the stickup and shooting took place in Plymouth."

"But you were at the trial?"

"Almost every day—I couldn't wait to get those two. They'd been giving me headaches for years."

"I guess you know that makes you a suspect," I teased.

"Yeah, but I've got a great alibi. I was on duty in the office—signed in and everything. You can take me off the list right now."

"I don't think you were really on it—just giving you the needle. What else do you have on this Harris guy?"

"Interesting individual—worked in local manufacturing for all his professional life, some kind of engineer. Not really sure where he worked but that wasn't germane in the trial. I'd say mid 50s, 6 feet tall, pretty good shape but not a workout freak or a runner—sort of Joe Average. Seemed pretty smart, but you'd expect that of an engineer. He didn't get very emotional at the trial—kind of typical, Minnesota Scandinavian stoic."

"Tell me about the trial. Anything interesting or that might point us in the right direction?"

"Well, I'll tell you, it was a circus. First off, it was Judge Mitchell's last trial. She was all set to retire and delayed leaving when this came along. I guess it was her last chance to 'right a grievous wrong'." Olson quoted the judge, known for her views on social injustice and what she believed to be the real cause of all crime involving minorities. "So she starts off by excluding all the ballistic evidence and the provenance of the four weapons that were found in the suspect's possession on technicalities. Then she threw out all evidence that the perps were even at the scene at the grocery store based on the idea that the scene was contaminated. It was pretty screwed up when the Hennepin County Crime Lab people got there due to all the people at the store and that there were EMTs all over the place taking care of the four other people who were hit. I guess she just wanted to be sure that these two weren't among what she called "the legions of innocents unjustly incarcerated by our seriously flawed system.""

I was more than familiar with Judge Amy Mitchell's concept of justice. I'd been in front of her more than once in my career. The key with her was jury selection. You had to have one that saw through her honor's blatant attempts to free every non-white suspect whose household income was less than $100,000 per year. It wasn't racial—it was economic. She was more than happy to lock up minorities who made big money.

"That's right, there were four other people hit. What did these guys do, just open up on everyone?"

"Um—no. They each had two handguns—a mixture of brands 9-mm brands, but all of them turned out to have been stolen. While Cirrus O'Leary-Sample was right in the middle of getting the teller to give them the dough,

Tyrone just pulled his two guns and started blazing away. As far as we can tell, he wasn't really aiming at anything or anybody—just making noise."

"And he managed to hit five people?" I couldn't help but think of that police dashboard video tape you could see about once a month on one of those police reality TV shows. You know, the one where two cops are trying to arrest two brothers driving a white Suburban—I think it was in Ohio—and the two brothers jumped out of the car, pistols drawn, and opened up. The four squared off and shot it out at a distance of about 8 feet—total rounds fired was something like 40 or 50 and nobody hit. They didn't even hit the freakin' Suburban. It was amazing.

"No, he got some help from O'Leary on that. When Tyrone started shooting, O'Leary thought something had gone bad so he pulled and started shooting too. Between them they hit five people. Nobody else was hit very bad, except one pregnant gal who was hit in the belly and lost the kid. We don't really know which one was using which gun because we have no prints off the guns and the witnesses couldn't tell a Glock from a 1911 from a revolver. Both of them had residue on their hands and the witnesses said both had been shooting."

"Yeah, I know how hard it is to get prints off a gun. What the hell kind of name is Cirrus O'Leary-Sample?"

"His parents are some kind of latent hippies who named their kids some pretty stupid names. He's got a sister named Andromeda. Anyway, his folks wandered their way through the late '70s, and then got involved with some people in the '80s who had some good ideas. They wound up hitting it big in the dot com surge in the '90s, but pretty much blew it all in the last 10 years. They've spent the last couple years trying to recapture a little income from the old days. How this hit Cirrus is that he was raised by affluent hippies who professed opposition to everything that made them money—so when the money ran out, they were right there to preach against society again. This left the kids pretty messed up. Cirrus turned into a hip hop rap fan—decided he was destined to join a gang and become the next great white rapper. The daughter, Andromeda, is in a convent considering marrying Jesus Christ."

I nodded, "Anything on the security cameras?"

"Of course not—there were cameras that were on but the tape was unusable due to bad quality. It's an old system that still uses tape instead of digital recording. The tapes hadn't been changed in years—just reused."

"That figures. After all, you can't be spending $20 on new video tapes every six months or so. What's with these companies? They install a couple-grand worth of surveillance equipment then don't maintain it—what's the use?" I pondered that for moment and asked, "So you're sure Tyrone did it?"

"Oh, yeah—him and that psycho Cirrus. But by the time the out-of-town hired-gun defense lawyer got done with that quack county attorney's newest and youngest prosecutor there was nothing left for a jury to consider. All the hard evidence was not allowed and the circumstantial just didn't have the teeth for first-degree armed robbery that resulted in a homicide. The jury let them both walk."

"Didn't the DA ask for lesser charges?"

"Only Second Degree Intentional and the jury couldn't make that fly either. Oh—there was a weapons charge. Six months suspended."

"What was he thinking?" The DA would normally have asked for everything down to jaywalking on a case like this.

"Well, as you know, he is up for re-election and I guess he figured it was in the bag. It would have looked good on the election campaign too—cleaning up the suburbs for the voters."

"So—what was this Harris guy's reaction to that?"

"You know, I watched him throughout the trial. Here was a guy whose whole life had been shattered by this and he took it pretty well. She was his whole life—no kids—no other family. He was Minnesota stoic. He wasn't going to be called as a witness since he didn't see anything, so he was allowed to attend the trial. He could see where it was going—everyone could—but he just sat and watched. After the verdict, I saw him leaving the courthouse and the press was on him like white on rice. He ignored 'em—just walked out into the sun and strolled away. But, like I said, he was in Fargo last night."

# Chapter 6

We arrived at the morgue and went inside to view the mortal remains of one Tyrone Hill. I grabbed a cup of coffee on the way down to the autopsy room. I've seen enough dead bodies that it doesn't put me off my feed. Although I still get pretty uncomfortable if the victims are little kids. You never get used to that.

The medical examiner was already into the procedure when we walked in. Another investigator from the crime lab was there to maintain chain of custody if anything was found that would be used in the investigation. They'd already drawn blood for toxicology screening. It would be interesting to find out what Tyrone had in him before he went down.

I greeted the ME, a woman I'd known for years and had contemplated dating for a while. She was cute, smart as a whip, and had a reputation of being a fun-loving kind of woman, if you know what I mean. But it just never happened. I don't know, maybe it was that I lost some of my interest after I saw her practicing with an MP-5 submachine gun at the range. She was as good with that as she was with a scalpel and it sort of turned me on and off at the same time. I mean—I consider myself a modern, sensitive caring kind of guy—her proficiency with fully automatic weapons shouldn't bother me, should it? I don't know. I've dated women who could shoot before—women who didn't have anywhere near her looks and smarts. Anyway—I digress—again.

I also introduced myself to the crime scene investigator, a new kid just out of school. Departments were getting a lot of applications for these positions now, with all the TV shows making it look like that a glamorous crime-solving life. The idea of working in a nice clean lab—with the latest, and in many cases, not-yet–invented lab equipment and a bunch of co-workers who could double as body models—was very appealing. I mean, really, who wouldn't want to be able to stop by a crime scene, take a few photos, pick up some trace blood and other fascinating stuff, head back to the office to squeeze a confession out of a child molester, and have a murder solved before dinner. Never mind the fact that DNA analysis still takes weeks—you can't get prints off half the stuff they do on TV and most real-life bad guys get lawyered-up and stop talking before you get back from the men's room. In fact, the CSIs still solved a lot of crimes from a technical point of view, but I'd never seen one with a gun in his or her hand. They didn't go rushing into potential danger like they do on TV. After all, that's what you have the SWAT team for.

"Before I show you the inside, you might want to take a look at the entrance wounds," the ME said with typical detachment. She had saved the skin from the area where the bullets struck— "Nothing but net," she added.

I cringed a little at her basketball metaphor. I knew she was referring to the accuracy of the shots, but it was a little cold even coming from her. I mean, here is this great looking intelligent woman who, I was sure, could throw a hell of a roll in the hay, commenting about technical skill in what was basically an assassination. Maybe I should ask her out? She was slim and tall, for a woman, wearing dark maroon scrubs that set off her auburn hair, and with a remarkable anatomy all her own. Anyway, I took a look and, just as Olson had said, you could cover all three entry wounds with a quarter. I do a lot of shooting, usually 15,000 rounds a year or more. So I knew that it would be difficult at best to get three shots like that from a moving car. The distance wasn't that great, only about 30 yards, but a tight group like this would be good shooting at 30 yards at the range, shooting off-hand standing still. Of course, a good marksman with a good rifle could put three under a dime at 30 yards shooting from a rest.

"Yeah, real nice work—what about the ammo?" That's what I'd really come to check out.

"Got some if it right here. I'll have to dig around some to find it all." She showed me a tray with about 20 bullet fragments in it. "Really did a number on his insides. With the placement of the shots, I'd say Tyrone was dead before he hit the ground—pretty much shredded his heart."

I looked at the fragments and knew immediately that it was frangible ammunition. It's my specialty. I'd been through the FBI's very extensive training on ballistic forensics and knew what was what when it came to exotic firearms and ammunition. I knew two things about his case: first, with multiple rounds recovered—there was virtually no chance of a ballistics match to a rifle barrel. If there had been only one shot, they could then piece the fragments back together like some kind of puzzle and would have a good chance to make a match, if they found a gun.

No—I knew that wasn't true either. Ballistics matching was of a spent bullet to a gun barrel, not to a particular gun. Gun barrels were interchangeable and the type of rifle I believed these bullets came from was very common with many sources. It would be easy for someone to have obtained replacement barrels and changed out the barrel used for this shooting, if he held on to the gun at all.

Second, I believed I was looking at the work of someone who also had extensive training in firearms. The level of skill in the shooting wasn't the only thing that told me that—there was no brass left behind.

A little explanation about ballistics might help here. "Brass" is what we call the spent shell casings. When people talk about bullets, they often are talking about the whole round or cartridge—that's what you buy at the store. What you load the gun with is not a bullet—it's a cartridge. The cartridge is made up of four parts—the casing, sometimes called the empty shell, which is usually a shiny brass tube that usually gets left behind—the primer is the little button you can see on the bottom of the cartridge—the propellant is the gunpowder inside the cartridge—and the bullet, which is the thing that comes flying out the end of the gun barrel.

If we could have recovered the casings, we'd have something to tie the crime to the gun itself. Changing the barrel wouldn't impact that. When a gun is fired, many things have to happen to make the bullet come flying out of the barrel. First, the firing pin strikes the primer. When it does that, it leaves a unique mark that we can tie to the individual firing pin. When the primer goes pop, it's kind of a little cap that starts the gun powder burning. When the gunpowder burns—so fast that it sounds like an explosion—it pushes the bullet out of the barrel.

But, as the laws of physics demand, for every action there is an equal and opposite reaction. Most people would call the reaction the kick or recoil of the gun. But that kick is caused by the cartridge casing slamming backward into something called a breech block. When that happens, any little scratches or imperfections in the block are transferred onto the bottom of the casing, further tying that cartridge to that firearm. Even if we couldn't get a ballistic match off the bullet fragments, we could tie the rifle to the scene if we had a casing. But no casings were found at the scene. The brass must have stayed in the car. Was that just a fluke or did the shooter arrange the shot so the brass would stay in the car? To figure this out, we had to know the origin of the weapon and the ammunition. For now the question was—*Why?* Why would a shooter go to the trouble and expense of finding and using this unusual type of ammo? I could only think of three real possibilities.

# Chapter 7

## Monday Morning, June 16th
## Moorhead, Minnesota

Ben Harris was attending to the day-to-day chores of living out of a motor home. His 40-foot Winnebago Journey had all the comforts of home, and one quality home didn't have—it moved.

Today was moving day. Ben had been grocery shopping and had stocked the big RV with everything necessary to live out of it for the next two weeks or so. He had plenty of food, dog food, water—bottled and in the supply tank—snacks for driving, full LP tanks, empty waste tanks. The diesel fuel tank, which supplied the engine and the generator, was full. He could now effectively drop off the grid for a while. Of course, that's not what he wanted, he needed to show up somewhere to make the time accountable. He had a way to do that, too.

He pulled out of the Moorhead, Minnesota, KOA Campground and turned west on the frontage road. He took his time on the gravel road every KOA camper had to endure to get back to the civilization of hard-surface road, only a mile or so away. When he got there, he went to the abandoned farm homestead he'd scouted out. It was a risk to leave the trailer there, but one he was willing to take. He didn't want the trailer to be seen at the campground—didn't want it noticed anywhere—but had to have it to haul his car around.

The impromptu storage site was only about 12 miles from the campground. He backed the RV in behind the old barn using the rear-looking TV camera and hooked up the trailer. Now he was ready for the road. He pulled back out onto the county road and headed south to pick up I-94. There, he turned for Fargo and points west. He had a long drive ahead of him.

The day took him through the vast extents of North Dakota. As most people who've never been there believe, it is flat. But it has its own beauty. The horizon is visible miles away. The air is clean and bright in the summer heat. The gentle roll of the terrain is just enough to require attention to the speedometer. He passed Jamestown, Bismarck, and Dickenson. He watched the scene change from the flat agricultural plains of northern Minnesota to the sugar beet and potato fields of eastern North Dakota to the badlands of the west. Teddy Roosevelt loved this country so much that he started the National Park system out here. North Dakota was about 350 miles east to west. As he drove he was reminded of what a professional acquaintance had said years ago. They were at a convention in Denver and Ben had invited him back to Minnesota to visit his lake place for some fishing. The friend had agreed and the weekend was planned. The friend, a man who lived in Massachusetts, with a common east-coast perspective, looked at a roadmap and assumed everything was less than a day's drive. He had looked at a Midwest regional map and seen that it was only a few inches from Denver to Northern Minnesota, so he rented a car in Denver for the trip. Two days later, he arrived at Ben's, exhausted, and thoroughly pissed off. The quick half-day drive had turned out to be around 1,200 miles.

With the one-hour time change, Ben made Montana for a late lunch. The RV could keep up with most of the traffic, around 5 over the posted limit of 75, but he was comfortable at the limit. He had no intention of attracting any law-enforcement attention on this trip. He and Anne had planned this trip for years but had never gotten around to it. A "Lap of the U.S." they had called it, with side trips to see friends and historical points along the way. Ben with his dog would be making the trip without Anne now, and he would be making some side trips they hadn't planned.

As he drove, his mind went back to the trial. He was consciously reliving it. He didn't want to, but this was better than not sleeping. He'd found that if he thought about it during the day, he could sleep. If he didn't, he'd dream about it. And the dreams were frightening, even compared to what he'd seen in real life. He'd see Anne there, alive, and not shot. He'd see the robbers without their hoods, laughing and taking aim, even though all the witnesses said that the gun fire was random, just shots going off in every direction. The worst was that he'd see himself running from the back of the store, armed, even though he didn't carry a gun. He would be running as fast as he could, but his feet were in mud—he couldn't get there in time. When he finally did, he'd shoot and miss. Over and over he'd miss from a few feet, even though he was an expert shot, or see his rounds go through the robbers without effect —all in slow motion. And then, when his gun was empty with its slide locked back, that's when Anne would be shot.

It was better to think about the trial during the day than re-live the crime at night.

# Chapter 8

**Minneapolis**

Olson and I were driving back to the Police Department and his office. The discussion centered on the case—motive, suspects, and why the frangible ammunition.

"I still wonder about that ammo," Olson said, "you're the expert. Throw me a bone here. Why would someone use that?"

"I only see three possible reasons. It could have been in the gun when it was stolen, assuming it was stolen, so we have to check all stolen and lost property reports involving AR-15-type guns. I'm already ruling out anything else that shoots that size ammo because the witnesses said the shots came so fast. A couple of them said there was only one shot and there's no way anyone could have cranked a bolt action gun that fast. That leaves ARs. We don't know if it was a rifle for sure, and there are pistols that shoot that caliber, but I don't think anyone could shoot that group with a pistol from a moving car.

"Second reason—the shooter had an uncommon regard for fellow human beings and didn't want to risk any misses penetrating nearby homes and taking out little Suzie while she was sleeping. As you know, this was the reason frangible ammo was invented. It has a lower muzzle velocity and breaks apart on impact with anything remotely hard surfaced to prevent thru penetration. The stuff was developed for SWAT teams who had to go into urban building environments after bad guys—they didn't want rounds going through the bad guys and through walls and hitting innocent bystanders. This assumes he was willing to take the time and effort and spend the extra money to locate and buy this type of ammo. This almost sounds plausible if you assume that our shooter is basically good hearted—someone who actually thought about these possibilities before dropping old Tyrone. For reason two to be correct, a gang banger would have these kinds of thoughts. I doubt that. I also don't think that our shooter had a good heart because he is such a good shot he didn't have to worry about misses. So that pretty much rules out this reason.

"Which brings us to—?"

"Third possible reason—the shooter knows that we can't get any ballistics evidence off frangible fragments. That's not very well known so I don't think it's the reason. The interesting fact about this type of rifle ammunition is that, when they hit a human body, the shape of the bullets makes them tumble.

This almost always causes the round to disintegrate, which also makes ballistic identification very difficult with plain old full metal jacket. I think that anyone who knows shooting like this guy does would know that he didn't need to go to frangible to prevent ballistic identification. He'd know it was nearly as hard with regular full metal jacket."

"So, which possibility do you like?" Olson asked.

"For now, I think we are looking for a stolen weapon that came complete with the ammo. We need to look for a gun that was taken from the home of someone who bought it for home defense and took the time to research ammunition. Then, they bought a lightweight AR-15, shot it a few times for familiarization, bought a few boxes of frangible, stuck the whole thing in a closet, and then forgot about it until the house was broken into. That's where this weapon came from."

# Chapter 9

**Tuesday, June 24th**
**On the Road in Utah**

Ben and his dog, Mikey, cruised down I-84 between Salt Lake City, and Provo, Utah. They had been on the road for almost two weeks and, including the weekend in Fargo and the quick four-day side trip Ben had taken alone, it was about time to resupply. The trip had taken them west all the way to Seattle, then down through Portland, Boise, and Twin Falls. It was close to dark and he wanted to get to another private campground soon. Shopping would have to wait until tomorrow.

He was using small privately-owned campgrounds on this lap of the western states. He'd correctly assumed that they would be less likely to have the formalities of a central login system. They wouldn't be tracking his moves and sending him emails informing him of great deals along the way. For this reason he also avoided the biggest chain camping supplier in the country, World of Camping, because he already knew of their marketing ability to know where you were.

Mikey was enjoying the trip. He got to ride for hours up on the front dash of the big Winnebago and watch the country go by. Ben didn't think he minded too much that he had had to leave him with some old friends in Seattle during his side trip—a small but reasonable risk. He told his friends that he was going hunting in the mountains, a statement that was true, and asked them to watch Mikey for him. This friend had a lot of secrets and knew how to keep them.

Mikey was the third Shetland Sheepdog Ben and Anne had owned. Like the first two, he was named for a Minnesota Twins player. The first two, Kirby and Jack, had been Blue Merles and had shown all the great Sheltie characteristics. The only exception to this was that Kirby, like his namesake, had died young. At only nine years he had kidney failure that left Ben and Anne with the choice of extensive medical treatments, with no guarantee that he would live longer, or letting him go. It was the most difficult decision of their lives but they let Kirby go. Fortunately, they still had Jack to welcome them when they came home. He missed Kirby, still looking for him for years after he was gone. Jack lived to the ripe old age of nearly 14.

Mikey was not named for a superstar, as were his predecessors. He was instead named for a backup catcher that had joined the team along with an upcoming superstar. The young phenom spent more than his share of time on the DL, so Mikey got plenty of playing time. His reliability as a pinch hitter had earned Ben's admiration. Now his Mikey was riding along, keeping him good company as they explored the west.

As they rolled across the vast expanses, Ben's mind kept wandering. He remembered the hours of waiting during the trial. Procedural issues, schedule conflicts and interruptions would stall the progress of the trial. When they did he would sit on a bench in the hall outside the courtroom and look into the offices across the Atrium. The building appeared to have been built with steel columns and cross braces from a huge erector set. The interior of the Government Center was an open atrium from the floor to roof with all the courtrooms on one side and what looked like regular offices on the other.

He had looked into the glass-walled offices across the way and made up stories about the people working there. They could have been offices from any business in Minneapolis. One day he looked over and saw an office decorated with a big "Over the Hill" banner and balloons. Apparently someone had turned 40. Another time, he watched as a woman packed all her things into boxes, hugged what must have been co-workers, and then left. Was she changing jobs, retired, promoted, or fired? At least she had friends who were sorry to see her leave.

Ben had friends in business too. His co-workers had all come to the funeral, along with some people that were strangers to all but Ben. He had deep roots in the industry in which he worked, and those people knew the importance of supporting a colleague at the time of a death. They knew it better than anyone. A few of the people he worked with in Minneapolis had an idea who the strangers were, but none knew them like Ben did. He had spent many hours in difficult conditions with them, had backed them up from behind the scenes as they did their jobs, and they were here to back him up.

After the service several of them waited behind to have a word with Ben, assuring him that if there was ever anything he needed, anything they could do, anything, they were there for him. He told them he was sure he'd be okay, that the law would be served, and thanked them for their help. The strangers left their cards and left the funeral.

Tomorrow Ben and Mikey would guide the RV south to Hwy 89. That would take them south through some of the most beautiful country in the nation. Ben wanted to see it, but didn't want to leave a footprint on the grid there. He was picking and choosing the places where he wanted to leave a trace and he'd pick a solid one tomorrow. Until then, he would continue using small, out-of-the-way places to stop or just a rest. After tomorrow, they'd be near their next layover and his next visit.

# Chapter 10

Two weeks had gone by and things were getting hotter in the weather, and the politics. We were getting nowhere on the case and the mayor was now pushing.

I was wearing what was summer casual for me—lightweight khakis with a brightly colored golf shirt. There was the problem of where to conceal a weapon, but I look good in orange. On day-1 of this case, two weeks ago, Olson gave me an overview of the Hill/O'Leary-Sample trial. Now he filled in more details.

"The trial didn't start for over a year. The two suspects had been arrested almost immediately after the robbery, with the proceeds and the weapons still on them. Only about $7,500 had been taken, but it was apparently enough for these two. That's when the circus began. The two suspects were both the children of two of the Twin Cities' leading families. I'm not sure how, but this attracted the out-of-town defense attorney, Richard Ronald Davis, like a moth to a flame. You know this guy—he has a reputation for taking cases that will result in big fees and/or big TV time. He's gotten a lot of bad guys off with theatrics and questionable tactics. He knows the American system better than most defense attorneys and prosecutors, and he can manipulate a trial with the best of them.

"He flew in from Atlanta with a team and worked on the media, the judge, the evidence, and the jury pool. He couldn't keep himself from claiming that both Hill and O'Leary-Sample were the victims of neglected childhoods, bad schools, deprived diets, lack of employment opportunities, etcetera. In the weeks before the trial, he was on TV nearly every day. And you know what I think his greatest strength is? He's got a knack for releasing little tidbits over time so that by the time jury selection started the entire pool had seen and heard him enough to feel that they knew him. He was familiar—not just a celebrity out-of-town mercenary.

"Result—he asks that the two perps be charged as juveniles even though they're 18 and 19 years old because they were juveniles when the robbery took place. Same with their priors—juvenile, so that can't be revealed to the jury. He gets the evidence reviewed for chain of custody and provenance and asks for most of it to be thrown out. So the judge buys the whole package—hook, line, and sinker—disallowed most of the pertinent evidence. The jury bought *their* story—'spending time with one of their relatives'. The DA had assigned his newest, least experienced prosecutor to the case and she didn't have a chance. Not only were they not convicted of second degree murder, they weren't convicted on wrongful death or even the holdup. Somehow the jury bought the idea that they were just innocent victims of society and that, even if they did something they should not have, they deserved a second chance."

"*Complete* acquittal? And the DA didn't bring lesser charges?" I was at a rare loss for words.

"Not quite, they got a conviction on the weapons charge and six months in Lino Lakes—*suspended*. Like I said, they walked out of that room as admonished and contrite little boys who would go forth and do good deeds in the world. It was amazing."

That would really make Harris the number-one guy, and I was not happy that no one had been able to locate him since the day after the shooting of Hill.

Olson said, "I know you're still looking at him, but I'm telling you, he doesn't fit the profile. He's got no background in firearms—no hunting licenses, no firearms purchases, no firearms training classes, no military background. And he just didn't seem the type. I watched him the whole trial and he didn't seem to me like someone who was planning revenge."

"Okay, I'll go with that, even though I still have to talk to him and that O'Leary-Sample kid. But we're two weeks into this and we have squat. We've got no source on the weapon or ammo, we've got no other suspects unless you count every rival gang in town and we've got nothing else to look at."

Olson replied, "Last we have on Sample is the family went to Alaska on vacation right before the Hill shooting. They haven't come back and no one knows where they are. You know how these things work—something will turn up, it always does."

Neither of us knew how true that would be. Outside Glennallen Alaska, in the Wrangell-St. Elias National Park and Reserve, two hikers—well off the beaten path—had just found the partially eaten body of Cirrus O'Leary-Sample.

# Chapter 11

**Wednesday, June 25th**
**Arizona**

The Shooter was out west too. He left his RV parked at a nondescript roadside near Sunflower, Arizona. He trusted the RV's air conditioning to keep things cool inside. Temperatures in the 100s are common this time of year. He was plugged into shore power and had a switch that would kick on the generator if the shore power went down. He had paid cash for three day's stay. The owner of the RV Park didn't seem interested in many formalities such as IDs. Ben had one ready, but was glad he wasn't asked for it.

Dressed like a local in shorts and golf shirt, he backed his car out of the trailer and went into town. The sun was brilliant and the sky hazy, with a hot dusty wind blowing. He left the top up and ran the AC. He changed his hat, re-combed his hair, and added a large bushy Latin-looking mustache during the drive. In Phoenix, he parked a few blocks away from what could have been a rough-looking used-car lot. He had found the place in a local shopper-type paper. There was an ad and a phone number. The Shooter called the number and found it was a little side business that a mechanic was running next to his house and shop. There were about a dozen sand covered clunkers with worn paint, faded vinyl roofs, and tires that wouldn't have lasted a Minnesota winter. He walked the lot, kicked a few tires, and finally found the car he'd seen advertised. It was an older Mercedes Benz—a small 4-door with 4-wheel drive. Although it had a lot of years on it, it still had a good-looking paint job and could pass for "affluent but eccentric," which was what he needed. He took it for a test drive and bought it for $3,800—no ID was necessary as long as he promised to take the car down and transfer the title himself. The mechanic/dealer didn't care if he did or not. He'd never bothered to put the title in his name when he'd bought it from a guy who'd brought it in with a cranky starter.

The Spanish-speaking car jockey seemed impressed with the Shooter's use of the language, and knew that there were times to not ask questions. He signed the title with the name printed on the owner's line and handed the paper work to the buyer, who thanked him and drove out of the lot. He swung by the spot where he'd left his car. After transferring a package from his car to the old classic's trunk, he drove it to a long-term parking lot outside the Phoenix airport and left it, walking into the airport and taking a cab back to his own car.

He drove his car back to the RV. He loaded the car back into the trailer and removed the car's stable mate from it. It was a small motorcycle. The bike was more-or-less stock but had desert camo paint and was very quiet. It had saddle bags and he checked to make sure that the change of clothes he'd packed into one of them was still there before opening the fuel valve and starting it up. After a few minutes of warm up, he headed back toward Phoenix.

This time he went to the Northeast area of the metropolis. He had scouted his target on Internet satellite imagery and knew where he wanted to go. Approaching the target area from the north, he headed into private undeveloped land that was posted 'No Trespassers." He crouched in a depression to change into the desert camo clothes he'd brought. Now he and the bike were virtually invisible in the waning light of evening.

The Shooter rode to a spot just to the north and west of a very high-end neighborhood. Here, he found a parking place that would leave his bike out of sight and walked about a mile to a point where he could see into the houses. They were still a quarter-mile away, but he had a spotter's scope with him that let him look right into the windows. He compared the houses with the aerial photo's he printed off the Internet and picked out the one he was interested in. Then he watched the house for about an hour and a half. It was just getting dark and before long he had the information he needed.

He rode back to the RV, loaded the bike into the trailer, and prepared for some sleep deprivation. He planned on being home in a day and a half.

# Chapter 12

We were back at it with some ideas to follow up. I'd just gotten back from a one-day trip out to sunny and stinky Hollywood, where I'd been helping out on a TV show's story line. They wanted to have a bad guy shoot someone with a shotgun from a distance of about 6 feet and blow a hole in the guy about a foot in diameter. This is great video, I guess, but not reality. At that distance, a 12-gauge is going to make a hole about the same size as a large-caliber pistol. People who don't know firearms think that a shotgun is some kind of super weapon and don't realize, at six feet, the shot hasn't had the chance to spread at all. It will go right through someone, but it's going to be a small hole, about the size of your thumb. I'll give the TV people some credit for at least asking—in the end, they went with gory over accuracy and cut the guy in half.

Olson's digging had found there had been a burglary a few weeks prior to the Hill shooting, at a home in south Minneapolis and some firearms were reported missing. The thing that kept this case from popping up before was no mention of a rifle. That's because the homeowner hadn't known it was gone. He thought he'd left the rifle at his cabin. He later revised the stolen goods report to include the rifle.

We arrived at the home of the robbery victim a little after 10:00 a.m. It was a nice one-and-a-half-story house in south Minneapolis with what real estate agents call "great curb appeal." Tudor styling, vines growing up the fireplace, and a winding paver sidewalk that must have been a bitch to shovel when it snowed—looked nice though.

I rang the bell next to a massive oak door. A face appeared, peering through leaded glass that obscured my face as well as theirs. I called out, "Minneapolis Police."

The homeowner opened the door and Olson asked, "Jim Swanson?"

The man said yes and let us in. I started right in on him.

"Mr. Swanson, did you report a burglary about three months ago?"

"Yes I did. And your people haven't had any luck in finding the jerks that did it."

"I wouldn't say that—but that's not why we're here. You recently added an AR-15 rifle to the list of items taken. Why did you wait so long?"

"I didn't know it was missing. I don't usually keep it here—I leave it at our lake place. Then, when we were there last weekend, I couldn't find it and I remembered that I'd brought it home to take it to the gunsmith for some work."

"What kind of work?"

"Does that really matter? I've reported it missing now."

"Just curious—Mr. Swanson, we believe the gun may have been used in a shooting. Did you own any frangible ammunition?"

"Any—what?"

"*Frangible ammunition.* As the owner of an AR-15, wouldn't you know what frangible ammo is?" If he had it—he'd know what it was so I watched his face as I said it. If not—actually, I would have been surprised if he had it or knew anything about it. But if he did—this is what makes police work so much fun.

"I have no idea what you're talking about. The only ammunition I had for it was regular target rounds—you know—full metal jacket, I think they're called."

"Mr. Swanson, if your gun and ammo was used in this shooting and you're holding out on us, I'm going to have you charged as an accessory. You could be looking at 20 years in Oak Park Heights." This was an empty threat but I figured he wouldn't know—the best I could hope for was knowingly filing a false police report and that didn't amount to anything. Besides, Oak Park Heights is Minnesota's high-security facility. That's where the bad guys go after they've been sentenced to somewhere else and have done something there to warrant a trip to OPH. People I know who work there and say it's like the old Smith-Barney ads—you can't get sentenced to OPH, you have to earn it.

"Detective Neumann, I am a law-abiding member of this community who has reported a crime. I don't appreciate being threatened in my living room by the people who can't seem to solve that crime."

Olson cut in—time for some good cop—"Jim, we don't think you had anything to do with the shooting—we just need to find the gun that did it. Why did your gun need to go to the shop?"

"Like I told you, it needed some work. I was going to have a scope mounted. I never keep it here."

Olson stepped toward Swanson, handing him his card, saying, "I'm sure that was it. If you think of anything else, please be sure to call me."

"I'm sure I will."

As we walked to the door together, I got one last shot in—"I'd really be disappointed to learn that there was anything else you knew about now but was conveniently left at the lake."

Olson pushed me out the door.

"You know what that was all about, don't you?" I asked.

"Of course—he didn't want to get nailed for having an assault rifle in the city limits."

Like a lot of big cities, Minneapolis has a ban on citizen ownership of so-called assault weapons. This description has always bothered me. I said to Olson, "It's really the German's fault. Toward the end of World War II they developed a lightweight rifle that would fire fully automatic. Hitler was so taken with it he named it the *Sturmgewehr*—German for storm rifle—as in to storm the enemy's position. This was later adapted to assault rifle in English and we've been stuck using Hitler's label ever since."

Personally, if I'm being shot at, and it's happened a few times over the years, I feel that I'm being assaulted—regardless of what kind of gun is shooting at me. I don't care if it's an AK-47 or a .25-caliber pocket gun—it's a gun. It's kind of like the whole "weapons of mass destruction" thing. If a hand grenade lands at your feet, or a mortar round lands on your head—those are weapons of mass destruction as far as you're concerned. You become the "indiscriminate victim" if it's your ass that gets blown off. To define one weapon as somehow more destructive than another speaks only to the skill of the hand that employs it—not that it's more dangerous in itself. That belief underlies the sort of attitude you get as you move closer to the tallest buildings in the country. But—I digress.

"Pretty stupid law if it winds up getting in the way of people reporting that they've lost one." Olson checked his voice mail and listened to his messages. "You're going to love this—"

In my best Clint Eastwood I said, "Go ahead—screw up my day."

"I've got two messages. One says that Ben Harris has called for an appointment tomorrow. The other one said that they found the Sample kid."

"Yeah?—where's the kid?—I want to talk to him right now."

"Going to be a little tough—he's in a body bag in Alaska."

# Chapter 13

**Friday, June 27th**
**Minneapolis**

Olson and I waited in his office to see if Ben Harris would keep his 10:30 a.m. appointment. The information desk at the old city hall building would confirm his call from yesterday and direct him down the hall marked "Police Offices." When Harris walked in to the office—he would learn that I was there, too. Olson made the introductions and the verbal skirmish began.

"First off—Mr. Harris, we're both very sorry for your loss," Olson started, "we both have lost loved ones and know what you are going through."

Ben nodded and said nothing—he'd probably heard plenty of condolences in the year and a half since it happened. Olson beat around the bush—asked how he was getting on with his life and what he thought about the trial. It's an old technique—trying to get the person to feel that you are on their side. Ben was having none of it. So Olson got to the point and brought up Tyrone's drive-by death two weeks ago.

After pausing, Ben replied, "I was on vacation but I read about it in *USA Today*. It didn't exactly break my heart."

I decided to get into the discussion, but set us back when I asked him point blank why he had killed Hill.

"You know, I know you have to play your games—good cop—bad cop—whatever, but do you really want to start this by pissing me off?" Ben challenged.

Obviously set off, I rose to the bait and said, "I'll talk to you any goddamned way I want! This is a murder investigation. I suggest you start taking it seriously." This was a rough start on what I felt could either a very short or possibly a very long relationship.

Olson cut in before I did any more damage or Harris could say anything— "We just need to check on your whereabouts when the incident occurred. I understand you were in Fargo. Can you prove this?"

"I was registered at the Moorhead KOA. I was there for three nights. During the day I attended an old car show—I have a car that was entered in the show. After the third night I checked out and left. I believe, from what I read in the papers, that the killing took place on Sunday night. That would have been the last night I was there."

I came back at him, "Where did you go?"

"I went for a trip. Anne and I had bought the RV to see the country, and that's what I decided to do—alone of course."

"And you just got back now?"

"Last night."

"Do you have any way of proving where you were?"

"Most nights I stayed at a regular campground, but some nights I didn't. Sometimes you just pull over wherever you are—and there are the Wal-Marts."

I didn't get this. "What about the Wal-Marts?"

"Most Wal-Marts will let you stay in their parking lots. They figure that if you're parked there you'll spend some money there—they have very good camping departments."

"And you were alone for the entire time?"

"I visited some friends. And I had my dog with me. You could check with him if you like."

I ignored that—"Where did you go?"

"I assumed you would ask me this, so I have prepared an itinerary. It shows where I've been for the last 17 days." I looked at the list and didn't see the place I was looking for. "Didn't drive up to Alaska—did you?"

"No," Ben replied, and left it at that.

I tried a new tack. "Listen—you know we're just doing our jobs here—we're trying to solve a murder so a criminal can be brought to justice. You know you are our best suspect for this. You have reasons to want Hill dead. He killed your wife. He didn't get convicted so you had to take care of business yourself—that would be very understandable."

Ben paused and answered with steel-edged irony, "You're looking to bring a criminal to justice? I've seen what kind of justice our country has come to expect—it's a compromise."

I started to see some steam come out of his ears—he wanted to talk about *justice*.

Harris continued, "I had time while I was at the trial to look in on some other trials. It seems to me that they are very nearly all compromises—neither side gets what really they want. The victim in the rape trial wants the guy castrated but, of course, we can't do that. The defense wants the jury to believe that she said yes and just changed her mind afterward and the accused should walk but that's not what happened either. I saw parts of a trial where a guy beat his wife to death with a hammer. He pled guilty to second-degree murder with intent. He got 25 years—if he serves it all—he'll probably be out in 12 or less. I guess the defense was happy with that. But the best known lawyer in this town couldn't preserve his professional record by getting him off, and the family of the lady who was killed was certainly not happy. Every verdict is a compromise. I guess if no one is happy, then justice was done—except there was no compromise in my case."

He looked at Olson—"You were there for that circus they called a trial. It was a farce. They had these guys cold, but someone powerful didn't want them convicted. The judge disallowed all the best evidence. The prosecuting county attorney didn't have a chance against that hired gun the defense brought in from Atlanta. I had three and a half months of watching our judicial system in action. I was nauseated. Sure I wanted them dead—but after the trial I wasn't sure who the real criminals were. I wouldn't know where to begin if I was going to try to right a wrong. So I gave up and went camping—wouldn't *that* be very understandable?"

Olson and I looked at each other. I still thought Harris might be the guy but I'm pretty sure I got what he was saying. I'd seen plenty of bad guys go free in years past due to lack of evidence and a botched arrest or search. Still, we'd have to look at the trial transcripts to really get a feel for where Harris was coming from.

I pursed my lips and nodded to Harris "We'll be checking out this list. Please don't go anywhere for awhile—we might need your help again soon."

They rose and escorted Harris to the door. "I'll be here for a few days if you need me. But I'm going to keep my word to Anne and see the rest of the country," he resolved.

When he left, I asked Olson for the details he'd gotten on the Sample kid. Olson said that the family had gone to Alaska after the trial for "a rest to recover from the injustice done to our son," according to a quote from the father. The son had disappeared about a week after Hill was shot in front of the party house. On Sunday the 22nd, he'd been hiking in the Wrangell-St. Elias National Park and just never came home. The parents hadn't reported it right away because it was summer and they assumed he had decided to stay out overnight—then the body was found. So far the coroner had no cause of death, but said that is looked like he took a fall—which either killed him or injured him so badly that he was easy prey for whatever came along.

"I guess we'll have to go up there and see for ourselves?" Olson said.

"I guess—but let's give them some time to get the cause of death. I'd really rather not have to make that trip."

I really don't like flying and Olson knows it. I'd rather drive—it's my preferred method of travel for any trip under about 800 miles—about one really long day.

# Chapter 14

**Saturday, June 28th**
**Plymouth, Minnesota**

The Shooter packed a small backpack and pulled his bike from the hooks in the garage ceiling. He casually rode it 4 miles over the city trail system through French Lake Park. It was a fabulous Minnesota summer morning—78 degrees with a partly sunny sky and lots of bikers out riding. He blended right in. He swung out the southeast side of the park and cut over to the road that ran down the west side of Medicine Lake.

He cut through the neighborhoods, crossed Northwest Boulevard, and rode to the nearby Radisson Hotel, looking more like a sightseer than someone getting exercise, and stashed the bike in the woods north of the tennis courts. He walked into the back of the hotel and found the public bathrooms off the lobby. He knew from experience that hotel lobby bathrooms got very little business and felt quite comfortable changing out of his biking shorts and into khakis. He donned a comfortable golf shirt and stuffed his used clothes into his backpack.

Taking just a few minutes to stop into one of the toilet stalls for a little privacy, he applied a mustache and pulled a short wig over his very tightly cropped graying hair, which gave him a blond Minnesotan look, and then left the bathroom. Walking through the lobby to the front, he asked the front desk to call a cab, which he took to the Mall of America in Bloomington. There, he hopped the light-rail to the Humphrey Terminal at the airport. At the Sun Country counter he produced identification showing he was Gil Cederstrom, a resident of Blaine, Minnesota. He paid cash for a round trip to Phoenix—leaving in 45 minutes and returning to Minneapolis at 9:37 tomorrow morning. Then he went to the gate to wait for his flight.

The flight took just under 3 hours—a tailwind helped things along. The Shooter deplaned and headed out to long-term parking, where he knew he'd find the car waiting. He unlocked the door, got in, and drove to the pay booth. He paid in the cash line for a number of reasons, but especially because there'd be no credit card record of his presence. From the airport, he headed east to Highway 101 North and took that up to East Shea. Along the way he swung through a quick car wash to knock off the dust that had accumulated during the time the car was parked. He was trying to pass the car off as old money eclectic. It could be old but not dirty. From Shea he went north on East

Palisades into one of the most affluent neighborhoods in the United States. He hoped the old Benz looked good enough to pass for a local among all the high-end foreign cars.

He turned off at North Eagle Peak Trail. This was a dead end but he was prepared for that. The paved two-lane road had a center island but turned into a real trail after it passed a high-priced condo and town house complex. Just after a rise in the road, he came to a gate. It was just below the horizon—placing it out of sight of the residents, presumably to spare them the notion that they were at the end of the world. He pulled a bolt cutter from the package of items he'd left in the trunk and made quick work of the cable that locked the gate. He drove the car through and closed the gate—replacing the cable with a new one. It wasn't locked but he didn't need for it to remain unnoticed for long—just a few hours.

He drove the Benz north on the dirt path—glad he had the 4-wheel drive. He pulled off what he was mentally calling "Eagle Peak Two Rut Goat Path" into a depression—deep and far enough from the road to hide the car—where he shut off the engine and popped the trunk. In the trunk he found a change of clothes in desert camo, a very good pair of boots, and the rifle. He changed his appearance and hiked eastward—up the side of a small mountain for the mile or so—to the vantage point he'd scouted by satellite. Satellite photos of virtually the entire planet were available on the Internet, and he was expert at reading them. About 300 yards before he got to his perch, he changed his footwear.

Approaching his perch, he switched to a combat crawl and inched his way the last 20 or so yards to what's called "The Military Summit" of the hill he'd use. That's the term for the highest point you can get to without being seen from the other side. He crept up, found a spot he liked, and built a little support from rocks that were scattered about. Then he settled back to wait. Might as well have a little nourishment while I'm waiting, he thought, and he un-wrapped a candy bar. He waited at this over-watch point for some activity. His target had very routine habits and he was counting on them now.

Retired judge Amy Mitchell was going through her usual evening routine. She had purchased the home in Scottsdale in the early '90s—before any kind of land boom—and was already sitting on a tidy bit of appreciation, even with the recent decline in values. She had no intention of ever selling the place, but it was nice to know it was increasing in value.

The house was typical Arizona rich and had a bit of a Frank Lloyd Wright look to it—horizontal lines, wide-high windows and overhangs. It was built of native materials and blended nicely into the surroundings. The house was laid out to take advantage of the winter sun angles. The builder correctly figured it would be the cold season home of some snowbird. It was all on one level—no basements in Phoenix—no one wants to dig down into the rock—but there were some steps between different areas of the house as it rose and fell with the roll of the terrain.

On the north side there was a broad covered patio that overlooked the swimming pool. The remarkable pool had sold her on the house. The edge on one end drops off into a lower catch-basin level. From the other end, it looks like it just goes on forever and from the drop off edge you get a little water fall—like a vanishing horizon. Feng Shui before it had a name.

Mitchell's habit was to have a glass of wine and take a dip before bed every evening. Her years on the bench had made her an early riser and, oddly enough, the summer sun rose later and set sooner here than in the higher latitudes in Minnesota. It was about nine o'clock when she went outside with her glass.

The Shooter watched as she came out of the house and appeared in his sight picture. As she went about her daily swim routine he tracked her movements around the pool. She dropped her robe and, still wearing a towel, appeared to be in exceptional shape for her 58 years. Early retirement was possible if you made enough and kept things under control at home. The Shooter's background work told him that she might have some other sources of income that could have helped finance this place. He had no second thoughts or anxieties about what he was going to do.

Mitchell took a deep sip of the wine, her favorite 10-year-old Merlot, and set the glass on the table by the pool. Then, taking advantage of the other reason she loved the place, she slipped out of her towel. She knew that the vast expanse of desert to the north would provide privacy—at least until it was ultimately developed. No doubt she hoped she could buy enough of it to keep it private.

Mitchell had stopped moving. The Shooter took one last check of the wind and settled on target. It was a very difficult shot, but not impossible. He took a deep breath, let it half out, and smoothly squeezed the trigger.

Just as she was going to plunge into the deep end, she felt a sharp pain in her belly. It felt as though she had been hit hard by a full fist. Looking down, she saw a small hole about 4 inches below her left breast. The wind went from her lungs as if it had been sucked out by an enormous vacuum, and she dropped straight down to the tile. She lay there, still, wondering what had happened and beginning to feel cold. She couldn't breathe or cry out, and no one would have heard her. It took 3 minutes for enough blood to drain from her internal organs—plenty of time to wonder what had happened to her life.

As the Shooter watched Judge Mitchell die through the rifle scope, he began to have a sickening feeling in his stomach. He remembered a childhood experience. When he was 13 years old, his family had been visiting friends who lived on a hobby farm. After spending the afternoon plinking cans with a single-shot .22 rifle, the farm-family's mom told her son, "Why don't you two go and shoot that darn rabbit that keeps getting in my garden?" So the Shooter and his buddy went in search of the pesky rabbit.

They had found it outside the barn, munching on some recently stolen greens. First, the farm family's son took a shot, but he missed. After reloading the rifle, the son handed it to the Shooter and said, "It's your turn. You'll probably get him—you're a better shot than I am."

The Shooter had taken the ancient firearm and the two boys stalked the rabbit again. They found him again, this time on a path going down to the creek. Just before the Shooter took his shot the family's son said, "Be sure you get him good. If you just nick him, he'll yell."

The Shooter had taken aim and squeezed of the shot. But just as he pulled the trigger, the rabbit moved. The shot hit the rabbit in the rear legs, disabling it but not killing it.

The farm-family's son was right—the rabbit emitted a shrill howl that pierced the Shooters soul as he tried to reload. After first dropping it, he got another shell into the rifle and stopped the rabbit's awful cries. The screaming had stopped, but the Shooter's life had been changed forever. He vowed—hoped—to never again pick up a firearm. For years he would occasionally have nightmares about the screaming rabbit.

The Shooter had lived up to his self-promise until he was an adult. In the course of his work, however, it became necessary for him to learn to shoot and he discovered he was very good at it. But that had been with paper targets—not living beings. Now, as he watched a human being die as a result of his actions, he began to wonder if this could be justified. The memory of the rabbit came back and, for a moment, filled him with heart-wrenching remorse.

He shook it off. He knew what he was doing was necessary and justified. He knew that the person he'd killed deserved to die for what she had done to others, and for what she had not done. He packed up the rifle and other equipment and started the long hike back to the car.

He drove out to the north, not wanting to travel past the same houses again. There was no sense in giving anyone a second look at the unfamiliar car. Stopping at a quick-shipping kiosk, he bought a box in which he packed the gear and his change of clothes, then went to another shipping drop off point, and sent it to a friend near his home. He would recover it from the friend later. His final stop was to park the car in a rundown neighborhood near the airport. He left the keys in the ignition, expecting the car to be taken before he got home. He walked to the corner and caught a cab to the airport for the flight home, still fighting off the sound of the screaming wounded rabbit.

# Chapter 15

**Sunday, June 29th**
**Robbinsdale**

I didn't wake up bright and snarly the next morning. Instead, I slept in until after ten o'clock. I'd been up late working on my next book. This one is supposed to train forensic field investigators what to look for at shooting scenes, besides shell casings and projectiles—that was covered in the first book. This one was supposed to hit topics like blood spatter and wounds, shooting positions and firearm types. I wasn't sure I was getting the points across and would have to have a few people look at it. I had an appointment scheduled with a friend who is a trauma specialist in St. Paul, hoping that she could better describe what different wounds looked like. So far, all I had was bad, gross, painted red, and really gory. She's one of the smartest people I know and not bad looking either. Maybe—

There had once been women in the picture. I'd married too young—full of energy and lust, if not true love. We had been together for about half of our first year at the university and just couldn't wait. I don't think it was anything more than my need to keep filling in boxes on my life resume—high school, college, marriage, career, kids, house in the burbs, and the Golden Retriever. She was just trying to prove to her overbearing father that she was as good as her brothers and could get more out of the U. of M. than the MRS degree he figured she was there for. She wound up in law school—that showed him.

I finished a BS in Abnormal Psychology and got interested in police work. That didn't set well with anyone. Here she was in law school—getting ready for a great career and a home in Edina or on Lake Minnetonka—and I wanted to ride around in a car chasing bad guys. One thing led to another, and I wound up alone. At least we hadn't gotten to the kids-part yet.

As I've aged, the sex drive has become more of a chip shot. I still chase around a little, but I've accepted the fact that the chance of having a family has pretty much passed me by. I've got a sister with kids, so I can get an "Uncle" fix every once in a while if I need it. And it turns out I like kids, for the short time I'm with them. I don't know if I'd make much of a dad, but taking my nephew to a Twins game is a kick.

I think the main thing is that there are some nights when it sure would be nice to have someone to just talk with—someone who isn't a guy. Corny—I know—but I've had my share of great days, and some not so. It would be nice to have someone to make dinner for after they had a crappy day, or maybe they'd make dinner for you when you came home dragging. It would be nice to have someone to share the success with and to divide the pain with. Anyway, regarding sex—if you just stay in shape, don't smoke, don't drink too much, and don't look like you're looking—it can find you. I'm not saying I'm a player or anything, but I get enough activity to keep the edge off.

It was Sunday morning and it looked like another hot summer day was brewing. I didn't relish the thought of leaving my nice cool home. I live in Robbinsdale, a first ring suburb of Minneapolis that has aged gracefully and is experiencing a small renaissance in the 21st century. The city had purchased many of the older rundown homes, torn them down, and sold the lots to private builders or to the local vo-tech, which had a building trades program. These homes were among the best in the metropolitan area—built by students and their instructors. They took much longer to build than other homes but were in demand. I waited two years to get in one of these—a modern, modified two-story with a two-car attached garage and a four-car garage out back on the alley. This was the clincher for me—I have two snowmobiles and a Harley. There was once a boat but that's gone now. I also have a nice wood shop set up out back.

I got up and did a cursory set of exercises—50 quick sit ups, 50 pushups, some stretching, and promised myself that I'd get on the treadmill today. I had my usual breakfast—orange juice—I'd stopped calling it OJ after that trial—Honey Nut Cheerios and a piece of wheat toast with raspberry jam.

It was about eleven o'clock when I went out to the shop to work on a shelving project begun five months ago. I wanted to get some work done on that before it got too hot. I thought I could make some real progress with today's open schedule. Of course, that's when the phone rang.

"Danny me boy—you are not going to believe this one." It was Olson and he had a really startled sound to his voice.

"Yeah, go ahead you Scandinavian bullshit peddler—I'm up to anything you've cook up."

"I just heard from Rademacher over in information. She said someone popped Amy Mitchell last night."

"Judge Mitchell!—I thought she retired?"

"Yeah—got her outside her home in Arizona—looks like a long rifle shot but that's preliminary. I thought you'd want to know, since she was the presiding judge on the Harris murder case."

"You bet I'd want to know! Hey—grab your car and pick me up—let's go over to that guy's house right now!"

# Chapter 16

Olson picked me up 10 minutes later and we shot out County Road 9 from Robbinsdale to Plymouth with the lights flashing. Harris's home sat in a copse of trees on a 1.5-acre lot in a part of the suburb that was just beginning to sprout town house developments and upscale track housing. Olson had killed the siren a few miles back and now flipped off the lights as we approached and turned up into the property.

The long drive circled to the left of the house and went past the garage doors to the rear. There, we could see Harris's RV with a covered trailer hooked to it and the ramp down. I could see the rear end of a burgundy-colored, mid-50s Mercury convertible in the trailer. Harris was working underneath the RV. He had one of the big storage doors open and was apparently packing things into it. We got out of our car and a dog that looked like Lassie in miniature came running out from under the RV to bark a greeting to us. Harris looked up to see the unmarked car and came out to meet us.

"Good morning officers. I didn't know you were coming or I would have planned lunch," Harris smiled. "Is this a social call or business?"

I answered, "It's going to be all business. Where've you been since our meeting yesterday?"

"Right here, of course. I have no way of proving that other than a few phone calls."

"Who'd you call?"

"I tell you what—I'll let you do your detective thing and figure that out for yourselves. That way you can feel like you're actually doing something to solve a crime."

That was enough for me—I went off—"Look, smart guy, you'd better be able to prove your whereabouts for every second from the time you left city hall to this minute or I'm going to have your wise ass in county lockup on murder charges." Olson stayed out of it for now—he'd seen me like this and knew that I had a pretty good chance of getting a suspect to talk.

Harris calmly replied, "We've been over all this—I was in Fargo for three days, and who cares where I was last night?"

"There's been another murder. Judge Amy Mitchell was shot to death at her home in Arizona last night. Right now you are our prime suspect—so where were you?"

Ben appeared startled and seemed to chuckle, "Hmm—Judge Mitchell? How about that—I sure hope it wasn't one of those so-called unjustly accused she let off the hook. I've been right here. I imagine you have the ability to discover any way I could have possibly gotten from your office to Arizona and back by now. Why don't you go do some checking?"

"Why don't we go inside and I'll have a little look around?"—my turn to smile.

"I will not consent to a search of my property. If you go inside, it will be without my consent and anything you find will be the first thing thrown out of court by whatever fine member of the judiciary gets this case. Further—I decline to allow you to search any of my vehicles or the grounds of my property and hereby request that you leave my property now. If you return with a warrant—be prepared for a challenge to its veracity."

I could barely control myself and Olson foresaw an imminent explosion. There's a fine line between when I'm a really good "bad cop" and where I go off the edge when I'm dealing with someone who I think is pushing my buttons. So he put his hand on my shoulder and stepped in—"Ben, there's no need to get pissy here—we haven't asked to search anything and your attitude is only aggravating the situation. People who have nothing to hide are usually more than happy to allow a search. It helps us eliminate them as suspects and we can get on to looking at someone else."

"That may be so, but I learned enough about the law in that courtroom to know what my rights are. If you can't get a warrant—you can't search. It shouldn't be too hard for you to figure out that there is no way I could have gotten to Arizona and back by now—why don't you go do that? That should eliminate me as a suspect quicker than going into my home."

Olson answered, "We will—we just wanted to see if you were here. Are you planning a trip?"

"Yes—I told you yesterday that I was going to continue my tour of America, with or without your permission. I'll be leaving in a day or two—I'll even keep you informed of my whereabouts."

"That's good enough for me," Olson said. "Just drop us a line every now and then—say—every 12 hours and let us know where you are."

"Email okay?"

"Sure—just stay in touch."

I looked at Olson as if he was speaking Martian but said nothing. We got back in the car and drove away in silence.

About three miles down the road I said, "I can't believe we're letting that guy go. He's in on this somehow—I can feel it."

"He may be, but we've got nothing on him and we've got a lot of other things to track down. Let's see if we can prove his story."

"Yeah—pull his phone records and see if he really was in town last night. If he was, we've got a road trip."

"A long one," Olson nodded, "Where to first—Alaska or Arizona?"

I replied, "I think—Arizona—that one's fresh. In fact, we should call travel and get booked out this afternoon if we can. We'll go on to Alaska from there."

# Chapter 17

The Mitchell murder had made the headlines in Minneapolis, or would have if there still had been an afternoon paper. It would be one of the top stories on the evening news shows, which now started at four o'clock. Even though it was a big story with local implications, Olson had a little trouble getting the trip approved until he pointed out that the acquitted suspects in Mitchell's last case were both currently awaiting burial. It could have been a coincidence but, like most cops, the assistant in the travel office didn't believe in coincidences and we got the trip approved.

We had new info by the time we got to the airport. An investigator in the office who specializes in phone work had confirmation that two calls had been placed from Harris's home number last night. One was to an RV dealer and the other was to a veterinary office. They followed up by checking with the RV dealer and found that Harris had ordered some items for his rig by phone last night. The other call was to his vet this morning. The vet's office confirmed that Harris had called to order some flea and tick repellant and heart worm preventative for pickup today. This put Harris at home last night at six-thirty and this morning at eight. There was no way he could have gotten to Arizona and back in that amount of time. Still—we had someone working on pulling all the airline passenger manifests for yesterday to see if there was any way he could have made the trip.

We parked at the airport and made our way through security to the gate. The whole security thing has become even more of a hassle for cops on the job than it is for normal people. I mean—here we are trying to get through the bottleneck without going through the lines, metal detectors, and body searches while carrying a firearm. We get some long looks from some of the other travelers.

We made it to the gate and had about 20 minutes until boarding. This is where I start getting nervous. I've never liked flying and the larger planes haven't done anything to make me feel better. Anything that has to weigh as much as one of these aluminum coffins does just isn't meant to get off the ground—the fact that they do is just a tease. Sooner or later—I figure I'll get mine in one.

We cheated death again and arrived intact and on schedule in Phoenix. With the two-hour time change, it was mid-afternoon and mid-summer. As we walked out of the airport terminal to find our rental car, we were hit by a wall of heat—felt like someone had opened an oven door in my face.

"Good grief, Olson—this is pathetic!"

"Yeah, I saw the thermometer in the airport—it said 118 degrees. I guess we didn't exactly come to town during the tourist season, did we?"

We found the car and headed for the crime scene in Fountain Hills—a very upscale development on the northeast edge of Phoenix. On the way, we talked about the judge. As with any criminal trial judge, Amy Mitchell was sure to have made some enemies along the way. Even though her sentencing was at the light end of the scale, she had sent a lot of people to Stillwater. What made this messy was the coincidence of the two acquitted and now dead robbery suspects—one now murdered and the other dead from unknown cause.

As we drove, Olson started up one of his trademark commentaries. He has a reputation in the department for being the guy to have on a stake out because he can keep up a running conversation with himself for hours.

"Will you look at this stuff? We've been on this road for 10 miles and it's climbing higher and higher and the income levels have to be going up with the altitude. Look! There goes a Ferrari. Hey, check out that strip mall—nail and hair salons—Pilates—tanning—really! Who needs a tanning parlor here? And a dog-grooming joint—don't these people do anything for themselves? What a cesspool of self–indulgence. Man, I'd hate to have to try to get up one of these driveways with a little snow on it. I mean, they go straight up. Look at that! A lime green Lamborghini, I mean *Lime Green* —."

Olson was right about the altitude though. Shea just kept going up. I estimated we were at least 3,000 feet above the floor of the Valley of the Sun. The houses were obviously expensive but drab. They looked as if the only colors available were on the Beige page of a Pantone book. They ranked in shade from sand to taupe to terracotta. In fact the entire scene was either the Beige page or one of 47 shades of sage. Tan and green—that described upper-end Phoenix.

The judge's home was north-east of town—past Frank Lloyd Wright's Taliesin West, which was out in the desert when he built it. The home site had a great view to the east and was very privately situated. I looked around and could see that it was privacy that a killer would love.

We were met by Detective Maria Fernandez of the Maricopa County Sheriff's Office. She was the investigating officer on the case. She was also a real beauty—classic Latin features—about five foot four and slim. She had a large-caliber 1911-type automatic on her hip in a well broke-in holster. It had a worn look that it didn't get hanging in the closet—it was active duty.

Introductions were made and she took us to the back of the house where the body had been found.

"She was here when the maid came in this morning—right out here by the pool."

The home had one of those Infinity Pools—the kind that seemed to go off into the horizon. It was definitely a high-end property.

There wasn't any outline of the body, although there was a very large pool of blood. The outline thing had pretty much gone out of fashion in crime investigation. Instead, there were already pictures available and these were laid out on the patio table.

The body had been found next to the pool—by the shallow end. Also next to the pool was a glass of wine, a towel, and a robe. The judge had apparently been getting ready for a little skinny dipping.

Fernandez said, "According to the maid, she had a glass of wine and took a swim every night before bed. This time of year it would have been about ten, The maid said that she waited until it was fairly dark and had started cooling off. Cause of death looks like high power rifle fire—one shot—entering the just below the left breast and exiting the lower back abdomen. We believe she was standing here—facing north—so the bullet passed through and went out there somewhere"—she pointed south to an area of scrub and desert. The exit wound was also quite small, which rules out hollow points." She paused and said, "Or, the shot might have come from the south and exited to the north—we're not sure yet. Probably not the south though. There are just too many houses that way. We are obviously looking both ways, but the only hope we have is to find the shooter's stand and try to calculate the trajectory from that. We haven't found it yet."

We looked both ways and tried to put ourselves in the shooters place. Which way would I rather be facing—where is the best escape route—where would the sun have been—if it had been daytime, which way is the prevailing wind? These are the questions a sniper would ask and I knew that this had been a very prepared and skilled marksman.

I pondered a few more moments and asked, "Was there any blood splatter?"

"Very little. We believe that the shooter was to the north and west—out there somewhere," she said, pointing—"because if the shot came from that direction the blood splatter would go into the pool."

"Good assumption. What's the road situation there? Could he have gotten away easily?"

"No, not really. There's no way in with a vehicle and it would be a 2-mile hike, and I mean *hike*. The terrain that way is very difficult. On the other hand, that would give the best overlook and the sun would be to the shooters back. Plus he'd have to hide a vehicle somewhere and people in this neighborhood would notice a strange car if it was on the street. The car could have been anywhere out there"—she said, pointing northwest—"because he had to walk so far anyway."

"But if the shot came from there—wouldn't there be blood spatter here on the pool apron?"

"Yes, but that's also where the body fell. If the shot came from that direction—the body could have fallen into the spatter and flooded it."

"But you think he shot from the north?"

Fernandez paused in thought—"Yes, because on a long shot like this, it's quite possible for the body to just drop when hit in the lower abdomen like she was—they just fold up. When she hit the patio she opened up and that's how we found her. It just depends on which way she was leaning when the shot came."

I said, "I think you're right. We should be looking out there for the stand"—I pointed northwest—"my reasoning agrees with yours on the sun angle. He would have had the best light to deal with from that direction. You look like a shooter—I'll go with that."

Maria fixed me in a hard gaze. "Why do you think I'm a shooter?"

"You have the look in your eyes—the way you talk about it—your holster—different things. Hey, I'm not one of those guys who think that the only range a woman should stand in front of is one with burners on it."

"I get out at least once a week and compete in USPSA shoots. I shoot about 30,000 rounds a year."

I figured that the competition level she was shooting was as high as mine, maybe higher, and I had just gotten there. She was starting to sound very interesting. "How about rifle shooting?"

"I teach and coach our SWAT guys. I was on the team for four years."

"So—what do you think he used?"

"I saw the entry and exit wounds—small holes. My guess is less than .30 caliber, solid core, jacketed—not hollow point, probably bolt action with a scope—maybe .243 or even .170. As for the rifle—something like the Remington 700s we use on the team. But the size of the exit wound, and the fact that it isn't obvious which wound is entry and which is exit, makes me nervous." She paused and looked me over. "You probably know that all those calibers are tumblers and the exit wound should have been a mess. I don't know what would leave that nice neat little hole."

That was already bothering me too.

"Any chance it was an AR?"

"I doubt it. We'll know more when we find the stand."

# Chapter 18

There were two groups searching the possible shooting stands—one south and one northwest. I went with Olson and Fernandez out to the northwest area. As we climbed out through the scrub brush and rocks, I kept looking over my shoulder back to the house and pool. I was trying to see it through the shooter's eyes and thinking about where he would have been. We reached the search team and I knew immediately that we were in the wrong place. I saw a small rise about 75 yards west and went over to check the view. It looked good to me.

"He might have been here."

Fernandez and Olson came over as I found some ruffed-up tracks. There were also some rocks that had been disturbed.

"Why here?" asked Olson. His total outdoor tracking time amounted to whatever it took to find where his dog had dumped in the yard—not a real tough scouting-type problem, unless it was snowing hard.

"Take a look here at the ground. The sand's been scuffed around and this looks like a track in and out. These rocks have been moved—the dirty sides are up. No trash or brass or footprints though."

"Yes there are, "Fernandez studiously disagreed, "we just won't get anything from them. Your guy dragged his feet in and out—what I can see looks like he was wearing slippers or moccasins or something without a sole print. Your guy knows what he's doing."

The heat was getting to me. I could feel sweat running down the insides of my shirt. "First off—please don't call him *our* guy. The only reason we're here is because the judge is from Minneapolis. Second—you're right—he knows the woods."

"Oh, he's your guy, all right, if he's a guy. Why else would you two be here before the good judge is even cold?"

I had lain down on the sand behind the spot I thought was the makeshift gun rest. She was right—there was no reason to assume that the shooter was male. But it was a *woman* making that observation—meaning what—that she believed a woman could do it? That sort of translated into a belief that she thought she could do it. Yes, there was more to Fernandez than I'd seen at first glance.

I could see the line of fire perfectly. It would be about 375 yards—sun behind him—prevailing winds down range—piece of cake for someone with talent. I had a thought, "How long since it rained here?"

"Not for about three weeks. This time of year we might go a month or even two without any rain. You're right to ask—these tracks could be weeks old," Fernandez said. She lay down next to me to get my perspective.

"It's a pretty long shot for a light-caliber AR—even with a long barrel." Fernandez looked pensive. "Actually, it's a pretty long shot to have that kind of hitting power for anything as small as the entry wound looks. It might have been something else, but—" she paused, "I'll do some checking on that."

Fernandez looked a bit distracted, like she was formulating something in her head. I thought she was going to add something, but she didn't. I wondered too—that was a long distance for a small bullet.

"With this spot, a good rifle, and a little ability, he could have made a head shot. Why the center shot?"

"Only one reason I know," Fernandez said, "he didn't want a clean kill. She'd drop and bleed out—you know—give her a little time to think about it."

# Chapter 19

From the presumed shooting point, the forensics team started a trajectory search. This would give them the line of flight of the bullet to the target and, barring any change in direction caused by hitting something solid in the target, a continuation of flight path after it left the body. Fernandez said they'd search the line thoroughly, but not to get our hopes up. I knew it was a long shot, no pun intended, but also knew they had to try. Who knows, maybe they'd get lucky.

As we walked back to the house, I thought that luck was really a big part of it. Most criminals just weren't that smart—they left all kinds of trace behind. They used credit cards and their own cars for getaway vehicles, they let themselves be seen at the crime scene, they kept the murder weapon, and they took easily identifiable things from the scene as souvenirs. The list was endless. The homicide investigators at the MPD had started a list of the stupidest things they'd come across. Near the top of the list were bank robbers who wrote holdup notes on their own deposit slips, complete with name and account number. Another bank robber used a city bus for a getaway. A woman held up a liquor store with her baby in her arms, then stopped outside long enough to strap the kid into the car seat. There was a case where a guy broke into a house and the home owner was home, awake, and armed. After he took a shot at the robber, the bad guy ran out and stole a truck off the street, leaving his own car at the crime scene driveway. After a recent convenience store robbery, the cops followed a trail of 20-dollar bills right to the guy's house. When he opened the door his first words were, "How'd you find me so fast?"

I know from experience that intelligent people can commit crimes. But most crimes are committed in the heat of passion. This makes for mistakes. I've investigated crimes committed by criminal attorneys—people who should have known the system well enough to know what not to do—who were caught because they'd done the same stupid things their clients had done. I know that a thoughtful, careful, and patient criminal can get away with murder. All it took was time, patience and money to do what had to be done, and you could kill with impunity in this country. Most Americans think that murderers are usually caught, but that just wasn't true, forensic TV shows notwithstanding. I know that serial killers have gone on killing for decades and that first time killers could walk if they were careful.

Maria got a phone call.

"You're sure on that?" she asked. After a few more one-word responses, she hung up. "This is strange."

"Okay. I'll bite—what's strange?"

"That was the ME. He said that cause of death was blood loss due to severe traumatic shock to the abdomen."

"That sounds about right to me. Getting hit in the gut by a high powered rifle round would qualify as severe traumatic shock."

"Yeah, but he said it was weird. No vital organs had been hit in a way to cause all that bleeding. He said he could find the entrance and exit wounds and that it looked like the round passed straight through without hitting a bleeder. He said that the organs in the abdomen looked like they had taken a severe shock and just exploded like you see in someone who jumps off a building. And that the organs above the diaphragm showed shock too, even though the bullet didn't go through the ribcage. He said it looked like she'd been in a car wreck because both her lungs had collapsed. She bled out internally without hitting an artery."

That was strange. Most bullets cause damage by hitting something important. Most bullets don't go right through people, they break up and scatter and hit a lot of important stuff along the way. If a bullet passes right through someone, it's called a "flesh wound," one that isn't a real problem. But if it hits something important, like a femoral artery, you'll bleed out in minutes. Plug the hole with your finger long enough to get help and you'll be back on your feet in a month or so.

We made our way back to the house and exchanged business cards for follow up. Olson asked Fernandez to let us know if they found anything along the lines of forensic evidence. We needed something to tie this to someone in Minnesota. We got in our car and headed back to the airport.

At the airport we made the arrangements go to Alaska. While we waited for the flight, I called Andrea Bartholomew, an investigator with the Minneapolis PD. She was working on tracking down the flight manifests for every possible way of getting to Phoenix and back last night. Andrea answered after about seven rings.

"I've got just about every way figured out and Harris wasn't on any of them. And there's no other way he could have gotten there and back."

"Okay," I answered, "Finish that up and if you haven't got a match, try private plane charters. And just to make sure you don't run out of things to do today—start cross-matching the passenger lists to Phoenix last night with flights to Anchorage—plus-or-minus three days of the date the Sample kid disappeared." I paused as a thought was coalescing in my head. "Also, please find out where Harris worked and what he did. Get contacts, co-workers, associates, and anything you think I'd be interested in. And get Rademacher in to help on this. She's real good at this stuff." She said she'd get on it.

We boarded the flight to Anchorage and settled in for the 5 hour journey. No drinking, of course, since we were traveling armed. I tried to read a book I'd bought at the airport, a good story about how super sleuth Mitch Rapp saves America, again. I liked the local Minnesota-born writers' books like those of John Sanford, especially since those were based in the Twin Cities. But I couldn't keep my eyes open and wound up sleeping, a blessed event for a nervous flyer.

# Chapter 20

**Monday, June 30th**
**Anchorage, Alaska**

I woke up in a jet-lag-induced, false sense of awareness in a generic hotel room in Anchorage. It was bright daylight outside and I was ready to go. I sat up on the bed, remembered I was in Alaska, and looked at the clock on the side table—4:45 a.m. What's with this place?

We had landed at Anchorage International at 10 p.m. local time after a 5 hour fight. That would be 1 a.m. in Minnesota, which was where I'd woken up yesterday, so I was understandably a little messed up. We got a car and went straight to the hotel and crashed, even though it was still light outside. I got up for my mid-sleep visit to the biff and it was still light outside. The clock had said 1:30. Now it was 4:45 in the morning, 7:45 in my home town, and I was raring to go after only about five and a half hours of sleep. Olson could count on me dozing off over lunch.

Alaska is a neat place, whatever time it is. I'd never been here before and the all-night sun was weird and cool at the same time. Just think of what you could do with that kind of daylight. According to the chamber of commerce default-TV channel, you could hunt or fish all night, or you could grow the biggest vegetables on the planet, but you've got to cut your grass every other day. I thought it might give you more time to stalk someone and kill them. No time limit on murder.

I showered, dressed and was heading out the door for the hotel's complimentary breakfast when Olson, in an adjoining room, called me to say he'd heard from Fernandez in Arizona. They had thoroughly searched the trajectory line and had nothing. She was following up another idea and would call us when she had something. I rang up Bartholomew.

"Find anything on his employment?" I asked.

"Just the name of the place where he worked—something called AMES Services. I dug a little and found out that the A, M, and the E in AMES stands for Advanced Micro Electronics. They make some kind of special radios. I'm digging to find out where they are and what kind of radios."

"Good work. I've never heard of them, but they are probably buried in the Twin Cities ordnance industry. Look there." Most people didn't know this, but there is a long history of manufacturing in the Twin Cities that specializes in military products. The big guys are well-known—Honeywell made the famous Norden Bombsite during World War II or FMC, who made ship cannons and rocket systems. But there is a large and very quiet group of companies specializing in military products that exist to support the big guys. Many have non-descript names—my favorite is an outfit called DPMS, which stands for Defense Procurement Manufacturing Services. What a great name. It could mean anything. They make really good AR-15-type rifles. I've even got one that I've got all tricked out with—but, I'm off the topic again.

Alaska. The place was overwhelming—Colorado with an ocean. The mountains literally run right down to the water. I met Olson for the aforementioned breakfast in the hotel restaurant, got in the rented car, and drove over to the Alaska State Patrol's local office. We had an O-six hundred rendezvous with destiny. It was a three hour drive up to the park where the kid's body was found so the ASP had offered to fly us up there in a helicopter. Apparently flying is the preferred way to get around up here but that didn't make it any easier for me. I don't like flying and had never been in a helicopter in my life. I once heard a friend describe helicopters as 20,000 parts all moving in different directions. That was reassuring—and this guy was a pilot. Olson was excited about the prospect of an aerial tour though. In deference to him I agreed and figured that I could always just close my eyes and hit the scotch, if I'd had any. As is turned out I was entranced by the grand vistas of the valleys and mountains. With the headphones on the noise was gone and conversation was possible. Somehow—I enjoyed it.

Andy Kahler of the Alaska State Patrol met us at the landing area near the park's entrance. He was a wiry guy with big hands and a firm handshake. He had the typical bear sunglasses, but apparently the ASP was a little more relaxed on the rest of the dress code. We climbed into his SUV and headed into the park.

I asked, "Doesn't this come under the jurisdiction of the National Park Service, since the body was found on park land?"

He said, "We handle most of the crimes that occur there, and there isn't that much of it. You'd be surprised how tame hikers are. The ones that come all the way up here to camp are usually very experienced and careful. They pack out their trash, don't cause fires, and follow the rules. This was a pretty big deal for us."

"You mean you don't have many bodies found in the park?"

"No, we get bodies—not many murders."

That got my attention. "You think it was a murder?"

"Coroner's pretty sure, after he found the bullet hole."

This was news to us. I asked for details.

"Yeah," Kahler said, "there was a bullet hole. But I hear it was pretty hard to find, just nicked one of the ribs. And, of course, with all the damage to the body, we really couldn't tell anything when it was picked up."

"Tell me about that. Who found the body and what was the condition?"

"There was a pair of hikers in the area. They stopped at the overlook to take some pictures of themselves. One of them dropped a pan out of her pack, apparently wasn't hooked on right, she said it had fallen off before, and she was backed up to the edge so over it went. They climbed down after it and there he was. If she hadn't dropped the pan, there wouldn't have been anything left. He couldn't have been down there more than a day or two or the scavengers would have picked him clean."

Now, there's a happy thought. That's why I don't go camping. I asked what he knew about the bullet forensics.

"Well that's a little strange. The coroner said that it looked fresh, as opposed to an old wound that had healed up, and that it couldn't be very high caliber—maybe a .22 or smaller. That's strange for out here because everything you'd hunt or be worried about in this state takes .30 cal. or higher. And there's no hunting in this park."

I'd already jumped to that conclusion. Despite prohibitions against weapons on federal park land, if I was going out for even a short walk in these woods, I'd be carrying a Smith and Wesson .50 Magnum—the new hand cannon. It's replaced the Dirty Harry model .44 Mag as the most badass gun around. You ought to see it—barrel's about a foot long and looks like you could drop a golf ball into the hole in the end of it. I was pretty sure it would stop a bear. But—I digress.

I asked the trooper what he thought of the scene.

"It's a beautiful spot—nice scenic overlook with some picnic tables and fire boxes, above where the body was found. We collected evidence of a little recreational drug activity, but no real way to connect that with the body."

Olson chimed in, "This guy was a known user—probably taught by his parents."

That got him one of those weird, but knowing looks from Kahler. We got to the point of closest approach for a car and got out to walk. It was about a half mile to the overlook. I stepped over to the place where Cirrus would have been standing before his step into eternity. Kahler said that they didn't know which way he'd been standing because there was no evidence of either the entry or exit wound. Probably bear shit by now. Anyway, I looked around and took in the scene, looking for a sniper stand. "Come on Cirrus," I thought to myself, "talk to me."

There were several fire pits and picnic areas scattered around the overlook. It was like multiple groups of people could be here at the same time without bothering each other much. Of course, someone had bothered Cirrus, so I started looking at the individual spots. Each one had a fire pit, a few logs pulled together in a circle that you could sit on while your lunch was being prepared, and a trash can. I asked the trooper how often the trash cans were emptied.

"I guess I'm not sure. As needed, I suppose."

I looked in the cans as I walked around. Most had something in them. I don't know what I was looking for. It's one of those investigative techniques I like to use—I call it investigating by walking around. You don't know what you're looking for until you find it.

And—I found it.

# Chapter 21

In one of the trash cans I noticed a little color on a piece of paper discarded and half buried. It was a familiar red and green. I reached in but couldn't get it, so I flipped the can over, dumping the contents on the ground. Olson and the trooper saw me and came running over. "What'd you find?" Olson asked.

"Take a look at this." I held the wrapper out for both of them to see.

Olson took one look and said "Whoa—you don't think?"

Kahler was lost and asked, "What is it?"

I said, "It's the wrapper from a Nut Goodie—or at least part of a wrapper. It looks like about a third is missing." I held it out for Kahler to see. "Are these sold around here?"

"I don't think I've ever seen one of those before," the trooper replied. "You say you've seen them?"

"These are made in St. Paul, a local candy company that has a loyal following. I've heard that people have them shipped all over the country, or, Sample could have brought it with him from home so it could just be a coincidence." Of course, as I've said before, I don't believe in coincidences, but since we were all cops I didn't need to add that to the discussion.

"You think it means something, or you wouldn't be standing here holding it," Kahler said.

"Yeah—Olson, check it out locally. Have Sharon call Pearson's Candy in St. Paul. See if anyone around here sells them. It could be a coincidence, but we've got to be sure. I think someone brought it from Minnesota."

Kahler went back into trooper mode, produced an evidence bag, and took possession of the wrapper. "I'm not sure if there's any way to get prints or DNA off this thing, but our lab will sure try. If there is anything, we'll let you know."

Mentally, I was trying to put the event together. "Okay—let's say Sample was standing here, enjoying the view, maybe having a little doobie. Someone walks up to him and pops him in the chest and he goes over the edge. So, he must have been comfortable with whoever else it was that was here. But we don't know which way he was facing?"

Kahler said, "That's correct. The body was down there, but there's no way to know what happened up here."

"You said the reason the coroner ruled murder was a bullet hole in a rib?"

"Correct. There was a fresh nick on one of the ribs. I believe it was lower and on the back part of the rib." He pointed at his lower back just above the kidneys, to demonstrate.

"So he could have been shot with a little .22? Did you find any bullet fragments or other ballistic evidence?"

"No, and we excavated the area under and around the body. That's standard procedure here when we find a body that's been down for a while."

I knew the reasoning behind that. There were often times that evidence on the body could get washed off or moved by animals disturbing the body. "So someone walks up and pops Sample in the back and over he goes?"

Kahler replied "I don't think he was shot in the back. I think the nick was an exit wound."

"Why?"

"The coroner said the nick had chipping on it, like when you drill a hole. He said that indicated the bullet had to have passed from front to back."

"But you didn't find any bullet fragments?"

"Nope."

I'm going into thinking out loud mode right about now. This didn't make sense. "But if he was shot front to back with a .22, the bullet shouldn't have exited the body. Even close up, a .22, going through several layers of clothing, and then a torso, wouldn't have enough energy left to nick a rib and exit." Unless—.

Olson and Kahler stood there while I went through my head process. Olson knows me well enough to let me go and Kahler demonstrated a level of experience that showed he'd been through this with investigators before. Sometimes you've just gotta let the processing happen.

"Okay—I've been thinking that this must have been done with a little .22 handgun. If that were the case, you should have found the bullet in the remains, or under the body. You didn't, so it must have been a through-and-through. That means the weapon must have been something a little bigger than a .22—maybe a 5.7. That might get a through-and-through at close range."

The FNH—Five-seveN—was a relatively new gun that had developed a devoted following. Reportedly being used now by the U.S. Secret Service, it is a super lightweight handgun that shoots a 5.7mm round that looks a lot like a rifle round with its stepped neck cartridge. But its popularity with law enforcement is largely due to the fact that the bullet is a tumbler and not a penetrator. That means that it won't go through people and hit other things you don't want to hit—that, and the 20-round magazine. I've got one of those too. "What's the procedure for a firearm purchase up here?" I asked.

Kahler replied, "Just like anywhere, you have to be a state resident to purchase a handgun. Long guns are another story though."

I knew that the drill for getting a gun through airport security—records would exist if our guy had flown up here. The TSA requires a declaration document that includes the make and model of any firearm being transported. I didn't believe our guy would be dumb enough to have filled that out truthfully. But the gun would have been in a locked case. All the person transporting it has to do is declare its presence. It was unlikely TSA would go to the trouble of having the traveler open the case. And I was sure that lots of hunters brought long guns up here on the airlines. He could have tried to sneak something else like a pistol through. On the other hand, if you got caught fibbing you got a "go directly to jail—do not pass go—do not collect $200" card. The alternative was driving up and bringing it with you, but that meant going through Canada. And those Canadian guys are no fun at all when it came to firearms declarations.

I took another look around and saw a place that could have been a shooting point. "Let's take a walk," I said to the other two and we headed up a slight incline away from the overlook.

We'd gone about a half mile up what was the best line of sight, talking about the probabilities of being confronted by some wild animal, when Kahler said "It's really not the bears you have to watch out for—it's the moose."

"Moose—you mean like Bullwinkle?" Olson asked.

"Yeah. The moose are more trouble than the bears. Mostly, the bears are only a problem if it's a female and she has cubs. Otherwise, they pretty much stay away from you. The moose, well, they don't see too well—they're kind of stupid too—so they let you walk right up on them. Then, they'll paw and snort and charge you. They're plenty fast too. And they're pretty tough to stop with a pistol, even one of the big ones."

We came to a place where a path crossed our vector. I noticed a spot that looked good to me. The crossing path went back down in the direction of the parking area that was pretty well covered with trees that would shield someone from being seen from the picnic overlook. It was perpendicular from the line we'd taken up here. I took the laser scope I brought out of my pocket and looked back down the hill. The readout on the scope said the possible sniper nest was 1,400 to 1,500 yards from the overlook. Nearly a mile—a long shot, even for an expert.

I borrowed Andy's binoculars and handed him my scope. "From this spot, a shooter would have a perfect view of anyone on the overlook without having to worry about being seen themselves. And from down there, you probably couldn't even hear it."

"Yeah, but this is too far for a shot," Kahler said. "Only an expert sniper could make a shot from here, and he'd have to have used a .30 magnum or maybe even a .50 caliber to have any hitting power at this range."

"My thoughts exactly, except we may be working with some other kind of rifle here. I'm not sure what's going on, but I'm going to find out what kind of gun was used."

We looked around. It had been at least a week since the shooting, so there was little left in terms of footprints or bi-pod prints. There was the trail though. I sent Olson down the trail toward the parking area and Kahler and I walked back to the overlook. Along the way he made some observations.

"If that was the shooting spot, your guy can really shoot. I was in the Army and shot a .50 cal Barrett. They're real steady but you have to practice a lot to make shots like that."

I hypothesized that the shooter could have made the shot, and then walked back down here to check his handiwork. That would have given him the chance to drop a candy wrapper in the trash. We walked back down to the car. Olson was standing next to it when we got there. In his hand was the rest of the candy wrapper.

"I found it along the trail."

"I take back everything I ever said about you not knowing anything about tracking," I grinned.

Kahler retrieved the first part of wrapper and, sure enough, the parts fit. Before he bagged it with its partner, I wrote down the lot number. We'd check that out to see when it was made and where it was sold. Now we could put someone on the trail to the shooting sight and at the overlook—but whom?

# Chapter 22

We rode with Kahler back into town to the hospital. There we saw the photos of what was left of Cirrus O'Leary-Sample. Not much. One whole leg was missing and the rest was pretty well torn up. After the autopsy, his mom and dad wouldn't have to spend much on air freight. The coroner, a happy guy about mid-40s with a prematurely receding hairline and a *pipe* in his mouth, strolled into the morgue.

"Andy Hatcher," he said as he stuck out his hand, "glad to meet you."

Is everyone in Alaska named Andy? We went through the usual trading of names and cards.

"So, you guys are up from Minnesota?"

His accent was pure Minnesotan. I had to ask, "You a local?"

"Oh sure—all my life—except when I went to med school at the U. of M."

"You went to the University of Minnesota?"

"Yah-sure you betcha"—I thought I was hearing soundtrack from *Fargo*—"There's a strong Minnesota connection here. Palmer was settled by a bunch of Minnesota refugees after World War II. Buncha farmers were promised that this was the new Garden of Eden—grow bigger crops here than anywhere else."

I couldn't resist—ever happed to you? "So your people are farmers who believed Alaska was better for farming than Minnesota?"

"And they were right. This part of Alaska holds the world records for the largest of all kinds of vegetables. We get 22 hours of sunlight all summer."

You stay in this business long enough and you'll learn everything. I didn't voice the next obvious question, "You mean all three weeks?" This guy was proud of who he was and where he lived and why would I challenge that? I asked about the bullet nick.

He had the rib out and tagged as evidence. I could see he took this part of the job seriously.

"Got it right here. As you can see, there is evidence of a bullet nick. I estimate that it occurred at the time of death because there is no sign of any healing, and that it was a front-to-back shot with a very light-caliber weapon. No other evidence of the wound or projectile."

I looked it over and had to agree. I've seen enough busted bones to know that this one had been hit by a small-caliber bullet from the front to back. I didn't like that at all. I asked about cause of death.

"Well, we can't really be sure. He was apparently hit by this bullet that passed straight through, then tumbled over the precipice, and then was eaten. Can't really say when he died, but I'm going to put homicide as the cause. Without being shot, he wouldn't have gone over the cliff."

"Could you tell anything else about the internal organs? Is there any unusual damage?"

"Answer is no, I can't tell because they weren't there."

That's a good way to get rid of evidence—feed it to a bear. Now all we had to do was go out and find where the bear shat. I'd start by looking in the woods.

Hatcher had one more bomb to drop. "You might want to take a look at this—" he led us over to a table that held Samples' clothing, "this is his T-shirt." It was an Under Armor long-sleeve job that cost a bunch but really kept you warm. I had a few of them for winter activities—mostly snowmobiling. They fit tight. This one had an unusual star-shaped hole in it.

"Yeah, that's it," Hatcher said. "That hole is kind of weird. I looked at it under the scope and it's a hole about 3/16 inch across with 5 little lines coming off it, like spokes. Nice clean cuts too."

The fabric the shirt was made of is a very high-quality fine-weave material. It showed a neat, small hole surrounded by cuts, like spokes from a wheel. Now I had something to grab onto, even though I didn't know what it was. But I'd solved cases with smaller starts than this.

Kahler drove us back to the ASP offices where we got copies of the pictures of everything important and started the goodbye process. I asked Kahler and Hatcher to let us know if anything else came up. They asked the same of us. Olson and I headed out to the parking lot where we'd left our rental car nearly 6 hours before and started the drive to the airport. While Olson drove, I made phone calls. First, Bartholomew.

"Whatcha got?"

"Well, I've located the company he worked for, that AMES Services outfit I told you about. They have a research lab and offices in Medina and apparently do some manufacturing there and in Arizona. Harris was one of their top research guys, who also happened to work closely with customers. Their customer list is very short but includes the U.S. Army and Navy."

"That it?"

"No—I also found out that the product line Harris worked most on had to do with something called the Land Warrior project. He worked closely with the Special Forces people at Fort Bragg on radios that their men could use in combat."

"Get any names of people we can talk to?"

"Yeah—I'll have a list when you get back. When will that be by the way?"

"Not sure yet—might have to go back to Arizona on the judge's murder. I'll let you know."

# Chapter 23

I called Fernandez in Arizona.

"I was hoping you'd call. I may have something for you."

I was thinking, "That would be nice." Maybe what she wanted to talk about would warrant a return trip. I was surprised to hear myself think that, but hope springs, as they say. "What do you have?"

"On a hunch, I re-sighted the possible trajectory line to allow for a longer-range weapon. By adjusting the line about 15 degrees clockwise, I found a better shooting site and there was evidence that someone had used it."

"What kind of evidence?"

"I've got boot tracks in and out and some spots that look like bi-pod prints."

"Where is the spot?"

"That's the tricky part. It's a 1282 yard shot from here."

Shit—1282 yards is only possible for a real expert. "You're sure this is the spot?"

"As sure as I can be. This line is right and the tracks are right."

I was thinking I should ask her about the star-shaped hole in O'Leary-Samples shirt when she said, "There is a possibility of a new and different kind of weapon in use here."

"What do you mean by new and different?"

"Well, like I said when you were here, I've worked in the past with our SWAT team and I've trained with some of the Special Ops guys at Ft. Bragg. I stay in touch with them to keep up on the new and different. The Army has developed a new type of rifle round that has great punch and penetrating power. It's a sub-caliber round with a discarding sabot."

I had the phone on speaker and Olson asked, "A discarding what?"

Fortunately I'd had just enough exposure to know what she was talking about. I said, talking mostly to Olson, "Sabot, spelled S- A-B-O-T, that's pronounced Saw-Bow, is a French word for clog or shoe. It's also used to describe a projectile that is smaller than the barrel that launches it. You know the Army's M-1 tank, right?" Olson nodded. "Its primary tank killing weapon is basically a depleted uranium spike about 1.5 inches in diameter with fins to stabilize it. It looks like a big dart. In fact, it's called an "Armor Piercing Fin Stabilized Discarding Sabot Penetrator." The barrel on the M-1 tank that launches it is 120mm or about 6 inches in diameter, meaning the projectile is much too small to be shot from that barrel. So they wrap it in the "Sabot," which is kind of like the plastic cup that holds the pellets in a shotgun shell. When the shotgun shell leaves the barrel, the plastic cup opens up like a flower and falls away. With the tank gun, the plastic cup holds the projectile the same as a shotgun shell. The result is you can fire a much smaller projectile from a bigger barrel. This allows you to put a lot more push behind the projectile."

Olson continued nodding as Maria chimed in, "That M-1 tank round can cover a mile in less than a second. In fact, the thing is going so fast it doesn't even need any explosive on board. It's like a big fast bullet. I've seen these things work at the Army's test range. When it hits the target, it just goes right through it. It's going so fast and weighs so much that it goes through the heaviest armor. It turns the armor into molten metal on the way and drags that molten metal into the interior of the target. The depleted uranium they make these things out of is pyrophoric. That means it disintegrates going through the armor, and the particles that come out the other side of the hole self-ignite when they hit the oxygen in the air. This immediately lights everything—ammunition, fuel, and people—on fire."

Now there was a nasty thought. I added, "There have been rifles that fire sabots for years. There is what is called "flechette" rounds, which are really nasty anti-personnel weapons. They have a sabot that holds a bunch of tiny razor-tipped darts that spread out like shot gun pellets and rip people apart. In fact, shotguns that shoot slugs are firing a sabot round. If the rifle in question could fire a single penetrator-like projectile, it would have a much longer effective range."

Olson had a look on his face that told me he was hitting information overload.

"Maria, the kid killed up here was wearing a very tight undershirt and the entry hole is shaped like a star."

"Oh, boy—that sounds just like what you'd get with a dart."

"A dart?"

"Yeah, that's what the Army guys call their projectile. It's made of tungsten and is about 1.5 inches long—.17 caliber with 5 fins. You fire it from any .30 magnum-caliber rifle, but good old standards like a Remington 700 seem to work best."

Holy crap. Now I've got a bad guy who is not only a sniper-quality shot but also has access to latest-technology weaponry. I wondered what could make this worse.

"Oh, there was one other thing I found at the possible sniper perch," Maria said, "There was a piece of trash."

"What kind of trash?"

"A wrapper from a candy bar."

Then she had my undivided attention. "A candy wrapper?"

"Yeah, not a locally available one either. But we have a lot of Minnesota people here part time—some probably get them from back home."

I felt my throat tightening up. "What's the brand?"

"Pearson's Nut Goodie."

"Shit—shit—shit!" I muttered. I had Fernandez read the lot number and it was the same as the one we'd found here in Alaska. Coincidence? Not likely. I decided we'd better go back to Arizona, but not right now. We needed to get home. I called the airline and made the arrangements while Olson drove. As I watched the scenery go by I kept thinking about Ben Harris. What is the connection? How would he get this kind of weaponry? Could he make a 1,400+ yard shot? I had lots of questions for Mr. Harris. They'd have to wait until I got back to the Cities.

# Chapter 24

## Plymouth, Minnesota

While the Minneapolis detectives were touring Arizona and Alaska, Ben Harris followed Mikey up the stairs into the RV and closed the door behind him. The rig was loaded up and ready for the road. He pulled out of the driveway and settled in for a long leg. He was heading east this time—going to see some Civil War battle fields and visit the Smithsonian. Mikey took his normal place on the dash and rode shotgun.

They crossed the Twin Cities on I-94 and headed into Wisconsin. He'd left at 10 a.m. to avoid most of the rush-hour traffic and that put him outside Madison in time for an early dinner. He kept out of the Chicago area by going south on I-39. He got a good night's sleep in a Wal-Mart parking lot on the outskirts of Bloomington IL, rose early and caught I-74 to cut across to Indianapolis, where he picked up I-70. The RV rolled into Dayton, Ohio, in time for an afternoon tour of the National Museum of the United States Air Force. He was an honorary member of the Air Force Retirement Society as a result of some of the projects he'd worked on when he was in the business world. It was a special time in his life, when he traveled and worked with warriors. He was lucky enough to attend some of their special schools in order to better understand their unique problems and needs. As he walked through the giant hangers of the Air Force Museum, he looked at the history of mankind's efforts to destroy each other from the air. There were a few systems here he'd helped design and perfect. He knew that his was an esoteric profession—he prevented conflict by making it too fearful for others to start.

Ben spent the night between Columbus and Pittsburgh parked in a large truck stop near Zanesville, Ohio. He fed Mikey, and then made dinner—grilled pork chops, instant mashed potatoes, and a green salad. It was important to eat properly when in the field, he'd been taught. After dinner, Ben called a number back in Minnesota and spoke with his counterpart about progress on the rest of the program. Thus far, everything had gone off without a hitch. But he knew that no plan survived first contact with the enemy, so the phone he was using was untraceable on both ends He also called ahead to a North Carolina number and checked arrangements there. Again, everything was prepared.

Over the next two weeks he visited Gettysburg on the Fourth of July and witnessed a re-enactment of that horrific battle. He took two days to work his way through the Smithsonian and other DC highlights. He hiked the Blue Ridge and Cumberland with Mikey, and Stone Mountain and Chickamauga on his own. He stopped in central North Carolina to see friends and do some more hiking and other outdoor activities. He drove a bit farther south and spent some time in Atlanta checking out the downtown skyline. Then he made his way back to the west through Tennessee and Kentucky, making a side pilgrimage to Bristol to indulge his surprising—for most people—love of stock car racing. He drove back north through St. Louis and took the scenic route up the west side of the Mississippi to Keokuk, Iowa, and Iowa City. Arriving home refreshed but exhausted, he parked the rig and settled in for some catch-up sleep.

Gil Cederstrom had been making plans for a trip too. Two days after Ben got back, Cederstrom would be traveling eastward.

# Chapter 25

**Monday, July 14th**
**Atlanta, Georgia**

The Shooter was hard at it. He had repeated his trip to the airport, this time driving to a busy Holiday Inn in Bloomington to leave his car and then taking a cab to the airport. He went to the Delta counter and bought a round trip to Charlotte, North Carolina, and passed through security without a problem—he had nothing on his person that would set off any alarms. He read a book on the flight and thought about the approach for his objective. In Charlotte, he rented a car and drove west on I-85 through South Carolina. At the first rest stop in Georgia, he pulled in for a break. He went to the men's room and then went out the back to a historic-spot overlook. He waited until there was no one else in the rest stop, then vaulted a low fence, and hiked down a steep incline to a ledge. There, in a crevasse in the rock, he found the wrapped package he was looking for and removed it, climbed back up the hill and nimbly stepped back over the rail. He carried the package out to the car and put it in the trunk, climbed in, and drove away. It was only a short hour and a half to Atlanta.

In downtown Atlanta, he found the address he was looking for and parked in the public garage. He retrieved the package from the trunk and went into the building. There was a maintenance elevator on the back side of the building and he took it to the highest floor. He walked up another three flights of stairs and found the door to the roof. When he stepped out onto the roof, it was 5:30 p.m. local time. He was about six blocks from his target, which was just about right.

He walked around the deserted roof and found the spot he had located on the aerial photography. After setting the package down on the gravel, he took out a small ceramic composite knife he had brought with him. The material in the knife was non-metallic, making it invisible to the airport security devices and the blade was razor sharp. He slit open the package to reveal the rifle case inside and removed a Luepold 10×50 scope from the case to take a look at his quarry. He had a good view of the west-side penthouse balcony of the office building six blocks away and across the street. Among its many tenants were the law offices of Davis, Powers & Styles. His target was Richard Ronald Davis, Esquire, Attorney at Law. In the judgment of the Shooter, this was the man who obtained the acquittals that so undermined justice. He knew that Davis, or "Big Dick," as he preferred to be called by his inner circle, liked to have a one-drink happy hour every evening before going home. He visualized himself joining a couple of TV-character Boston lawyers on their office balcony, commiserating over scotch and cigars. The Shooter was counting on the Dick's affectation—"name on the door"—to be his undoing.

Sure enough, at 6:10 Davis appeared, glass in one hand, cigar in the other. There were two people with him. The Shooter recognized one as Davis's closest associate. The other was a stranger. "Oh well—they'll get a show," he thought. He had assembled the rifle, a somewhat ungainly looking thing with its heavy over-long barrel, had mounted the scope, and had chambered the special round. He had brought a hand-held Kestrel 4000 mini-weather station. He measured the wind, humidity, and temperature. These data were input into another device that looked like an ordinary calculator. It was a ballistic computer—the same model used by the military. He measured the distance with a laser rangefinder at 874 yards. This final piece of information went into the computer. The results of the calculations gave him settings that he dialed into the scope. It would be a very difficult shot, but not impossible. He steadied the rifle on the bipod legs—back from the edge of the roof, just in case some sharp-eyed person happened to be looking up. He swung the weapon out on the line of fire and found Davis in the reticle. He stopped and repeated his appraisal of the weather and wind—no changes. He had the humidity accounted for and the drop was only 22 feet over the line of flight. He rechecked the wind with the hand-held anemometer and it held steady at 14 mph and was a quartering tail wind.

He dialed a few final clicks into the scope to account for the fact that Davis was standing instead of sitting, as he had expected, bringing the target about 18 inches higher. The shooter took a deep breath, held it for about 2 seconds, slowly let it half out, held it again, and squeezed the hand-tuned trigger. There was a reassuring buck as the rifle jumped in his hands. He held on target, watching through one of the world's best optical systems. And less than a second later—the Shooter saw Davis's head explode.

# Chapter 26

Luther Robinson was one of Davis's most trusted associates. He was always close at hand when decisions were to be made and was standing only four feet or so from Davis when it happened.

The current strategy under discussion was whether or not to get involved in a case between the City of Cincinnati and a local individual who was suing the police department for assault and battery. The plaintiff in question was a 24 year-old white male who was arrested for drunk & disorderly after a traffic stop. He wasn't driving—his wife was—but she was drunk too. She had been cooperating with the two traffic officers. She admitted that she'd had a few beers and had an outstanding warrant for a minor drug bust. But the husband was belligerent and started challenging everything from the officer's authority to their ancestry.

After putting the wife in the patrol car, the police officers removed the man from the passenger's side of his car and started asking him questions. It was clear he was too impaired to drive himself home, but he kept insisting they had no reason to hold him and he should be allowed to leave. The officers couldn't allow that, he wouldn't co-operate, and ultimately he was arrested and received charges including drunkenness, disorderly conduct, and resisting arrest.

The officers put him in the back seat with his wife and started searching the car. While they were waiting in the squad car, the two drunks contrived a plan. They didn't know that the dash camera was still on and, although it wasn't photographing them, it recorded every sound.

Husband: "Hit me quick—hit me in the mouth!"

Wife: "I can't do that."

Husband: "Come on. They didn't cuff you. Hit me in the mouth as hard as you can. We'll get them on a brutality charge."

Wife: "Yeah—that'll show them."

The next sound was a bone crunching blow to the guys face.

Husband: "Ooow—that smarts!"

Wife: "Well—you said to hit you."

The man was now bleeding profusely from a broken nose. Apparently he'd forgotten that his wife had a pretty mean right cross. And they'd both been unaware of the recorder.

At the fatal moment on the balcony, Davis, Robinson, and the third man, were discussing the pros and cons of interceding on behalf of the couple.

Davis had said, "It's a high-profile national case. I don't care if we lose—it's a lot of air time."

Robinson, always cautious, disagreed, "The fact is, we will lose. And losing is losing even with national press. In fact, this one may be worse because of the press."

Davis countered, "We don't know we'll lose. Look what we did in Minneapolis. That was a loser too—until we got into it. We were the ones that found the holes and got the evidence dumped and the jury stacked." There was a bit more to it than that, but neither mentioned it.

This was how they processed decisions—back and forth like two boxers feeling each other out for a weakness. Davis thought he'd found one.

"It's the dash tape that's key. The traffic stop is suspect since it was just for a busted taillight. The arrest of the wife shouldn't have happened since she incriminated herself without the benefit of Miranda, and the tape was made without their knowledge. Without that tape—they've got nothing."

Robinson pondered. There was a lot of money involved in a victim-suing-city-type trial. He knew Davis was going to take it with or without his approval, so it was important to be sure he'd covered all the possible down sides.

Davis was happily sucking on his cigar, leaning out over the rail, and looking down on the city of Atlanta. "This is what it's all about," he thought, "I've worked my ass off for all of my adult life and now I get to decide who walks and who goes directly to jail. What could make this better?"

His internal dialogue ended instantly as the dart impacted the left side of his head. It was traveling at about 4,200 feet per second, a little more than 2,800 miles per hour. This is much faster than the speed of sound, so there was no warning that it was on the way. The tungsten dart was very heavy for a bullet at 884 grains, or about two ounces—almost five times the mass of a typical sniper rifle bullet. At that velocity, the impact was the same as hitting someone in the head with a common household hammer going 350 miles per hour. It made a small, five-pointed-star opening above his left ear, where it entered Davis's head. Its impact created a supersonic, hydraulic shock wave that traveled through Davis's head like a tidal wave. It would have left the same signature mark upon exiting the other side, but that tell-tale mark was obliterated by the shock wave. When the wave hit the inside of Davis's skull, it transferred the energy of that 350-mph hammer blow to the bone, which vaporized.

Robinson heard a sort-of splat, like the sound made by a dropped melon, and saw Davis's head simultaneously blow up. Later, he was asked if he heard a gunshot, and he couldn't remember. In fact, he couldn't remember much—just that they were standing there talking and Davis's head exploded. There was no other way to describe it. One second it was there—the next it was a cloud of pink mist. The rest of Davis dropped where he had been standing.

# Chapter 27

## Robbinsdale

I was enjoying the televised Twins game and a cold beer with Pete Anderson, a guy I went to high school with very long ago. Somehow, we'd stayed pretty close throughout the years even though we'd gone completely different directions in our lives. He'd also gone on to the University of Minnesota but, after two years, a couple of his buddies talked him into transferring to a local college whose football team had the dubious distinction of holding the NCAA record for consecutive losses. He signed up to play. He was a pretty fair football player—six foot seven and could catch almost anything thrown in his neighborhood—but not Division One quality, so he wasn't playing for the Gophers. So he tried out and made the team. On the final pre-season practice, he broke his collarbone and was out for the season. Of course, they broke their losing streak that year. He missed being on the winning squad, but he made the team picture.

Pete had charisma—not just with the girls in college—so after college he went into sales, representing local manufacturers. Pete got into the lucrative, if underpublicized, military-related manufacturing that has flourished in Minnesota.

Pete was doing multi-million dollar deals in his later twenties. And, since most of what he did was paid by a percentage, he was doing well. Now, in our dotage, he was living in a big house on Lake Minnetonka and taking it easy. Someday I will too—I can hope.

We were on my deck, which is behind the porch attached to the rear of the house. It was Tuesday evening and the temp was above 90 degrees. Summers in Minnesota are kind of weird. They come late and leave early and simmer you in between. The light was flat and promised thunderstorms before morning. We were cooling off in the unheated hot tub, counting the minutes until the sun starts going down and the mosquitoes come out. I have a nice flat screen in the porch that is easily visible through the screens, so we were drinking beer and enjoying life away from the realities of homicide investigating. I was picking his brain about military weaponry.

"So," he asked, "this hot tamale is telling you that she thinks the judge was hit by some science fiction bullet and you don't know who to believe?"

"I'm not sure, but she sure is. She checks out as far as I can find on her credentials—working with the feds and her own SWAT team." I was uncertain about where to go with her, other than knowing I'd like to see her again.

"Well, I'll tell you what I've heard from some of the guys I know. The whole idea is miniaturization of the basic tank round—makes it man portable, so to speak. You really wouldn't want to use it on people because it's just too expensive. There are already other types of rounds that can give you that kind of reach without going to tungsten—just too expensive," he repeated. "I know that they've already done it with an armor piercing round for the M2 machine."

I asked, "The M2—that's the old World War II .50 caliber?"

"Yeah, it's been around for a long time, but it's still a great heavy machine gun. This new round is a discarding-sabot armor-piercing round to take out lightly armored targets like helicopters. The army found out the hard way that those Russian Mil 24s are pretty tough to shoot down with regular machine gun rounds—in fact, anything less than a missile—so they came up with this new thing. I hear that it's good out to two miles."

"This so-called man portable rifle—is there anything usual about the gun?" I asked.

"Yeah, it has a very distinguishing characteristic. It will have a relatively long heavy barrel and the barrel will have little or no rifling."

"How do you get that kind of accuracy with no rifling?" This was science fiction.

"That's how it works. Just like on the tank cannon, the projectile is fin stabilized. Spinning would actually screw it up. You find a rifle with a long barrel and no rifling and it's either an active-duty Special Ops guy or your guy—or maybe both."

"*Maybe both?*" that got me wondering, "What do you mean by that?" I asked.

"Come on, Dan. You said your prime guy is the dead gal's husband—Harris—right?"

I acknowledged that and he said, "I know who he works for—at least worked for. They're one of the biggest Special Forces suppliers in the state."

"Who is that and what do you mean *worked* for? I thought he was still working."

Pete chewed on a pretzel and answered, "As far as I know, the story is that he has a couple of very important patents. He's on the payroll, but that's only for insurance coverage benefits. He's living off his royalties."

"How much can a guy make off royalties?" I asked.

"At his level—it could be maybe $200K-plus per year, per patent. We're talking breakthrough products here."

That would be enough to own the RV. "Why is he still working?"

"We can't all retire like you buddy. Besides, believe it or not, some kinds of work are fun. I've had some very interesting experiences with the military guys over the years."

"Yeah—like what?"

Pete elaborated, "I've seen live fire exercises that would set your hair on fire—live cluster munitions dropped—rocket launches. I even got to shoot a tank with an anti-tank rocket myself once."

"Why would they let you do that?"

"It can be several things. If you are the guy selling the thing to them and it's not working right, they'll happily hand it to you and say, 'Go ahead, hot shot, show us how'. If you know them really well they may let you give it a dance just for fun. Plus you sometimes get to go out on training missions, which can be neat. I know a guy who spent three weeks on an aircraft carrier once, just so he'd be there to see a new missile tested."

I agreed that would be a blast. "You think this guy Harris ever did that kind of thing?"

"I don't know. Most of the stuff they make is radios and such. I don't know if there'd be any reason for him to spend any kind of field time on that. It sounds more like lab time."

If Harris was going out on field trials, maybe he met people who could get him this super gun. And if he had, someone else was involved. I'd have to start over on his acquaintances, friends, relatives, and co-workers—anyone who might know who he worked with on the user end.

# Chapter 28

The Twins had just taken a lead that should ensure they kept their winning streak alive when the phone rang. It was Olson.

"Hey, you got a TV on?"

"Watching the Twins. They keep this up and we'll have another Series here."

"Yeah, they're hot—turn it quick to Fox news."

"What's up?" I knew Olson didn't get excited about the news unless it was big.

"Just *turn* the *channel!*"

I flipped over to 30 and found a live remote going on in front of some office building somewhere. Office buildings in this country all look the same to me—it could have been anywhere in the country. The reporter was wearing the station-issue blouse and skirt, blond hair, bright lips, and an excited look in her eyes.

"Again—in breaking news—famed criminal defense attorney Richard Ronald Davis was shot in the head by a sniper this evening as he enjoyed his usual after-work cocktail on his 14th floor balcony. A co-worker was right next to him when—in the words of the co-worker—Mr. Davis's head *exploded!* There is no sign of the sniper or where the sniper was when Davis was killed. Police have surrounded all the adjacent blocks and sealed them off for searches. All the people in those buildings are being questioned and identified. The police were called in immediately after the killing and they are certain that they will find the sniper among the people they have in custody."

"Holy Hannah!" I erupted—"Wasn't he the guy that defended Hill and Sample?"

Olson confirmed, "Right on the nose—looks like our boy has hit again."

"Where are you?" I asked.

"At the office—you going where I think you're going?"

"Right now—meet me there. But first, call the cops down there and tell them they'd better expand their lockdown perimeter to at least 1,000 yards."

I ran into the house to put on some long pants and a sweatshirt and shoved a little backup pistol into my pocket. I ran out the back door and told

Pete to lock up when he left, and then ran to the garage for my city bike. I've got two motorbikes, one city, and one country. The country bike is a full-dress Honda Gold Wing Airbag. Yeah—it's got an airbag. But it is 1,800 cc, 6-cylinder smooth, and fully set up with plenty of storage for road cruising. You can get on it and go 1,000 miles like nothing. I grabbed my city bike. It's a Harley Davidson VRSCDX, also known as a Night Rod Special. This thing is just plain scary—to look at or to ride. It's got the same engine as the HD racing bikes, is painted all black, and is loud. I jumped on and shot west on County Road 9 toward the Plymouth home of my prime suspect.

# Chapter 29

I goosed the black bike up to cruising speed and headed west, and activated a few special accessories on my motor scooter.

All Harley Davidson owners like to add things to their bikes, sort of personalize them, and I'm no exception. The amount of aftermarket stuff that bolts onto a Harley would fill a semi-trailer, but I've got some things you won't find in the catalog. The city PD motor department put some very small but effective LED lights on, front and rear, and a tiny all-electronic siren that you can activate with a thumb switch. I hit the lights and used the screamer at intersections as I roared west on 42nd.

The Police in Robbinsdale, Crystal, New Hope, and Plymouth must all have been watching the Twins game so I didn't have to explain anything to any of them. I know most of them and they all know about the bike. Even so, no suburban cop likes anyone running twice the posted limit through their little burbs. I crossed I-494 without being intercepted and made the turn to Harris's place.

When I got to the end of the driveway, I could see the big Winnebago RV sitting in the backyard. There were no other cars around and I parked the Harley and walked up the drive. I took my pocket gun out and slipped it under my belt in what the firearms instructors call the Mexican carry. As always, I was hoping I wouldn't need it. In fact, if I was right, Harris wouldn't be here at all.

I walked around the house calling Harris's name and banged on a few windows, just in case the dog was around to wake him up. No answers, no barks, no one home.

Olson rolled up the drive a few minutes later as I was walking back around toward the front of the house, figuring no one was home. I was just starting the decision process on whether or not the take the door when I saw his car.

Olson got out and motioned toward the house—"No one here?"

"Nope—you want to go in?"

Olson thought it over and said "How are we going to explain the busted door?"

That's always the problem. You can say that there was a phone call about a prowler in the area, but that would have brought the Plymouth Police. You can say you were just driving by or even that you'd come out to see the guy and thought you saw him laying on the floor inside, but all the blinds were closed and I couldn't see anything. And Harris had been pretty insistent about us not going in before and I didn't think he'd buy any story. But his resistance was the main reason I wanted in. I looked around and found a small sign stuck in the landscaping near the front door. It was a sign notifying the world that the house was alarmed and the name of the alarm company. Great, just my luck, and this would be the one guy who both pays the bill and turns the thing on.

It's a little-known fact that alarm companies are one of the great money makers in our country. Think about it. Most cops will tell you that many people have them, are paying the fees, but they don't turn them on. Most cities will give you one false-alarm police visit per year. After that you get charged anywhere from $75 to $150 per visit. So if it goes off because little Johnny forgot to turn it off, or forgot the code, or they forgot that the cat sets off the motion detectors if it's not locked in the basement, they may just leave it off all the time. Cops know that maybe 10 percent of alarms are actually on when people aren't home. Burglars know this too, but they don't know which ones are which, so just having it is still a good idea. Anyway, if you own an alarm company and only have to monitor 10 percent of the systems that subscribe, that's not too bad a deal for you.

I gave one last thought to trying a break in and had an idea.

"Olson, didn't this guy have a cabin?"

Olson, who is a walking file cabinet when it comes to case information, pulled out his Blackberry and took a look. "Yeah, up on Bay Lake. I got a phone number too."

He gave it to me and I asked "You sure this is a land line and not a cell?"

He said "Yes—checked it out myself with the phone company."

It had an old-type number prefix and the area code was 218, which is right for northern Minnesota, but that didn't mean it wasn't a cell. The problem with cell phones is they didn't necessarily have to be at home to get a call. I called it.

Seven rings went by and I got an answer. "Harris."

"Mr. Harris, this is Dan Neumann of the Minneapolis Police."

"Yes—?"

I really didn't think I'd get an answer. I scrambled. "I—uh—just had a couple of questions you may be able to clear up for us. Do you think you could stop by Detective Olson's office this evening?"

There was a pause. "While I'm impressed with the hours you are apparently keeping, I just put a steak on the grill and I'm planning on fishing after that.

How about tomorrow—say mid-morning? It's a pretty good drive from here, but I was going home tomorrow anyway."

"That would be fine. We'll see you around eleven o'clock."

The phone went dead. Apparently Harris had nothing else to add to the conversation.

"He answered?" Olson asked.

"Yeah, he's there. There's no way he could have done the job in Atlanta and gotten back here already."

"Or—there's more than one," Olson said.

That's always been a possibility. In a case like this there was always enough anger to go around and there could be someone piggy-backing a copycat crime on top of the one we were looking at. We'd have to check really close on the methodology used in Georgia to see if that killing was similar to any of the others.

"You are going to have to come up with some questions by the time he comes in tomorrow," I said.

"*Me?* You invited him—you come up with something."

"We need to start going after some connections here. Let's ask him about his work history. I was watching the game with my buddy Pete Anderson and he says this guy's employer is into a lot of military stuff. Maybe we could look at that and see if he has any friends who could be doing this for him."

Olson thought it over. He had been in the Air Force as an AP, or Air Police, for about four years. Not exactly Special Forces, but at least military. I'd never been in.

Olson said, "Some of those bonds can go pretty deep, especially the SOCOM Special Ops guys. They'd do things for each other, but I'm not sure they'd do anything for an outsider."

Either way, we needed to start looking at that. They were the only ones who had the apparent skills necessary to do what was being done.

# Chapter 30

## Along the Highway in South Carolina

The Shooter put down the phone. It was a call he had expected and was ready for. He'd pulled off the road to quiet the car and make the connection more stable. He answered the questions as planned, hung up, and pulled back onto the highway. It was a bit of risk that he had to take. The whole plan depended on the cops accepting things at face value and not digging any deeper—at least for now.

As he drove back east through South Carolina he made a quick stop in Greenville at a UPS store. There he shipped a long flat package labeled "Golf Clubs" to an address in Procter, Minnesota, a small town just outside Duluth. Back on the road, he thought about his time in this part of the country. He had spent nine months at Ft. Bragg, more specifically at the Kennedy Special Warfare School. This was where America took already highly-trained and experienced NCOs and Officers and turned them into the finest warriors of our time. You'd get a justified argument out of the guys from Coronado Beach and Hurlburt Field, but the Green Berets still had a claim on being the first and the best.

The Green Berets and SEALs became famous during and after Viet Nam. But that fame was the wrong kind. Despite the 200-year history of Special Forces, they were on the cutting block during post-war downsizing and went the way of the B-1 bomber—a great idea we just can't afford. That changed during the 1980s. Reagan was a big fan, as Kennedy had been, and the funding came back. Good thing too, as a bunch of minor conflicts requiring a small but well trained and equipped force came up on the radar. Special Forces gave presidents a capability to perform very precise missions under covert conditions that most Americans never knew about. It was during this period that the Shooter got involved.

# Chapter 31

1988
Fort Bragg, North Carolina

Ben Harris was a hot commodity. He had recently designed and developed a new radio system that was small enough, light enough, and used so little electricity that battery operation could go on for 20 hours—a lifetime at this point in battery evolution. He had started with a simple system and made it even simpler, driving down the size, weight, and cost to a point where every soldier could be equipped with it—at least every special warrior. But, as with all things new, it had led to some controversy.

Ben had been born in Minneapolis at Abbott-Northwestern Hospital in February 1956. He grew up the only child of two very average Midwesterners, Roger and Angie Harris. Roger worked in the burgeoning food industry that is centered in the Twin Cities. General Mills, Pillsbury, and Cargill are all based in the area. Roger was a marketing specialist who spent his years thinking up new ways to design, package, and sell cereal. He was successful and worked 42 years for the same firm, something unheard of in the current atmosphere of go wherever you wish and change jobs every seven years. Back then, job security was for real and companies made sure they held onto their top people by giving them new assignments, good pay, and a sense of belonging.

Ben's mother, Angie, was the head of the home and stayed there even when the women's movement started to kick in during the 'sixties. She didn't feel unfulfilled—she was happy with her husband, her son, her church, and her life. She nurtured Ben in a way that made him inquisitive. He was taught to never accept that something couldn't be done—that just meant that the solution hadn't been found yet. She encouraged him to believe that he should never close a door, that he should always consider every possibility. That, combined with his father's work ethic, produced Ben—a man with intelligence, motivation, consideration of others, and the willingness to sacrifice.

Ben grew up in the suburb of Minnetonka. He attended public schools at a time when things were changing rapidly in the school systems. Suburbs were growing and adding schools by the score, so, without the family moving, he wound up attending two grade schools, two junior high schools, and two different high schools as the school district grew and the boundary lines shifted. This meant that every year he made new friends to go with the old ones he kept and met new teachers as well. He excelled in science and math and also was in the band and orchestra. One year he dabbled in theater. Ben didn't go in much for sports—the only real team sport he participated in was grade school football and that was because the football coach was also the band director. In high school he skied on the downhill team one year but wasn't a standout, and the next year he was too busy with other activities.

Those activities included the opposite sex. As a member of the band, he spent a lot of time in mixed company and there were plenty of chances for dating, but he was a little on the shy side. One of his best friends was considered the Don Juan of the group and by the time they were juniors in high school, he could regale the gang with tales of his exploits. By the time they went to college this guy had earned the nick name "Frito" by the girls who said all he wanted was for it to end in "-*lay*."

College for Ben was the University of Minnesota's Institute of Technology. He became immersed in the science of electricity and radio wave radiation. It was the mid-1970s and the computer industry was still centered in Minnesota. The first real computer was built at the Univac Company during WWII. Ben excelled in this new discipline and took additional classes in radio and radar. By the time he graduated in 1980 he had a double degree in Computer Science and Electrical Engineering. He finished his MS in a year and a half and went to work for AMES. It was his work there that had brought him to Ft. Bragg.

Ben was dressed in camouflage fatigues, something he'd never worn in his life. He was standing alongside a jeep in mud up to his ankles. The colonel in charge of the training exercise was holding forth on what he thought of Ben's invention in terms that were as complimentary as the mud they were standing in.

"I've got to tell you, Mr. Harris," he said very formally, "these radios aren't worth the powder it'd take to blow them to shit. And it wouldn't take much—small as they are."

Ben answered, "I understand Colonel, but you've got to give us a little more time. This is a great new concept and will give your troops a capability they've never had. We foresee a time when you'll be able to get locations from these as well. You'll be able to sit back in a command and control vehicle with a screen in front of you that shows where every one of your men is, his physical condition, and his ammo load. After that, we're working on equipping every man with a tiny TV camera so you'll be able to see what he sees."

"That sounds like Buck Rogers to me. In the words of Gus Grissom, 'If we can't talk between two buildings, how are we supposed to talk between the earth and the moon?' "

Ben cringed and told the colonel to give him more time. He'd have them up to par by tomorrow even if he had to stay up all night.

A sergeant came over as the colonel drove away. "Don't worry about it, Mr. Harris. We'll get this thing figured. And you're right—these things are worth their weight in gold. I can't wait to get a set into a real situation and see just how big the advantage will be."

# Chapter 32

That chance came sooner than anyone would have believed. In August 1991, Saddam Hussein invaded his sovereign neighbor, Kuwait. The United States assembled the first-ever Middle East Alliance to go in and root the guy out. In preparation for this, the United States Army's Special Forces community went into high gear. Ben Harris was right in the middle of it.

Ben moved into Fayetteville, North Carolina, with a lot of ideas and a creative approach. His company sent him there to coordinate with the Green Berets and their cohorts, who were getting ready to go to Kuwait and Iraq. He was there for 10 weeks, working in the field with the warriors that would be using the communication equipment he designed, under very real-world conditions. As a part of his work with them, they took the time to indoctrinate Ben into some of the skills they used.

Ultimately he was invited to go through what the warrior short course, a quickie training regimen they reserve for other service members who need a familiarity with the capabilities of the Special Warrior, but not the actual abilities themselves. Most people who take this course are basically along for the ride as observers, but Ben wanted to participate. He was a good student and thought a lifetime of water and snow skiing had left him in good condition when they started, a belief that was immediately crushed. The physical requirements placed on Special Forces personnel are torturous. Fortunately his still-young—35 years—body kept up and by the end of the training he was being asked if he would like to sign up. He could run all day, rappel down a rope from a helicopter, and sneak through the jungle like one of them. Also—odd for a lifetime non-hunter—he turned out to be a natural shot.

A natural shot is someone who has an inherent ability to pick up a firearm and put lead on target. The process of shooting has many steps—target acquisition, identification, tracking, sight picture, and finally the shot itself.

Target acquisition is just noticing that the target has presented itself—identification is determining whether the thing you've noticed is a valid target—tracking is bringing the firearm to bear— sight picture is the final alignment of the firearm before the shot—and taking the shot, which is more than just pulling a trigger. A natural shooter is one who has the gift to be able to do all this with little or no training. Just like throwing a football, hitting a baseball, or martial arts, there are people who have a gift when it comes to shooting. Ben had the gift, even though it had never been awakened. And his real talent was in the area of long shots. He was that most rare of shooters—a natural sniper.

# Chapter 33

**Tuesday, July 15th**
**Bay Lake, Minnesota**

Mike Clancy—the human—told Mikey, the dog, "Just about finished with this." Mike thought it was funny that Harris's dog had his name. He was working on the assembly of the remote controllers he needed to finish the job. Another couple of hours and he'd have them ready to install in the light airplane they'd be using. The controllers had to work perfectly—all his systems had to work perfectly—lives depended upon it.

It had been a long year and a half for Mike. He had been in Afghanistan when the grocery store bank was robbed—long-distance tears. When he got back, he'd stayed on the periphery, not getting close to the Hollywood circus that the trial became. He did attend one day, and noticed Ben Harris there in the front row. He wasn't sure who he was but felt that he'd seen him before, and not just on TV.

About a week after the verdict, he received a phone call. The caller proposed an idea that would change Mike's life and give him a feeling of retribution—a feeling that he'd be doing something that needed doing—although it went against everything he previously believed in.

Mike grew up in St. Paul, near what is called the Midway area. Born in 1975, his family was a bit atypical for the time— mom still married to dad. Mike was an athlete, but not in it for social status. He played hockey on a bad inner-city high school team and went out for track and cross country at a school where neither were considered cool. He did well in school, especially math, and was interested in all things electronic. The 1990s were the beginning of the electronic revolution and Mike was fascinated by computers, CDs, personal stereos, and cell phones. After high school, he went to Dunwoody Institute, a Minneapolis vo-tech with a long history of turning out some of Minnesota's brightest technicians.

At Dunwoody, Mike learned the technical skills that ultimately brought him to the U.S. Air Force. He took classes in two areas—Electronics Technologies, and Automated Systems and Robotics. He graduated a few years after the '91 Persian Gulf War and, like a lot of young people, was attracted to the suddenly popular military. Of course, most of those who were signing up didn't think there'd be another war very soon. As part of his enlistment, he was assured he'd be offered training in his field and given the opportunity to make it in a technical specialty. Unmanned Aerial Vehicles (UAVs) were just getting off the ground and he wanted to be part of that.

That is where he was when the news came. He'd just rotated back to Afghanistan for his second tour there. In his first tour overseas, in 1994, he'd become expert at fixing the UAVs the Air Force now used to patrol the skies. After that tour he came back to the States for more education, Officer Candidate School, and worked on the design of the latest control systems. He knew the systems and how to build them and fly them. Then, it was back to Afghanistan. He routinely flew his Predator high above the Al Qaeda and Taliban forces and directed the flight of the weapons that would ruin their day. Once, he had control of a Maverick missile-armed Predator that took out the vehicle of an insurgent leader and four of his top aides. Now, on his second tour, he really had something to go back home to. Susan, his girlfriend since his first year at Dunwoody, had agreed to marry him. Good thing too—neither of them knew it when he left, but she was now expecting their first child.

Susan was from Edina. She grew up in relative affluence, going to one of the top-rated school systems in the country. After high school, she attended the College of St. Katherine in St. Paul and took a part-time job working in a popular bar and grill on Selby at Snelling Avenue. She was working one night when three young men walked in to watch the Twins game over a couple of cold ones.

Susan went over to take their orders and endured the usual games of introduction that she had come to expect from boys her own age. After several trips to the table, she was starting to notice the quiet one. Two of the boys were very open in their interest in her but one was just there, looking at her and offering little in the conversation. When she brought their beers, she set his down first, which prompted some ribbing from his friends. But they began to get acquainted—trading information on where they were going to school, what they were studying, how the Twins were doing, and such. Susan was entranced by the quiet young man and did something she had never done before—she slipped him her phone number.

Mike didn't know what to do. This had never happened to him before, so he stuck the slip of paper in his pocket before his friends could see it and thought about what to do. "Finish your beer," he told himself, "and call her while you've still got the nerve. "

He didn't call her until two days later. Never a lady's man, but he had dated in high school. He had enjoyed his share of the necking and the clumsy groping that was typical when nobody really knew what they were doing. He finally got up the nerve and called her and she answered.

Susan picked up, "Hello?"

"Uh—hi—this is Mike Clancy. We met the other night at O'Gara's. I just thought I'd give you a call and see how you're doing."

She paused just a second—she thought he'd never call—"Sure, I remember you. You're the only customer I've ever given my number to."

"Really? I mean—wow!—that's great. Well, how are you doing?"

"Doing great. How about you?"

"Doing great too. Listen—I was wondering if—maybe, if you weren't busy— maybe you'd like to go to a movie."

"I'd love that. What do you have in mind?"

Mike scrambled. He hadn't planned on the conversation getting this far. "How about," he thought hard for the name of a chick movie they could go to, "how about *Sleepless in Seattle*?"

"That sounds great. When?"

It was Thursday afternoon—Friday seemed good to him—"Tomorrow night. We could go to the early show then grab some dinner afterward."

"Okay. Pick me up at my dorm. You know where that is?"

He'd already checked the map—details were his strongest point. "Sure do." He was flipping through the paper now, looking for the schedule. "How about 5:30? That will get us there for the 6:10 show and we can get dinner by 8:30."

"I'll be ready at the front door."

And so began a true romance. They dated exclusively through college, always true to each other. As Mike's interest and expertise in electronics grew, he attracted the attention of some of the faculty at Dunwoody. One of them was always on the lookout for new talent, and he took Mike under his wing and mentored him toward the military. When he graduated, it was a natural next step to go see an Air Force recruiter. Ten years and two tours of Afghanistan later—he was one of the Air Force's top UAV Pilots.

# Chapter 34

**Tuesday, July 15th**
**Minneapolis**

I needed a mental health break. We had Harris coming in at eleven o'clock and I needed to be ready for that, ready in the sense of having my stuff together. Davis's death had come as a shock, yet, looking back, I guess we should have foreseen it and warned him. Not that it would have done any good. Olson had a hard time convincing anyone in Atlanta that they needed to expand their perimeter so, by the time they did, the shooter was long gone. In fact, they still didn't know where the perch was and it had been more than 12 hours from the time of the shooting. I'd called this morning and the detective in charge said they had nothing but a body. No perch, shell casings, trace—just lots of people with a motive. There had to be a couple of hundred people in the country who would light up when they heard Davis had been painted red, so where do you start with that?

I decided that I would run over to Bill's Gun Shop and Range, my favorite local place to make holes in paper. Everyone has a way to unwind. Some people play sports, some read a book, some drink—I make holes in paper. What can I say?

Bill's is located in a little strip mall here in Robbinsdale. In fact, if you weren't a shooter, you'd probably never even know it was there. Upstairs on the mall level, tucked in between a sandwich shop and a dental office, there is a well stocked and manned store. Downstairs is the range, offices, and classrooms. The market for firearms classes and concealment holsters really took off after Minnesota became one of the majority of states that has passed a Concealed Carry law. The Minnesota Personal Protection Act, a "Must Issue" law, took effect in 2003.

Most people don't know what a Must Issue law is. Must Issue means that if a citizen applies for a handgun carry permit and that person meets the legal requirements, the Sheriff's office in that person's county of residence *must issue* a carry permit. It is at the center of ongoing right-to-bear-arms-versus-public-safety debates. The NRA and their opponents are involved in every one of these legislative fights across the country. It's very simple—if you are a citizen, have no criminal or mental health record, are of age, have taken the proper classes, and can afford it, you may carry a handgun.

As with all interpretations of a citizen's second amendment rights, this one attracted attention from pro and con forces across the country. The opponents contended that it would be the Wild West with gunfights in the streets, dead bystanders, and no harm would be done by keeping the status quo or adopting a more restrictive "May Issue" law as have other states. The pro side of the fight produced the statistics from other states where Must Issue was already the law. In every case violent crime was down and the number of shootings involving permit holders was negligible. In Minnesota, now five years into the program, there have been no fatalities and only a couple of minor mishaps involving Concealed Carry holders. One of those was a guy who was ticked off at his brother and shot up his car. The car was in the shooter's driveway at the time and, even before Must Issue, you could carry on your own property.

I turned into the lower level parking garage adjacent to Bill's. You can come over here in the middle of the winter with your car wet from the car wash and park inside, underground, in a nice warm garage. If you go in and shoot for an hour or so, your car is dry and the doors will still open when you return to it. Of course, there was no problem on this day of sun and 78 degrees. I parked, pulled my bag out of the trunk, and went in.

I was greeted with the usual security-system door chime and the young guy at the range counter. He recognized me, gave me a wave, and went back to cleaning the Glock he had spread out all over the counter. Bill's has a nice collection of demo guns that get a lot of work and need constant upkeep. There was one guy in the range, typical for the early hour.

I dropped my bag on one of the tables and walked back to the offices to say 'hi' to Tom and/or John, whoever was in. Tom was on the phone so I waved and went back out to grab a lane. The range guy wiped off his hands, went over to the register, and took the required card I had filled out. I handed him a range token, which I buy by the gross, grabbed a couple of targets, and picked up my bag. I pulled my ear muffs on and turned on the switch for the sound suppression circuitry.

These ear muffs have got to be one of the great inventions of the twentieth century. They look just like regular ear muffs but they have an electronic gizmo that acts as a microphone and speaker so, when you have them on, you can still hear. When a loud sound is detected, like a gunshot, the circuit shuts off and they act like regular sound muffs and deaden the sound. I like them so much I wear them mowing the lawn.

Wearing the muffs and a pair of safety glasses, I went over to the range doors. They are like an air lock but, in this case, it's a sound lock. You pass through one, wait for the door to close behind you, and then go through the second.

I set my bag on the counter behind my favorite lane—number 13. I've got a fairly large gun collection. I try to give them all a trip to the range occasionally and today's selection was a Para Ordinance LDA Hi Cap. This gun looks just like any other 1911 type gun that can be traced to the legendary John M. Browning back in 1911, but it has a double stack grip. That means more bullets in the gun—something I never argue with—and a very light action trigger. With all the road time I've been getting lately, I decided I'd better carry this one and that means some practice. I loaded up the magazines, hung a target on the carrier, and sent it down range.

I always try to duplicate a tactical—*dangerous*—situation when I take the first shot of the day. You only get one first shot and you'd better be ready for it. I could close my eyes and imagine a bad guy coming out of a bank with a gun in one hand and a bag of cash in the other. Some cops and other people with tactical training actually start yelling *"POLICE – DROP THE GUN!"* at the target down the range, but that can be upsetting to other people there. The fellow down on lane 4 looked like he was just getting the hang of firing the .22 he had, so I skipped any yelling. I just held the gun in the low ready position with hands lowered and muzzle down range. Then I took a breath, opened my eyes, and went into my drill.

My first shot goes—spot the target, raise the gun, both hands on the grip, squeeze it as tight as I can with my left hand over my right, front sight, and then shoot. After that, it goes front sight—shoot, front sight—shoot, and so on. I start with single shots then go to double taps. Next comes something called a *Mozambique* drill. This involves a double tap to the body followed by a head shot. It got its name from Lieutenant Colonel Jeff Cooper, a guy who is known as the father of modern handgun shooting. He got it from a cat named Mike Rousseau who developed it while fighting juiced up insurgents in Mozambique. This is for use in situations where the bad guy is either wearing body armor—not completely unheard of these days—or—as happened in Mozambique—is stoned on something that turns him into superman. After that I always do some one-handed shooting—strong hand first, which is my right, then weak hand. While I was doing the weak hand, I got an idea about the dart case that would need follow-up. Nothing like a little relaxation to get the thought processes moving.

About 140 rounds later, I finished up and went out to the lobby of the range to pack up my stuff. Tom was still in his office, and I stopped in to talk to him about a few things.

"Tom, you guys follow the firearms new-product development business pretty closely—don't you?"

"We sure better," Tom answered. "It's our bread and butter. What do you have in mind?"

"I'm researching a case and it's looking like the murder weapon was one that either doesn't exist or should only be in the hands of the military."

"Okay—I'm interested. What are you looking for?"

"I've got at least two, maybe three, victims, who have been shot at very long range with something that went right through them. It looks to be small-caliber, high-powered rifle, possibly a handgun, but the distances are just too long for that."

"Have you looked at—maybe a 22/303 or 6-mm PPC?"

"Yeah, I considered that, but this thing—I don't know. The wounds are even smaller than .22 caliber and the hitting power is off the scale. I've been talking to some people and one source thinks it's a new type of rifle round. It's a sabot'd tungsten dart."

"You know, I have read something about that. Let's see, where was that—?" He started digging through some trade journals on his desk. "I think it was in this one that specializes in military hardware."

He looked through the magazine and found an article from about two years ago. "Yeah, here it is—a project that started at Ft. Belvoir and wound up with the Special Forces guys. It's basically a miniaturized version of an M-1 Anti Armor round, except it's a lot smaller and isn't made of depleted uranium. Fires from a standard 30-magnum rifle chamber," he was rambling on now as he re-read the article. "Says here that it gets up to 4,000 feet per second at the muzzle, and you know how these articles are—usually a little under what they are really getting. Good against vehicles and light armor to 1,500 maybe 2,000 yards."

That's the one I was looking for. I asked, "Where could a person buy one of these—could you get one?"

"Not a chance. This stuff is military only—not even law enforcement can get this stuff."

"But you can shoot it out of a regular rifle?"

According to this, it's basically a regular 30-cal, but, hang on—well that's different. It says you shoot it from an unrifled barrel. And it's a long one too, maybe 32-plus inches."

"Could someone make something like this?"

"Beats me," Tom replied. "I'm a gunsmith, not a specialist in exotic metals. The only time I've ever heard of using tungsten for is beefing up steel—tungsten-carbide steel—supposed to be tougher than regular."

I let this sink in. "Thanks Tom, I really appreciate it. If you think of any way someone could get these rounds, let me know."

# Chapter 35

I drove downtown for the interview with Harris. It was a hot Wednesday and the Twins had their final game ever at Yankee Stadium coming this evening. It couldn't be too soon for Olson—he hated that place. The Twins were 3 and 18 there since the current manager took over. I don't know that much about baseball, but is seems there are places and teams that can hex another team. The Twins used to do it to a very good Royals team back when George Brett played for them in the '80s. They beat everyone but the Twins.

I got to Olson's office at 10:45 and we went over the plan. We'd be really nice until Harris slipped on anything, then it would be fangs out. I also wanted to try to get him to write something so I could find out if he was left handed. The direction of the questioning would include the murder of Davis in Atlanta and our attempt to get some info on his past business associates and his work history—what exactly did he do?

Harris showed up right on time, at eleven o'clock. His punctuality was unnerving. It also takes away the possibility of using tardiness as an excuse for a little rough treatment. I don't mean to imply that we'd beat him up or anything, just that you can act a little put out when someone is late. Olson led the way.

"Good morning, Ben," Olson started out. "If you don't mind my saying so, you look a little beat."

"I agreed to be here at this time and that required an early rise this morning," Harris said.

"Well, we really appreciate it. We were wondering if you could give us a little background on what you used to do for a living. We've been checking on AMES and there really isn't much out there on what you guys make or do or anything."

"With good reason. AMES is involved in many top secret development programs for the military and having that on the Internet would be counterproductive."

I was already thinking that this interview might not help much. The only reason we were having it was to explain the call last night.

Olson continued. "We know that AMES makes some kind of radios, but we were hoping that you could fill in some blanks for us—what kind of radios, what are they used for, and who buys them."

"AMES is involved in the research and development of specialty radio sets for the military, industrial, and commercial markets. They specialize in highly secure, small-network individual radio sets to provide direct communications between two or more individuals in a real-time situation."

It sounded to me like he was reading from the company's product catalog. "Ben, could you put that in regular English that a regular cop can understand?" I asked.

"Sure. You know those little radios that hook on your vest with the mic hooked up by your collar? Lots of police departments use them. We make those and we also make smaller ones for the military."

Olson continued, "Did you work with the cop or military side of the shop?"

"Primarily, I worked with the military side."

"And what exactly did you do?'

"I'm not sure of the purpose of this line of questioning. Could you explain that to me?"

I was ready for this one with a non-answer answer. "We are just trying to get a feel for who you are. We are interested in any items in your background that could have led to you or your wife being the target of a murder attempt. Since the previous trial didn't resolve the case, we are still looking for your wife's killer."

Harris replied, "Kind of like 'I didn't do it, but I'll check all the golf courses looking for whoever did.' Is that it?"

Inwardly I chuckled at that one. I wondered if that guy would ever find anyone. Maybe he'll just find his missing trophies.

"Yeah, kind of like that."

Harris was willing to play along but I could see he wasn't buying it. "My job was to invent, design, build the prototypes, and then field test new systems."

I took over. "So, in your work, you had contact with military personnel?"

"Yes."

And did your work take you out of town on these field tests?"

"Yes."

"And when you were out of town, any chance you might have been getting a little on the side?" This was a long shot. This guy was about as straight a guy as I'd ever met.

"No—and I resent your implication." That hit a mark.

"I'm sorry Ben, but we have to look at every possibility."

"Perhaps if that had been done in the first investigation, we wouldn't have to be here playing these games. I don't understand or appreciate this entire line of questioning."

It was time for me to drop the other shoe. "Ben, how do you feel about the fact that Big Dick Davis got it?"

"Got what, another chance to go on TV and brag to the world that he can get anyone off?"

Olson answered. "Davis was shot—right on the balcony of his office."

You always watch the suspect when you deliver news. You have to see what their reaction is. Harris didn't even blink.

"I'm not surprised. I'm sure he had many enemies."

"Not many who could have done him the way he got it," I said.

"And how did he *get it*?"

"Assassinated—one round right through the head—dropped him like a stone. He was dead before he could know he'd been hit."

"That's too bad," Ben said.

"Why is that too bad?" Olson asked.

"That he didn't have to suffer like my Anne did."

There's not really much you can say after that. Obviously, if Harris knew anything about it, including having done it himself, he wasn't showing it. He had no hard feelings at all, but also didn't show any glee or satisfaction. His only regret was that it was too quick and painless.

After the pause Harris said, "Gentlemen, while my grief for Mr. Davis knows no bounds, I'm sure you didn't call me here to ask about that. Obviously, I can't be under suspicion for his death as I'm sure you know where I was last night."

"Who said anything about it happening last night?" I asked.

"That's the only time it could have happened. I don't watch TV or listen to the news at my cabin, and I listened to some music during the drive down this morning. It must have happened between yesterday morning around nine o'clock—when I left for my cabin—and about 30 minutes ago when we started this interview. Otherwise, I would have heard about it."

I couldn't argue with that kind of logic. I guess it was time to let him go. "Thanks for coming in, Ben. We really appreciate it."

He rose with a surprised look on his face. I said, "We'll let you know if there's anything else."

He started for the door—I added, "Please let us know if you're going out of town or anything. Just so we can get a hold of you if we need to."

He agreed and pulled the door open. I said, "Oh—and if you think of it, could you please jot down the names of a few of your colleagues so we can check out your background? You can send them in on an email."

He stopped and said, "I can do that right now." I handed him a pen and paper and offered him my chair. He sat down and started writing. He was left handed. I looked at Olson and he nodded that he'd seen it too. We looked like Gannon and Friday on the *Dragnet* TV show, nodding at each other. He was left-handed.

Ben wrote out the names and numbers of three people as work references. Then he stood, we said our goodbyes again, and he left. I said, "I like him for this—more now than ever."

"But he couldn't have done the one last night. He wasn't there," Olson said.

I knew that had to be correct, but I also knew in my heart that he had something to do with it.

# Chapter 36

I got on the phone and started checking out Harris's work contacts. They all worked there but all said they didn't do much with Harris. One was in personnel and all he would say is that Harris worked there. Another worked in production and was in charge of the manufacturing plant that made the radios Harris developed. All he knew was that Harris was, in his words, "a freaking genius." He had little actual contact with him. The third was another designer who worked in development with Harris and, at least, might have something I could pursue. His name was Bill Dunn.

I got him on the phone. "Mr. Dunn, this is Dan Neumann with the Minneapolis Police Department." I went through the usual introduction routine. "I'm doing some follow up on the grocery store bank robbery that resulted in the death of Mr. Harris's wife."

"Oh yes. That was a tragedy—so young and a beautiful woman too."

I wasn't sure if that made her loss any tougher or if it was easier to get over the loss of an ugly spouse. "Yes, I agree. Could you tell me how Ben was doing after the trial? What I'm trying to determine is if Mr. Harris would be inclined to—you know—to do anything about the obvious injustice that was done him by the trial." You have to fish a little when you're trying hard not to let on that this guy's co-worker was your favorite for a murder. You can't just ask a guy to tell you why his buddy isn't a killer.

"Oh, I don't think so. I heard about that, that the killers had been killed—so to speak—but Ben wouldn't hurt a fly. I don't think he even owns a gun."

"No chance, huh?"

"Not him. Of course, some of the people he worked with were certainly capable."

"What do you mean? Who did he work with?"

"The military guys. He was the specialist in our military systems and had a lot of friends in the Special Forces. Those guys could do it, but they have a real reputation for self control. They have to have self control to do what we ask them to do."

"What do we ask them to do that would require so much control?" I was curious, as much as following a line of questioning.

"They have to go all over the planet to rescue people and kill bad people and they're out in the field for months sometimes, cut off from oversight and command control. I know that they are expected to make their own decisions based upon their training and they do a damn good job of it."

"And Ben had connections with these people?"

"Well, I don't have firsthand knowledge of this, but I know Ben was out of town a few times when there were things going on that we weren't supposed to talk about or even speculate about."

"Where did he go when he was out of town?"

"Supposedly, he went with them."

"He went out on missions with Special Forces?" This was new.

"Yes, that was the word that was going around. I don't think he was actually out in the field—just behind the scenes. Some of the systems we make were very early in their development and needed constant care to keep them running. Plus, it's a good way to make sure that the product is doing what it's supposed to."

"Do you know any of these people so I could give them a ring to check on Ben?"

"Not really. They aren't very public people. They were here at the plant a few times. I did see three or four of them at the funeral."

"Mrs. Harris's funeral?"

"Yes, I'm sure of it. They sort of stand out in a crowd. Very fit young men with short haircuts. You'd notice them if you saw them."

I'm sure I would. I thanked Dunn and hung up. I yelled over to Olson and asked him if there were any photos of the funeral. Police will sometimes take photos at funeral of crime victims to see who shows up. You'd be surprised at how many bad guys like to go to their victim's funerals. "Yeah, I think we did, even though I thought it was stupid at the time."

"Well, now you know why you did it." I'm never amazed at what will turn up down the road in a murder case. Maybe even a different murder case.

Olson started digging through the files. You'd think this would all be on computer by now, but it's not. Olson had the photo file out and was looking near the back of it. "Here we go—funeral photos."

Olson handed them over. There were about 50 8×10s. As usual, most are taken before the start or after the service was over. We want to know who was there and who they talked to. I flipped through them until one caught my eye. "Here—look at this one. Who are these guys?" I handed the photo to Olson.

"Beats me—good looking couple of guys?"

I'll say—late 20s or early 30s, short hair, fit, and well dressed. I kept looking through the file and found another one. In this shot they were talking with Harris. "Looks like they know each other."

Olson agreed and flipped through the others. "I don't see them talking with anyone else besides Harris and each other."

"They've got to be military. Nobody's that fit unless they're working as personal trainers at Bally's."

"Good guess. So how do we figure out who they are and where to find them?"

"They aren't going to talk to us. They're covered. Anything they're involved with is going to be covered by national security. We're going to have to dig them out and catch them off guard."

"But where to start looking?"

"I think I'll call my buddy Pete. He might have something we can use."

# Chapter 37

I got Pete on the phone and asked straight up, "Pete, I need to find some guys who were here for Harris's wife's funeral. I've got pictures from the funeral. I think they're military, maybe Special Forces guys who Harris worked with. How can I find these guys?"

Pete took a moment to answer. I had a feeling he was trying to decide whether or not he should. "Finding them would not be impossible. But they will never talk to you. You are not part of the brotherhood. Even though you are a cop and sort of on the same team, you are not one of them."

"What team are you talking about?" This was pissing me off.

"Dan, I've known a lot of these guys. They don't talk about what they do. Not usually to each other, not to their own wives, never to civilians. It's not going to happen even if you can find them and get them in a chair with a subpoena. They'll claim national security and they won't talk to you."

"I really need some help on this. You sure they won't give me anything, even if it looks like I'm trying to help their buddy?"

"They'd see through that in a heartbeat. There is one thing—I know a guy who was with the Berets and lives here in town. He's a good guy and might be able to give you some insight at least."

"You think he'd come over for a beer or something?"

"Yeah, I'll ask him. Come out to my place tonight and we'll put the game on and crack a few. The Twins are at New York for the last time. Ride that nasty bike of yours—he likes motorcycles."

About 6:30 I mounted up on the black bike and headed out to Lake Minnetonka to Pete's house. He lives on a little island that's about as far from civilization as you can get and still be on the Minneapolis local phone service. I road south on Hwy 100 to I-394 and went west. It was a great evening for a ride, about 85 degrees and a little hazy from the humidity. I took the County 19 cutoff for its two-lane, twisting, and scenic riding perfection.

I pulled over and took off the half bucket helmet that I use for city riding. I wanted to feel the wind and enjoy the moment. From here I rode past some of the oldest and grandest homes in the state. They go back to when there was streetcar service all the way out here and people would have summer homes on the lake. The streetcar used to run from downtown Minneapolis to Excelsior, where you transferred to a steam-powered boat that was part of the streetcar system. They would deliver you right to your own dock. The boat service went away with the streetcars, but the last one, which had been sunk on purpose way back when, was raised from the deep a few years ago and has been restored and put back in service. It's a time warp that will take you back a century. Names like Pillsbury and McMillan were on the mailboxes then. Now it's rich athletes and hip-hop producers who have some of these grand old homes.

I motored past Brown's Bay and Smith's Bay on my left, took the bridge over the channel to Crystal Bay and rode past the Lafayette Club. I went through the city of Spring Park and turned toward Enchanted Island. From here it's another 10 or 12 minutes to Pete's. His wife's message on the phone system is, "We've gone to town for supplies and should be back in a day or two."

I rolled into Pete's driveway just after seven o'clock. There was a Hummer in the drive already. Pete drives a Denali, so I figured that the guest of honor had already arrived. I let myself in, as usual here, and went through the house to the patio by the pool. Pete was there with another guy. He looked fit and large enough to take care of himself with just a look. Pete made the introductions.

"Dan, this is Wolf," he said. Nothing else—just, Wolf. "Wolf, this is Dan Neumann." He stood and I shook his hand.

"Pleasure to meet you," I said. He was a pleasant looking chap, about six foot three and I guessed his age at 50-ish.

Wolf spoke. "Pleasure's all mine. And my name is Fred Hutchins. You can call me Wolf if you prefer."

We sat and Pete passed around beers for everyone. We made small talk for awhile about the weather, the Twins, the usual. During a pause Pete brought up the reason for our meeting.

"Wolf, Dan's a police detective with a problem I thought you might be able to help him with."

"And what's that?" Wolf asked.

I said "It's kind of a sticky situation. I'll give you the story." I went on to relate the tale of the botched grocery store bank robbery, the murder, and the trials. As I told him about the trials and the acquittals, I could see him focusing and becoming intense.

He asked, "How could they get off with nothing? If the prosecution had all that evidence, shouldn't they have been convicted of something?"

"You're right. Usually, even if the county can't get the most serious charges, they will have charged some lesser offenses to be sure there was something to fall back on, just in case. In this case, the prosecution was confident that they'd get their convictions and didn't charge the lesser offenses. But when the trial started, about half the evidence was thrown out on procedural grounds and the defense presented a great case. Of course, the Judge went along with nearly everything the defense asked for, starting with jury selection. The final result was they were each convicted on a weapons charge and given a 6-month sentence—suspended."

He was quiet. "Okay— what happened next?"

I went on to tell him of the killings of the two hoods, the judge, and the defense attorney. He had a look of some satisfaction when I told him of the last two. Then, I started to tell him about Harris and my suspicions.

He asked, "Does this man have any military or firearms expertise?"

"No—none that we can ascertain."

"Does he have any friends or contacts who would have the skills to do this?"

"Maybe. He worked with some Special Forces guys in the early 'nineties."

"By Special Forces, who exactly are we talking about?"

"He worked with a group at Ft. Bragg, in North Carolina."

"Yes, I know where Ft. Bragg is, I was stationed there for more than twenty years. What business did he have with them?"

"His company makes some kind of special radio that the Army uses. He was the inventor and the technical field rep."

Wolf paused. He was wondering if he might have known this mystery man at Bragg. He chose his words carefully. "So, he has no skill himself, but has connections in Special Forces. I'll tell you one thing right off—no Special Forces personnel are involved in this."

"How can you be so sure? I mean, it's pretty clear to us that Harris can't be doing this himself—at least alone. He doesn't have the skills."

"Special Operators are an elite group of men. Yes, they are highly trained, but that's not all. They have to have the self control to obey orders at any cost—no matter what they think the right thing to do would be. That doesn't mean that they can't think for themselves. In a combat situation they may be out of touch with higher command and have to change how they were going to do something. But that doesn't override the mission. The mission is always first. No Special Forces guy would start killing civilians—no matter how attractive the possibility would seem."

I guess I had to agree with that. Our country had been cranking out these specialists for years and I couldn't recall even one case where one went rogue.

"While he was at Bragg, did he do any—field work?" Wolf asked.

O.K., I'm impressed. How'd he jump to this? "Yes, apparently he spent some time on field exercises with the guys he was working with. This was to help the development of the radios."

"It was for something else too," Wolf answered. "When working with suppliers, there is often someone from the manufacturer whose sole purpose is to work with the operators. They are usually former military, but occasionally, an exceptional non-military representative will be allowed into the so-called Club. I think it's very possible your man could have received some training while he was at Bragg."

I already knew about the "Club." I just wanted to find out how to get into it, or into someone's head who could tell me about it. I pushed just a little. "What training would he get? I mean, the guy's a radio designer—he has a degree in electrical engineering."

"To keep up with the people he was training, he would have to work in the woods with them on field exercises. This would involve, at minimum, basic field craft—things like how to move through the woods, self-concealment, and maybe making fire by rubbing two sticks together," he said with a smile. "He may also have gone to the ranges and had some firearms training."

"But he was there to work on radios."

"Yeah, the people he was working with are shooters and they would be going to the ranges nearly every day if they weren't in the field."

"Every day?" I was impressed. I try to get there once a week and most cops get there only as required for annual qualification.

"It's common for these people to shoot more than 50,000 rounds per year. Machine gunners shoot more. Snipers don't shoot that much but they shoot at least 20 rounds every day regardless of training schedule."

Wow—50,000 rounds per year—our tax money at work. Of course if there's anyone who needs to hit what they're aiming at—I went back to Harris, "Okay, so he might have learned how to camp. Come on, this guy is our prime suspect and we know he can't be the one doing the killings."

"And how do you know that?"

"You haven't met him. He's a geek. Okay, a fit geek, but his whole history is individual sports, music, a little art—nothing that says warrior."

Wolf leaned back and smiled. "What you've just described would be the quintessential biography of a Samurai. They were musicians, poets, and artists. It was considered a requirement for their craft since they couldn't be out fighting every day.

"Let me tell you about warriors. I'll tell you from my own point of view, since that's the one I'm most familiar with. I went into the Army in 1968, just after the Tet Offensive. I had just graduated from the U. with a degree in Military History, with a minor in Psychology. Also, I was a product of ROTC when that was becoming unpopular. I owed Uncle Sam four years for my education. I went through Basic Infantry School and went to Viet Nam in the fall of '68. I spent one tour in the field. In February of 1970, I came home and went to Ranger School, and then through the Special Warfare School to become a Green Beret. I went back to Viet Nam in the spring of 1972 with an A Team. My job was to assist in the training of South Vietnamese units as we were turning over the war to them.

"After we left, I was back at Bragg and wound up training guys for the next 12 years. My degree consigned me to the field I wound up in—Psychological Operations. Psy-Ops is interesting though. My unit was responsible for developing new ways of messing with the enemy's heads. With my Special Ops background, I got to go to Panama when we were trying to get that clown, Noriega. I was on Granada and in Somalia. During the first Gulf War, I went back to Special Forces and was with the group that went in early to locate Iraqi anti-air assets. I've seen a lot of different kinds of action and worked with a lot of guys and the one thing I can tell you is that you can't tell who's a warrior until the chips are down."

I asked, "Come on—you're telling me that you can't look at a guy who's six foot six, has monster pipes for arms, can chew nails and spit tacks, and tell me that he'll be a warrior?"

"No. You can't," Wolf said. "There is a warrior ethos. Some people have it but most don't. All throughout history this has been true. Look at many of this country's Medal of Honor winners—like Audie Murphy. He was five foot five, had to lie to get into the Army, and had no history of being a fighter—just a loner. He gets into the Army as a private, goes to North Africa, then Italy, and earns the Medal of Honor by jumping on top of a burning Sherman tank and manning a .50-caliber Browning. He held off an entire German regiment.

"Almost all warriors displayed no great pre-disposition toward bravery or heroic behavior. It just happened when it had too. I've known many men who looked like they should have been the ones to earn the medals in combat but didn't. I've also known many little geeks who turned out to be the best natural leaders in combat. Later, after the battle was over, they'd have all kinds of head problems I'd have to work out with them. But during the battle, they were natural warriors."

"What about Harris? I persisted, "he had no formal training, no firearms experience, and no *warrior ethos* as you put it. He's just an electronics engineer."

"Actually the background you've described doesn't tell us anything about whether or not he is a natural warrior. But we are talking about two different things here. One is the natural warrior and the other is the individual who reacts to a terrible situation by becoming something he previously was not. There's plenty of historical precedent for this kind of thing. And I'm not saying your guy is the one who is killing off these people, but, let me give you an example.

"In the late 1870's, there was a man who went west with his family and his fiancée. They were traveling into the southwest, through Texas and New Mexico to start a new life. His name was John J. Clanton. His party was attacked by Apache Indians and his fiancée was brutally murdered and scalped before his eyes. As a result, Clanton—a man with no military training, little experience with firearms, and who by every account was a peaceful religious man—went on a rampage, a personal crusade against the Apaches. The government was paying a bounty for Apache scalps, and Clanton started collecting them. He was merciless and brutal.

"After about two months of Clanton's efforts, the Apache were so decimated that they withdrew from the area. Unfortunately for Clanton, he now lost his source of income. So, he started going south of the border and killing innocent Mexicans for their hair. The government figured this out and wouldn't pay him so he had to go deeper and deeper into Apache country where, ultimately, they killed him. The one event of seeing his fiancée killed turned him into a government-sanctioned psychopath and led him down a trail from which he could not return. Do I think your man Harris could do these things? Yes—I'm sure he could."

"How can you be so sure?'

"There is something at play here that you may not have considered. Every one of us has two sides. The eastern religions refer to it as the yin and yang. Freud called it the ego and the alter ego. I prefer to call that other place the dark side—that place inside each of us that we keep buried. It's stronger in men than women, but women have it too. This is the primal part of each of us that was necessary for our species to survive and to dominate our world.

"Most people are raised by whatever society they are in to understand a difference between good and evil. Religions foster this belief—explaining that the good is what our creator wants us to embrace and that there will be punishments for embracing the bad, evil, or dark side. And whether or not you believe in religion regarding this is irrelevant—the fact is that knowing the difference between good and evil is fundamental to organized society.

"Before what we call civilization, this dark side helped us to kill to eat and to kill each other for breeding rights, among other things. But, as human social organization evolved, these primal urges had to be controlled. All civilization requires a sense of right and wrong. We depend upon a shared belief system to control our primal urges to acquire and procreate.

"We raise our children to share our beliefs. We teach them early on to respect other people's belongings and that they should expect the same respect in return. We teach them that harming others is forbidden, that killing someone is the lowest, most awful thing they could do.

"But we all have this other side lurking beneath the surface. The side of us that wants to covet your neighbor's property, the side that wants to procreate with any available member of the opposite sex, willing or not. Certainly early in our evolution, this drive to breed was necessary, but it's not acceptable now. And the taking of another life is the highest crime one can commit against both your god and fellow human. For some people this alter ego is lying just beneath the surface and can come out without warning."

I could hear what Wolf was saying and I understood the implications for crime. Many rape victims have let their assailant in the front door. In the cases of date-rape I'd worked, the bad guy was a really nice guy until a few drinks and the wrong circumstances finally evoked his dark side. I could also see how a professional criminal or a sociopath could use this to their advantage—look normal, act normal, and people will let you walk right up to them because they want to think that everyone is sharing their benign intentions.

"Now, look at this from the point of view of the military professional. I dealt with this as an instructor for the Army. Although by the time I got them, most of the men I worked with had been conditioned out of it—."

"Conditioned out of what?" I asked.

"The natural resistance to taking someone's life. Think about it—when we send an 18-year-old to boot camp, we do our best to break down the societal constraints that preclude him or her from killing someone. But to produce an effective soldier, we have to teach them that murder is still a sin but killing can be necessary. It's a hard thing to get across. After World War II, a study found that most of our soldiers never really aimed their weapons. Training on bull's-eye targets didn't prepare them to shoot people—even the best shots had a hard time when the target was another human. So, after Korea, the Army switched to human silhouette targets. This vastly improved accuracy but, even with the human silhouette targets, most infantrymen in Viet Nam simply pointed their weapons in the general direction of the enemy and let 'er rip."

I'd seen the film of Viet Nam showing guys holding their M-16s over the top of a berm and just letting go on full rock and roll.

Wolf went on. "After Viet Nam, a study was done to figure out how many rounds had been expended to inflict one casualty on the enemy. You have any idea what they came up with?"

I guessed, "one thousand?"

"You're off by a factor of 250. One study showed that there were approximately 248,000 rounds of rifle ammunition expended for every VC or NVA soldier who was hit—two hundred and forty eight *thousand*. This was a phenomenal finding—the main result of which is that the current model M-16 has three settings on the fire switch—safe, single shot, and burst. The burst setting allows only a 3-round burst to be fired. No more rock and roll."

That news was shocking to me. I'd always thought that soldiers were shooting at someone, even with all the news coverage showing guys just hosing down the forest.

"Most people can never overcome this resistance. Even those in the military for their entire adult lives have a hard time when it comes to putting their sights on a living breathing human and pulling the trigger. Often, they can the first time, and then never again. Only when faced with death—their own or someone close to them—can they actually do it without catastrophic consequences to their own personalities. Career snipers who have trained for years are often good for only that one shot. If they are involved with a situation that requires them to do what they've trained for, they can do it. But many have to be reassigned afterward because they just can't do it again—and they knew it was life or death. The Germans had a problem with this during World War II. Many of the technical developments they made in their attempt to exterminate the Jews, and anyone else they saw as unfit, included insulating their men from the ordeal of killing. They had to dehumanize their victims.

"So, back to your guy—is he a psychopath? I think not. I think he is someone who is in full control of his faculties and is well adjusted but sees things in white and black, as right and wrong. In fact, I think he would be a natural warrior given different circumstances. He is among the small percentage of people who have the balance to understand that, although killing is inherently wrong, there are times when it is necessary. There have been many times throughout American military history where those were the exact words that were used to explain offensive actions. It should be the motto of the sniper—'I'm sorry it was necessary'. Have you ever been involved in a shooting?"

In fact I had and I still see the bad guys. "Yes."

"Then you know what I'm talking about. There are times when a clear violation of everything that we have been taught since we were born is necessary for the greater good. It's that way all the time in combat. But even with that knowledge, many men have permanent nightmares."

He was right-on there too.

"In the case we're discussing, your suspect counted on the system to avenge his loss by punishing the evil, and the system failed. And that's all he could hope for—vengeance. Some people now call it closure, but it is vengeance. While I am a believer in the death penalty, I know that it will not prevent even one killer from doing what they are going to do. It's a societal version of vengeance that is important only to the survivors, but that's getting off the point. So—does he lash out against the system or those who did him wrong? Good question— which is which? The only thing I'm a little confused about is the fact that the two boys who did the crime were killed. I'm not sure he did that. He may have concluded that justice was up to him, or you may have more than one person involved here."

This was helpful. All along we'd been looking at just Harris and now this guy says maybe two guys are doing this. I asked about his current occupation. "You mentioned that you're out of the Army now. What are you doing now?"

"I had a good education in the Army that included combat medic. All Special Forces members are cross-trained in at least two other fields besides their primary field. So, when the opportunity presented itself, I applied to and went to medical school. I'm a medical doctor."

"What field?"

"I thought that was obvious—I'm a psychiatrist. I specialize in post-traumatic stress disorder and work primarily with our vets."

"Primarily? Who else gets post-traumatic stress?'

"You'd be surprised. First responders for one—firefighters, trauma doctors and nurses—cops. You mentioned that you had been involved in a shooting?"

"Yeah—twice."

"Didn't they give you a few days off and have you talk to someone?"

"Yeah, but not a doctor—some kind of counselor."

"Counselor—Doctor—." He weighed the difference in his hands'.

I leaned back in the chair, to center what was weighing on my mind. Could it be that I was looking for a *professional*? Did he see himself as some kind of avenger—some sort of real-life Batman? How to reconcile that? It's part of a cop's career—the times when you might overhear someone after a shooting say "nice job—saved the taxpayers a bunch of money" or "asshole got what he deserved." That may be the case, but isn't it our job to take the high road and bring the bad guys in for justice? We don't dispense justice, we preserve it. How would I react to a situation where I knew I had a guy cold—a guy who deserved a couple rounds in the 10-ring? Would I preserve the peace, or dispense justice?

In fact, I'd had to face that question at least once. I'd been involved in two shootings on the job, one clear and one not. Had I visited my own dark side on the second one?

In both of the shootings I'd been involved in, the bad guys just opened up on us first. I had no chance to stop and think in the first one. And afterward, I didn't feel any remorse or have trouble sleeping, although I do have an occasional bad dream. Like Wolf said, is there some primordial being inside me just waiting to get out? Am I in control of my "Dark Side?" If I found a kidnap, rape, or murder suspect and had the chance, would I just shoot them? Well—I've been there too.

We had a few more beers, watching the game and the boats go by. I reached my beer cut-off point for motorcycle riding at two and switched to diet Pepsi with a lemon twist. Pete was holding forth, commenting on the babes on the boats. He can be very descriptive and I've always thought he could make a living writing soft porn. Wolf chuckled at the comments and offered a few of his own, but I could see that there were depths to him that weren't going to be revealed. Certainly, he'd experienced things I never would. Toward the end of the evening, I asked for more about *his* dark side, his experiences with others, and how you can tell.

He said, "On my first tour in 'Nam, I was a green infantry lieutenant. Fortunately, I was assigned to an experienced platoon with good sergeants. As you may know, sergeants make the world go round in the U.S. Army. Anyway, I understood that the sergeants were the ones with the experience and know how to get the job done and get as many of the troops home alive as possible. I would meet with them after I had received our platoon's orders and together we'd come up with a plan that would best-chance the mission and keep people alive. I'd let them decide who in the platoon had the experience to do something, then I'd give the orders."

"One afternoon I got orders to conduct a night recon patrol into an area we knew was crawling with NVA. We'd been there two days earlier and there had been a nasty fire fight. We'd go in, shoot it out, then go back to our camps, and the bad guys would stay where we left them. There was no reason to believe that they'd left. I got the distinct impression that the regimental staff-wienie that came up with this idea hadn't been in the field since Korea, and had no idea what we'd be running into. There was just no way to do what he wanted and not take casualties.

"Basically, we were supposed to go out and march down a marked trail until we ran into them, then pull back and call in our location for artillery support. It was called "movement to contact" and was a standard method employed there. Fortunately, my sergeants knew the area well and we were able to get off the trail to where we could scout our way in and find them before they noticed us. We flanked them and launched a two-pronged attack. One of the new guys—in country about two months—was in the flanking group and when they went in, he went—nuts."

"Nuts?" I asked.

"Yeah, it was his second firefight in three days, and I guess that was all he needed to go over the edge. It was like that sometimes. Usually guys would be there six or seven months before they started what we termed "going native." When they started getting short, counting the days till they were going home, they'd become cautious and I couldn't send them out anymore. At about two weeks to go, you just left them behind to polish mess kits or something.

"Anyway, this little runt of a guy was just in from the world, as we used to say. He was from the Midwest—had been in college on an English major program and had slipped up by missing a semester's registration and his draft board got him. Never played sports, never hunted, and probably never been in a fight in his life. I thought his only chance to make it was he'd never get hit because he was so small—he goes running into the flank of the NVA positions with his M-16 blazing and tossing grenades. He killed about 30 of them—never took a scratch. We had to send him to China Beach."

"Why'd he go to China Beach?" Was that a real place? I thought it was a TV show.

"When we'd get a guy who'd gone over the edge, we'd send him there to chill out. A few days on the beach with good food and nice weather, and no one shooting at them, and they'd be okay. It was pretty much standard procedure for guys who'd earned Silver Stars and higher—pretty strange though for a guy to go there after only two months in country. Anyway, I was with the flanking group and while he was doing it, I saw his dark side. He was an animal—running flat out, shooting NVA at close range right in the head and guts—had his bayonet mounted and was slashing at them. All the while he was screaming and had this look of pure visceral rage on his face. That's another way you knew they were gone, the look on their face."

I thought back to the two times I'd been involved in a shooting. Any cop involved in a shooting is a rare thing. Most cops serve 20 to 30 years and never even pull their service piece from the holster. Many are, frankly, not very good shots and the only practicing they do is right before annual qualifying. But not me—I got to pull it a total of five times and twice had to use it.

The first was when I was a fairly new patrol officer, only a year and a half on the force. I was riding with Ken Winters, a 12-year veteran and we had a call on a silent alarm at a stereo store and went over to check it out. It was about two o'clock in the morning and what happened reinforced my belief that nothing good happens between one and five o'clock in the morning.

We pulled up alongside the place, it was a corner lot, and got out to look around. There were two other units on the way, as this place had been broken into twice before. My partner took the front and I took the back. Just as I was rounding the rear of the store, I heard Ken yelling, "Down on the ground!

Police! Down on the ground now!" Two guys had just burst from the front door with their arms full of high-end audio gear. They didn't know we were there and were as surprised as my partner was. They had the presence of mind to toss the stuff to Ken and he had the natural reaction of trying to catch it. They were able to take off around the store toward the rear. They ran right into me.

I had pulled my service revolver when I heard Ken yelling and had it ready when they rounded the corner. I yelled, "Down now! Police!" Everything slowed down, just like they show in the movies. The first guy looked up, saw me, and slammed on the brakes. The second guy came around him and I saw the gun in his hand.

"Drop the gun! Drop the gun!" I shouted. He brought the gun up as he slowed down. I still don't remember how many shots I fired, just that I did. He got off one as he raised the gun, but he rushed it and the round went low and to the side. My constant practicing paid off and I went into automatic mode. I had the gun up and on line, front site on target, and I fired. Down he went. The first guy dropped to the ground too.

When it was over I didn't know if I'd shot one or both of them. Turned out I got lucky and only shot the armed guy. I hit him three times center mass and once in the head with a .357 magnum—he was dead before he hit the ground. But I'd fired the gun dry. We were maybe 12 feet apart and I'd completely missed a man-sized target with a third of my shots. To this day I don't know where the other two rounds went, we never found them.

This was a typical police-involved shooting. It starts and ends so fast that all you have time for is reaction. I was placed on administrative leave for a week and sweated out the investigation. When the ink dried on the forms, I was exonerated and it was ruled justified.

The second was more problematic. I was 37 and a detective with the vice and drugs division. We had been working a case in which a local drug ring was using college kids to mule the merchandise from place to place. Mules are selected because they have no reason to be hassled by the cops. They have no prior history or record and they aren't involved in anything that would attract attention. Sometimes they travel to other cities and sometimes they just make local deliveries. Either way, they are getting paid, and often in drugs.

They can get into trouble if they are caught or if the merchandise disappears, and I don't mean with the cops. That is what had happened here. The mule, a Hamline University student, had been robbed by members of another gang while she was bringing back a load from a spring break trip to Daytona Beach. The other set of bad guys had figured out what the Twin Cities bad guys were doing and put a tail on the girl, waited until she had picked the stuff up and was about to head home, and then grabbed her. The gang back home didn't care about her—they wanted their drugs or money back. She disappeared.

We had a pretty good track on where they would have taken her and set up for an assault team entry. The gang had taken over an abandoned building in the warehouse district north of downtown Minneapolis. The main floor was empty—they were upstairs on the fourth floor where there was bit better lighting and ventilation that hot summer night. The local SWAT guys are very good and they went in hard and fast and started the rush up to the occupied floor. I went in with them as the lead investigator on the case. The gang had lookouts and as soon as we headed upstairs, the gunfight was on.

We had been aware of this woman for eight months. We hadn't contacted her or tailed her but she was on our list of probable mules. She was about the age of my sister's daughter and I had begun to identify with her—not a good thing. She was 21 years old and well on her way to a biology degree and probably grad school after that. She had typical blonde-Scandinavian good looks and her whole life ahead of her. I was pumping pure adrenaline as we went in and, between the flying bullets—I lost it.

I went up a back staircase we had located on the building drawings. Two steps at a time, I ran up to the fourth floor. As I made the landing, I could see into the room where they were holding the girl. She was tied to a chair, naked, and covered with bloody welts. One guy was holding a gun on her and the other was holding a bamboo switch.

The gunman raised his weapon toward me and I dropped him with two rounds. The other guy just stood there and said, "Guess you got me, dude. Too bad for her though—bitch already dead." He had a gun in his belt but didn't make a move for it. He just stood there and smiled—I put two in his chest and one in his head before he had time to fall.

A moment later when the rest of the team burst in, I had my gun on both bad guys and they both had their guns in their hands. That was the night I met my dark side. Strangely, I never lost any sleep over this one. It was the *first* one that occasionally kept me up.

About nine o'clock, the Twins were losing so we made our farewells. I strapped the brain bucket back on and headed home. It had been an education, all right. I had plenty to think about and a few more things to chase down, starting with the idea of a second bad guy.

# Chapter 38

**Wednesday, July 16th**
**Robbinsdale**

The next morning I went through a quick workout, showered, and headed downtown. I'd had so much fun with my motor yesterday—I decided to ride the bike again today. The weather was looking cooperative, and in Minnesota, you only get so many days per year. You'd better use every one you can.

I walked into Olson's office about 9:30. He was already hard at it and had the coffee on.

"Top of the morning to you," he said with a much too cheerful bad Irish accent.

"And to you, you perky scandehoovian. We got anything new?"

"Sharon Rademacher came up with one name that might fit our profile. Some guy named Cederstrom was on a flight to and from Phoenix the night before and morning after Judge Mitchell was whacked."

"Okay. There were probably 20 people who went to Phoenix and back that day. So how does that interest us?"

"Sharon has been trying to find anyone who might have gone to both Phoenix and Anchorage. This same individual was also on a plane from Seattle to Anchorage and back about the time the Sample kid got it."

"Same guy?"

"Yup. And on the Seattle trip, he checked a rifle with his baggage. But there's no record showing that he flew to Seattle. He just showed up there. Also no record of any firearm checked to Phoenix. No record of going to Atlanta either. I told her to start checking nearby cities and she said she was already on it. He lives in Blaine. Want to go see him?"

We jumped in Olson's car and took off across the Mississippi and up Central Avenue. We were there in about a 20 minutes. The townhouse was in one of those new developments that have four or five different floor plans and some single family homes too. It's just off Central, which is called Highway 65 up there and adjacent to a big sports center, where they have a national soccer tournament around the time of the summer solstice every year. Naturally, that's about the hottest time of the year, so we get these kids and their parents from all over the country that come here expecting a break in nice, cool Minnesota. Then they get here and get hit with 95 degrees, 75-percent humidity, and some of them get heat stroke.

We turned off Central into the complex and even the GPS couldn't find it. I once tried to get my dad to move into a single-level town home complex and his main objection was, "How will anyone find me?" And he was right. These places need to do something to help strangers locate addresses. After five minutes of circling around, we figured out the system and found the house. There was no back door to cover so we both went to the front. It was an alert but casual approach. I knocked on the door from the side wall for cover.

No answer. I rang the bell and knocked again, hard and loud. Nothing. A neighbor had just opened his garage door and looked at us curiously. He walked over.

"I don't think anyone is home," he said.

To put the intruder in the right frame of mind, I identified myself and asked him, "You know Mr. Cederstrom?"

"Not really. I've seen him maybe twice, but I don't think he's here much. The story is he travels a lot."

"What story is that?"

"You know—you get to know your neighbors and when someone new moves in, you check around to see who he is and what he does."

"So, who is he?"

"What's going on? What do you want him for—is there some kind of problem?"

"Just a routine investigation," I said. That was true enough. But if the police tell you that you are the subject of a routine investigation, call your lawyer. It means the police like you for a crime. "You know—just background."

"Well, what I heard is that he renting the place for a year while working here. He's some kind of salesman and he travels a lot. That would seem to be right—I've only seen him those two times."

"What's he sell?"

"Beats me. But he drives a salesman's car. Not sure what it is, but it's blue."

"What's a salesman's car?"

"I'm not sure exactly. He's got a Camry or a Taurus—new but nondescript—they all look pretty much the same. But I know it's dark blue."

I guess that was something. I asked "Do you know who owns the house?"

"Some Asian guy. I think he bought it as an investment, you know, to rent it out. The association has a rule that up to 15-percent of the houses can be non-owner occupied, so he rents it—one year minimum though. We don't want people moving in and out every week."

I thought, "What are you—the Chamber of Commerce?" but held my tongue. I asked him how he knew these things.

"I'm the president of the homeowners association."

Good news. "Could you get us the owner's name and address? We're going to have to talk to him too."

"Well, I'm not supposed to but, since you're police, I guess I can. I mean, if you wanted to, you could get a warrant, right?"

"Yeah or just look it up in county records on the computer. It would save us a little time."

The helpful nosey neighbor went back to his house and came back in a minute. Either he'd changed his mind or he was the most organized guy I'd run into in a long time.

"Got it right here—George Wong. He's listed with a business address in Roseville. Looks like he owns three other units here—must be a professional landlord."

We thanked the helpful guy and headed for Roseville. While we were driving, I got on the horn to the office and had them look up Wong. I got Tony Nguyen, one of the other homicide detectives, on the phone and he confirmed Wong's office address and some background. Like most professional landlords, it turned out that he had a few encounters with law enforcement over the years.

The last one involved an apartment-building fire. I remembered the case from the news. It was a building in Hopkins, which he had purchased about five years ago. The place was built in the 'sixties and had no fire sprinklers in it. The building met code when it was built and there is no requirement to add them now. Two people died in the fire.

The survivors sued the city for not requiring the sprinklers, the city fire department for not saving the victims, the alarm company for taking 38 seconds to notify the fire department, the original builder's estate for not putting the sprinklers in, and, of course, Wong for not adding the sprinklers.

The guy, who was convicted of arson for setting the fire in revenge for his girlfriend hooking up with someone else, wasn't sued. Apparently he had no money or insurance and his chances for future fortune were severely limited by his current work situation in the state prison system. Only deliberate arson could have gotten the fire started so fast and spread so far before the fire department got there. On a hunch, I asked them to check and see who the presiding judge was in the case. They said they'd check and call me back.

The office called back after about three minutes. They said that Wong had lost the wrongful death suit after the fire and had been ordered to pay $1.6 million dollars to the families of the two people killed. That would come from his insurance company, of course, but still, he lost and it would cost him in the long run. Tony said the presiding judge was *Amy Mitchell*. We suddenly had our choice of going for a warrant, notifying the Roseville PD to get their assistance to make a felony arrest, or just going in on our own right now. You can guess which one I picked.

The office building was one of those typical suburban units that ran four stories high with parking on both sides. There was a main entrance in the middle on one side and a second door on the other. Olson asked if he should go to the back in case Wong makes a run for it.

"I don't think so. I don't think he's expecting us and if he is, I don't want to try to stop him. If he's our guy, he knows how to shoot and I'd just as soon not start something right here."

"Okay," Olson replied, "but if this gets messy, you know we're going to have a bunch of people to answer to."

That was an understatement. If Wong was our guy and he got away, we'd have our department to answer to. If he came up shooting, we'd have our chief, the Roseville chief, the State Patrol, the State Bureau of Criminal Apprehension, and all the news media second-guessing us. Maybe he wouldn't be here. You can always hope—.

We walked into the front entrance like a couple of guys coming for a business meeting. I wished I had a briefcase just to complete the picture. I found the office number while Olson pushed the elevator button. Wong's office was on the 3rd floor.

It was a small office about halfway down the hall. A nice-looking young woman at the reception desk greeted us.

"Good morning. Can I help you?"

"Yes. We're looking for George," I answered with as much familiarity and good humor as I could muster—as if George and I were old buddies. Apparently I was convincing.

"Hang on a second and I'll see if he's available." I guess asking our names was not SOP.

She disappeared around a corner and was back in about 15 seconds.

"You can go right in."

"Thanks a bunch," I said with a big smile.

We walked back where the receptionist had pointed and found an Asian man in a golf shirt, sitting behind a big desk in a well-appointed office. There was a comfy-looking couch and overstuffed chair and a coffee table. The usual college degrees were on the wall, along with some family pictures, a few photos of apartment buildings, and a rather mean-looking five-foot-long tarpon. As Olson slid to the side in a flanking move, I walked right up to George, pulled open my coat to show him my shield and my gun at the same time, and identified myself. He took it well.

"Yes officers—how can I help you?"

He seemed oddly calm. Most people, when you move into their space as quickly as we just had, and then show them a badge and a gun, are at least startled. I introduced Olson. He just sat there.

"Mr. Wong, we're here to talk to you about the murder of Judge Amy Mitchell."

"Of course—I have been expecting you."

"And why is that?" I wondered if the place was wired to blow or something. If this guy really had a trump card somewhere, I wanted to know what it was.

"When I heard about her death on the news, I presumed that, sooner or later, you would come around. Unless you found who did it, and then you wouldn't need to talk to her past victims."

Well, that sort of set the tone regarding his position. "George—is it okay if I call you George?"

"That's what all my friends call me."

I always try to put my new good buddies at ease right away, regarding what we are going to call each other. It helps to have that to fall back on later if the suspect starts thinking that you aren't the buddy he thought you were.

"George, it's my duty at this point to tell you that we have very good evidence that you are involved with Judge Mitchell's murder, as well as three other murders."

"Dan—it is Dan, correct?" I nodded. This guy knew the game better than I did. He continued, "Dan, I can understand your interest in me and many others who have not found justice in Judge Mitchell's courtroom. But I have no idea what you are talking about in reference to three other murders. Is this a preliminary discussion, or should I call my attorney?"

"I don't think we need to bother with attorneys at this point. You are not under arrest and we are just here to ask a few questions." That sounded reassuring, even to me.

"Why don't you start from the beginning and ask away. Perhaps that will clear things up faster than you think."

His comfort level was unnerving me. "Okay, where were you the evening of June—"I paused and turned to Olson—"Olson, what was the exact date?"

Before Olson could answer, George said "It doesn't matter what the date is if it was in June. I was in China the entire month of June. My family had a reunion that I attended. You can check my passport. Should I get it from the safe?"

That was convenient. "Gone the entire month? Exactly when did you leave and return?"

"I left on May 28th and returned July 1st, in time for the Fourth. Would you like to see my passport?"

"We can hold off on that. Who is Gil Cederstrom?"

"I have no idea—should I?"

"As a matter of fact, you should. Do you own rental property in Blaine?"

"Yes, but I can't see where this line of questioning is going. Should I call my attorney now?"

"Let's hold that thought. Where are your properties in Blaine?"

"I own an apartment building off 109th, a strip mall at 114th and Central and four town homes in the development called Pastor's Greens. It's adjacent to the Pastor's Walk golf course. I bought them when they were new and they are barely holding their own. I'd sell them, but you know how the townhouse market is right now."

Actually, I didn't know how the townhouse market was, and didn't really care. "Gil Cederstrom rents one of the townhouses."

"That could be, but you don't expect me to know the names of all my tenants?"

"We have solid information that places Cederstrom in position to have committed two of the four murders—and he is your tenant. How would you read that?"

"Sure—I could have motive—as could you, if you had ever appeared before Judge Mitchell. But murder? I hardly think so."

"I'd say you had 1.6 million reasons."

"My business has expenses and the lawsuit was one of them. My insurance paid and I put it behind me. Whatever could I hope to accomplish by killing the judge or the others you mentioned?"

Actually, he had no reason to go after the others.

"Dan—we are still on a first name basis, no? Dan, I own a company with $35 million dollars in revenue per year, with assets in excess of $50 million. As I said, it was a cost of doing business. I would never jeopardize that with something as personal as murder."

I had to agree that murder was, indeed, personal—it is as personal as it gets. But I already was past George doing it himself. He must have hired Cederstrom.

"George, I don't think you did it yourself. I don't think a man with your resources would get your own hands dirty. I think you hired it out."

That sank in for a moment. George replied, "I'll tell you what—let me pull the records on your Mr. Cederstrom and we'll see who he is."

He picked up the phone and called Miss Sunshine from the front desk. He told her what he wanted and, after he hung up, said, "I presume you wouldn't want me to go get them myself."

"You are very perceptive, George. So, what's the story on the fish?"

"It was a great experience. I was fly-fishing on the flats south of Port Charlotte, Florida, about four years ago. A friend of mine there took me fishing and told me that there were big tarpon and I didn't believe him. I thought we'd be lucky to get into some ladyfish or something. We were in the Boca Grande Channel that goes into Charlotte Bay tossing out pretty good sized flies. This hog caught my line and the fight was on. It took four and a half hours to get it into the boat. What a fight—the best time fishing I've ever had and I've done a lot of fishing."

If I would have closed my eyes right then, I could have seen the Al Lindner fishing show on TV. This guy had switched from business formal to good old boy fish-speak in the blink of an eye—sounded like he'd lived here all his life, which he probably had.

The receptionist came in with a report literally hot off the printer and handed it to George. He looked it over and said, "This should have everything you are looking for. Mr. Gil Cederstrom, moved here from Indiana and works for a company there called Advanced Information Systems. We always do a background check on every prospective tenant. He checked out fine. Credit—785, Social Security number, criminal check here and in Indiana, and not even a traffic ticket. He signed a one-year lease and paid in advance with a money order from his company. Subsequent checks have shown that he has paid his utility bills and credit remains the same. In fact, it's exactly the same, which is a bit unusual."

"What do you mean, unusual?"

"For most people, credit ratings change over time as they use credit or pay off debt. This looks as if Mr. Cederstrom hasn't bought anything or used any credit since he moved in."

"And when was that?"

"Let's see. It was early June. He's been with us a little under two months."

I looked at Olson. June—just in time for this little project. "George, you are still someone we will want to talk to from time to time." I handed him a card. "Please keep us informed of your whereabouts."

George showed us out, chatting on the way. "Be sure to keep me informed if you decide one of my tenants is a killer. That would be a violation of his lease," he said, with a straight face. "I'm certainly curious about the coincidence that one of my tenants should be your prime suspect in the murder of a woman I had such a distasteful encounter with. It's hard to believe that could happen, isn't it?"

I remember thinking, "What is this guy—a mind reader?" Once again, cops believe in coincidences about as much as they believe in the tooth fairy. I told him, "Please don't go on any long trips without notifying us. I'd consider that provocative."

"And why would that be provocative, Dan?"

"Because, if I come looking for you to chat, or discuss fishing, or to arrest you for murder, I'd like to know that I could find you without having to resort to something messy like a nationwide APB. You know how that can get—SWAT teams and everything. Plus if you're out of the state, then the Feds get involved and it costs more and you know how tight the city budgets are these days."

"Yes, I can understand that. I'll let you know if I have to go anywhere, like—say—China."

"Try to not plan any trips to China soon. Okay, George?"

# Chapter 39

On the way back to Olson's office, I called Tony Nguyen to see if anything else interesting had come in.

"You got a call from some guy in Atlanta. I've got the number right here." He read it off with the guy's name—Franklin Bushard. "Guy said he was with Atlanta PD and wanted to talk to you about Davis."

I thanked Tony and made the call. He answered and the connection was amazingly good. Sometimes I really wonder about all this cell stuff. I can't get a decent connection in my living room, but here I was talking to a guy in Georgia from a moving car clear as a bell.

"Bushard," he answered.

"Franklin, this is Dan Neumann in Minneapolis. I heard you called—you have a moment?"

"I'm on the highway so I might loose you. Are you the guy who called about spreading out the search area after Davis was shot?"

"Yeah, my partner called—you find something?"

"Sure did, about six blocks away. It was about a 900-yard shot. What we're wondering is why you thought we should look that far away."

"We are looking into the possibility that there is a trained sniper involved in the killing of Judge Amy Mitchell. She used to be here in Minneapolis but had just retired to Phoenix. Her last case involved Davis as chief defense counsel. The shot that got her was at least 1,200 yards. Plus, there was a killing in Alaska that's possibly connected to ours. Might have been the same guy, but we didn't have much left for forensics."

"What do you mean, *left*?"

"A bear must have found the body before we did. What can you tell me?"

"You were right on the nose with the search. Found the probable perch, but by then the guy got away. Hell of a shot—caught Davis just above the left ear—blew up his head. It had to be a high-powered rifle to do that."

"You go to the autopsy?"

"Yeah—why?"

"Anything unusual about the entry wound?"

"As a matter of fact, yes. Hey—you're making me think that I should get you down here. You come up with one more coincidence and I'm going to slap a warrant on your ass. The entry wound was still clean, after a fashion. It was in the one fairly large part of the skull that was left, a chunk about three inches in diameter. All the rest of the skull was blown to shit. Anyway, the one chunk we found we cleaned and it shows a very small entry hole—maybe point one five to point two zero inches in diameter."

"Any other distinguishing marks around the hole—anything like a little star?"

"That's it, buddy, I'm going to arrest you right know—you know more about this than I do. Yeah, there's kind of a star-shaped marking around the entry hole. What's that all about?"

"Not sure yet. Here's what I have—I have a killing of a retired Minneapolis Judge in Arizona and possibly a hiker in Alaska. These shootings may or may not be related to the judge's last case here. The hiker was a defendant in the last case she had. Your guy was the defense counsel in that same case. The person or persons doing the shootings may or may not be military personnel or military trained. The high level of skill needed for these shots seems to make that likely. The exact type of weapon may be something not even available to the public, but some kind of experimental military weapon. That's where the little star-shaped hole comes in. Here's what I don't have—I have no physical evidence, I have no witnesses, and my prime suspect is not former military. He's not a hunter, has no known firearms expertise, and has very good alibis for the time periods of the shootings. All he has is a motive."

"What's his motive?"

"That last trial the judge had was of the suspected murderers of his wife. They walked and Davis was the defense."

"That's motive all right."

"Okay," I said, "keep us informed if you find anything else around the perch."

"It's pretty clean, like whoever it was took their time and cleaned up. No shell casings of course. Gravel on the roof was scuffed around some. We're checking the door knobs and handrails on the staircases up to the roof but I don't have anything yet. There were lots of prints but we're trying to run an elimination of other people who would have been in the building. We did find a wrapper for a candy bar."

Oh-boy—"What kind of candy bar?"

"Never saw this kind before. Something called a "Nut Goodie."

"No shit—that's our guy! He left one in Alaska and in Arizona. It's his signature. Do you have a lot-number off the wrapper?"

"Yeah—hang on a second."

Bushard came back on and read me the number. It was the same as the two previous wrappers. I gave Bushard the bad news.

"Well at least we know we're only dealing with one guy," I said.

"Neumann, I don't know what happened up there but we've got something else going on here. I've had Davis under investigation for the past two and a half years. I even got an undercover guy into his office. We were investigating him for corruption."

"Corruption of what? He was a defense lawyer, aren't they all corrupt?"

Bushard chuckled. "Yeah, I hear you. But this was something real. He wins too many of his cases—almost never loses—even cases the prosecutors thought they had locked up tight. Your case is one of the ones we are looking at. We think he may have been either blackmailing or bribing judges, police, investigators, and whomever he could to get inside information on his cases."

This was a serious charge, although not unheard of. About 99.99 percent of all defense lawyers keep it clean and don't lose any sleep over losing a case when some slime ball gets what he really deserves. They have to do their best in order for the system to work and if the State gets him anyway, well, that's the way the cookie crumbles. But every once in a while, there is someone for whom winning is the *only* thing.

Bushard was still driving and had to ring off. "Listen—I gotta run. Good to meet you—thanks for all the info. If you need anything from me, or come up with anything else, just call me back." I gave him my cell number and we hung up.

# Chapter 40

We got back downtown and went inside to Olson's office. There was a message to call Bill Dunn.

"Dunn, this is Dan Neumann from the Minneapolis Police Department. You called?"

"Yeah, I got to thinking about who else you might want to talk to. One guy comes to mind. He used to work with Ben Harris when Ben was making all those trips to Ft. Bragg. His name is Sterling Whitehead."

"Got it—Sterling Whitehead. And why would I want to take up Mr. Whitehead's time?"

"He was Ben's assistant. A very bright young man right out of Iowa State with a degree in electrical engineering. Ben used him as a gofer and helper when he was building new systems. I know that he went with Ben to North Carolina at least twice. He might know some more about what Ben did there, who he worked with, that sort of thing."

"Thanks. I'll give him a call right away."

I hung up and called Whitehead.

"Hello?"

"Is this Sterling Whitehead?"

"Yes, who's calling?"

"This is Dan Neumann of the Minneapolis Police Department."

Before I could say any more, he cut in—"Okay, okay—I know I've got to get those parking tickets paid, but you just have to give me a little time. Maybe I could work something out to pay them over time."

This could be interesting. As quickly as I could, I started looking him up in the Department computer. "You know, Sterling—okay if I call you Sterling?"

"Yes."

"Sterling, that's not really what I called about. What I was wondering was,"—"Holy crap," I thought. He had 47 outstanding parking tickets. Almost all were from the same area in Uptown. It's the yuppie capital of the city—"I was just wondering if you could stop by our offices here on your way home from work. We have a case we are working on that concerns some people you know and I'd like to ask you a few questions."

"What kind of questions?"

"It's just routine. It will only take a few minutes."

"If I help you out, is there anything you can do about my parking tickets?"

Not really, I knew, but wanted to keep him hopeful and cooperative. "I can take a look at them—maybe give you some pointers on how to resolve your issues with the traffic department."

"Sounds great. Where's your office?"

"Right downtown—the old city hall building. Ask for Robert Olson's office. I share one with him."

"I can stop by after work. Is there parking somewhere around there?"

Good question for someone who's about to get his car impounded. "Right across from the government center there's a ramp. Bring the ticket and we'll validate it for you." This guy was in for a real surprise. It's about $20 an hour to park over there and I can't validate anything but my birthday. "I'll be here waiting for you." I gave him my cell number in case he got lost and looked at Olson.

"You get him to come in?"

"Nothin' to it," I bragged.

"How do you do that?" Olson asked.

"Simple. You just give them a straw to grasp and they grasp." I'm no expert in human behavior but, like most cops, I know how to use diplomacy get people to do things they might not want to. It's a gift.

# Chapter 41

## Atlanta

Franklin Bushard was confused. He'd been on this case for two years. It had started out as a corruption case involving a local judge, who had handed down an awful lot of surprising acquittals. That led to some insiders within the records department of the Cobb County courthouse, and then to Richard Davis. With a lot of good police work, he was able to piece together a case that showed that Davis's office was in the business of bribery and extortion, along with criminal defense work. The mechanics of just how this was occurring were not clear yet. He had parts of it but not enough to bring charges and he knew that once charges were brought all the sources would dry up.

He called Brian Pritchett, a county prosecutor who was working the case.

"Brian, we need to talk. Have you heard anything about the Davis shooting?"

"Nothing I'm sure that you haven't. He was on his balcony and got his head blown off—that about it?"

"So far. But I just talked with a cop in Minneapolis who thinks he has two other shootings that are connected with ours. He says the shooter is a sniper who is using some kind of weapon not readily available to the public. He says it's some kind of new military weapon. I don't know where he got that, but he knew about the star-shaped entry wound."

"That's more than coincidence. I think we should talk to this guy in person. You want to go up there?"

"Let me think about that. Hmm—go to Minneapolis in the middle of the summer. You mean leave Atlanta and go anywhere north in the middle of the summer? Okay, I'll go."

# Chapter 42

**Minneapolis**

Sterling Whitehead was on time. I guess when you're trying to swing a deal to get out of jail time for aggravated parking, you show up. A uniformed officer showed him to Olson's office.

"Sterling, come right in. I'm Dan Neumann and this is Robert Olson. We're very interested in straightening out your parking issues."

He came in slowly, as if unsure of the protocols. Should he sit, stand, speak, or salute? I helped him out.

"Here—sit right over here and we'll get your file."

Olson dug through the crap on his desk and found Whitehead's file. Of course, he had no file on Whitehead, so he used another file. It was really an old file on a long-term drug operation he had busted two years ago. It was about three inches thick and looked very intimidating. He opened it and started piecing through the many pages of notes, while emitting some sounds of shock and awe and shaking his head. The idea was that it would put Whitehead in a cooperative frame of mind. From the look on his face, it worked.

Sterling broke the silence and got the ball rolling. "Well, gentlemen, how can I be of service?"

"Sterling," I said, keeping up my buddy demeanor, "we are looking into that grocery store bank robbery that resulted in the death of your co-workers wife."

"Oh yes—Ben's wife. She was a lovely woman—such a loss."

"Yes. What we're wondering is if you can give us some insight into Ben Harris.

"Ben Harris? Why are you interested in him?"

"Well, as you may have heard or read in the papers, the two individuals who were tried and acquitted for his wife's murder have been murdered themselves. We are trying to see if, perhaps, Anne Harris's death wasn't random—that maybe someone else happened to be in the store that day that had a grudge against Harris. Or maybe she was having an affair or something? You work at AMES, right?"

Whitehead nodded.

"What do you do there?"

"Wait a minute. First off, I can't even begin to believe that Anne Harris would have an affair. She and Ben were totally in love. And Ben, well the man is the soul of integrity."

"I'm sure he is. What we're wondering has more to do with AMES."

"All you want is some information on AMES?"

"Maybe just AMES—maybe some other things—we won't know until we get there. So what do you do at AMES?"

"I work in product development and design."

"And what does that involve?"

"Just what I said. I help design new radio products and then work on their development."

Olson answered. "Yes, we get that but you have to understand, we don't know what radio development involves. Do you solder up radios and call your buddies on them or what?"

Whitehead chuckled. "No, nothing like that. Most radio design is done on a computer. We lay out the circuitry on the computer and even test it on computer. By the time we actually make one, we have a pretty good idea if it's going to do what we want it to."

"And what do you want your radios to do?"

"Talk to other radios. We make specialized, encrypted short-range person-to-person and person-to-network communication systems."

"And who are your customers?" I asked.

"I don't think I can answer that. Many of them are classified. Is that going to screw up my parking ticket deal?"

"Not yet. I appreciate your concern for security. We're pretty sure who your customers are. They're military, aren't they?"

"Well, I guess since you already know—yes, the Army."

"And in your design and development, especially the development part, do you find yourself working with the military in the field?"

"Yes. It's very important to work with the end users so you know if the systems are doing what they're supposed to do."

"And when you are doing this, you may occasionally go out of state?"

"Yes. I have taken trips to North Carolina to work with our customers." He was really warming to the experience. I was glad I'd made that special effort to call him Sterling.

"Anybody go with you?"

"Sometimes—actually, most times. I was kind of new at this at the time and the relationships are very personal. I thought that it was based more on who you knew rather than what you knew. Same thing with the other guys I worked with. Most of them have never been in the military, so they don't understand the value of the personal relationships."

"Were you in the military?"

"No, I went right from high school to Iowa State, and then to AMES. I always think that's kind of funny, since Iowa State is in Ames. I went from Ames to AMES. Anyway, not many of the guys at AMES have military time."

"So who did the field work with you?" This was the keystone question. Whoever had been at AMES had access—had been close to the military. We needed those names now.

"I know that Ben Harris did a lot of field work. He wasn't military, but he was very close to the Army personnel he worked with. I went with him once to Greece. It was an education for me. We worked with our Army guys and the Greeks. I went to Ft. Bragg a few times too. That was nothing but work."

I asked, "How so?" as conversationally as I could.

"In Greece there was a lot of socializing. It was important to the Greeks. We did mostly classroom stuff and a little field some days. At Bragg we worked on field testing a new personal com system. It was really neat—but it was all work."

"Was it all classroom?" I asked.

"No—mostly field. And that was real work. These guys would take us out into the forest for three or four days at a time. We slept on the ground, ate sometimes, and crept around all the time just like we were on a mission. They wanted to test the radios under as real world conditions as possible. It wasn't just camping.

"And you and Harris did this?"

"Yes."

"Harris is a bit older than you are. He must have been dragging his ass." An observation, not a question, but you do this now and then to keep the subject going in the right direction.

"Are you kidding? He ate this stuff up. He had been through what they call the *Short Course*. That's training they have for non-special-forces military guys and non-military people who just need the understanding. It's two weeks of hell, from what I've heard—classroom in the morning and field in the afternoon and evening for a week, followed by the *problem*."

"What's the problem?"

"They give you a field exercise to work out. For example, they'll tell you to go to this place and pick up that equipment, then make your way to a point on the military reservation maybe 30 miles away and place a demo charge on a bridge by a certain time. Then you make your way to another point, maybe 25 miles away, and rescue a hostage and bring them home."

"Sounds like I could do it in a day."

"I don't think so. You're on foot with two or three other guys—one is a secret instructor who's planted in the class, though you don't know that. His job is to make things as hard as possible for you. He's always dragging his ass and complaining about everything. And what I've heard is the instructor usually gets hurt somewhere along the way so the team leader—Ben—has to decide whether or not to try to take him with or just leave him. If you leave him you flunk, though they don't tell you that. I heard that Ben's guy supposedly twisted his ankle and had to be carried by Ben and the other two guys the last two days, and he was a big guy. Plus it's the foothills of the Appalachian's so it's hard terrain to cover. On top of it all, there are guys out looking for you. If you're even spotted, you flunk."

"And Harris went through this course?"

"Go through it? He aced it! You'd think he'd been in the teams for years, from what I heard. He didn't talk about it—he's not the heroic type. But the people at Bragg knew him and considered him one of theirs. I think that's why they took him to Afghanistan in 2002."

"Harris went to Afghanistan?" This was incredible. I'd known a lot of military types over the years and none of them would have even considered taking a civilian into the field, especially not a place like Afghanistan.

"Yeah, and not just to stay in the background and talk on the radios. He went out on missions with them—carried a weapon and everything."

This was so far over the top I was getting dizzy. I'd heard from my military friends that Special Forces operated by their own rules, but this—a civilian out on patrols? I asked if Sterling knew what kind of weapon Harris carried.

"An M-4, I think. But it could have been a regular hunting rifle. He has the reputation as being a hell of a shot."

Oh shit. Ben Harris just changed from suspect with motive but no ability to suspect with motive and means. "Sterling, what kind of a person is Ben Harris?"

"I'm not sure what you mean by that."

"You know, loud, quiet, boisterous, introverted, family man, party animal? What kind of guy is he?"

"I guess he's just a regular guy. Great wife, really too bad what happened to her. He's one of the smartest people I know, takes care of himself, works hard. I'm not really sure what you're looking for."

"I'm wondering if you think he could kill someone—you know—if he was in combat. Did he ever have to shoot anyone?"

"Not that I know if. I think he just carried the rifle because everyone else did. You know, if you're going to field test a radio, you have to be carrying all the gear everyone else does in order get a realistic feel for whether or not the thing is useful. If all you're carrying is the radio, you don't know if it's too heavy or cumbersome or if you can reach it and use it. Besides, I don't think the guys with him would have let him get into a bad spot. They really liked him and the radios worked very well. They knew that he was working on their behalf and they'd keep him out of trouble."

"So you don't know if he could shoot someone? How about if it were something else, how about if he were to confront a burglar in his home or a mugger on the street? Could he shoot him?"

"That's a hypothetical that I don't think anyone could answer until happened to them. How about you, Mr. Neumann? Could you shoot someone?"

Of course, I would and could and had. But I'm a trained police officer who is expected to do that if necessary. The timing was bad, but suddenly I couldn't stop myself from reflecting back on my conversation with Wolf.

Wolf had said that everyone needed the good and dark sides to function—it was important to our development as a species. But now the dark side had to be controlled. I'd certainly seen the dark side come out of people, but there was always some underlying background in a person that made them more likely to commit a crime. Abuse, neglect, substances—a whole list of reasons why people do bad things. It's the same list used by bleeding hearts and defense attorneys to explain why the bad behavior isn't really little Johnny's fault. He's really a victim of the society that made him.

But there are true psychopaths and sociopaths out there. These are the four or five percent of people who understand that doing something is wrong, even criminal, but who think those rules just don't apply to them. They can personally justify robbing a bank or, more commonly, committing murder. They are weak in the good side—little or no conscience. Many of them can function in a community for years, while committing their crimes and no one knows who they are. There have been cases like the BTK killer in Kansas or the Atlanta child killer—men who killed indiscriminately in their home areas for years without anyone ever suspecting them. These are the criminals who are most feared by law enforcement because they are so hard to find. They also are the ones who caused an entire field of criminal research to be created—profiling.

I didn't think my guy or Harris were psychopaths. I thought he was that other person Wolf talked about—someone who had reacted to a great evil done to him by taking action to correct what he saw as a mistake by society. It was clear in his mind that the two boys, the judge, and the defense attorney were the ones who should be punished for the crime committed against him and his loved one.

Perhaps he saw two crimes here—the first was the bank robbery and murder, the second was the trial. Maybe he wasn't just correcting the mistake of the court—he was correcting the court itself. Maybe he killed Davis to be proactive—to prevent him from getting any more criminals off. Perhaps he believed that Davis was evil and had somehow rigged the case. Could he have found out about the investigation Bushard was running? Did he have some connection in the Atlanta Police force or DA's office? If he did, that would further explain going after both Davis and Judge Mitchell.

But by killing the judge, who had retired and would never again sit on a case, he wasn't preventing her from making another error. She was done anyway. No, her murder could only be described as revenge.

Wolf had said that capital punishment doesn't prevent murder, but it avenges the survivors of the victims. I agreed with Wolf, it didn't stop people from committing murder because killers don't think they'd get caught.

This was where American society differed from others, especially eastern societies. I had spent a year in Japan as an exchange officer, and the Japanese told me that their crime rate was low because they were so good at solving crimes. They had a case closing and conviction rate in the high 90-percent range and were justifiably proud.

But other American law enforcement pros I've met since say that Japan is different because the Japanese criminal expects to get caught. When they do, they don't spend 10 years and millions of dollars worth of Yen fighting it. Their attitude is "well, you got me" and off they go to jail.

American criminals think they won't get caught and when they do, they fight it tooth and nail. Many rationalize their crimes because they think that society has treated them unfairly and that they are only doing what anyone would do. When caught, they regard themselves as victims. This results in a lot of surprised convicts in our prisons, some of whom are busy in the prison library studying to be lawyers so they can represent themselves in their re-trials.

But there was that other possibility—that the shooter somehow knew that Davis had co-opted Mitchell. If he knew that Mitchell was dirty, her death wouldn't just be revenge for letting his wife's murder go, or to prevent her from doing the same in the future. It would be payback for her turning her back on her duties to society. Bushard said that Davis was bribing judges. Was there any way that the shooter could have known that? Another talk with Bushard was needed—.

Sterling was looking at me—waiting for an answer. I nodded yes, giving myself time to reel my mind back completely into the present, and said, "Without going into details, there have been times when I've had to draw my service weapon. But you're right—we shouldn't be speaking hypothetically. Regarding Harris, do you know if he did any hunting or owns any firearms?"

"I don't know the answer to either of those. I know that he liked to shoot with the Special Forces guys at Bragg and that they would settle bets at the club after hours. The bets were always paid in drinks and I never saw Dan have to buy. I only saw him shoot once and that was an M-16. He was pretty good with that."

"So your experience in North Carolina was just a couple of trips with Harris and you think he's a pretty good shot?"

"That's about the size of it. Is this going to help me with the parking tickets?"

"Like I said when I called, that's not what I was calling about. You do need to do something about the tickets, and soon. They're kind of like savings bonds—the longer you keep them, the greater they mature. When you add up all your fines, it's a pretty big number and that's what a traffic court judge will look at. I can walk you down the hall and put in a good word for you. I think you'll still have to pay the fines, but we might be able to get the penalties waved and make sure they don't issue a warrant for a felony arrest."

"I guess that's something. Can I go now?"

"Yes, but let us know if you have any more trips coming up."

Sterling and I left. The walk to the traffic desk was short and silent. I told the officer on duty what Sterling was there for and that he'd been cooperative in an investigation I was running. That was about all I could do. People think cops can and do fix tickets, but that's not quite how it works.

Back in his office, Olson asked, "Where were you? You were out for a while."

"I was down at traffic with Sterling."

"No, I mean while we were talking to him—you zoned out."

"Oh that—I know—I mean, I don't know. I just got to thinking. What if the shooter is out of Atlanta and knew that Davis was dirty? What if there's some kind of connection between here and Atlanta that we don't know about? Could be someone that Harris knows down there let him in on Bushard's investigation and that he knew Davis and Mitchell were dirty. We could be in the wrong state. Wha-da-ya say we call travel and get us tickets to Atlanta?"

Before he could do that, the phone rang and he picked it up. After a couple of minutes Olson hung up and said, "We don't have to go to Atlanta. They're coming here."

"Now *that* is what I call a coincidence—when?"

"Tomorrow morning—should be here by 10:30. I'll pick them up at the airport."

"Great. Then I can take off and go try to make some sense out of this."

I left and headed for my second-favorite mental-health center—Bill's.

# Chapter 43

I rode out of downtown and headed north. The afternoon was blistering and the sky had that hazy look that could build into a nasty thunderstorm later. I hoped for the storm. It would clear the air and cool things off for tomorrow. I'm always hoping for a better tomorrow.

I parked underground—nice and cool in here, and found John inside.

"Hey Dan, how ya doing?"

"Great. I've got a nice afternoon for the scooter and I'm hoping for some answers. What could be better?"

John laughed and said "Okay, that's a tough first question. What kind of answers? I watched *Jeopardy* today so I'm feeling really smart."

"Fair enough. Only I'll give the question and you see if you know the answer." Question one—for $500—if I wanted to make a long gun with a smoothbore barrel, where would I find the barrel?"

"Too easy. Smoothbore musket barrels are available all over the place. You can get them in anything from .45 to old big bores like .67 caliber. Next question."

"How about a 32- to 40-inch smoothbore in a .30 caliber?"

"That might be a bit harder. I'm not sure if you can get a bore that small. Are you sure that's what you need?"

"Hell, John, I'm not sure I'm even asking the right questions. It's so bad that I don't *know* what I don't know."

John chuckled at that. "Hang on a second while I Google it." He turned to his computer. About 30 seconds later he had a screen up for Wild Mountain Sporting Goods, a firearms supplier in Idaho. "Take a look here, this outfit has smoothbore barrels for black powder guns and antique replications. It looks like they can make them to fit." He paused and scrolled down, "Here it says you can buy a 42-inch, .45-caliber smoothbore barrel for 196 dollars. Here's one in a smaller caliber, but it's shorter." A little lower on the page was a comment that said you could order custom barrels.

I asked, "Any contact info?"

John found it and read it off and I asked him, "Any other places that might have this thing?"

We spent another 20 minutes looking for barrel supplier candidates. When we were done I had eight companies in eight states from New Hampshire to Alaska.

"Thanks buddy. I'll give them a call and see if they have any Minnesota customers."

"Good luck. You'll probably have to serve them a search warrant in person. This type of outfit isn't likely to give you that info over the phone. They take privacy and confidentiality seriously."

Great, Idaho is that last place I wanted to go. "Okay, I've got another question for you."

"Fire away."

Let's say I want to make a sabot round that I can fire from a .30-caliber barrel. The projectile will be some kind of a heavy-metal dart, maybe made of tungsten, about .17 in diameter with some fins."

"Dart, huh?"

"Yeah, that's what I'm calling it. What would I use for the sabot?"

"You need something that will stand up to the pressures and heat of the firing. You said you had an idea on the muzzle velocity of this round?"

"About 4,000 feet per second."

"All right, we'll go with that. You need something that will seal the barrel well enough to get the projectile up to that speed and then it has to fall off to release the dart. There are a lot of plastics that could do it. Does your guy have any experience with plastics or modeling?"

I didn't know and said so. That was one more thing on the list of stuff to check out.

John said "Okay, so we assume he's got plastics experience. Then he'd need some way to make the darts, mold the plastic, and assemble the rounds. He's also going to need a way to do some gunsmithing."

"Why gunsmithing?"

"If he can get a barrel, he's going to have to bore out the chamber to accept the round. Your guy would need a whole lot of powder to get her up to 4,000 feet per second with a projectile that weighs as much as you think this one does. The formula's pretty simple—X amount of weight needs Y amount of powder and L amount of barrel length to go Z fast. That's also why you need the long barrel—more muzzle velocity—same as a rifle."

"So I need to find a guy that can machine his own barrels and the darts, make his own plastic sabots, be a world class shot, and can kill people and sleep at night with no problems. Sounds simple."

"Yeah, but if you find him, you'll know you've got the right guy. It would be a lot simpler if he just got the gun and rounds from someone. Any chance of that?"

"My contact says no. He's a retired Special Ops guy and he says *no way* would the military let that happen. Every barrel and every round is accounted for."

"I'm not talking about the military," John said soberly. "They aren't making these things. Someone else is."

"I asked about that too. He said that the manufacturers are all under super-tight control."

"Sure they are. Come on Dan," he said, pointing at a cabinet stocked with fully automatic machine guns. "I've got stuff here it takes a special license to own, but I've got one. That doesn't mean that there aren't people out there who also have the proper license and who would sell you one of these for the right price. If there's a will, or a dollar, there's a way."

That was an angle I hadn't thought of. What if the shooter had gotten a gun from the original manufacturer? Or even just the barrel? Who was the original manufacturer? John said he thought the gun would be a standard-looking .300 magnum. If the shooter got his hands on a barrel, could he fit it to a standard rifle? What if he was getting the rounds from a manufacturer too—or just the darts and sabots? Could he load his own rounds if he had the correct projectiles? There were many questions to check out. John saw me out the door.

I rode home thinking about how to get a search warrant served on these barrel manufacturers without having to do it myself. And who was making the guns and rounds? And who is this man-of-all-trades?

# Chapter 44

**Thursday, July 17th**
**Robbinsdale**

I got up the next morning with my head spinning. It had been a tough night. All the information from yesterday was scrolling through my mind like tickertape, and I couldn't make one story out of it. It was time to get up and get over to Olson's office. The guys from Atlanta were coming in today.

It was only 6:15, so I jogged a quick lap of the neighborhood and hit the weight machine for a half hour. I do some of my best thinking while working out.

I made another mental list of what I did have—four murders, all connected by the botched bank robbery. We had some forensics and witnesses from the first shooting but nothing from the others. The bullet fragments from the first shooting were worthless ballistics-wise. We had motives for each of the killings, but only one thing that ran through all four. And what was up with the candy bar wrappers?

I finished up and made my once-a-week big breakfast. I used to do this more when I was lucky enough to have company for breakfast, but now I just make it for myself. It consists of buttermilk pancakes from scratch—never got into mixes—eggs, some kind of sausage or bacon, coffee, juice, and fruit. It doesn't take that long and it keeps me going all day, lunch or not. Anyway, I stay in practice just in case I do get a visitor.

I flipped on the news channel my TV is stuck on. Usually, I'll watch while cooking so I could stay up on the rest of the world's happenings, but today it's the same old fixation on the presidential election. This stuff is driving me nuts. I mean—who needs a two-year election campaign? I think we should do what the British do, call the government un-viable, and have elections within two months instead of on a regular schedule. Might cost the TV stations some ad money, but I'd pay higher cable bills to get rid of this. I turned it to the Food Channel and watched some guy talk about the history of pasta making.

While I was whipping the batter, I continued reviewing the case. Two different methods—one a not-so-simple drive-by, the others very complex and skilled sniper shots. The drive-by involved a type of ammo that wouldn't normally be used in a drive-by-type shooting. Why? The other three may have used a type of projectile I wasn't sure even existed. If it exists—how to find the source? Where did the rifle come from? Did the shooter buy it, steal it, or make it? Who has the skill to make this shot? Harris? Maybe he does. Is there someone else involved? Maybe. Who are the other possible shooters? Is the killing over or are we racing the shooter to the next target? And what's up with the Nut Goodie bars?

I finished breakfast and was working on my coffee when the phone rang. It was Rademacher.

"I got another hit on Cederstrom," she said.

"Whatcha got?"

"He was on a plane to Charlotte the day of Davis's killing, and then came back the next morning. I did the math on the mileage and he would have had time to drive to Atlanta and back. Also, he rented a car and it came back with enough mileage to have gone from Charlotte to Atlanta and back."

Who the heck was this Cederstrom anyway? "Any hits on his employer?"

"Nothing. The phone number is a dead end and I can't find anything on them in the usual industrial publications."

"You're the best, Babe," I said.

"Yeah—you always say that. When are you going to stop talking big and find out just how good I am?"

"No way until you dump that husband of yours. He carries a gun." Sharon was married to a county sheriff who could bench press about 550. But, if she ever did dump him—.

Sharon laughed, "Fat chance. He's the best and he's only got three years to go until retirement."

"Well, thanks anyway. Do me a favor?"

"You know I can't say no to you, Danny." The game continued. Good thing HR never got a hold of a recording of Sharon's phone conversations. She was an old-fashioned girl who could never understand why a little workplace teasing was out of place.

"Call Pearson's Candy and ask them what their numbering system is for lot numbers or expiration numbers on Nut Goodies. Give them the number we have and find out who bought it—where and when."

"Got it. Anything else?"

"Yeah, and this is going to take a little time. Look online for outfits where you could buy smoothbore musket or rifle barrels. There are about eight of them. I'm looking for a 32- to 42-inch, .30-caliber, smoothbore rifle barrel—don't need the rifle, just the barrel. Make sense?"

"No, but when did that matter?"

"These outfits may give you trouble on this, but if they have what we're looking for, I need a list of anyone they've sold that to. The list shouldn't be long, but getting it may be a problem. I'm told these suppliers are very protective about their customers."

"I'll charm 'em. Don't worry—I'll get it one way or another."

"That's what's got me worried, Sharon," I said with a chuckle. She may have been in her late forties, but she was still a hottie and knew it. Plus, on the phone, you'd never guess her age. I hung up, scooped up the dishes and headed inside. It was another nice day for motoring, so I took the Harley again.

# Chapter 45

I got to Olson's office about ten o'clock. Olson called and said that he'd just picked up Bushard and Pritchett at the airport and they were on the way. I had just enough time to check in with the chief and let him know where we were—nowhere. We had a lot of information but it wasn't going anywhere. I told him about the leads we were following and facts we were chasing down. Maybe the Atlanta guys would shed a little light for us.

Pritchett and Bushard walked in ahead of Olson at 10:45. Pritchett was a typical prosecutor, at least in my eyes. He was a slender white man of average height with a stylishly long hair cut, impeccably dressed in a very nice chalk-line three-piece suit. Bushard, however, looked like a cop on vacation—khakis, a golf shirt, and the indispensible blue blazer—just what I would have worn. He was a tall black man who looked like he could have had a career in the NFL. I knew from moment one that the lawyer would be a problem and I'd like the cop. He and I would hit it off because we had the same frame of reference. After introductions we got coffee and sat down in one of the conference rooms.

I led off with a quick review of what we had, which was still not much. "We've got a few ideas we're chasing down—where did the gun come from, and what's up with the candy wrappers, but not much else to build a case. We've got a lot of good motivation for the guy we like, Harris, but nothing that's going to get a conviction."

Bushard asked, "You haven't said anything to the press about the candy wrappers have you?"

"No, and I want to keep it that way. Actually, the press isn't paying much attention to this and I like that. If they find out about the candy bar thing, they'll go nuts and we'll have to deal with them too."

"Right—I can see it now—The Candy Man, or The Goodie Nut," Bushard replied. "We brought a copy of our case file on the investigation we were running on Davis. We know he was bribing and extorting little bits and pieces here and there to get what he wanted from judges, prosecutor's offices, and others on some cases. I'm pretty sure he was doing something on yours too, but unless we can get bank records we're going to have a tough time proving anything."

"How would bank records help?" Olson asked.

"We've got Davis's bank records showing that he was dispersing cash to places he wouldn't normally have to. He was smart and it's pretty well hidden—going through several banks including some off shore—but the timing is what locks it. If we can show that he sent money the same time your judge received some, that coincidence is going to look good to a grand jury."

That sounded good to me. "But getting a warrant on a judge is going to be tough. We'll have to play it as part of the murder investigation and something to do with dirt."

Pritchett agreed. "Right, but I think we have to down-play the murder part. If the judge and Davis are already dead— where's the case?"

I figured he was playing devil's advocate, like most prosecutors—they have to. Still, he had a point. If the suspect of a crime is dead, there's no trial—just a ruling. "You guys still have the rest of Davis's office, who may be complicit, right?"

"Sure, but Davis was the big fish. We'll have to focus on other judges, prosecutors, and the like to keep this alive. Actually, finding that Davis was dirty might help the defense in any trial on Davis's murder."

There's a thought. I decided I'd still have to check this out and see if it will help us. If we had to hand it over to the defense later, that's the way it will go. So I asked, "If we could prove that Harris knew about the corruption, wouldn't that add to motive?"

Bushard answered by bringing us up to speed on his end. "We had that same problem in Atlanta. We had to find the right judge to get the whole package—wire taps, bank and phone records, even to get a guy inside Davis's office. We set that up ahead of time so there'd be judicial oversight on the case right from the start. What you need is a judge that still believes in the integrity of the bench and will go after anyone who is dirty. An upcoming election might help too."

We kicked around the rifle thing and got nowhere. Both Atlanta guys thought the shot was incredible.

Bushard said "I stood there right where the shooter must have been and I could barely see the balcony where Davis was hit. With the swirling winds around those buildings and the 2-floor drop, it was an amazing shot."

Pritchett spoke up and said, "I'm a bit of a shooter myself," surprising Olson and me. This guy looked like he didn't know which end of the gun the bullets came out of.

But Bushard just nodded. "This shot would have been nearly impossible for anyone without military training. Even with a special weapon like the one you're looking for. It's the kind of shot that snipers and SWAT shooters practice a lifetime for. Whoever made it had great skill and that skill has to be practiced. Look for someone who practices."

That hit me like a fast ball. Of course, anyone who can shoot like this has to practice. Did Harris practice? And if he did, where did he do that? This wasn't something you could practice down at Bill's. You'd need a 500-yard outdoor range, and 1,000 yards would be better. And I didn't think there was one of those in the state. Not public, anyway. I suppose you could find a place on private land somewhere—.

We packed up and went to lunch at Runyon's, a little place I like. They have good food, reasonable prices, and you can usually get in at lunchtime. Pritchett went off to the men's room and I asked Bushard about Pritchett's shooting.

"He was in the military and served in the first Iraq war. I know he doesn't look like it, but he can really shoot."

He sure didn't look like it to me. I remembered what Wolf had said about the warriors being indistinguishable from the regular guys. I asked, "What did he do in Iraq—JAG office?"

"No, he went to college and law school after Iraq on the GI bill. He was in the Marines—Scout Sniper. I heard he made a 1,400 yard kill with a Barrett M-107."

Holy crap. I've fired an M-107. It fires a .50-caliber Browning machine gun round. The round is about seven inches long and the bullet is the size of my thumb. With the proper scope, it's good out nearly two miles, but most shots are less than 1,000 yards. It's usually used to stop vehicles—not people.

"What did he shoot at 1,400 yards?"

"Apparently—I heard this from a guy who was there with him—he and his spotter were on a rooftop in a little village on the Kuwaiti coast when their unit started taking mortar fire. A guy with good eyes can actually see the mortar rounds in flight and they were coming from another rooftop way far away. So he got on his scope and found it. The laser read 1,400 yards so he dialed it in, got set up, and waited for the mortar men to show themselves. They'd been watching to see what they were hitting. So, when the next round went up, the three guys manning it stood up. Old Brian had his semi-auto M-107 all ready to go and boom—boom—boom—they're all down. They couldn't have heard what was coming to send them to paradise. Then, just for fun, he hit the top of the mortar tube sticking up over the parapet, to knock it out of service—hit a 5-inch tube at 1,400 yards."

Wolf was right. You can't tell a warrior by their looks.

# Chapter 46

After lunch we sent the Atlanta guys back to the airport via the Mall of America and told them we'd work on those bank records. The Atlanta contingent was staying overnight and both had shopping lists provided by their wives. That mall might be the greatest thing that happened to Minnesota tourism since the Walleyed Pike. During the holiday shopping season, plane loads of Brits fly in for two day junkets, take the light-rail from the airport to the mall and shop straight through. They never even bother to get a hotel room. Unbelievable.

I started thinking that this bank record search might necessitate a trip to Phoenix. I called travel and asked them to book it. They said the earliest flight was at 5:30 that afternoon. Then I called Maria Fernandez and asked her what she was doing for dinner. She laughed and asked, "Are you in town?"

"Not yet, but I'll be wheels down at 6:50 local time." I filled her in on the plan to get Mitchell's bank records.

"Okay hot shot, you're on. I'll even pick you up at the airport. You need a place to stay?"

"Yeah—any ideas?"

"We have a place here where we put visiting dignitaries. I'll set it up."

With that I rang off and headed for the door. I hollered at Olson, "Pick me up at my place at four o'clock." I hopped on the Harley and raced home for a quick change and to check my go bag. Then I set out for Harris's. I wanted to try one more time to get him talking about the case.

I took the Harley again, this time enjoying the ride as a motorcyclist in a cold-weather state. You really enjoy something when it's not always available. I went helmetless—just my sunglasses on for protection.

There was a car I hadn't seen before in Harris's driveway. A two- or three-year-old-dark blue Buick 4-door. Could that have been the car the shooter drove in the Hill killing? No way to tell now unless he'd left the shell casings inside of it, and I doubted that. The big Winnebago was still there. Hopefully, Harris was home.

I had to knock on the door to find him. He answered and came outside. "Great day isn't it?" he observed.

"Great day for a ride. I thought I'd come out and see if you had any new thoughts on the murders."

"No new thoughts. What did you have in mind?" He held the door open and we walked inside. I guess today wasn't a show-me-the-warrant day. The house was decorated in typical Minnesota up-north—modern colors on the walls, Scandinavian-style furniture, a big flat screen hanging on the wall above the fireplace, and a mixture wildlife prints and modern paintings. This is what happens when both the man and woman of the house buy the artwork.

"Can I get you something to drink? I have just about anything from the bar or soda."

He was downright cordial. I love these games when you're talking to a guy you know is right for something but you can't come right out and say it. We'd see how the play went today. I asked for a diet cola and found a seat in the living room. His dog came over and gave me a quick sniff. Harris was back in a flash and the sparing resumed.

"We've got some pretty interesting information that I'm trying to develop. It looks like the shooter switched up and went long range after Hill was shot with frangible ammo from an AR-type rifle. He or she used something that must be military on the last three victims."

"You don't say? And why should that interest me?"

"You have motive and I found out, as you should have expected, that you have some very good shooting skills. You never said you'd been through the Special Forces Short Course at Fort Bragg. I found out that you have a reputation as a skilled sniper."

"Don't kid yourself. I could never do what those guys do. They can do things you can't even imagine and shooting is only a small part of it."

"Maybe—but you do admit you're a hell of a shot."

"Well—I can usually hit what I aim at."

"That's why I'm here. Hypothetically speaking, can you tell me why someone would go to all the trouble of getting frangible ammo for the first shooting then switch to some exotic firearm for the next three? I don't get why they wouldn't just use a .308 or some other typical hunting cartridge?"

"Hypothetically speaking, there could be several reasons," he said, seeming to warm to the subject. I wanted him to open up, in conjectural terms. He continued, "The first shooting—you told me—was in an urban setting. As you know, frangible ammo was developed for situations like that, where there was a possibility of hitting non-threats with missed rounds or rounds that had passed through the target. Perhaps the shooter was trying to mitigate collateral damage."

"Why would I know about that?"

He smiled. "I read your book—I know you're an expert on ballistics and odd ammunition."

"Why did you read my book?"

"When you started investigating me, I did the same to you."

"Sort of a know your enemy strategy?" I probed.

"It worked for Patton."

"True enough. So what did you find out about me, Ben," I said, turning friendly on him.

"You are a semi-retired homicide investigator with a department-leading case closure and conviction rate, which are not the same thing. You attended the FBI's ballistics school and became the Midwest's leading specialist on ballistic forensic evidence. You give paid testimony all over the country but the bulk of your income now comes from consulting on TV and movie sets. Your income is substantially greater that it ever was as a cop. You live in Robbinsdale, have no long term relationship with a female at the current time, were married once, and your ex is now a corporate lawyer. You have no children that you know of and you also seem to be able to get justice served most of the time."

This guy had done his homework. I wondered if he had any contacts in Atlanta that could have filled him in on what Bushard was doing down there. I was starting to think that the Internet wasn't such a great thing after all. I felt a nudging at my leg and looked down to see that the dog had brought over a toy and was pushing it into my leg.

"That's Mikey. If you take the toy and throw it you'll have a friend for life, but he won't leave you alone as long as you're here." Harris called Mikey to him and the dog trotted over. He took the toy and said, "Not now, buddy—I'll play with you later." Mikey went over to lie down in the sun in front of the patio.

I turned to Harris. "What do you think about this case, Ben? Do you think justice was done?"

"No. I don't think justice was done. I think a mistake was corrected by someone. But justice can't be repaired. It is either done correctly the first time, or it's lost forever. Any attempt to fix it just makes the mistake worse."

"You really believe that?" I was stunned. I thought I'd get some long argument rationalizing what had happened. I thought I'd get some defense of what I suspected he'd done. "You think what's been done to the bank robbers and Judge Mitchell and Davis will make what happened to your wife worse? I would have thought you'd be glad that these people were dead."

"I am not glad. What happened to them wouldn't have been necessary if the bank robbery had not happened in the first place. None of this would have been necessary. But people are people. Humans do bad things to each other and there has to be some consequence to their actions. Otherwise society will collapse."

"So you're sorry that Mitchell, Davis, O'Leary-Sample, and Hill are dead?"

"No, I'm not sorry they're dead, I'm sorry their deaths were necessary."

"You are sorry their deaths were necessary?" I felt like Mike Wallace, looking for that ah-ha moment on *60 Minutes*. I also remembered what Wolf had said about what should be the snipers motto, "I'm sorry it was necessary." This was getting serious.

Harris went on, "I'm sorry that someone felt that their deaths were necessary and they acted upon that feeling."

"Why were their deaths necessary?"

"The robbers perpetrated an evil act against society. The fact that my wife became a victim of that was just a coincidence. That they had the opportunity to do what they did was a mistake. Both had long prior records of illegal activities. They should have received some kind of rehab attention or, failing that, incarceration. Many people along the roads of their lives could have intervened and prevented the ultimate act—but didn't. The four parents, and the village, such as it is, were all too busy to properly raise these children. And no one ever held them accountable, so they, reasonably, had the belief that they could get away with the bank robbery.

The Judge, by her actions, reinforced the idea held by some in our society, that the kind of behaviors the bank robbers were exhibiting were somehow excusable because they were victims of a society that made them what they were. So then—with whom does the responsibility lie? Personal responsibility is the cornerstone of everything that makes our society work. Without it, you can trust no one."

Again, Wolf's talk came back to me. Harris was echoing Wolf's assessment of trust in a society. I also thought it was ironic that Harris says the boys' defense was based on victimhood. Is he now using that same victim status as his justification or rationalization for the shootings? He had to be conflicted. This would haunt him for the rest of his life—if he was the shooter. I went back to the firearms question.

"In your experience with the military—have you ever seen or fired a rifle that shoots some kind of sub-caliber dart rather than a conventional bullet?"

"I'm not sure what you're talking about."

"The gun used to shoot the last three victims was not available over the counter. It was an unconventional rifle shooting experimental ammunition."

"Really? I'd love to hear about this."

I suspected he could write his own book on the subject—not only how well it worked but results of actual field tests. I decided to work that angle.

"This rifle would have a longer-than-usual barrel, be chambered in something like a .30 caliber, but would fire a discarding sabot sub-caliber dart. I'm not sure what the dart is made of but it's something heavy, maybe even depleted uranium."

"There is a sabot'd sub-caliber armor-piercing round for the M2 .50-caliber machine gun, but that's not anything new. Can't say I ever saw or fired that at Bragg. It sounds interesting though. Why that weapon?"

"That's what I'm asking you."

"Good question. What are the ballistic qualities that this weapon delivers that you wouldn't get from a .308?"

"It seems that the projectile passes straight through whatever it hits. Like any bullet, it's a kinetic energy weapon, but it doesn't rely on tumbling to deliver its energy. It basically strikes so fast and hard that it sends a shock wave through the target, destroying all the tissue the shock wave hits—very destructive."

"I'll bet. And the victims chances for survival?"

"None."

"You said the last three victims were hit from quite a distance."

"Over 1,000 yards."

"But a 1,000-yard shot is not the shot it used to be. Military and civilian police snipers make that shot every day. A Canadian corporal made an antipersonnel shot in Afghanistan that was a bit over 2,600 yards. I think he made the Guinness book with that one."

That was true—1,000 yards used to be a kind of benchmark for long-distance shooting. Now, a well-trained hunter with a good rifle and scope could take an antelope in Montana at that distance.

"Could you make that shot?"

"In my sleep."

That was something I did not expect to hear. "You sleeping okay these days?"

"Like a baby."

"Did you make that shot?"

"I think we've gone from discussing the hypothetical to asking me a real question. If you'd like to do that, we'll have to go to your office and I'll call my lawyer."

You have to respect an opponent who stays in the game with you. I figured it was time to change the subject. "Ben, you have a place up north, don't you?"

"I'm sure you know that I have a place on Bay Lake, just north of Mille Lacs. You called me there when you asked me to come back in for more questioning. If you don't remember that, you're not the investigator I took you for."

I wondered what else he was taking me for. "You're right. Now, this lake place, you go there often?"

"As often as I can. It's good for decompression. There is good fishing. You should come up sometime."

"I think I will. You have any other property around there?"

"No, but I assume you'll check that out too?"

"You can bet on it." I looked at my watch and decided I'd better get going if I was going to make my flight.

"You know, Ben, we are going to sit down and hash this all out at some point. You said it yourself—I have the department's highest closure rate and this one will be closed."

I was about to go off the path of accepted interrogation practices, but I couldn't think of any other way to try to crack his veneer. Sometimes, confronting a suspect with the truth will shake them so bad that they'll come clean, just to correct details you messed up in the story. I took a deep breath, and gave it a shot.

"I'll tell you what I think. I think that when I scout around a little up at Bay Lake, I'll find some field that's owned by some ex-Army guy farming up there and that he just happened to let you use it for thousand-yard target practice. I think there were two possible oversight positions in Phoenix because you went there when you were on your RV vacation out west to scout the place out. I think that you were in the vicinity of Seattle at the time O'Leary was shot. And that when I get the security tapes from the Seattle Airport I'll see that you are the guy we know as Gil Cederstrom and that you took that flight to Anchorage. I think that it will have been you that took that flight to Charlotte too. I think that if the TSA boys had looked in that locked gun case that Cederstrom took to Alaska they would have found a Remington 700 with a detachable 42-inch smoothbore barrel, a box of goofy ammo, and a supply of Nut Goodies. I think that you like Nut Goodies and are using those just to mess with my head. I don't like to have my head messed with, and that motivates me to muster whatever it takes to send you to prison for the rest of your life. You just said you were sorry it was necessary that these people were killed. That could be taken as an acknowledgment of guilt."

"I said I was sorry that someone felt their deaths were necessary. I'm also sorry that this will be one of your failures. You may solve this case, but your own mixed feelings, the same feelings you had when you shot that drug dealer—oh yes, I've done my homework—and the lack of evidence will prevent you from ever making an arrest."

*My* feelings—what was this crap. That druggie had it coming all day long. I had no feelings except to get the bad guy. Harris was pushing buttons he shouldn't have pushed. Before I said something I'd regret, I got up to leave.

He cocked his head to one side and said, "And what are you talking about—Nut Goodies?"

I realized I might have let a cat out of the bag there. "This isn't over, Ben. There will be a reckoning some time."

"Perhaps. But whether or not that happens will depend a lot on you, won't it?"

"You can bet your ass on that. And I'll be right here when the time comes."

"I don't think so. The time may come—but it won't be here. Good day, Detective."

With that cryptic farewell, I headed out to the Harley. As I rode back into town, I wondered what he meant by "it won't be here." He had to be leading me to something. I just had to figure out what.

# Chapter 47

Whatever else can be said of Olson—he's always prompt. "I got your itinerary from travel. You've got e-tickets, so you can just head to the gate with your bag."

"Thanks a bunch, buddy." He knew I kept everything I'd need in my carryon. We both always kept them packed. In this business you never knew when you'd have to spend the night on the road or in some crappy stake out.

It was going to be close on the flight, what with rush hour and all. Still, this was one of those moments when time can't really be scheduled. Olson drove and I thought about the case. The possibility of an Atlanta connection was intriguing.

While we were driving, Rademacher called. She said that she'd found four possibilities for the rifle barrel and had called them all.

"No go on the barrels Dan. Every one of them said they only make stuff for black powder and those are all .45 caliber or higher. One guy said that he was pretty sure that was all they made, but the boss was out for the day and he'd have the guy call me tomorrow."

"You sure you're getting the straight poop?"

"Oh yeah. I said I was looking for a birthday present for my husband and he really wants this special barrel for the rifle he's designed. It even sounded plausible to me."

I laughed as I imagined some guy in rural Montana or West Virginia getting the Sharon treatment. It must have made the guy's day.

"Oh—I did get a hit on the candy wrappers," she added.

"What kind of a hit?"

"The number is from a batch that was sold to a distributor here in the Cities. I called him and he said most of his customers are local convenience stores—no customers more than forty-two miles away."

That was something. The candy wrappers in Arizona, Alaska, and Atlanta all came from here. That pretty much ties it to us. I'd better make sure that this tidbit of evidence didn't get out.

I thanked Sharon with the usual praise and feigned sexual tension, as we rolled onto the airport grounds. We pulled up to the upper level departure drop off and I jumped out and trotted in to the security station with my badge in my hand. The lead TSA guy saw me coming and had cleared a little path by the time I got there. He was still pretty careful checking my IDs. Call them what you will, but they have a miserable job and hell to pay if they screw it up.

I made the flight with about 10 minutes to spare. The only seat open was back in the noisy section. I stuffed my bag into the overhead and grabbed a magazine.

I was uncomfortable in my seat. I'd switched to an inside-the-pants-holster for my FN 5.7, which is the thinnest full-sized gun in the collection. It's also the lightest, and the 20-round clip is handy if you run into trouble too. But even with a thin gun, the coach seats really weren't designed for my widening posterior with a gun strapped to it.

The flight was a comment on the U.S. air industry's gift of consistency—boring, dry, and just long enough for my butt to fall completely asleep. I really don't like flying. The only thing this one had going for it was the person waiting at the end.

Maria met me at the plane and actually gave me a little hug, which was very nice. She said she'd let me take her out only if she got to pick the restaurant.

"Sounds good to me—what do you have in mind?"

"How do you feel about a little Mexican?"

Actually, I have rather strong feelings about Mexican food—about ethnic food in general. God save me from chain restaurants. But if it's a little hole-in-the wall, family-run joint where everyone on staff looks and sounds like they belong there, I'm okay. "Something authentic, I presume?"

"As authentic as it gets. I know a place that's so authentic that you'll walk out singing in Spanish."

"That's for me. Let's go."

We walked to the front entrance of the airport where Maria had parked her car in a police only zone. This was very handy because the air was as hot as I remembered. She drove to a neighborhood about 15 minutes from the airport and parked on the side of a place I would have picked myself—hole in the wall, adobe construction, old Chevy's and Fords parked all around. I mean, Hollywood couldn't have decorated this set any better.

Maria ordered for both of us in Spanish and I absorbed the ambiance. Spanish music was playing from what had to be a nicely restored and operating juke box. It was smoky, but all the open windows helped. The waitress appeared with two beers. I knew they were coming, I understood that part of the order. My Spanish is limited to hello, goodbye, thank you, and *dos cervezas, por favor*. The small talk turned to the usual—cop talk.

"I read your book," Maria announced.

That was out of the blue. "My publisher and I thank you. That must have been the reason for the royalty check I got last week."

She laughed and said, "Oh, I don't think so. We have a copy in our forensics library."

"Well, thanks for reading it anyway."

"You're very good, you know. The information is spot-on and the copy in our library is worn. They wouldn't be using it if it didn't get them convictions."

Everyone wants to hear that they're good at something, so I bit. "What part did you like the best—trajectory analysis or bullet striation matching?"

She laughed again. It always feels good when someone laughs at your jokes.

"Actually, the section on ammunition and weapon selection fascinated me. I'd never put much thought into why bad guys pick the guns they pick."

I'd put a lot of theory into that part. It's a lot of mumbo-jumbo about why a crook would pick a particular type of weapon. As cops, we used whatever is the department standard. But the young bad guys, gang bangers and such, really pay attention to what's in the films and on TV. When some new firearm comes along, they want it, for style reasons. When Bruce Willis made the first *Die Hard*, one of the bad guys used an unusual looking gun made by Styer. After the movie, the gun became sort of a fashion statement for those who could get it. Nowadays, cops look for more than stolen .38's and 9's. They have to watch movies too. And the gun stores are getting very picky whether or not to have any of those fashion-statement guns in stock. If it has to be ordered, that buyer may move onto something else.

Dinner arrived and, while I wasn't sure what it was, it tasted great. Maria had ordered something a little less spicy for me, in deference to Midwestern tastes. It looked like a couple of enchiladas and hard tacos with beans and rice. Maria's plate was literally smoking when it arrived and she attacked it with gusto.

"This is really very good," I said, wiping my eyes.

"What would you expect?"

She seemed to be glowing. How do people get that kind of heat down anyway? I washed it down with beer but that didn't seem to help much.

We finished eating and decided to see a little night life. She took us to a noisy cantina a few blocks away and, once again, walked fairly tough-looking streets with the confidence of a native. I asked her if she grew up here.

"Very astute, Mr. Detective. My family lives about five blocks that way—. My folks are still there with my younger sister and her kids."

I'd placed Maria at around 40, so the math worked if her mom and dad were in their 60s. "Do you want to go see them?" I asked.

"No, I'll see them Sunday at Mass. If we go now, they'll want to feed you and wonder if you have evil intentions for me."

Well, I hadn't really thought about it much—only about 20 times since she answered the phone this afternoon. Meeting the parents would not be considered an advancing step along that road. Of course, like most single, more-mature men, the thought of a little intimacy is always nice. But over the years I've found that planning it is usually the kiss of death. Better to just go with the flow and if it happens, it happens. Besides, I'm not usually the kind to go for a one-night stand, even out of town. Maria fascinated me in ways I hadn't considered in years. I decided to play it cool and light and not do something stupid that would make tomorrow a very long day.

Maria broke my thoughts. "Tomorrow's going to be a bitch—a lot of hurry up and wait while we try to get the subpoena, then more of the same at the bank. We'd better get some sleep."

My mind registered that she said get some sleep as opposed to get to bed. Oh well. We walked back to her car. I asked about the VIP quarters she said she would set up for me.

"Here's the deal. I like you—you have a certain appeal that most men don't. The fact is that most men that appeal to me are in our line of work. And I'm sure you can understand the complications of getting involved with someone in the department. So, it's your choice. I can drop you at a hotel we have a department rate with, or you can come to my place and stay with me. No strings—no expectations. But I'll expect you to be able to keep a straight face tomorrow."

Mrs. Neumann didn't raise her boy to say no to an offer like that.

# Chapter 48

**Friday, July 18th**
**Phoenix**

"So what's the plan for today," I asked, "how are we going to get those banks records?"

We were riding to Maria's office and the bright morning sun washing over my face was a bit unsettling. Or maybe it was the way the morning had gone so far that was unsettling. We had gone to bed and had even managed to get some sleep, but this morning didn't have the usual morning-after awkwardness that often accompanies an impromptu romantic evening. Somehow, today was different—comfortable in a disconcerting way. That's the only way to put it.

I've pretty much given up on the idea of soul mates. I tried marriage at too young an age and the other relationships I've had over the years have ranged from long and dreamy to polite rutting. There was nothing that had commitment attached to it. No regrets or sense of loss—just move on with life and go to work. Not so today.

I couldn't tell what Maria was feeling but I'd only had a few fleeting glimpse of her so far this morning. So, there I was, making omelets in her kitchen, and she was showering and dressing like it was nothing at all. I was so comfortable that I was uncomfortable.

She had come out of the bedroom wearing a light sun dress and looked fabulous. She sat down across from me at the kitchen table, with the sun coming through the window at her back. I swallowed and stared, stunned by her appearance. Then I wondered where she was concealing her firearm. Cop love—it's a wonderful thing.

We'd eaten and watched the morning news on the TV, noting that the world had survived the night without our intervention. Then we loaded up and headed out, with Maria driving me pondering what part of my world might have just shifted under my feet.

She spoke first, "First thing, I think, is to get with the DA and get paper for the subpoena to take over to the courthouse."

"Right—anyone in mind that might sign off on this thing?"

"There's one woman who is usually on our side. The thing is—you are investigating another judge, retired from Minnesota or not, and setting a difficult precedent will be on the mind of whomever we ask."

"That's the sticky part. We need someone who really won't tolerate any hint of graft or corruption—maybe your boss?" I was thinking of the County Sheriff, a guy who had a well-earned reputation as an exceptionally tough bad guy buster. He was proud of it, too. On the Sheriff Department's Internet site he had pictures of the tent city they used for lock up and lists of the bad guys currently incarcerated there. The MCSO website kept daily pictures of who had been arrested recently, deadbeat moms and dads, and the like. They had over 3,000 people signed up as a posse that was available for volunteer patrol work, searches, and traffic or crowd control. Of course, he had the aging population of the county to draw from and many of those folks were lifelong NRA members, hunters, retired military, and others just concerned about security. Maria chuckled at the idea.

"Yeah, he'd sign this subpoena without a second thought. Nothing makes Sheriff Joe's day like busting a public official."

We rode on a bit farther and I felt the need to disclose my feelings about last night. I don't know why. In other similar circumstances I'd have been happy to never talk about it.

"Maria, about last night—I want you to know that what happened was very special and unusual for me. Last night was a different sort of experience."

She said, "I'm not sure what happened either, but it was very nice and it's very sweet of you to say that. Like I said last night, I really like you and would like to get to know you better. It was special for me too." She looked at me, reached over, and touched my hand. It was electric. She added, teasing, "Don't you worry baby, I'll call."

I couldn't help myself and had to laugh at that. I guess it did sound like I was playing the traditional female role, worrying about future contact, and she was reassuring me that it was more than a one-nighter. I ruminated on that too.

We arrived at the MCSO Building on South Lewis and she parked in a reserved slot. The guy at the back door gave Maria's ID a quick look but was all business for me. I had to check my weapon and he carefully scrutinized my ID, even though I had an obviously well-known escort. We went up to her office. So far so good, not even a second glance from anyone.

"I've got the file right here," she said as she unlocked her desk.

"You have to keep desks locked around here?"

"House rules. The Sheriff is serious about all kinds of security, not just Homeland."

She opened the big file and dug through it. "Here it is. I want to have the summary ready for the judge to go along with your request."

I pulled my bag open and the request for the subpoena was right on top. It was attached to the paperwork from Atlanta. Maria looked it over and had a suggestion. "You know there's a chance a judge will look at this and say the status of three states involved makes it federal?"

"I'm open to ideas on how to keep the federales out."

"That would keep things more streamlined. Sooner or later we'll have to let them in if there's been interstate banking involved. But for now, I think we can get what we need with just our local case. I'll call Randy Goldsmith over at the prosecutor's office and see if we can't just walk this through."

I agreed. I'd known that federal involvement would be inevitable, but just the same, I'd like to get as much of this done as possible before they came in. I've worked with them enough to respect and fear them. I respect their lab, their analytical ability, their nice clothes, and their budgets, but I feared losing the case as soon as they were on the scene. This was *my* case—Arizona, Alaska, Atlanta, and all. And I didn't want someone else closing it.

We walked over to the county prosecutor's office. When Randy Goldsmith greeted us, I sheepishly realized that his black hair, dark features, and golden-brown Hispanic skin were not what I had visualized.

"I'm sure we can get anything you want. The Sheriff wasn't very happy when this happened and the word's out to support anything Fernandez wants."

"The Sheriff has pull over here too?" I asked, impressed.

"Oh, yes. We are a team and everyone is proud of our record in both prosecution and conviction. An unsolved murder would be a bad thing."

Randy made a couple of phone calls and we headed over to the court house. Fifteen minutes later we had what we needed. Then it was off to the bank to see the records officer.

# Chapter 49

By the end of the afternoon, we had the records we needed from three different banks. I called Bushard and told him I'd fax and Fed Ex a certified copy to him. He said he was ready for it and they were considering pushing up the timetable on their arrests. There were people in Davis's office who must have known what was going on and were either accomplices or were turning a blind eye.

It was 5:45 and there were two more flights to Minneapolis today. Maria and I hadn't talked any more about last night since getting to her office and the last thing said was her joke about calling me. I wasn't ready to leave it there.

"Maria, I've got to make a decision here. Either I've got to get to the airport or find a place to stay. I'm not asking for a reprise of last night, so—"

"Why not?" she cut in, "I'm okay if you want to stay. Tomorrow's Saturday—why not stay the weekend? What I'm trying to say is—I really enjoyed having you over last night. Look, I'm not expecting anything from you other than company. We're grownups—no strings attached. It's just nice to spend some time with someone who shares my interests, who is smart and good looking, and not bad in the sack either. The clincher is you don't live here. I'm sure you know how office romances can turn out."

Indeed I did. I'd tried one of those when I had just moved into plainclothes and it sizzled for three weeks. After that, well, we both knew it was over and neither of us had expected otherwise. But seeing a former lover at the office every day can be very awkward. I guess I'm not quite adjusted to modern mores. And neither was she. She eventually asked to be transferred. After that—no more cops in my bed.

"Yeah, I know how that goes. Ms. Fernandez, may I take you to dinner tonight?" I asked formally.

"Yes, you may and I'll let you pick the restaurant this time."

That weekend was a wonderful blend of sightseeing, restaurants, and romancing. We took in a Diamondback's game on Saturday night, drove up to Sedona on Sunday morning for breakfast, and then got up to the Grand Canyon for a late lunch. The scenery, both inside the car and out, was spectacular. I hadn't let myself have this much real fun in years, and I didn't want it to end. Of course, we both had to assume this couldn't last but—still guardedly—we both started talking like it could. Who knows? Maybe all I needed to get on the monogamous track was a change in destination.

## Duluth

Gil Cederstrom was having a busy weekend. He spent Saturday in Duluth sightseeing around the harbor and included a walk through the Canal Park. This is a combination of tourist attraction and a functioning gateway to an international shipping point. Years ago it was only the shipping gateway, but tourists now flooded the place every summer. Many up-scale hotels and restaurants lined Lake Drive as it carried traffic to Duluth's most well-known landmark—the Lift Bridge. Cederstrom gave the bridge a close examination. It connects Duluth to Minnesota Point Island by spanning the shipping canal. He had some ideas that he would later confirm on the Internet. At the end of the island sits Sky Harbor Airport, a field for light aircraft. This was Cederstrom's last stop.

# Chapter 50

**Monday, July 21st**
**Phoenix**

Monday morning I was on the 9 a.m. flight home—too soon for me. The morning had been a repeat of Friday, only I made homemade buttermilk pancakes this time. Everything seemed too easy. Maria drove me to the airport and we made our goodbyes like a pair of longtime partners. No mushy stuff—a quick kiss on the cheek and a promise to stay in touch. And it felt real. Before I was through security, I was thinking of reasons why she should come to Minneapolis.

**Bay Lake**

Ben Harris was deep in thought while he was working on an electronics package that was different from any he had previously designed. He didn't really know much about this one. He had obtained the specs and an education in the basics from a contact in the business. He had made cash purchases of parts and components from eight widely separated sources. It was quite a collection—several specialty circuit boards, linear actuators, power supplies, ribbon cables, and sensors. The two small TV cameras had a remote sending package that operated in the military band widths, and could send a signal a minimum of 100 miles. In addition to this, there was a complete communications package, which he had built from scratch. All the components were off the shelf and ready to go. All Ben needed to do was assemble them into the system he needed.

He was working in the garage of the lake place he and Anne had bought before prices started jumping up. It sat on a 1-acre lot at the northeast end of Bay Lake. The lot was rectangular—about 400 feet deep with 110 feet of lakeshore. It was lined on both sides by tall pines that screened it from the nice retired couple to the north and the rowdy water-skiing hillbillies to the south.

The house had originally been a cabin. A previous owner had added an A-Frame structure to the front, or lakeside, part of the cabin. It was now a roomy enough to sleep up to eight or so, if you were good friends. There was a wood-burning fireplace, a complete kitchen, and no air conditioning. Anne had always said, "If you're hot—go swimming."

An over-sized two-car garage sat to the rear of the house. A complete shop was set up in the corner—a work bench with a vise, a wall with some tools hung on it, and a jar full of orphan nuts and bolts. Mike Clancy was working with him.

"This should be everything we need to build the system," Harris said.

"That's your end. Tell you the truth, I really don't know the guts that well, but I understand the operational end," Clancy replied with modesty that understated his expertise.

What they were doing was a bit of technical sleight-of-hand. Clancy had been the one to come up with the idea after Harris had seen him at the trial. No one else at the courthouse knew who he was, but Harris could identify his type easily after the years he'd worked with them. Clancy was military. He had the bearing, physical appearance, and demeanor that proclaimed it.

They had chatted between sessions, had dinner, and gotten acquainted out of mutual curiosity. They shared a tacit agreement on the possibility of what the outcome might need to be. Each would be amazed and grateful for how aligned their values would prove to be. Both had felt it and knew what they must do, and both knew that a partner would make things easier and more satisfactory. Clancy checked Harris out through contacts and Harris did the same, resulting in a stunning revelation. By the time the trial ended, both knew they had a partner to work with to the end.

They knew what had to be done and had ideas about how to do it. For the two months after the trial, they gathered the tools they would need and set up the false trail that would keep the police off of them during the operation and afterward. Finally, on that stormy morning in June, they put the plan into motion and started a sequence of events that would remedy several injustices the American system was unable to correct.

# Chapter 51

**Monday afternoon**

I landed at MSP at 3:30 p.m., after a three and hour flight that included a two-hour time zone change. The day was pretty much shot, but I called for my messages and there were several. There were the usual appointment reminders and one from Pete saying that he was having a party on the water this weekend and when to be at the dock. There was also one from Rademacher. "Dan, this is Sharon. I tracked down that last smoothbore barrel guy, the one that was out two days ago. He said that he didn't make them either but that I might be able to get one here, in the Cities. When I asked him where he said that there's an outfit in Arden Hills that makes them for the government. So I got a number for them and started working that angle. The company is called BFG Industries. Their sales department says they make special order gun barrels for many different uses and needed to know exactly what I was looking for. When I said I was just getting background information, they said they'd need me to submit a request in writing and they'd look into it. Then I told them who I was and then they said I'd need a warrant. I thought you'd want to know. Call me when you can."

This really pissed me off. It's one thing to worry about industrial or national security, but this was a murder investigation. I called Sharon.

"What's this fresh bullshit about a warrant for the gun barrel guys?"

Sharon replied, "They said that their customer list is proprietary and that it's also a Homeland Security issue and that they would consider our request if and when we supplied them with a warrant."

"Where's Olson?"

"He's in, I saw him earlier."

"Go find him and tell him to grab a prosecutor and get a warrant and meet me at this place? What's the address?"

Sharon said she'd email it to my phone. These new phones are pretty good once you get used to them. Never want to lose one though.

I took a cab home, telling the cabbie to step on it for a tip, and we made non-lights-and-siren record time. I didn't even go into the house, just went to the garage, and got the GMC. I bought the Denali, which is a gussied up Suburban, when I had a big boat to tow. The boat's gone now, but I just can't part with the big fuel hog. It only gets 16 miles per if I baby it but it can get through anything Mother Nature dreams up. Plus is has the lights and siren. It was a 12 minute drive up to Arden Hills and I rolled into the parking area right behind Olson.

"You get the paper work?"

"Yeah, got it right here," said Olson as he handed me a warrant.

We headed for the door. It was nearly five o'clock and I figured they'd be locking up soon, which wouldn't stop us, just make things harder. We crashed the lobby as the receptionist was turning off the lights.

I held out my badge and said, "Minneapolis Police."

She looked flustered and asked how she could help us.

"I need the top, on-site officer of this company out here right now."

"That would be Mr. Corey. He is the vice president of Human Relations."

Great—everyone was gone except the head of personnel. What was he going to know about gun barrels? "If he's all you've got, please get him out here."

She picked up the phone and hit some numbers. A few minutes later Mr. Cyril Corey came out. He was a ruddy-faced guy who looked like he spent a little too much time on the golf course. And he must be taking the cart. We did a quick exchange of cards.

Olson started in, "Mr. Corey, we're with the Minneapolis Police Department and we're investigating a murder. Our investigation has brought us to the conclusion that a very special weapon was used in a series of killings. This weapon may have a connection with your company. Just how much do you know about what you make here and who your customers are?"

"Actually, I'm one of the founders of the company and I am intimately familiar with our product line and our customers. Am I going to need to have counsel present or is this a preliminary and unofficial visit?"

"It's official all right," I answered. I produced the warrant and handed it to Corey. "It's as official as a heart attack. You can call counsel if you wish but it's not really necessary. We don't think your company did anything wrong, just that one of your products might be involved. What we are looking for is information on a military rifle that can fire a sabot'd sub-caliber projectile accurately out to 1,500+ yards. Do you people make anything like that?"

Corey paused. He looked around the lobby and out the windows, obviously deliberating. Finally, he said, "Why don't we go into a conference room and discuss this?" He turned to the receptionist and instructed her to round up coffee and something to munch on. "Would either of you like anything other than coffee?"

I would have dearly loved a scotch right about then, you know, single-malt good stuff, but we both said no.

We walked down a hallway that was lined with beautiful light paneling. I asked what kind of wood it was.

"Bamboo," Corey answered. "It's very lovely, hard as nails, and low maintenance."

We turned into a small conference room. There was a table for six to eight people, a paneled wall that was open to reveal a large white board, and windows that looked out onto a garden courtyard. The courtyard was filled with colorful perennials and a few benches and tables. It looked like a great place to move the meeting if we didn't care about getting anything done. We had just taken seats when the receptionist rolled in a small cart with a coffee and donuts. Corey sat at the head of the table.

"You mentioned a particular type of weapon. Our firm manufactures many types of gun barrels as well as other ordinance parts, subsystems, and materials. Perhaps you could fill me in on more of the details of the crimes. That would allow me to know if any of our products might interest you."

I briefed him in the three murders that had been committed with the long-range shots. He listened to each with interest and asked a few questions along the way.

"Was there any evidence of ballistic tumbling of the projectile within the bodies?"

In my world, that's what is known as an insightful question. "No. The projectiles appear to have passed straight through."

"Was any brass recovered from the shooting position?"

"No. No brass."

"And no sign of the projectiles themselves?"

"No." I hadn't said anything about the possible connection to the military that Maria had told me about. I wanted to see if this fit anything in this guy's catalog.

"Mr. Neumann, there is a weapon that could do the things you've described. We manufacture a specialty barrel for the U.S. military that is part of a system designed to take out lightly armored vehicles and other soft targets at great range. This system is classified top secret and I'm not sure I can discuss it with you."

The last thing I wanted was a delay. We had only so much time before the feds were going to jump into the game, and I had to have this nailed before that clock ran out.

"Mr. Corey"—we were still on a formal basis, so I couldn't lay my familiar first name game on him. Besides, I hadn't looked closely enough at his card and didn't know what his first name was—"we have a warrant that authorizes us the right to search and to seize any and all records, gun barrels, and other items as we see fit in the investigation of these crimes. I can have a forensics team here in fifteen minutes if that's the way you want to go. In addition, the fact that these crimes were committed in three different states is surely going to attract the attention of the federal government soon. I don't think either of us wants that." I was playing on the hope that he wouldn't want the federales in here anymore than I did.

This threat seemed to work. Corey looked at my card and he said, "Dan, if we can go off the record, perhaps I can fill in some gaps for you that would help you in your investigation."

He was showing that he knew the rules of the information disclosure game. I took his card out of my pocket and made a show out of reading it. "Cyril, I think that's a good idea."

Cyril thought for a moment and said, "If you could wait a moment, I'll round up some things I'll need to show you that will help in our discussion."

This was the point where a bad guy would bolt if you let him get out of your sight, but I was getting okay vibes from my new buddy Cyril and I didn't want to spoil that. So I smiled and said, "Go ahead, but don't disappear."

Cyril nodded and left. Olson was less satisfied. "I'm not sure I would have let him out of the room. It's pretty clear he knows something we need to know and he could be heading for Canada by now."

"I don't think so. He knows about the weapon all right. His questions were spot on, especially the one about the bullet tumbling. No, I'm betting he'll be back in a few minutes with some show and tell."

I was right.

# Chapter 52

**Bay Lake**

The component assembly was going well. The system was basic. You needed a two-way radio to handle communications between the vehicle and the operator, some kind of computer to interpret the commands from the ground into actions in the vehicle, some kind of mechanical device to perform those actions, a way to feed the results back to the operator so they knew what was going on, and a power supply to provide electricity for everything.

In the earliest remote-controlled vehicles, the feedback was from maintaining eye contact. You moved a lever on the remote radio controller and watched to see what the vehicle did. As radio performance grew, and the mission changed, a way to get feedback from outside line of sight became desirable. Some of the earliest television work was done in the area of getting a picture from the inside of a vehicle back to the operator, who was miles away. The first work in TV-guided weapons was done during WWII. Airplanes were set up with remote controls and a rudimentary TV camera pointed at the control panel, sending a picture of the instruments back to the operator who was usually in another airplane following at a safe distance. The operator then navigated the unmanned, explosives-laden airplane right into the target. Early on, the target was most often missed and the entire program was eventually scrapped as too expensive for not enough results. But development revived, and now remote control weapons are some of America's most-feared tactical assets.

Of course, what was going on in Bay Lake had nothing to do with taking out a target, except in a philosophical way. Mike Clancy and Ben Harris were building a very modern remote-control system to eliminate someone else's target.

Mike had been working toward this moment for his entire adult life. It seemed that everything he had done had been preparing him for this one operation. All of his schooling, his military training, and his military experience had brought him to a place where he and Ben could pull this off. He had gone through the U.S. Air Force's training program for advanced electronics systems. He had received pilot training and held a pair of wings as part of his uniform decorations, and then he became one of the top remote pilots. They are a group of men and women who stand watch over some of the most desolate country on the planet, flying their Global Hawks and Predator drones from miles away. They do the take-offs, fly the drone to the target area, and then sit and wait for something interesting to happen.

Interesting things do happen. Mike Clancy was one of the first to fly an unarmed drone over southern Afghanistan. He was one of the first to discover its ability to spot targets of opportunity. Satellites flew over on a schedule that the human targets knew. They would lie low during those flyover times. Drones are not on a schedule, are virtually invisible, and could be kept overhead for hours. This brought some valuable pictures to people who wanted to do something to those bad guys in the photos. Mike was one of the first to think, 'If I had a few bombs or a missile, I could nail this guy right now.' And that resulted in his being the first remote pilot to target and destroy a moving truck with a Maverick missile. He became Air Force's go-to remote pilot, and considered an ace for having taken out more than five vehicles with missiles. The mission he and Ben were working on should be much simpler. All they needed was to get the timing right.

Ben came back out to the garage carrying their dinner. "I've got the actuators ready to go. Holes are drilled for the hardware to connect everything and the wiring looks good. I was just about to test them."

"Go ahead," Ben said.

The linier actuator is one of the most common devices in American life today, although most Americans wouldn't know one if it was dropped on their foot. It's a long skinny pipe-shaped thing with a way to connect both ends to something you wish to move,  and a couple of wires coming out the end to hook to the control system. These are the things that open car doors and tailgates at the push of a button. They're cheap, strong and reliable—perfect for a remote control system to fly a light airplane.

Mike threw the power switch on and took hold of the remote control panel he'd built for this project. He had the actuators laid out in a row labeled "left foot," "right foot," "yoke," "fore," and "aft," "yoke–rotate," and "throttle." He said, "Okay—we are started and at the threshold of the runway. One by one, then again, and then again, he tested each control and its actuator, and their simultaneous operations. Every maneuver, especially the turns, was smooth—just what any observer on the ground at the airport would expect.

Ben nodded his appreciation. The work was professional and the flying would be smooth. "Looks great. Let's eat before these brats get cold." Everything tastes better with a dash of success.

# Chapter 53

## BFG Industries, Arden Hills

Cyril Corey returned with a rifle tucked under one arm and two boxes, one about six inches square and flat, the other a four-inch cube, in the other. Olson was a little unnerved, or so it seemed—he started to reach for his weapon when he saw the rifle. I sat still and Olson got the message. Corey laid the rifle and boxes on the conference table and sat down. He said nothing, just sat and looked at me.

The rifle was like none I'd ever seen. It had an extremely long barrel, like a Revolutionary War musket you'd see in a movie or at a battlefield museum, and a modern synthetic stock that was adjustable for length and height of the butt pad. It had a large scope and a pair of flip-down legs mounted on the fore stock. It was a bolt action that looked like other hunting or sniper rifles. It was entirely matte black.

"It's based on the Remington 700, as are most military sniper rifles," Corey pronounced. "The barrel is 40 inches long. The scopes vary, depending upon mission. The bi-pod legs are required for nearly every shot."

I looked at Corey and then stood and picked up the rifle opening and clearing the action to ensure it was unloaded—a Pavlovian action for a life long shooter like me. I looked it over closely, scrutinizing the chamber and barrel. I asked Corey, "What caliber is this?"

"It's a special caliber. Basically, the barrel is .30 caliber but the chamber is more like an oversized .300 magnum. You'll notice the thickness of the material around the chamber is greater than you'd expect."

Indeed it was. The barrel was quite a bit larger in diameter at the loading end. This would make it able to withstand much higher chamber pressures than a normal rifle.

Corey continued with the description of the rifle. "As you know, higher chamber pressure is what makes a bullet go faster. But there are limits. You can't just put more gun powder into the cartridge. Sooner or later you'll reach a point where the barrel can't take it and the gun blows up in the shooter's face. But by adding more steel around the chamber end of the barrel, we've ensured the safety of the weapon. This will allow it to take a higher pressure without exploding. Combined with the long barrel length, this rifle can get a projectile up to a very high speed."

I was enjoying this lecture. There was more to this guy than I'd first thought.

"As you probably know, in firearms, everything that is going to control the shot has to happen before the bullet leaves the gun. Once it departs the barrel, Sir Isaac Newton is in control. By that, I mean physics. It's all inertia, wind resistance, and gravity all at once. But when the projectile leaves the barrel, you can't add speed, spin, or control over the direction it's going. That's what is meant by "going ballistic"—you are no longer in control—the projectile on its own."

Ballistics is my strong suit, but Olson seemed to be paying the same rapt attention that he does to my intermittent elucidations.

"So your barrel will launch this dart projectile faster so it will go farther, correct?" I asked.

"Yes and it improves accuracy by getting the projectile to the target sooner. The faster you get to the target, the less you have to worry about wind, temperature, and humidity. But the biggest thing a shooter has to consider is gravity.

"As soon as the bullet leaves the barrel it is falling. Serious shooters know that gravity is the most important thing in their world. Just take a bullet, hold it in your hand with your stop watch ready, and drop it. The time it takes the bullet to hit the floor can be the same whether it's dropped or fired from a gun over level terrain."

I liked his analogy. Maybe I could use it in my next book. I asked, "So in order to improve accuracy—it's desirable to make bullets go faster?"

"Absolutely. And as firearm technology has progressed over the centuries, bullets have sped up. Typical handgun bullets leave the barrel at about 700 to 1,500 feet per second. Sounds fast, but that's nothing compared to the 2,000 to 3,000 fps that rifle bullets travel. This is important because, if you can get the bullet to the target in less time, you don't have to compensate as much for gravity or movement."

Olson spoke up, "That makes sense. It would be like a video game where you don't have to lead the target at all."

Another good analogy—I thought—if I stayed with these two long enough, they'd write my next book for me.

Corey concluded, "And there's one final advantage. The faster it's going when it hits the target, the more energy it will deliver. Think about this—if you throw a bullet at someone, it does nothing. That's because it's not going fast enough to bring any energy to the target. But deliver the same bullet at 2,000 fps and it's lethal. Same bullet—different speed."

Three for three—I'm writing a new book. I had to get back to my agenda. "Mr. Corey, my experience tells me that a rifle in my hands is capable of delivering a bullet accurately at a very high speed. So what is the projectile? Do you have cartridges for this in that box?" It seemed the logical question.

Corey answered, "Yes. I'll show them to you, but I first need to tell you that under normal circumstances I would not be able to. However, since this weapon system has been deployed to the field and you are conducting a homicide investigation, I believe we're okay in this case. We do have the authority to disclose its existence to persons on a need-to-know basis and your warrant establishes a need to know. You will have to sign a security disclosure first."

He slid a security agreement across the table to each of us and continued. "Since I know who you are and that you are an expert in the field, I'm willing to show them to you with the understanding that they are classified secret by the Pentagon and this is not to be disclosed to anyone."

I nodded ascent and signed the form. I slid the form over to Olson and, while Olson signed, Corey slid the box over to me. It was filled with rifle cartridges, standing at attention in a styrofoam base just like a box you'd buy at the store. I took out one of the cartridges.

It was much like any other rifle cartridge I'd seen—brass cartridge case necked down from a large-diameter powder chamber to the end holding the projectile. But the projectile was a little weird. It looked like the plastic cup that comes out of a shotgun shell. Much more refined and possibly handmade, the material was harder than typical shotgun shell plastic. I could see the tip of whatever was inside just peeking out the end. "You don't happen to have one of these disassembled, do you?" I asked.

"Of course." Corey flipped open the flat box and slid it across the table. Inside was a disassembled round. "This is a display set we use to show the various interior structures of this unique round."

The cartridge case was typical. Nothing about it said anything to me. But the projectile was unlike anything I'd seen in all my years studying firearms. The plastic sabot was split open and laid to one side. It was a precisely formed part with none of the crude, quick-molded features of a shotgun shell. Next to the sabot was the dart.

I picked it up—it was heavy. It was also a work of art. About 1.5 inches long, about .17 inch in diameter. It looked like something made from a thick coat hanger—except it was not steel. It was tungsten. It had five little fins that had just a bit of twist to them. The fins made the diameter at the rear the same as the rifle barrel. I asked Corey, "What are the ballistic dynamics of this round?"

"The projectile weighs 884 grains, which, as you know, is quite high. It delivers a little over 4,300 feet per second 10 feet from the muzzle. The shape makes it very stable in all wind and humidity conditions. It has an effective range against soft targets out to 2,500 yards—about a mile and a half."

"You say against soft targets. What are you including in soft targets?"

"I'd say—unarmored vehicles, aircraft, unprotected shelters, and, of course, people."

Yes, of course—people. "And you make these rifles here?"

"No, we don't. We make the barrels. We ship them to the Army and Marine Corps and they build their own rifles. They are very specific about that. I believe that they start with stock Remington 700s and modify them to their own use. The modification process includes adding this barrel."

"Yet, you have one of the rifles?"

"We have to have one to test the fit and function of the barrels."

That seemed logical. "So, based upon what we've talked about concerning this murder case, do you think I should be talking to the military?"

"Yes, they are the only ones who have the rifles."

"Except for this one?"

"Yes."

"Any chance someone could—say—borrow this one for a long weekend or something?"

"No—none whatsoever. It is kept in our test lab and is inventoried three times a day. I can produce the records if you'd like."

I would have liked, but not right then. If it came to that—we'd get them later. Something was gnawing at me though. I couldn't quite put my finger on it. "I'd like to see how they're made."

"I'm sure you understand that this is a proprietary process and, warrant or not, I'll have to have you and Mr. Olson sign a confidentiality agreement, assuring that you will not reveal anything about our manufacturing process."

More paper work. I thought, "Sure we will—it'll be confidential right up to the testimony." But I said, "Of course."

We got all signed up and went out into the plant. It was very clean and well-lit. I've been in a lot of gun manufacturing facilities all across the nation, and this one was nice. Funny, I hadn't known it was even here, right in my own backyard, all these years. The building was standard late-20th-century industrial. The walls were painted white, the floor painted gray, and the windows covered. It was empty of employees. Corey took us out into the area where the barrels were made.

"We start by forging our own blanks—that's the steel rod the barrel will be made from. That's done in another plant so I can't show you that. But it's a very straightforward process and nothing special about it. When we get the barrels here, they are straightened and the bore-drilled. Gun drilling has a long and interesting history, if you'd like to hear about it."

Actually, I would, but that could wait for another visit. "That's okay—could you just show us what you do here?"

"Certainly. As the barrels are drilled, we re-straighten them several times—between every step in the process, actually. When the bore is finally finished, we machine the cartridge chamber and then there are several metallurgical heat-treating steps to ensure the barrel will be strong enough. The final step is to chrome plate the cartridge chamber."

As we walked past rows of machinery, I noticed there was no waste anywhere. Usually, in machining operations, there are tubs of metal chips, the waste material cut off the parts. This would be especially true in the drilling area, as there would be a lot a shavings coming out of the holes. I asked about this.

"We clean up every day before going home. Every operator shuts down their machine 30 minutes before quitting time for clean up. Any good shop will do that. You have to clean every day just to keep up with it."

That made sense. "How many of these barrels do you make in a year?"

"Oh, not many. I'd say we've delivered 48 total since we've been making them."

"Only 48?" This is the U.S. military we're talking about. They buy things by the millions, not dozens.

"It's a very special, low-use weapon system. My understanding is that they have only deployed six to the field. With training weapons and spares, 48 would seem to be the correct number."

I'm thinking that the low number should make my job easier, but it hadn't yet.

Corey interrupted my thoughts. "Naturally, we assumed we'd be making more. In fact, due to the length of the barrel, we had to make quite a few more blanks to get the yield we achieved."

"What?—more blanks to get the yield?" I'm just a cop but I thought I'd just heard something important. "What is your yield?"

"To get the 48 we shipped, we made about 200 blanks. Due to differences in metallurgy, not all of them survive the machining process. Those that don't are scrapped out."

"And you have records on the scrapped-out barrels?"

"Of course. Any DOD Supplier has to keep thorough records on their scrap. You can see those too, if you'd like."

I'd like. But I would send someone over who could understand that stuff. The thought of digging into scrap records just about made me ill. It had been a long enough day without starting an accounting project. I said, "I'll send someone over tomorrow morning."

There was a buzzing going on in my head as we walked out of the plant. I knew I had to sort out all of this fresh input as soon as I could. I thanked Corey for the tour.

"It's been my pleasure. I hope I've been able to answer your questions."

"You have, but there are a few items left. I'll send someone tomorrow about the records audit. One other thing—you mentioned you have to test the barrels. Do you do that here?"

"No, we need a longer range for that. We have a facility in Green Isle. It used to be an agricultural equipment manufacturing company. We bought it because the principle feature of the plant is that the building is very long and narrow. Most of it is used for storage, but we use the length of it as a firing range. It's about 400 yards long."

"Is 400 yards enough?"

"Mr. Neumann, this gun is spot on at 400 yards. Time of flight is about a quarter of a second, so drop is nonexistent. Yes, it's long enough."

"And you store the ammunition there too?"

"No, of course not. All ammunition to be expended is taken from stores here and accounted for."

"I'd also like to take a look at those records tomorrow too."

"Not a problem. I look forward to seeing your representatives tomorrow morning. What time should I expect them?"

"Bright and snarly," I grinned. "Good evening Mr. Corey."

In the parking lot I asked Olson, "I want Rademacher on this first thing."

Olson answered, "I'll call her tonight. Anyone else?"

"Yeah, send some muscle out with her. She might be able to charm them out of their pants, but if she finds something, I have a feeling that their cooperation level will diminish pretty fast."

# Chapter 54

**Tuesday, July 22nd**
**Minneapolis**

I made it to Olson's office first thing the following morning. Sharon was at the rifle barrel company, backed by one of the investigators on the case. She was doing some rifling of her own, going through the production records. She had left a note.

> *Dan:*
> *I found one other possible shooter on the case. The fiancé of the girl who was pregnant was in the Air Force. He was overseas when it happened, but he was back for part of the trial and is here now. His Military Occupation Specialty is UAV Pilot, whatever that is, but he had some training in firearms and his records show he is an expert with an M-16. Don't know if this helps, but you said to look for someone else.*
> *Sharon*

I didn't know if it would help either, but I was looking for anyone else who could be in on this. If Harris wasn't the shooter—who was? And who was Gil Cederstrom?

I called Maria in Phoenix, mostly to just hear her voice. "We have another lead on the case. We're digging up anything we can find on a Michael Clancy. He's apparently the fiancé of a young woman who was one of the other victims at the grocery store bank robbery. He's in the Air Force."

"Okay—anything that you want from me?"

Well, I could think of a couple of things right off, but I said, "Can you do some digging on your end into this rifle you were telling me about? I found out that the barrel for the thing is made here in the Cities and it looks like the company that makes it has all their stuff in one sock, so they aren't selling them out the back door. Can you contact whoever it is you know that might be able to find out if one of these rifles is missing?"

"Sure, I can make a few calls. But I'm telling you now, they aren't missing any."

"Could you try anyway? We're also talking about a task force meeting here with the guys from Atlanta, to follow up on the money trail. Can you fly up here for that?"

"Sure. Just tell me when and where."

That meant I'd better put together a meeting quick-like. "How about tomorrow? Can I pick you up at the airport?"

"I'll check with my boss, but I'd better get up there tonight. If I wait for a flight tomorrow, I won't get there until dinner time."

Better and better. "Okay. Call with the flight number and I'll meet you at the airport."

I hung up and called Atlanta. Luckily, Bushard said they'd make it too, but they'd be on the early morning flight. Olson agreed to pick them up like he did last time and we set the meeting at 10:30 a.m.

Meanwhile, I got going on the process of figuring out who Mike Clancy was and whether he had any involvement in the case. By early afternoon I knew he was a local who had attended Dunwoody Institute, was educated in computers, electronics, and robotics, had gone into the Air Force after 9/11, and was now a pilot of remote control airplanes. My buddy Pete was a pilot, so I called him to see what he could do to fill in more gaps in my education.

"Pete, I've got a line on a guy who flies remote drones for the Air Force. You know anything about that?"

"Yeah, I've had a little learning in that area. Most of the observation or spy planes these days are UAVs, which is acronym for Unmanned Air Vehicles. They can stay up practically forever and be directed to stay over a particular place for a long time. Why the interest, if I may ask?"

"One of the other people hit in the Plymouth grocery-store bank case was the fiancé of one of these pilots. I'm trying to figure out if he could be our guy."

"I kind of doubt it—those guys and gals are real techies. They aren't field people. If your victims had been hit with a missile, then I'd say maybe, but not with a rifle bullet."

"All right. I'm just trying to find someone besides Harris who could have done this."

"I thought you had another guy."

"I've got a name. But the guy doesn't exist. It's like he appeared, killed these people, and then disappeared. We're still looking for him, but nothing comes up."

"Stay on it, buddy. I know you and you'll get him—if it's him or Harris—you'll get him."

We rang off and I headed home to straighten up and throw a couple of spuds in the oven. It had been a long time since I had a house guest and I wanted things to look right for this one. At five o'clock, I headed out to the airport to pick up Maria.

# Chapter 55

### Bay Lake

There was a dinner plan on Bay Lake. Ben and Mike had finished their preparations and decided to go fishing.

Ben had two boats—a big pontoon for cruising and parties, and a state-of-the-art fishing boat. The 19' Alumacraft was fitted out with just about any kind of fishing gadget you could want—fish finder complete with GPS and memory so you could go back to a hot spot, an electric trolling motor with remote foot control to augment the 150-horsepower Mercury outboard, live wells, and full lights for night fishing.

They were parked over one of Ben's good walleye spots and had four nice fish in the boat. Mike hauled in his line and found that he was fishing without bait.

"They got me again. These guys are really sneaky."

"Yeah, they'll pick you clean every time you give them a chance. Ol' Walter knows how to get his meal without becoming one."

"That's it for me. We're out of leeches."

"We've got enough fish for dinner tomorrow, and that's what we came for. Anyway, even if we didn't catch a thing, at least we got to wet a line. That's more than most folks will get today. Let's head in and start the grill."

They stowed their fishing gear and hauled in the anchor. The sky was turning dark anyway, threatening to dump another summer storm on them. Ben fired up the big Merc and they turned north to his place. Mikey hopped up on the foredeck to keep an eye out for whatever it is dogs look for with their hair whipping and ears flattened. Both men and dog enjoyed the wind and spray on the ride home.

Five minutes later, Ben turned in toward his dock. He guided the boat into the covered boatlift. As he centered the boat on the lift, he hit a button on the dash and the lift came to life, cranking itself up under them. When they reached the full up position, it hit a limit switch and stopped. Mikey hopped out onto the dock and trotted up to the house.

"That is the slickest thing I've ever seen," Mike said.

"Had to have it after I saw one at the boat show. Of course, I just made one out of a garage door opener instead of paying what the guy at the show wanted."

In Harris's cabin on Bay Lake, a small electronic box woke up. It had noted the signal from Mike's phone as the boat drew near the dock and now it forwarded an incoming phone call to Mike's phone through a special cell repeater tower on the roof of the cabin.

Mike's cell phone beeped.

"That's a surprise. I didn't think there was any phone service out here."

"I rigged a repeater through that big antenna on the roof. You get service in the house and within about 150 yards. My neighbors love it." The system could also relay landline calls to Ben's cabin to any other phone he had programmed in—anywhere in the world.

It was a text message from a friend in the Cities.

*Hey bud - whr r u?*
*Thr was a guy here frm the Police*
*Dept looking 4 u and asking*
*If I knew whr u r.*
*FYI*

"Well, I guess the cat's out of the bag."

He showed the phone to Ben.

"Yeah, we better go ahead and do it tomorrow. As soon as I rent the plane, they'll get a hit on the credit card, so we'll have to have everything in place before we do that."

"I've got all the stuff in the truck. All that's left is the paint and to load up the bike—that'll just take a couple hours."

"All right—tomorrow it is. We'll have a big breakfast and head over to Duluth."

That breakfast would either be the first of the rest of their lives—or their last as free men.

# Chapter 56

## MSP International Airport

I parked the Denali in the airport cops area at the end of the lower level drive-through and tossed my Official Police Business placard onto the dash. One of the airport police guys who was keeping traffic moving through the pick-up lanes immediately came trotting down to straighten me out. I pulled my credential case out and had my badge up before he got there.

"You know—badge or not—you're not supposed to park here," he said.

"Hey, give me a break this once. I'm picking up some out-of-town VIP and I need to make an impression," I pleaded.

He was feeling magnanimous and let me off the hook with, "I hope she's worth it." He just might end up as a detective.

Maria was coming in on Northwest, which is now Delta but will always be Northwest to locals. I remember when there was a North Central and a Western and then feel older. The information board read five flights from Phoenix today. She was on the 5:30 arrival, due into gate F6. I had timed it just about perfectly—the flight had landed and was taxiing over right now.

Maria was one of the last off. Seeing her gave me a tingle I haven't felt in years. Hey, I'm old enough and have been around enough blocks to know better than to get excited by a little quick romance, so this was weird. But there I was, standing at the gate rocking back and forth on my feet and peering down the line of people getting off the plane like a teenager at a rock concert. When Maria appeared, my breath actually caught in my throat. She was beautiful—an angel had landed.

"Hey—Big Guy—how you doing?"

"Great! Now that you're here."

I grabbed her carryon and we headed up the concourse. We engaged in the usual weather and how-was-the-flight talk. It was fine. The flight, I mean.

I had to ask, "Is this your first trip to Minnesota?"

"Yes, it is—but not the last, hopefully."

I thought, "Be still, my beating heart."

"It's good to come in the summer for your first time. It's not quite as hot as Phoenix, but the humidity is a lot higher."

"I've heard that, mostly from people visiting Phoenix. They say that our weather is nothing like the heat here. I'm hoping to experience some of that sweaty heat."

"Okay—that's enough, I teased, "I've got to drive in traffic and you keep talking like that, I'm not even going to be able to walk!"

She laughed and put her hands up in mock surrender. We stepped out into the Minnesota heat, such as it was, and walked down to my car. The cop who I'd talked into letting me park there saw us and gave me a thumbs up.

We drove to Robbinsdale through the late afternoon traffic which, surprisingly, wasn't too bad. I parked in the garage, and pulled her overnight from the back seat. She never questioned my fairly presumptive behavior, which I took as her agreement as to the lodging arrangements. I pointed out the wood shop and, of course, the two motorbikes. Maria was impressed, or at least politely observant. We crossed the back yard and went into the house through the back porch, passing the hot tub along the way.

"Nice tub. We going to use that later?"

"If you'd like. You bring a swimsuit?

"No."

"That might be a problem. I don't have a lot of privacy out here and I don't want to start an incident with the neighbors. That'd bring the Robbinsdale cops and they're the last guys I want looking at you."

"We'll figure something out."

I'd left two nice New York strips on the counter to warm up and the potatoes would be ready in a few minutes, so I gave Maria the quick main-floor tour. I asked her what kind of wine she'd like with dinner.

"I'm not a big wine drinker. Have you got a little cerveza?"

"My kind of woman."

I pulled a couple of Leinie's from the fridge and handed her one.

"What's this?"

"Local brand—Leinenkugel. This is a Honey Weiss, which very loosely translated means honey wheat. Give it a try."

She took a long pull and gave a satisfied smack. "This is great. I'm going to have to get some sent to Arizona."

I tended to the steaks and started putting together a salad.

"I like your place. It's real homey," she said.

"I bought it for the garage layout—two attached and the big building out back."

"Yeah, that would be a plus. Too bad the building's not a little longer. You could put a range out there."

I knew she wasn't talking about a kitchen appliance. Like I had said, she's my kind of woman.

"Why don't you park in the attached garage? What's in there that so important?"

I led her through the kitchen hall to the garage where I blocked the door for the grand opening.

"Tah-dah!" I announced with a flourish as I swung the door aside. Maria looked in to see my pride and joy—my numero-uno toy—a 1969 Mustang 429 convertible.

"Wow! That's fantastic."

"It's my baby. If you're here long enough and we can get free, we'll go cruise the lakes, maybe pop over to St. Paul. There's sort of an unofficial cruising strip there—down University and up Snelling. There's even this old time drive-in where you can still get the best onion rings in town."

We went back out to the porch, set out some appetizers, and I flipped on the TV for the Twins game. After a bit, I lit the grill and started the steaks.

"You know, you haven't said anything about the case." she said.

"I was letting it sit," I conceded. "We'll get plenty of that tomorrow. The guys from Atlanta are coming back. They've got the bank records figured out and it looks like Mitchell was getting something from Davis."

"That should be interesting. I guess we'll have to get the feddies in on this pretty soon," she sounded resigned.

"I'd been holding off on that as long as I could. As soon as they're in, we'll lose all control and I want this guy—or maybe guys."

"Guys? Why do you say that?"

I told her about my conversation with Wolf and his statement that there might be more than one guy involved in this.

"I could see that. Who else are you looking at?"

There's only one guy who fits the profile. One of the other victims at the grocery store bank holdup was a young pregnant woman who was hit and lost the baby. She had a fiancé who looks interesting, but no one knows where he is now.

"Why is he interesting?"

"He's military, but not Special Forces. In fact, he's Air Force. Some kind of behind-the-scenes techie guy. But, like I said, he wasn't here for the robbery, was overseas but got back for part of the trial and has since separated from the Air Force and disappeared."

"Just because he's not Spec Ops doesn't mean he can't be our guy. You never know about guys, especially the techies. Some of them are the most dangerous guys out there—if they've got skills and techie brains, they're scary. What do you know about him?"

"White male, age 33, born and raised here, went to a local tech institute, enlisted in the Air Force after 9/11. He was in Afghanistan when the robbery went down. Came home for bereavement leave, and came back to attend some of the trial. We just became aware of him two days ago—we don't know where he is now."

"What about his fiancé? Can you talk to her?"

"Yeah. We could, if we can't locate him. Word is she suffered lots of psychological trauma though. She wasn't called to witness— that was probably the only decent ruling Judge Mitchell made in the trial—and she never showed up at the trial. We don't want to locate and interview her unless we have to.

"So how'd you get that info?"

"I talked to his parents. They still live in the area."

"What about his folks? Any chance they could do this?"

"Not a chance. They're in their late '70s."

"That's weird. He's 33 and they're nearly 80. He must have been a pretty late surprise. How about older brothers or sisters?"

"Didn't have any."

"He's an only child?"

"Yeah." I flipped the steaks. They were looking excellent. My cooking skills are limited to breakfast and steaks, but I'm my own favorite cook at both events.

Maria thought for a minute. She said "His parents must have been in their mid-to-late 40s when he came along. Hmm—an only child at that age. Any chance he's adopted?"

I hadn't thought of that, I admitted, "I'll call my records specialist and put her on it." I grabbed the phone and called Rademacher. "Sharon, could you check on that Mike Clancy's birth cert in the morning. I'm wondering if he might be adopted."

"Got it, sweetie. Need any help tonight with the dishes or anything?" She laughed. I'm going to have to kill Olson. Before I could muster a comeback, she said, "Hey, I spent all day out at BFG and I might have a hit for you on the barrel numbers. There are no actual discrepancies in the counts and the rejected amounts, but one shipment of scrap was light."

"What do you mean, 'light?'"

"They have a very good system. The right hand doesn't know what the left is doing. On the factory floor they keep a paper count on all the barrels, from receiving the raw forged blanks to the final shipments to the Army. But, they have a weight system that the people in production don't know about. The shipping guy weighs every shipment of scrap and records that weight. The accounting department has all the records but they only check them if they think there might be a problem or for an audit. I did a cross check and one shipment of scrap was light one barrel."

"When was the shipment?"

"It went out on May 22nd."

"How about the ammunition?"

"They have some record issues there too. When the ammo actually goes out to the range, there may be some differences between the number taken and the number of rounds fired and the number of rounds returned to stock. No one seemed to think that was a very big deal, because they also make machine gun barrels and those go through thousands of rounds in test. I guess a few rounds here and there didn't matter much."

"How many rounds are missing?"

"I figure at least twenty, which just happens to be one box. They only had a few thousand to start with, but at least twenty can't be accounted for."

"Three dead on three rounds expended, and twenty missing rounds—that means there could be seventeen still out there."

I hung up told Maria, "I don't want seventeen more bodies."

She said, "You won't have them. He's done."

"How do you get to that?"

"It's been at least two weeks since his last hit? He's hit all his targets, unless you think he's got it in for the prosecutor too."

"Good thinking, but—no, I have to agree. I sure do hope he's done."

"Well, we aren't. Let's eat—I'm starved."

We had a nice dinner, watched the Yankees hammer the Twins, and downed a few more beers. After dark, Maria said she was ready for the hot tub, so I changed into a swimming suit and got her a t-shirt. The air was still, so we had to stay under water to keep the mosquitoes off us. Ah—true romance in Minnesota. I won't bug you with further details, but the evening certainly surpassed my imagination.

# Chapter 57: Endgame

**Wednesday, July 23rd**
**Bay Lake, 6:30 a.m.**

Ben and Mike got up early. This was the day they had been planning since they first conceived the idea of what they called "The Exercise." In order to succeed, they had to perform the precise final steps in their plan, and then leave the authorities with just enough information to close the cases. Either they would successfully finish The Exercise in justice, today, or they would prepare to spend the remainder of their lives in prison. Either way—the game would be over.

Mike came in from the garage, where he had been wrapping up the last of their preparations. Last night Ben had helped him rig a temporary paint booth in the garage. It was basically a tarp on the floor with plastic drapes on four sides and a tented roof held up with strings to the roof trusses. Mike's truck was inside the enclosure and, when it was airtight, Ben painted the truck bright red. It wasn't much of a paint job but it would pass. After letting it dry overnight, he loaded the truck and prepared for the day's work. He gathered up the walls, floor, and ceiling of the paint booth and stuffed them into a large trash bag that he would drop off at the dump on his way to pick up Ben. The dump was unattended and had a burn pit where Mike could incinerate this parcel of evidence.

They had a hearty breakfast, as they would any other day. When they finished, Ben did the dishes while Mike loaded the bike into the back of his pickup. Mike double-checked the equipment they'd need. The radio system, antenna, generator, all the servos, linear actuators, and radios, and the TV cameras and transmitters were all inventoried and secured.

Ben came out of the cabin as Mike was finishing. "Looks good—everything ready to go?" Ben asked.

"Everything is here and tied down. I'm set to head over to the Lighter's place."

The Lighter residence was out of sight of his place and he knew that no one would be there. On the other hand, if the boat was spotted there, it shouldn't cause any concern. He visited them often—more often in the past few weeks as the plan for The Exercise came together. Nothing could look out of place.

"All right—I'm off. I'll see you over there. Don't forget the stop at the dump."

"No problem."

Ben headed back through the house to lock up, checked Mikey's water dish to see that it was full, and then walked out onto the dock. The lake was very shallow here at the north end, and some years the dock wasn't long enough. This year was okay though. Even with the recent rains, the water at the end of his dock was only a bit more than a yard deep.

He unlocked the lift and lowered the boat. He stopped before it was floating and climbed inside. He had left a hose dangling in the water and made sure it was still providing fresh water to the live well. He lowered the engine into the water and primed the fuel line. Sitting in the driver's seat, he cranked the engine. The big Merc caught immediately and he backed the throttle. He then finished lowering the boat into the water, which muffled the exhaust into a rough rumble. Ben removed the extra plastic hose he had rigged into the live well, stowed it and took his position in the drivers' chair.

Ben backed out about 50 feet to get a little more depth under the keel before cranking the wheel to swing the boat's tail around and point the bow to the south. He always drove the boat cautiously this close to shore, and there was no sense doing anything different today.

It took about eight minutes to get from his place to the Lighter's cabin. The morning was still and the lake calm, making docking a simple maneuver. He circled in, swinging the boat's nose out toward the lake with the right side toward the dock. He rigged a stern line and two center spring lines, checking that the fenders would stay in the right place, and headed to the house. One last check on the live well showed all was okay.

Mike was already pulling into the drive when Ben rounded the house. Ben climbed into the pickup and Mike threw the truck into reverse. They started the two hour drive to Duluth.

The day was perfect for flying—blue skies, little wind, and no real prospect of typical afternoon boomers. It was dryer than usual too, and that made the drive comfortable, even without the AC on. Mike had the XM radio tuned to Watercolors and they both enjoyed the jazz as they drove. The terrain in Northern Minnesota is the result of the last glacial age—gouged out, with plenty of low spots that collected water and became lakes, then grassy swamps, and then little towns with local bars and VFW's.

Ben and Mike said little while riding. They had become well acquainted in the past few weeks and there was little new ground to cover. They simply enjoyed the summer-morning weather.

They took Highway 210 across the middle part of the state, and turned north on I-35 for the last few miles to Duluth. They crested the hill above the city, with lake view continuing out of sight, but they took the Proctor exit. A friend of Mike's owned property on the north side of Proctor. There was a hill toward the back of the property that was out of sight of the road, but provided a sight-line to Duluth and the lake.

Mike stopped the truck by a pole barn and picked up a long flat package addressed to him care of this address. The package was labeled *Golf Clubs*.

They also made sure no one was home. They had several points in The Exercise that would rely on chance. But Ben believed in the rightness of their cause, and that things would break their way. No notice of his boat moored at Lighter's dock or their presence at this place were two major breaks they needed. They also needed one more crucial uncertainty to break their way.

They drove the last few hundred years to the crest of the hill. There the two men unloaded the generator—a two man job. Then they headed out.

The two drove back down the hill, back to I-35, and finished the drive down to the harbor. They drove past the high-priced hotels that now line the beach side of the Canal Park area, to the parking lot on the west side of the Duluth ship canal. They pulled on a couple of backpacks and locked the truck. Blending with the tourists, they walked about, checking the old anchors and the retired tug boat that is on display.

"Can you imagine going out onto the lake on that thing?" Mike asked.

"Not me, but then I never thought I'd be walking through southern Afghanistan with a rifle either."

"Me neither. Fortunately most of my time was indoors in a nice safe control center."

"I wish I'd known you then. I could have used your perspective for some of the ops we were assigned to."

They walked out to the end of the canal wing and back, looking at the lighthouse and taking pictures. When they reached the park, they stayed on the walkway, passing the Army Corps of Engineers building and walked under the lift bridge. At this point, the sidewalk passed just under the 386-foot moving deck of the bridge. A tall person could reach it easily.

Ben pulled a device out of Mike's backpack and handed it to him. Ben had scouted the area and had determined that this would be the place to slow down the pursuit. While Ben watched for other tourists, Mike switched on the power, nimbly hopped up onto the wall of the canal channel, reached out over the water, and placed the magnetic-equipped box on the side of the steel bridge beam. Then he flipped the contact rod up and over the electrical conduit, checked to be sure it had a good grip on the conduit, and then hopped down—all in less than ten seconds.

"Come on," Ben said, "I know a place with great sandwiches and cheesecake."

**Minneapolis, 9 a.m.**

The morning was bright and noticeably less humid for the time of year. We had breakfast out on the porch. I made waffles. With the pancakes, omelets, and now waffles, Maria would now have experienced my entire repertoire.

"These are great! Wow, you've got quite a collection of recipes."

"Actually, the batter recipe is the same as for the pancakes—you just double the oil and cook them in the waffle iron. I got it from Mom."

"It tastes different to me," she said. She insisted on helping, so we cleaned up just like old married folks and loaded up to go to the office.

When we arrived, Olson was already there with the Atlanta contingent. We got started immediately, even before the coffee showed up.

Bushard said, "We have pretty much wrapped up the money part of the investigation. It looks like Davis had sent some to Mitchell in an offshore account."

"Well that explains some of her behavior at the trial," Olson said.

I could see that but there was still no connection. "Yeah, but is there anything that would help you believe that Harris or anyone outside your investigation knew about it?"

"No, and that's what has us puzzled. If Harris found out about the connection from someone in my office, that would be additional motive for killing Mitchell," said Pritchett. What about the gun match?"

I replied, "We know where the barrels come from but not how anyone could have obtained one. The place that made them has a discrepancy in the records of how many barrels they were supposed to have. It's possible someone could have gotten one from them. And they also seem to be missing as much as 20 rounds of the ammunition. But if the shooter could have gotten the barrel and ammo, he would still have had to build the gun."

"How hard would that be?" Bushard asked.

"For someone with experience, not a big deal. For Harris, I don't think he could have. Other than some shooting experience with the Army, he's not even a shooter. We don't know if he has any gunsmithing experiences."

"What about this other guy?"

Olson answered, "We are still looking for him and are interviewing his known contacts. So far, no shooting or gunsmithing experience."

I added, "We'll stay on that, of course, but we are still mostly looking at Harris."

Pritchett had just been listening and finally asked, "How about this phantom—this Cederstrom guy? Anything on him yet?"

"We have no known employer, and—well—just his residence," I replied.

"Anyone search the place?"

I'd been so distracted by our visit to see the landlord, Wong, that I'd dropped the ball on that. I gave my head a smack and said, "No, we never searched the place." I picked up the phone to call Wong to set up a meet.

The rest of the team chatted while I called Wong's office. I got off the phone with the world's most obedient secretary. She said that Wong was out of town and that there was no one around who could take them out to Cederstrom's and let them in. She also said that she had been instructed to be as cooperative as possible if I called, but that did not include giving me the keys—I'd need a warrant. I told the team what was going on.

"I called over to the DA's office and they're getting us what we need. It's going to take a bit, so let's go get lunch," I announced.

We walked over to a lunch place a few blocks away. With its reputation as a cop joint, I knew we'd get a decent sandwich and could talk about the case.

## Duluth, 1:30 p.m.

After an overstuffed sandwich and a slice of the house cheesecake, Ben and Mike were back in the truck and heading toward the lift bridge. They heard the massive horns of the bridge exchanging blasts with an approaching ship. After the flashing lights and the lowering of the safety bars, they saw a freighter coming out of the harbor.

Duluth is an ocean port. Freighters from all over the planet visit here, transporting grain, freight, and, of course, iron ore, the rock that put Duluth on the map. It's just taconite now, the iron ore was mined out. But taconite still makes the northern Minnesota economy go round, which is why this was the last harbor for the Edmund Fitzgerald.

As the bridge went up, both men looked for the package they had affixed to the inside of the northern rail. It was there, blending in with the silver-gray paint as if it belonged there. While they waited, they timed the ship's passage at 12 minutes, start to finish.

Mike restarted the truck and they crossed the bridge to the island that, on a map, points like a thumb toward Wisconsin. This is the natural breakwater that creates the harbor that is Duluth's greatest asset. It's about seven miles long, and no more than a few hundred yards wide for its entire length. At the end of the slow seven mile drive sits Point Park and Sky Harbor Airport. They pulled into a parking area to ready their equipment.

Ben and Mike unloaded the bike from the truck bed. It was a Yamaha 250 dirt bike that could go just about anywhere. It had saddle bags and one other aftermarket add on that would make the difference later. They checked over all the other equipment, making sure everything was in place. Once initiated, their planned sequence of events wouldn't allow for a run to Radio Shack or Home Depot if something was missing.

"Looks good to me," Ben said. "Everything's right where it's supposed to be."

"Check," Mike answered, checking his watch. "It's 3:30. When do you want to go over?"

Ben had visited the airport's Fixed Base Operator last weekend while setting up the end-game strategy. He was a licensed pilot and had told the FBO he wanted to rent a plane to fly to Canada for some fishing. The FBO had two planes available for rental, one light twin engine and one single. The license Ben was going to use showed only a single engine rating, though Ben had more training and experience in a twin. He would need to allow time for the rental paperwork, and a quick hop around the airport to show the FBO that he knew what he was doing.

"Let's give it 45 minutes or so. I want to get there about 4:30. That'll be just enough time to sign the rental contract and make a touch-and-go with the operator."

"Sounds good to me. I'll do some more checking on the gear."

Ben knew there was little to do on the equipment at this point, but Mike needed something to keep his mind off what they were doing. Equipment readiness was the perfect distraction.

**Minneapolis, 1:30 p.m.**

The group finished lunch and walked back to city hall. When we got there one of the DA's assistants greeted us with the search warrant in her hand.

"Perfect timing," I said. "We'll take a Suburban and head up to Blaine right now."

Bushard claimed front seat privileges on account of his oversized frame. Olson scrambled into the back seat and Maria and Pritchett shared the center seat. We drove over to Roseville where I served the warrant on Miss Wonderful and got a key. She was charming to the last.

We were just heading north when Sharon called on my cell phone.

"Dan, you're not going to believe this—Mike Clancy was adopted. I had to do some real digging to get this info, but it looks like his birth mother was one Martha Brophy. The birth cert shows," she pronounced slowly and with emphasis, "the father's name as one Benjamin—J.—Harris."

I just about drove up onto the sidewalk! *Our* Benjamin Harris?"

"No way of knowing. She was Catholic and I had to get the info from Catholic Family Services. You know how tight they need to be with adoption records, but I went over there and talked to them and you just got a big break in a small world, pal. It turns out a friend of my sister Ruth works there. I'd met her at a party at Ruth's last winter. We caught up on the families and I told her about this investigation and that I'd really appreciate any help she could give me. I didn't tell her what we were looking at or why we needed Clancy's parents names, just that we had important info for all concerned. She didn't really let me into the files or anything, but I found out about Clancy's birth parents. She looked it up and told me the names. Nothing else—no current addresses or anything—but isn't this a strange coincidence? If this ever goes to trial I'm pretty sure she'll forget who I was and what she told me."

I hung up shaking my head in wonder at Sharon's skills and luck. And for a moment, I felt something new about Ben. I wondered how I would feel if, under already devastating circumstances, I suddenly learned I had a son? And then learned that my son's baby—my grandchild—died when my son's fiancé was shot in the same criminal event in which my wife died? I can't even imagine that much emotional shock.

I told the rest about Maria's idea to check on adoption and the discovery. If Clancy was Harris's son, that could change everything in this case. Maria took it in stride.

"It's not that big a surprise," she said. "The remaining questions are whether or not Clancy is Harris's son. And—if he is—did they know each other before the robbery? And do they know each other now?"

"Good work, Fernandez. That was a great read. If we can put them together, maybe that will go somewhere," Bushard said.

I said, "That would give us two guys and that would solve some of the logistics problems of how one person could get to all the shooting locations while Harris was apparently still here."

"That it would. We also need to check Clancy's military record again to see if he had any special shooting skills," Bushard said.

We pulled into the drive in front of Cederstrom's rental. I used the key I'd received from Miss Wonderful and we all pulled on gloves as we looked around. The place was a typical, contemporary town house—single garage in front and all the living spaces connected. All were sparsely furnished. There was only a two-seat couch, one chair, one stool by the breakfast bar, and an empty refrigerator.

"I don't think he's spending much time here," I observed.

"Sure doesn't look like it," Maria agreed as she looked in a closet.

Olson was checking the garage. "Nothing in here," he reported.

Bushard had gone upstairs to the bedroom level. He called down, "You might want to come up here and check this out."

We climbed the stairs together. The larger of the bedrooms had one of those self-inflating air-mattress beds you keep around for extra company, a chair, a table, and a floor lamp. On the table was a brown accordion-style storage file. Sticking out of the top were airline ticket folders. I picked one up by its corner.

Flipping it open I said, "Looks like this is the trip to Charlotte." I checked the others. "Sure enough, here's one to Phoenix and this one is Seattle to Anchorage."

"That only proves that Cederstrom went there. We already had that from the airlines," Olson said. He's always the optimistic one.

"Right, we need a crime scene team."

I called the office and asked them to send out a CSI team ASAP. We kept up the search. Sharon called again.

"I've been staying on this barrel thing. I think I have a line on a guy at the plant who might have taken one home."

"Why would he do that and why would he tell you?"

"Because I sweet-talked him, of course, to answer your second question first. I just told him that it looked like he was the only one who could have had access to the scrap shipment after it was counted and sealed but before it was weighed. I told him that it would be better if he copped to a little theft than start looking for a defense attorney on a murder charge."

Rademacher's logic strikes again, "So what did he do with it?"

"He says he sold it for scrap. I don't buy that because it only weighed a few pounds and even good steel isn't going for that much these days. It wasn't worth more than a few bucks as scrap."

"So what do you think he did with it?"

"I've got this idea—what if someone wanted a good barrel? How would they get one? They couldn't buy it off the shelf and the military is sure not going to sell them one. So what does that leave? I've been talking to the people who make these things and there are a lot of quality requirements that have to be met that may have nothing to do with the functional properties of the barrel. It could be about the interchangeability of one barrel to another. But if someone was building their own rifle with one of these, part interchangeability wouldn't matter. What I'm getting at is—a barrel might be scrapped and still work perfectly well. What if the person who wanted one had connections with the company that makes them, or had inside connections with the people on the floor. They might be able to get an inspector to scrap a good one, and then have the shipping guy grab it for them later. The records would be kosher and, if it didn't require DOD validation, it would be gone. Either way, someone could get a usable barrel that would be off the books."

I'd forgotten that Sharon had worked in manufacturing for a few years before she got the cop bug and joined the force. She had some kind of engineering certificate and could speak acronym when she needed to. Those analytical skills made her great at investigating crime.

"You think there might be two or more people in on this?"

"I don't know. I'm just thinking out loud. We need to check to see if Cederstrom had any connection with the barrel company."

"Get back to me as soon as you do." I can't imagine working this case without her.

The forensics team arrived and I had them start on the airline folders. "I need this first—prints or anything else you think is interesting."

The team leader set up his kit. He gloved-up and took the folder from me like it was a dead rat. Examining it visually first, he set it in a box and did a quick fingerprint check.

"It's clean."

"Exactly what do you mean?"

"I don't mean never touched. It's been wiped. Nope, I don't think we'll get anything off this one. I'll keep checking, but once you find one like this, the rest are almost always the same. If someone is this careful, they're usually thorough too."

So we had the goods, but no evidence. There had to be something usable here.

Olson and Bushard had been continuing the search. Olson called out from the kitchen downstairs.

"Hey, boss—you'd better get a look at this."

I went down the stairs with Maria behind me.

"What is it?"

Olson was looking in the cupboards. They were nearly bare—no house wares to speak of, and little food. Olson pointed up into the cabinet next to the fridge.

"Give me a break—" I said as I reached up and took down a red and green box. It was half full of Nut Goodies.

## Duluth, 4:30 p.m.

Ben got into the truck and headed over to the airport. Mike got on the bike, started it, and drove in the direction of the beach. They would meet later.

Ben pulled into the parking area for the airport's FBO, and went inside. The young fellow he'd talked to last weekend was there.

"Hi-ya, Dave, I was in last week about the Arrow."

"Sure, I remember. You're going fishing in Canada. Are you **going** today?"

"Actually, tomorrow. I'd like to get an early start so I thought I'd come over today and get the paperwork and test hop out of the way. I'd also like to load some stuff into the plane tonight. I'm planning on leaving at dawn, so I wanted to see if I could get a field pass for the morning so you wouldn't have to come in so early." The airport was small enough that it basically shut down after dark. Ben figured that Dave wouldn't want to have to get there any earlier than usual and would give him the combination to the electronic gate. He was right.

"Hey, that sounds great to me. I put in too many hours here as it is."

Dave brought the rental forms and Ben completed them. The plane was a three-year-old Piper Arrow, a single-engine, retractable-gear 4-seater that was easy to fly. The 200-hp Lycoming engine would give it a 137-knot cruise for a 900-mile range, plenty for someone going fishing in Canada. And its electronics package gave it GPS navigation to find those small, fly-in fishing spots. It wasn't a float plane, so it couldn't go right to the lakes, but there were plenty of airstrips near good Canadian fishing.

"I got her parked down the ramp a bit. She's been sitting for about two weeks. "I know she's fueled and ready to go, though. I run them up at least once a week whether anyone's using them or not."

Ben nodded as he filled in the blanks on the rental form. Odd to find a place that still used manual forms in this computer age, but that was a plus from Ben's point of view. Computers talk to each other and he didn't want that happening too soon. He showed Dave his pilot's license.

They walked out to a row of hangers. Parked in front of them in two rows on the broad asphalt ramp was a variety of light aircraft. All but two were single engine, and about a third of them were on floats. Sky Harbor is one of only two Minnesota airports that combine hard runway and water runway.

The three-year-old Piper stood out as one of the better looking planes, its modern paint scheme very shiny in the July sun. Dave opened the door, which, like most light aircraft, was on the passenger's side front seat. There was a control lock which Dave removed so the surfaces could be manipulated, and a fuel-test tube which he handed to Ben. Dave said "Go ahead start your walk around."

Ben did the safety walk around with Dave trailing him, showing that he had the procedure down. He properly checked all the critical items—the engine intakes, the oil level, and the control surfaces for ease of movement. He opened a small spigot under the wing and collected a fuel sample. This was to make sure that all the water that collects in the fuel tanks had been drained. Aircraft fuel is color coded and he checked the color too, to make sure that no one had put in the wrong octane.

Everything checked out okay, so the pair climbed into the plane, Ben first, so he could sit on pilot's side. Dave ran him through a quick familiarization of the panel. Dave then led Ben through the start up procedure. Ben opened a little window set into the main pilot-side window and, as pilots have done for more than a century, yelled "Clear!" to warn that they were about to start the engine.

Ben gave the 6-cylinder Lycoming a few minutes to warm up as he and Dave donned headsets and checked the radio frequencies and instruments. After listening on the local radio frequency for any local traffic, he released the brakes and let the plane roll forward. They taxied down to the end of the runway and Ben went through the uncontrolled airfield takeoff procedure on the radio. This was to let anyone in the area know that a plane was taking off from Sky Harbor.

Ben applied throttle and the little Piper jumped forward. It easily reached takeoff speed and climbed into the summer sky. They flew over the lift bridge and the harbor. Then they swung around to the south and east over Wisconsin and Dave started with some information about the plane.

Ben performed two touch-and-go landings, which seemed to satisfy Dave. On the third, they stopped and then taxied over to an open parking spot.

Ben keyed the intercom, "If it's okay, I'd like to load some things into her tonight. That'll save time in the morning."

"Sure, that's fine. When we get back to the office, I'll get you that gate code. I've got to get going pretty soon. My kid's got a baseball game tonight."

"Kid's are important—don't be late."

He parked the plane and shut it down. Ben stowed his headset and followed Dave out of the plane. They walked the ramp back to the office. Ben had intentionally parked as far from the office building as he could.

When they reached the office, Dave copied the gate code and handed it to Ben. Then, he asked Ben for the one thing that Ben knew would start the clock on the final phase of The Exercise—the credit card.

Dave ran the card and said, "Well, you're all set. We only burned a few gallons of gas, so you still have plenty for tomorrow. All you have to do is load up and go."

"Thanks a lot, Dave. This has been real smooth. I'll be sure to use you guys again."

**Blaine**

I couldn't believe it. Here was half a box of the same candy bars as those left at three of the shooting sites. All we had to do was check the lot number against the wrappers we'd found. It was a signature.

"This is nutty—and I don't mean the candy," I sputtered. This guy goes to the trouble to wipe down the whole place and leaves this? This is no accident."

Bushard was philosophical. "I suppose it could have been a mistake. A psychologist might call it a cry for help."

"Not a chance," I snapped. "This guy has us mystified and he knows it. Nobody this good makes a mistake like this. Come on, we gotta go see the guy at the gun barrel maker."

We all loaded up and drove over to Arden Hills. I pulled into the parking lot at 4:30—quitting time for hourly employees. I had called ahead and told my buddy Cyril to hold onto the guy we needed to see.

We walked in from the parking lot to the main lobby. I spoke again to the woman we'd seen two days before. I asked for Cyril Corey.

Cyril came out with a muscular young guy who looked like he had worked his way onto the shipping dock. We headed back to the conference room.

The shipping guy was introduced as Jim something, but I really didn't care. I was in no mood for good cop, bad cop. Today I was going with all bad cop.

"Jim, here's the situation. We know you sold that rifle barrel to someone. Now that, by itself, is only a minor theft charge. In fact, we'll leave it to Mr. Corey here to decide if the company wants to press charges. But that's all going to be dependent upon what you tell us in the next two minutes. If you can help us find the guy you sold the barrel to—that's as far as I will take it. If you don't, I'm going to get you charged as an accessory to murder in the first degree. So right now, you're looking at 30 to life for multiple counts of murder in the first degree. I suggest that you help us right now.

Jim blanched. He obviously hadn't a clue about the extenuating results of his action.

"I don't know what you're talking about. Murder? I haven't killed anybody."

"A barrel from a rifle—the type of barrel you make here—was used in three murders. You had access to the rifle barrels and one is missing. If you tell us who you sold it to, we'll see about leniency."

Jim's expression turned to a look of comprehension and then dread. "Murder—he didn't say he was going to kill anybody. He just wanted it for hunting."

"He?—who?" I demanded.

"I don't really know. Some guy who comes in here and calls on purchasing. I thought he was a hunter or maybe a spy for some other company or something. He didn't say anything about murder."

"No, I don't suppose he did. You think he'd tell you he wanted to kill someone with something that you'd have to steal for him? That surprises me, because you don't look that dumb."

Olson jumped in. "When did he talk to you about it?"

"I don't know. Must have been spring—maybe May."

"What does he look like?"

"Just—a guy. Maybe six feet, white, average, not a body builder or anything."

"How about hair, eyes, scars?"

Before he could answer, I dug into my pocked and showed him a picture of Ben Harris.

"Is this the guy?"

Jim looked at the photo. I couldn't tell if he knew him or not, he wasn't showing any signs of recognition.

"You know, it could be but I don't remember. Maybe his hair was more blondish, and I think he had a mustache—nothing really stands out. I've got his card back in the shipping office."

We headed out to the dock area. Jim was a vision of contrition and helpfulness. I think the impact of his situation was dawning on him. He sorted through a stack of business cards.

"Here it is—this is the guy," He said, handing the card to me.

I read it out loud, "Gil Cederstrom, Consultant, Advanced Information Systems. When did he get the barrel from you?"

"Like I said, it must have been around May. I was out with a bad ankle sprain for the first week and a half. So it must have been after that."

"So some guy comes in here and you just give him a barrel?" Maria asked.

"Well, no—of course not. He walked up to me in the parking lot after work one day and said he'd pay for it. He said he was a hunter and wanted one for his gun collection."

"How about ammo?" Olson asked. "This gun takes special ammo."

Jim answered, "He asked me about that too, but I don't have any access to that. I told him to check at the range."

"So, what did he pay you for this gun barrel?" I asked.

Jim hesitated. Finally he said, "Twenty-five hundred dollars."

"Holy!—Jim—didn't that seem like a lot of money for a scrap gun barrel?"

"Oh, it wasn't scrap. It was fine. It was marked scrap on the floor because there was something wrong with one of the mounting lugs on the end—I guess that's where you attach a silencer. But I asked Fred in quality about it and he said it would work just fine if you weren't using a silencer—the Army wouldn't buy it with the defect though."

Corey jumped in. "Fred didn't have any questions about why you were so interested in what was wrong with the part?"

Jim answered, "No. I guess since I'm always hanging around the QC lab he figured I was just interested. I've been taking classes on inspection at the Vo-Tech so I could apply up to be an inspector when the next spot opens."

And there it was. One of Sharon's predicted scenarios had come true. A part that was out of spec in one area but that was still perfectly usable was marked as scrap and tossed. That was what had been buzzing in the back of my head during our first visit. The only difference between a scrap part and a good part was a piece of paper. If someone could get a usable part that had been marked for scrap, it would be off the books as far as the Department of Defense was concerned. That was why they had the double-check system in place—count them and weigh them. Without that, we would have nothing. Even with this, we had nearly nothing—only that this poor sap had been duped into selling a good gun barrel. We still didn't know who Gil Cederstrom was.

We left the shipping guy with a uniformed cop who'd met us at the place. He would be booked on theft for now, but I had big plans for him. He was the only one that we knew had seen and talked to the shooter. Maybe if we could put a case together he'd remember what he looked like—memories improve in sight of the prison gate.

We exchanged thanks walked out to the parking lot. Bushard was interested in the picture of Harris.

"We have a fuzzy security photo of the guy we like for the Atlanta shooting. It could be this guy."

I said, "Yeah, and we've got some airport tapes with the guy we think he is. He's just too average. And the hair color is wrong, the mustache is there and he walks like a much younger guy."

Maria chimed in. "That could all be faked—the hair, mustache, and walk. You have any full-face shots?"

"No and that's the problem. I know you can make a pretty good match with a face shot that has his eyes—you can't change eyes—but we don't have that. Those cameras are all set to get face shots, but every time we think we have one of Cederstrom going through security at any of the airports—none of them catch his face. In every case, he's looking at his watch, or checking something in his pocket, or talking with the guy behind him."

Maria didn't think that was a coincidence. "It sounds like he was avoiding the cameras. Someone with a sharp eye could spot them and duck them."

"I don't know—"I doubted, "they're pretty well covered." He looks so natural that I don't think he's acting, but who knows?"

My phone rang—Sharon. There been a hit on a credit card registered to Gil Cederstrom. "Where was it used?" I asked her.

"Some airport in Duluth. I called and there was no answer there."

"What airport? Did he buy a ticket to go somewhere?"

"I don't think so. The place where he used it is called Sky Harbor Flight Services."

"Flight Services?" I wondered, out loud, "What is this fresh bullshit?" I yelled out to everyone, "Cederstrom used a credit card at something called Sky Harbor Flight Services in Duluth! Any ideas what he would have bought?"

"How much was the charge for?" Maria asked. I passed the question on to Sharon.

"The amount was $3,000 even, but there is an option to increase."

I told the team. Maria said, "Big round amount with the option to increase? Sounds like some kind of deposit."

"What's a Sky Harbor?" Olson wanted to know.

No one knew. I asked Sharon to find out—call the owner, the local cops, or whatever she had to do to find out what was going on.

"Hey, posse—he's in Duluth! That's only about an hour and a half at speed—what-say we go?"

We all loaded up again and made for I-35W, the closest northward freeway, where we could push the speed and get there as quickly as possible. Olson drove so I could work the phone. I notified the department of our destination and left the line open for when Sharon called back after about 15 minutes.

"Wha-cha got?"

"I found out that Sky Harbor Flight Services is what's called an FBO—stands for Fixed Base Operator. That's like a gas station for airplanes. They service and sell little airplanes. I got the number for the guy who runs the place. I called him and left a message to call you ASAP."

"Great. We're on our way to Duluth. Could you send me the address for the airport?"

"Will do, Babe."

**Duluth, 5:15 p.m.**

Ben had finished up with Dave at the airport, and Dave took off to attend his son's game. Ben got into Mike's truck and drove out of the parking lot. "Mike should be back in position by now," Ben thought. About a half mile back toward the lift bridge, he pulled over in a small parking area by Point Park. Mike stepped out from behind some trees and walked up to the truck.

"Any problems?" Ben asked as Mike hopped in.

"Not a one. I left the bike behind some washed-up driftwood so it wouldn't be seen from the water. It's just about 80 yards from the very northeast corner of the fence. I looked and there's even a nice hole in the fence where you can duck out. Just walk straight north from the hole to the drift wood and you'll find the bike. The key is in the ignition, helmet and jacket are right there, and the remote for the bridge box is in the saddle bag."

Ben turned the truck around and they went back to the airport. At the gate he punched the code into the gate control box and hit enter. After a couple of anxious seconds, the gate slowly opened. They drove through and closed the gate.

There was only one other person at the airport. Some guy was working on an antique Piper Cub. He gave Ben a wave as he drove by.

"He saw me," Ben said. He still had on the blond wig and mustache that he had been wearing when he played Gil. It itched. Mike had dropped down out of sight.

Ben stopped the truck behind the Arrow. Hidden from the Cub mechanic, they unloaded the equipment that would be going on the plane. Mike ran a long extension cord over to an outlet on the side of the nearest hanger. Ben had removed the pilot's seat and put it in a back seat. "Make a nice souvenir" Ben thought, but they wouldn't be keeping anything from this event. They had mounted most of what would be doing the flying on a flat aluminum base. This would be fastened down to the seat mounting bolts.

Mike handed in the equipment pallet and Ben helped him position it over the seat bolts. They'd made the holes oversized, just in case the pattern was off, but it slipped into position and bolted down securely.

Mike brought the power packs and radios from the truck. Ben strapped them into a back seat. He smiled grimly as he handed the nylon ties to Ben. "If this works, we might have to consider a career change."

"I don't think so," Ben replied, with his own wry smile. "Once should do it—besides, this isn't something we wanted to do."

Mike nodded in agreement. They both knew that they'd be happy to return to some kind of normal, if they survived this. But things would never be the same. Things hadn't been the same since that day in the grocery store. He returned to the work on the radio package.

Mike connected various control arms to the controls of the airplane. He first connected two linear actuators to the rudder pedals. This would give him control of the rudder pedals and the foot brakes. Then he connected one linear actuator to the face of the pilot's wheel, and then clamped a second one around the stalk that slides in and out of the panel. The first controller would turn the wheel left and right, and the second would slide it in and out, causing the horizontal elevator at the back of the plane to tip up and down. Finally, he connected one controller to the throttle lever.

Next he tied into the plane's electrical system in two places. One was just a switch and the other was a relay he connected to the plane's radio system. He made sure the radio was tuned to the proper channel so it would receive any calls made to it from the airport's local control frequency. These calls would be relayed to him at the control site they had named "Tower One."

They drilled a small hole in one of the side windows and Ben threaded a wire out through it for Mike to grab. Mike then attached the wire to a small antenna, which he glued to the roof.

Finally, Ben mounted and adjusted the two video cameras. One was looking at the main flight instrument panel and the other looked out the front windshield. Then he connected the cables for power to the front seat package and the radios.

He signaled Mike, who then checked each of the mechanical flight control actuators one at a time and took a look at the picture he was receiving from the cameras. After a few adjustments, he signaled Ben that he was satisfied with the view and Ben tightened down the mounting bolts to immobilize the cameras.

They had finished in 45 minutes. They had planned on being operational within an hour of the credit card read, and were right on schedule.

Mike shut down the radio package and retrieved the extension cord, tossing it into the back of the truck. He reached into the truck cab and handed the packaged rifle to Ben, who wedged it in between the plane's back seats.

"I hope it was worth all the trouble to get and use this thing."

Ben answered, "I knew the weapon would do the job and I thought that it would be bizarre enough to throw whoever would be looking for us off the trail. Turns out I was wrong. This Neumann guy is smart and tenacious—a dangerous combination in law enforcement."

"If you're right about him, we'll be seeing him soon."

"Keep his intelligence in mind if we wind up talking to him. He'll be doing his best to trip us up."

Ben climbed out of the airplane, shut the door, and gave Mike a hug.

"This is it. We either succeed or fail from now on."

"We'll make this work. We just need some help from the cops and from a boater."

"Call me as soon as you are in position."

"Got it. Good luck."

Mike got in the truck and watched for the mechanic working on the old Cub. When he made another trip into the hanger, Mike waved goodbye to Ben. He drove to the gate, entered the code, and drove out of the airport.

Ben now had to wait—the hardest part of any operation—for coincidence to make or break the plan. The only controls he had were the ones already in place. The cops had to come, but Mike had to get to nearby Proctor first. Ben had to get off the island, but a boater had to show up in order for the bridge to be raised. Everything either would happen—or not. He had done what he had to and was now just trying to "clear country," as the Spec Ops boys said. After the mission was accomplished, it was during this waiting period that most things went bad.

As he waited, Ben had some more time to sort through what he and Mike had done and what it could mean. His objectives had changed—maybe expanded would be a better description—since they had started this quest. At first, he had a very clear and simple understanding of what was necessary. They would do what hadn't been done by society—punish those responsible for Anne's death and the death of Susan's and Mike's baby. But as The Exercise unfolded, what had once been easily justified became muddled in rationalization and self delusion. In fact, their first target list had three more names on it. Those had become less important as the first and most obvious targets had been taken down. Eventually, somewhere between Phoenix and Atlanta, they had been taken off the list.

Ben still believed what he was doing was just, but was now dealing with the effects of post traumatic stress. Not from the event of the grocery store bank robbery that resulted in his wife's death, but from what *he* was doing. The first operation had been an academic exercise. Just as he had learned at Bragg, the target had to be scouted, stalked, and eliminated. But as the killings proceeded he began to lose himself. The first was the fastest and easiest, but the next three required patience and waiting. It was during those waits that he began to question himself.

"Should I have just accepted the verdicts?" he thought. He knew that sometimes justice fails to appear in court. The guilty often get lighter sentences than the victims desired, and you couldn't predict how any given judge would rule. He had chosen to be an avenging angel, but wondered if this was fallen justice. "Was it right"—he pondered—"or even good?" His parents had brought him up to believe in a higher authority and he believed that someday he would have to stand final judgment on his own for his actions. Would the good and bad he had done in his life be weighed, or would only his clearly sinful acts be considered?

Regardless, it was obviously too late to go back. Ben had always made decisions, accepted responsibility and lived with the outcome. But somehow, this chain of events had him looking back in doubt. It was the first time in his adult life that he had second thoughts gnawing at him.

He was prepared to accept the consequences if necessary. But he wasn't going to make it easy for the police. If they caught him—so be it. He wouldn't put up a fight that would risk anyone being injured. But he would fight it in court. As he had seen, justice as doled out in court isn't always about what the law says or what someone actually did. Sometimes it's about who or what you know and sometimes it's about what is right. But he regarded it mostly as a compromise—neither side's legitimate interests are fairly met, and all positions remain unsatisfied. Right now Ben was satisfied to have just gotten this far.

## In a Suburban on I-35, en Route to Duluth.

We were making good time heading north. I had called ahead to the Duluth PD and let them know we were coming in hot and why. They said they'd send a car out to the airport just to keep an eye on things. The cop I'd talked to said that the Sky Harbor Airport was at the end of the barrier island you reached by crossing the well-known Duluth Lift Bridge and that was the only way in or out. He had said they'd wait for us before doing anything. That was good, because I wasn't sure what we should do. My phone rang.

"Neumann here."

"Uh—this is Dave from Sky Harbor Flight Services. Someone left a message that I should call this number, but it was a woman."

"Yeah—Dave—how are you doing?" I feigned cordiality. "Dave, I'm trying to get some info on a guy who I think was out at the airport this afternoon." I could hear cheering and "hey batter—" in the background. He must have been at a baseball game. "Do you remember anybody charging something for $3,000 dollars this afternoon?"

"Well, yeah, I had one guy in."

"Could you tell me about him? What did he buy?"

"You know, I really can't talk about that. We have rules and I don't really know who you are. You could be anybody just trying to get information on somebody."

I looked at my phone like it was speaking Martian. This guy goes Mr. Security on me while I'm trying to stop the flight of a multiple murder suspect. Why isn't he working at the big airport?

"I'll tell you what this is about, Dave. I'm a detective with the Minneapolis Police Department. I'm trying to catch someone who we believe was involved in a multiple murder. I think he bought something from you for $3,000 this afternoon. I know this because we've had a watch on his credit card. Now,

I can understand your reluctance to give out information over the phone to someone you don't know, so how about this. I'll give you the general phone number for the Minneapolis Police Department. You call them and ask them who I am and where I am. They'll tell you. They'll even connect you back to me. Then you can talk to me again. Or you just tell me where you are right now and I'll have a Duluth squad car there in about 30 seconds. They can tell you I'm legit. But if I tell them you're a material witness and may be aiding and abetting, they'll probably arrest you on the spot." The bad cop in me took a chance and added "You want your kid's little league team to see that?"

"You don't have to do that. There was a guy in. He's rented a plane to go fishing in Canada."

Shit, too late. "When did he leave?"

"Oh, he's not leaving until tomorrow. He just came out today to rent the plane and get the test hop out of the way."

"What do you mean, 'test hop?'"

"Anyone who rents from us is required to take a test flight. This gives us a chance to make sure he's familiar with the airplane and that he can really fly. Sometimes we get guys that are really bad pilots and then we don't rent to them."

"Good plan. So, how good a pilot was this guy?"

"Very smooth, a natural. I ran him through myself. He was familiar with good pre-flight procedures and did a nice job on the touch-and-goes."

"You remember his name?"

"Yeah, Cedarberg—or something like that."

"What did he look like?"

"Kind of average—about 6-feet tall, blondish hair, and a mustache. He looks to be in pretty good shape—maybe 40. Pretty much like a lot of our customers."

"And he's not leaving until tomorrow?"

"That's what he said. He's going to leave at first light, which is before we open, so he came out today to take care of the paperwork and test hop. He said he would be loading up tonight to save time in the morning."

"Did you see him load the plane?" I had a twitch going now.

"No. He left before I did. I guess he'll come back, maybe after dinner or something."

Something was trying to formulate in my head, but it wasn't quite there yet.

"Listen, Dave—I'm in a car on my way to Duluth right now. We're just passing—" I looked out the window for a landmark, "—Hinckley. We'll be there in about 45 minutes. I want you at the airfield when we get there."

"I'll have to call my wife to come out to the game. I can be there 15 minutes after I leave here."

"Make sure you're there, Dave.

"You think he's going to steal it?"

"You said he told you he's going fishing in Canada, right?"

"Yeah—?"

"I don't think he's coming back."

"Well, I'll see you there."

I hung up and briefed the crew, "Dave at the airport says someone was in this afternoon to rent a plane to go fishing in Canada, but he said the guy wasn't leaving until tomorrow. Said his name was Cedarberg, or something."

"That's our boy!" Olson exclaimed.

"Yeah, probably. He said the guy filled out the paperwork today because he's leaving at first light and that's before the airport opens." I had a mental jolt—"He also said that the guy had to take a test flight to show that he was familiar with the plane." I speed-dialed Rademacher.

"Sharon, as fast as you can, please get someone from the FAA and find out if Ben Harris has a pilot's license."

"Got it—pilot's license. This is new."

"Yeah, I just thought of it, but I have to know if Harris can fly." I thought of something else—"Also, check and see if Gil Cederstrom has a pilot's license. By the way, Sky Harbor is an airport and Flight Services is a place they rent airplanes."

"Okay, that makes sense. I'll call you as soon as I have something."

I closed the phone while urging, "Olson, hit it. I have a bad feeling about this."

Olson hit the lights as the Suburban roared up to 100 MPH.

## Duluth

As Ben waited, Mike drove back up the hill. He was back at his friend's place in Proctor in about 25 minutes.

He pulled into the spot they'd scouted and got out. The generator was right where they'd left it six hours before. He started it up and plugged in the extension cable that was still attached to the radio package in the truck. Then he mounted a collapsible antenna to a bracket they'd made and attached to the truck bed, He ran the antenna up to its full height of 24 feet and switched on the radio. As it warmed up, he slid a loading ramp out and hooked it to the end of the tailgate. Finally, with everything operating, he called Ben on his cell phone.

"In position—ready to test."

"I'll start the onboard package now." Ben said. He hung up, stood up, and walked over to the airplane. For the last 15 minutes he had been checking the access road with binoculars. About five minutes ago, a Duluth squad car had arrived. The cop had stopped near the end of the park and was sitting on the front bumper. "Not very stealthy," Ben thought. He opened the plane's door, flipped on the power to the controller package, and then called Mike back.

"Package up and running. How do you read?"

Mike looked at the video displays on his end. The picture appeared and stabilized. It was in focus and in living color.

"Good reception here. I'll test the controllers."

One by one, Mike tested the actuators as he read off to Ben what he was doing.

It took about eight minutes to test everything. Then Mike asked, "Tower One—ready to execute?"

## The Suburban

We crested the hill that overlooks Duluth and, on this clear day, could see a hundred miles into Lake Superior. The postcard view shows the city hugging the hill to the north and the harbor spreading out around the lake. I could see the city's trademark Aerial Lift Bridge. As we coasted down the ear-popping-steep highway into the city, my phone rang.

"Neumann."

"Hi, honey. I've got what you want."

"Wha-cha got?"

"You must have some special intuition. Your buddy Ben does indeed have a pilot's license—for about 14 years. Complete with multi-engine and instrument ratings. But I came up empty on the other guy."

"Cederstrom doesn't have a license?"

"The FAA has never heard of him."

"Oh, boy." I thanked Sharon and told the group, "Harris is a pilot and the FAA has never heard of Cederstrom."

Nobody said anything. We were all racking our brains over what this meant. Harris was running.

We drove on for a few minutes, silent in the descending vehicle, until Olson spoke for all of us—"He's running."

We agreed. Harris had finished with the killing and was heading for Canada. It was hard to accept that this man, who had a life waiting for him back in Plymouth, would just drop everything and leave the country. Sure, he'd lost his wife and had no immediate family, but he had friends, associates—people who would help him build a new life. Everyone I'd talked to about him had said that he was a good American citizen. His work with the military had put his own life at risk for more than the sake of business—he was willing to into harms way for his country. Could a man so dedicated just up and leave?

But then the longer I thought about it—I wasn't so sure. That little tick had returned to the back of my head. Something was nagging at me. I pulled a state road map from the glove box, found what I was looking for, and called Sharon.

"Could you call the Crow Wing County Sheriff's office and have them send someone over to Harris's place on Bay Lake—do not approach—only to just see if he's there. If he's not, have someone watch it until he shows or until I call them back. Give them my number and have them call me."

Sharon answered, "Got it. You're thinking someone else is at the airport?"

"Well, partner, right now I don't know what to think."

We had just reached the exit for Lake Drive and were exiting the highway. We crossed the Lift Bridge and drove, as fast and safely as we could, to the Canal Park. There, we met a Duluth cop He had been sitting on the front bumper of his squad and got up to walk over when we parked.

"Hi there. You must be the folks from Minneapolis."

"Right, except we're from all over. I'm Detective Neumann and this is Detective Olson, also from Minneapolis—Detective Maria Fernandez of the Maricopa County Arizona Sheriff's Department—Detective Franklin Bushard of the Atlanta Police Department and Brian Pritchett of the Atlanta Prosecutor's office. Anything going on?"

"Nope—nothing. From here you can't see much, but no one can get past us in or out of the airport."

I looked over to the airport and could see the main building and row of multicolored hangers. In front of the hangers were a bunch of little airplanes, which I really don't like to fly in. I'll take a nice big 747 any day. I figure that if you're in one of these little airplanes, you just get a better view of where you're going to crash.

As we stood there, a battered Jeep rolled to a stop and a worried-looking young man approached us. He introduced himself as Dave, the airport operator, and I asked about Cederstrom. "Dave, you said that you checked the license of the guy who rented the plane?"

"Sure—standard procedure."

"And he was a good pilot?"

"I'd say he's a good one. Better than most I've seen."

"Do you check the license with the FAA?"

"No. I've seen enough licenses to know what one looks like."

"Well, buddy, you missed it there. We checked with the FAA and they've never heard of Mr. Cederstrom."

It occurred to me that I was hearing the sound of an airplane engine starting. We all looked in the direction of the airport saw a small white and red airplane taxiing on the runway. Dave pointed and cried out, "Hey—that's my bird! He said he wasn't leaving until tomorrow."

We all looked at Dave and I asked, "That's the plane Cederstrom rented?"

"There's only one on the field and that's it."

"Quick! We've got to stop him."

We rushed for the cars and I yelled at Dave to get the gate open. As we drove over, I could see the little airplane reaching the end of the runway and turning to take off.

## The Arrow

Ben squatted next to the red and white Arrow and answered Mike's "ready to execute" call. "Affirmative, Tower One." He looked toward the park and saw a black Suburban parked next to the police car. As he watched he saw the old Jeep he'd seen parked earlier by the airport's office pull up. "Our friend has been here for a few minutes and it looks like the party is getting bigger. I'll call you when I'm at the threshold."

Ben glanced around and climbed into the right seat. He hoped that the Cub mechanic, if he looked, wouldn't notice which seat he was in. He went through the engine start procedure, omitting the "Clear!" this time. After the engine had had a moment to warm up and smooth out, he released the brakes and taxied toward the east end of the runway. He began turning the controls over the Mike. When he reached the end of the runway he called Tower One on the radio.

"Tower One—approaching position."

"I've got the airplane."

Ben nodded at Mike's statement, he unlatched the cabin door and reached over to the control package that was mounted on the floor of the pilot's side of the cabin. He found the lanyard for the inflatable dummy and gave it a pull. As the plane made the turn around at the end of the runway, the blow-up doll inflated and he ducked down and out through the open door. From here on, Mike was in control. Ben slammed the door, rolled off the wing, and dashed into the bushes covering the end of the airport property. He looked back to see the plane weave back and forth a bit, as Mike brought it steady on the runway heading. Then, he heard the engine run up to full throttle.

## Tower One

Mike was watching the outside-view video feed as he straightened the little plane to the runway. Then, with a push of a lever on the control panel, he watched on the second screen as the throttle lever went to full forward. Mike's control set up was arranged much like the actual controls of the airplane. There was a lever to control the throttle, a joy stick instead of the wheel, and a set of pedals for rudder control. A few more switches completed the package. He watched the outside view to make sure the plane stayed centered on the runway, glancing at the instruments to check airspeed. When the plane reached take off speed, he pulled back gently on the joy stick and saw it climb into the air.

He took his left hand off the throttle controller, which had a friction slide and wouldn't move without his help, and flipped a switch. This sent a signal to the plane to energize the landing-gear retraction sequence. It had been easier to just patch into the wiring then to rig an actuator for this step, but there was no way to test it. He looked at the outside view screen and saw that all was going just as planned. He was in a gentle climb, flying right down the middle of the runway.

## Ben

Ben watched in awe as the plane climb away. When Mike had proposed the idea as a way to end The Exercise, he didn't think it would work. But now, seeing it happen, he began to think they might just get away with it. He snuck back to the perimeter fence and found the hole Mike had told him about. He scrambled to the pile of driftwood and, sure enough, there was the Yamaha under some branches.

Ben put on the jacket and helmet, uncovered the bike, stood it up, and did a quick check for the remote—right where it was supposed to be. He turned the key and gave the starter lever a kick. The engine fired after a few tense tries, and it was barely audible. That was the final alteration they had made to the motorcycle. It had a special muffler system like those used by Special Forces to quiet the engine. From 25 feet away, a person would be more likely to hear the crunch of the tires on the road than the engine. He climbed on and headed west toward the park.

## Dan

We stood there watching as the plane came down the runway. It lifted off and the landing gear starting to retract. I reached for my pistol, but common sense returned before I touched it. I wanted to catch this guy as much as I'd wanted anyone I'd ever chased. But I wasn't sure why I wanted him. Did I want him just to take him in and say I'd busted a multiple murderer, or did I just want to talk with him? I didn't know for sure. In some new, weird way, I almost hoped he'd get away. I made a mental note to self-examine my head—on that thought anyway—at the next opportunity.

Right now, though, there was someone working on one of the planes. I hollered a hello and waved him over. "Do you know who was in that airplane?" I asked.

"I don't know," he said, and looked at Dave.

"You're sure?" I asked.

"I only know he was here earlier and came back. His truck was parked down there," he said, pointing down to where the Arrow had been. "I guess he must have left when I was in the shop."

"You're sure he left?"

"He had a big red Dodge pickup down by the Arrow. I didn't see him leave but I don't see it there now."

"You're sure there was only one guy in the truck?"

"I only saw one guy come in. Course, it's a big truck—coulda been someone in the back."

"What was he doing down at the airplane?"

"Beats me. I couldn't see him from where I was."

We watched as the plane climbed toward the evening sun. Then it made a left-hand circle out over the harbor, which brought it back over the field at a right angle to the runway. As it crossed the airport, I could see the pilot in the window and I waved. The plane waggled its wings.

I asked Dave, "How can I talk to that airplane?"

"If he's got his radio on we can call him on the field's frequency. He might be listening."

We rushed into the building and Dave turned on a radio. After about 15 seconds, he keyed the microphone, "Arrow November 1735 Juliet—this is Sky Harbor field calling." We waited.

"Arrow 35 Juliet—please respond on this frequency."

A scratchy voice came back, "This is 35 Juliet responding your call Sky Harbor."

I took the mike from Dave. "Cederstrom, or whoever you are, this is Dan Neumann of the Minneapolis Police Department. I am ordering you to return to the airport immediately—return and land immediately!"

There was a pause—"Detective Neumann, how nice to hear from you. I thought you'd never figure this out."

That wasn't what I wanted to hear, but I listened closely to the voice. Was it Harris? I couldn't tell over the radio. "Cederstrom! I have a warrant for your arrest." I didn't, but we'd work out the details later. "If you don't return, things are going to be very bad—worse than they are now. If you go to Canada, we'll just have to extradite you and that will make me very upset."

"Detective Neumann, I don't think you'll be able to find me, so I'll take my chances and continue."

I looked around the room for help, but didn't find any.

"Is there any way we can chase him?"

Everyone obviously had their thinking caps on tight, but this wasn't moving fast enough for me. Finally Dave said, "I could get us up there in one of our other planes, but he'll have a pretty good head start and I'd have no way to really track him. We could call the Air Guard and see if they'd chase him—"

That rang a bell. The Duluth National Air Guard unit had F-16s. Maybe they'd help us if I waved the National Security flag.

"Let's find that phone number," I implored.


## Tower One

Mike was flying the plane out over Lake Superior now, and had turned northeast toward his final destination. They had located it using a standard lake maps chart that was available on the Internet from the Minnesota Department of Natural Resources. It would take about a half hour for the Arrow to get there. Mike and Ben had figured that would be long enough to make their getaway, especially if they got a little help along the way.


## On the Island

Ben turned the bike inland from the beach as he got to the park. When he reached the road he could see the plane passing over the field, waving its wings. He saw a group of people standing outside the FBO building. When they abruptly hurried inside, he surmised that they were the law. Without looking their way, he turned onto Lake Drive toward the lift bridge.

He rode on, carefully observing the speed limit. It took a little more than 12 minutes. At the lift bridge, he reached back into the unfastened saddle bag and felt for the small box. He found it, took it out, and pulled up a short antenna with his teeth. He rode onto and over the bridge, the steel mesh roadway buzzing under the bike's tires. As he passed midway on the bridge, he flipped a switch on the box. There was a small white light on the box and when it glowed, he turned off the switch and tucked the box back into the saddle bag. They had considered just throwing it into the ship canal, but had decided not to. No sense in risking any attention by littering.

Ben rode down Lake Drive and entered I-35 south. It took another 12 minutes to climb the hill to the Proctor exit. There, he made the turn up to Mike's friend's land.

## Sky Harbor

I found the number for the Air Guard first and called them.

"This is the 148th Fighter Wing—Master Sergeant Hawkings speaking." I told him what was going on and that we needed someone to follow the plane. He quickly made the assessment that what I was asking was over his pay grade. I asked to talk to the duty officer.

A sleepy sounding Lieutenant came on the line. "This is Lieutenant Bohling."

"Lieutenant Bohling, this is Detective Dan Neumann of the Minneapolis Police Department. I'm at the Sky Harbor Airport. An individual who is wanted for multiple murders has just taken off in a Piper Arrow. Can you to send a jet after it to follow it? We think he's trying to escape to Canada."

There was about a 10-second pause and I said, "Bohling—are you there?"

He answered. "Detective Neumann, I'm not sure that I can scramble fighters for a police chase. Could you please wait on the line?"

After another few minutes that seemed like an hour, but which probably gave him time to have me verified with the Minneapolis PD, Bohling came back, "Detective, we have the authority for a limited pursuit in this case. Can you describe the aircraft?"

"Glory be," I thought. I didn't actually think they could help, or would cooperate in time if they could. I had just thought it couldn't hurt to ask—.

I switched my phone to speaker and answered, "The plane is a Piper Arrow—white with dark red two-tone paint. The registration number is"—I looked to Dave for help and he whispered the number to me—"November 1735 Juliet. Got that?"

"Affirmative. I read back, white with red Piper Arrow—a single-engine low-wing retractable-gear light aircraft—tail number November 1735 Juliet. Do you have a heading?"

Again, I looked to Dave. "Heading?" I asked.

He said, "Tell him about O-75 degrees out over the lake."

I relayed the info and Dave added, "He might be able to get some help from Duluth Center. This guy's probably not checking in with them."

I passed that along too, along with the office phone number.

## Tower One

Mike was smoothly piloting the airplane toward the endpoint. Ben had found the spot they'd use, just offshore near Silver Bay. He had estimated total flying time at roughly 35 minutes at 130 knots. He checked his watch and estimated another 14 minutes until the Arrow would be there. According to the lake map, the water is more than 500 feet deep there and he and Ben hoped that would be deep enough.

Ben arrived and, without a word, pulled a garden hose off its roller on the side of the house and sprayed the truck. As the truck became soaked, the red paint ran down the sides to reveal that the truck's true color was white. Ben washed the truck very carefully to remove any pink traces of the water-based red paint. Hopefully, the police would be pursuing a red truck.

When the truck was white again, he rolled the bike up the ramp attached to the back of the pickup and secured it in place. Mike was sitting on a folding chair behind a camp table, on which sat the radio control package.

"All okay?" Ben asked.

"Fine so far. The GPS says we've got about 10 minutes left. Did the gear go up?"

"Just like downtown. Any word from those guys?"

"They called right after takeoff. I don't think they know who's in the plane. They asked for Cederstrom or whoever. I gave them the run around like we planned. I don't know if they're tracking us through Duluth Center or not, but so far no more calls."

"Fine, they'll know what's happened soon enough."

## Sky Harbor

The Air Guard called back on the office land line. Dave picked up and, after a few words and nods handed the phone to me, saying, "It's Lieutenant Bohling." We exchanged questions, observations, and contact information for a few minutes. When we were done, I hung up to wait for an update and filled in the others, who had been waiting and listening.

"He said they were scrambling two alert F-16s and sending them up the lake. Duluth Center is indeed tracking the bogey. It left Sky Harbor and never checked in with them, even though they were calling it on several different frequencies that should have been monitored. Estimated intercept time is eight minutes from take off. He told me they could only command the bogey to return and land, and only in U.S airspace. They said they were already briefing their Canadian counterparts."

Pritchett replied first, "That's better than shooting him down. That would be way too much paperwork, even for me." I managed a wry chuckle. I would have picked him last to provide a bit of comic relief for the tension we were all feeling.

Dave said, "They'll catch him for sure. He can make about 150 miles per hour and those fighters can make four times that. They'll have him quick, but then what. I don't want to lose my plane."

I was as reassuring as I could manage. "I think you might as well call your insurance company now. He's either going down or to Canada, and I don't know how long it'll take to get it back from them."

## Two F-16s over Lake Superior

"Duluth AG—this is Bulldogs 101 and 102—we are airborne and in pursuit—will let you know when we have a tally—"

"Bulldog 101—Duluth AG—Roger that—keep us informed."

## Tower One

Mike had the plane on a smooth course. It was only minutes from the goal now. He had no way of knowing that two F-16s were hot on his trail. Of course, that wouldn't matter. All they'd catch was a ghost.

## The F-16s

"Duluth AG—Bulldogs 101 and 102—we have a target on our scopes—estimate intercept in 60 seconds—"

"Roger Bulldog—let me know what you have when you get there."

"Roger that—tally the target—we should be on him momentarily."

Both fighters pulled back on their throttles and popped out their speed brakes. They would overshoot the little Piper in a few seconds. Even with throttles closed and speed brakes out, their airspeed was in excess of 300 knots when they passed the Arrow. But at that speed, with every bit of drag-inducing flap and speed brake hanging out, the F-16s were creating a tremendous amount of wake turbulence. Bulldog 101 passed a bit too close to the small plane, jolting the little plane like a huge invisible speed bump.

"Duluth AG—we just overran him—I report a Piper Arrow—tail number November 1735 Juliet with one occupant— requesting orders for procedure—"

As they made a break turn, bleeding off speed, Bulldog 101 looked back over his shoulder in time to see the Arrow roll inverted and point the nose

Dart | 215

toward the lake. He felt his throat constrict as the plane did nothing to pull out of the dive.

"Duluth AG—he's going in—" was all he could get out before the plane hit the water at more than 200 miles per hour.

## Tower One

Mike saw the jets pass on his outside-view video screen. Then, he saw the horizon start to tumble. A quick check of the instrument display showed that the plane had been tossed in wake of the jet. Mike made a snap decision, rolled the plane inverted, and dove for the lake. His last view was the blue water getting closer. Then—nothing. The plane was down.

## The Arrow

Light aircraft are built to take a lot of flight induced punishment but not the kind that occurs when hitting the water in a vertical dive at over 200 miles per hour. The engine of the Arrow continued straight down into the depths. The wings, rudder and elevator were torn from the fuselage and shredded into strips that would flutter down in an ever spreading pattern that would eventually cover many square miles of lake bottom. The fuselage itself was ripped open. The skin was shredded as the flight surfaces had been. The heavier items—instruments, radios, rudder pedals—would sink more or less straight down. The seats, including the detached pilot's seat, would spread in the debris field. The rifle's shape caused it to slice straight down through the cold clear water like a spear. It hit the bottom at about 20 miles per hour and stuck itself deep into the muck. Only a few inches of the stock protruded from the bottom of Lake Superior, never to be found.

## Sky Harbor

"What are you saying?" I sputtered into the phone. I couldn't believe my ears. The plane had crashed into the lake!

"Sorry about that. It looks like he took one look at us and dove in," Bohling replied. He wasn't sure what had happened but he had an idea and wasn't about to say anything that might later show up in a General Court or on TV. If his jets had caused the accident, he sure didn't want to help prove it.

I was incensed. Crashed? That couldn't be right. I thought hard, knowing that the answer had to be right in front of me. I walked away from the group and went outside. Going over everything I knew about the case, I kept thinking, "what is it?—what the hell is it?" I looked down the line of airplanes and saw the guy working on the old Cub. He was standing outside the plane, reaching in, and moving his arm forward and back. The elevators on the tail were going up and down, so he was pushing that control—the control—. Then the realization hit me—*Clancy*! Clancy was in the military, and his job was flying remote controlled airplanes. Could that be it?

I dialed up Sharon as I dashed back to FBO building. I burst in and was only able to holler to everyone, "I think I've got it—"before Sharon answered.

"Hi, Dan. What's up?"

"Did you get the Crow Wing Sheriff over to Harris's place?"

"Sure did. He called here and said it looked like no one was home. Harris's car was there, but the boat's gone. Maybe he's fishing?"

"Sure he is. He's live bait in Lake Superior. Call that guy back and tell him to sit on that place until we get there. And call every cop-shop between here and Bay Lake and have them pull over every red Dodge pickup they see. They're looking for Harris or Clancy or both, okay? Then check with DVS and find out if Mike Clancy or Harris has a red pickup. Got all that? Thanks."

I hung up and filled everyone in on what I had deduced. We agreed that this was our only immediate angle. "We have to go now!—I'll explain—I think Harris is alive and well and not fishing."

With Olson driving, I lit up the Suburban and raised my voice to share my reasoning over the siren. We were proceeding at a controlled roar down Lake Drive when Olson said, "Oh crap!" and we all saw the flashing barriers coming down—the Lift Bridge was going up.

A tall sail boat was approaching the bridge. I swore and slowed as the bridge went up, knowing we'd have to wait. "But it would be okay"—I thought—"it would just slow us down. If Harris was anywhere nearby, he couldn't get back to Bay Lake before I could, running with lights on. I had him now."

## On the Bridge

The device that Ben and Mike had attached to the moving roadway had been activated when Ben drove over it and pushed the switch on the box in the saddlebag. Inside the device, two large batteries started to charge up a capacitor. A capacitor is an electronic way of building a charge that can be released all at one time. A person is a capacitor when they rub their feet on carpeting and then touch something, the shock is the charge unloading. The capacitor in the device was building up a very shocking charge.

When the bridge started to rise, a small instrument known as an accelerometer was triggered. When it stopped, the device noted that and signaled the capacitor to discharge a huge amount of voltage through the arm that they had placed across the electrical conduit for the bridge. This surge popped the circuit breakers in the bridge control system and crashed the system's computer. So the bridge, the only way on or off the island, just stopped. It didn't cause any damage, but it would take the operators at least 30 minutes to figure out what had happened and another 15 to fix it.

Inside the device, one last command was sent. This went to the electromagnet that was holding it in place. It was turned off and the device fell into the ship canal, leaving no evidence on the bridge of what had caused the breakdown.

### Tower One

Ben and Mike finished loading the truck and headed off for Bay Lake as fast as traffic would allow. Again, they would have to be careful. A speeding ticket would ruin an otherwise well-planned and well-executed operation. They were silent as they drove, neither gloating nor remorseful.

### At the Bridge

I think we all have those moments, when it seems you are about to succeed—to win—and then, victory is vaporized by an unexpected event over which you have absolutely no control. This one left me apoplectic.

"What the hell is going on here?" I screamed at the windshield. The bridge had been up for at least 10 minutes and the sail boat had long passed underneath. I couldn't see any other boat traffic. A less-truculent Olson was on the phone to the Duluth PD.

"Yeah—yeah—well, we're in pursuit of a suspect in a multiple felony murder case and we'd like to get off this island. Any ideas?" Pause. "Yeah, I'll let you know." He hung up.

"Duluth says the bridge is busted, they don't know what's wrong, they don't know how long it's going to be up, and the only way off the island is boat or swim. They said they'd send a harbor patrol boat over, but their on-duty boat is way up the river by Fond du Lac chasing down a *fishing with dynamite* call. It'll take a bit to round up a crew for the other boat."

We got out of the Sub and milled around, looking at the bridge for something hopeful. Then I had my next epiphany of the day, in what was threatening to be a relentless series—I let it go.

It was a Zen moment. I think we also have moments when the best you can do is look at the predicament and decide whether or not to accept that it's out of your control, and that the only power you have left is your regard for the facts. Of course, I'm not usually able to quickly decide to not let something get to me. But I was amazed to realize that I was suddenly and simply okay with being stuck. And that notion was back—tempting me—"just let him go." I didn't know why, but I hoped for a chance to sit down with Harris and talk to him about—everything, if he wasn't on the bottom of the lake.

Maria, beautiful Maria, walked over to me. She apparently had been respecting my moment of soul searching, had noticed my change in demeanor, and sweetly took my hand. We walked over to the ship channel and she said, "This is a beautiful city. I never knew there were places like this in Minnesota. All we ever hear about in Arizona are the snow storms."

This was the moment I was supposed to seize—the opportunity to spend time with her. The others were leaning on the car, probably working the case. We walked up the island-side of the ship channel and I gave her one my famous travelogues, a brief version on Duluth and its shipping history and iron ore. I've always loved the place, spent many summer days here, toured the North Shore Drive for fall colors, and skied at Wild Mountain and Lutsen. Pretty soon I was thinking maybe we'd be stuck overnight and would have to catch a hotel room on the beach.

About an hour after it had stuck, I heard the bell that warns that the bridge is about to move. Sure enough, it started down. Maria and I ran back to the car and I took the wheel this time. We were the third in line, so I had to wait as the other drivers returned to their cars, started up, strapped in, and got going. Finally, we were moving.

We got by the traffic that was waiting on the other side of the bridge and reached the highway. The GPS was telling me to take it south to the 210 cutoff to get over to Bay Lake. I was on I-35 when my phone rang. I tossed it back to Olson who first said, "Hello," and then, "Neumann's Grill and Bar—first we grill you then we get you behind bars." It had to be Sharon.

"What's the deal, Bobby? Dan got himself a secretary now?"

"No, but he's driving about 90 in a 50 zone and I think this may be more multi-tasking than he can handle."

I gave Olson as mean a look as I could. He switched the phone onto speaker and went on.

"What do you need him for?"

"I checked the red pickup thing for him. Harris doesn't have any pickups but Clancy has a white one. Hope that helps."

I said, "Tell her to check on that bulletin for a late-model red Dodge pickup—one or two occupants fitting Harris's description—for everywhere from here to Bay Lake."

Olson repeated the instructions and got a confirmation from Sharon.

With lights on, but no siren except when needed, we cut across northern Minnesota to Harris's summer place. It'd be at least a 90-minute drive, even pushing it, so I tried my best to stay calm. After all, I'd gotten a chance to spend some time with Maria in a romantic setting. I decided that we'd get there when we got there and then—I didn't know what to expect.

I drove as fast as I thought the local Sheriffs would allow a Suburban with lights and a siren get away with. As we traveled west, we went over the spectacle of the airplane getaway.

"I'll tell you one thing—this guy had guts," Bushard observed.

"I think he's still got them. The probable partner in this scheme is a young guy who flies remote control airplanes for the Air Force. I think there wasn't anyone in that plane."

Olson said, "But we saw the guy in the window. He even waggled his wings at us."

"Maybe at us—maybe that was just part of the plan. In any case, the Coast Guard is going to be on that crash site pretty soon and they'll find out who's in that plane," I said.

"I don't know," Olson cautioned, "I think the lake is pretty deep there."

"What are you Olson—a lake detective?" Pritchett asked.

"My family has a place on the North Shore. If he went in up around Silver Bay, Lake Superior is about 600 feet deep there. The Coast Guard may never even find the wreck. Plus a light plane like that—going straight in. Might not be much left of it."

We all agreed that until we found out who was in the plane, we had no case. If the Coast Guard couldn't find the plane, then we were done.

## Mike's Truck

Ben and Mike had the lead they needed. Traveling back the way they'd come that morning, they pushed their speed but didn't take any chances. It took about 15 minutes less to get back than it had taken that morning.

First Mike drove by Lighter's place. Still no one there, as Ben had presumed when he laid out this part of the plan. They parked the truck behind Lighter's garage, hidden from the road, and walked down to the dock. The Alumacraft was right where Ben had left it. Ben went started the motor while Mike untied the lines. Ben checked the live well one last time. Everything looked just fine so they pushed the boat away from the dock and headed out.

Across the lake, the Crow Wing County Sheriff's Deputy was still on watch near Ben's place. He had parked in the driveway between the garage and the house, but could see the dock from his position. Anyone coming in from the lake would have a hard time seeing him, but if someone drove in he was busted. He had been working on a Sudoku puzzle book when he noticed a boat approaching the dock. He started the car, backed out of the driveway, parked on the road, and walked back in time to see Mike and Ben landing the boat on the lift.

### The Suburban en Route to Bay Lake.

We had made the turn down 169 toward Bay Lake when I got the phone call.

"Neumann here," I answered.

"Detective Neumann, this is Deputy Sanderbock with the Crow Wing Sheriff's office. That place you have us watching—well, the boat just came back."

"That's great—we're about three minutes out, so keep an eye on it and let me know if it leaves again."

"Got it—I'll call if anything changes here."

"Deputy Sanderbock, how many people are in the boat?"

"Two."

I pushed the pedal as hard as I thought I could without endangering the locals. We arrived in two minutes and I waved to the deputy as I pulled into the driveway.

We all hopped out of the Suburban in time to walk around the house and see Ben Harris and another man I assumed must be Mike Clancy unloading the boat. With Olson about 10 feet behind me, and the rest fanned out along the shore, I walked out on the dock. I resisted the urge to pull my piece, and just walked out on the long creaking dock.

Ben looked my way and stopped what he was doing. Both men stood up and faced us. I could see that they had nothing in their hands. There was something else I could not help noticing.

They were carbon copies of each other, one just younger than the other. Their faces, their build, their posture—everything was the same. Clearly, they were father and son.

"Just in time for supper," Harris said.

"I'm sure. Where have you been all day?" I asked, taking the last few steps between us.

"Fishing." Ben said. And to prove it, he held up a basket of flopping walleyes. There were indeed enough for supper, at least until uninvited guests had shown up. I stopped in my tracks and laughed—oh, man. For that moment, I lost focus on the case, all that had happened, and what was to be done with these two. At that moment, I didn't care—all I wanted was the story.

Maria was standing behind me now, with Olson and Bushard behind her. Pritchett and the deputy were watching from the front yard. She came around me and held out her hand. "I'm Detective Maria Fernandez of the Maricopa County Arizona Sheriff's office, since it seems no one else is going to introduce me," she said as she looked at me with wonder. I was sure she was thinking I'd lost my mind when I started laughing, but she was playing whatever was happening very well. I regained my composure and introduced Bushard and Pritchett. Bushard offered his big hand and Pritchett waved from the beach.

"Arizona and Atlanta? You guys are pretty far from home. Here on vacation?" Harris asked.

"Not vacation—more like a goose chase," Bushard answered.

"We've got enough fish for everyone to have a taste and I've got some brats in the fridge. Why don't we clean these fish and get going on supper?" Ben invited.

Bushard, Olson, and Pritchett were all looking at me as if I'd lost all my marbles, but Maria was congenial. She said, "That sounds great," and started back for the house. I thanked the slightly perplexed deputy, and he hurried off to respond to an emergency call.

We walked back up the long dock and up to the house. There was a fish cleaning table nailed to a tree at the side of the yard. It showed signs of many years of service. Ben hung the basket of fish from a hook on the tree and went into the house. I nodded to Olson to follow, but Maria was already up the two steps leading into the house, chatting away with Harris like they were long-lost cousins. I guess she had figured out that, unless someone spilled the beans, no one was getting arrested tonight. As the door to the cabin opened, Ben's dog trotted out and greeted everyone with a single loud bark.

Bushard and Pritchett sidled up to me, looking very perplexed. "What are we doing here?" Pritchett wanted to know.

"We're having a little late supper with the host," I replied—then quietly— "I don't know exactly what happened and I don't think we'll ever have enough to go to trial, but I want to sit down with this guy and pick his brain. I think he and Mike did the killings, and now they've made our number-1 suspect go away. I don't know if anyone is lying at the bottom of the lake, but I sure want to find out how they did that."

Bushard asked, "And what did you say Clancy did in the Air Force?"

"He's a UAV Operator. That's someone who flies planes by remote control and Harris is a radio specialist."

Bushard brightened. "You don't think—" he said with a chuckle.

"Yeah, I think."

I left it at that. Maria and Ben came back out of the house with Olson right behind them.

Mike had finished up with the boat and he was walking up from the dock. Everyone had gathered around the fish cleaning table. Mike said, "I'll start a fire." There was a fire pit about 15 feet from the table.

Ben said, "Good idea. With this wind, the smoke will help keep the skeeters away." He went right to the fish cleaning, finishing the job as the fire began to crackle and roar.

Ben said, "Come on into the kitchen and grab something to drink from the fridge." We made our selections and sat back down on the picnic table on the porch. Maria stayed in the kitchen, ostensibly to help out with food prep, and I sat down with Olson, Bushard, Pritchett, and Mike on the porch. We all had beers in our hands.

It was getting dark—about 9:30 this time of year. There was a nice breeze off the lake and there was an occasional cry of a loon. The smell of brats and fish frying was coming from the kitchen, along with snips of Maria and Ben's conversation and the clatter of utensils. If I hadn't been sitting with a murder suspect I would have thought I was on Golden Pond. I tried to remember if the Twins were playing.

We made small talk with Mike about the lake place, the weather, the Twins—Minnesota lakeside talk. Finally I asked how long he'd known Ben was his father.

"That was a surprise. I saw him at the trial and just knew he was the one. I was adopted, but my adoptive mother stayed in touch with my birth mother. When I was in college, they let me in on the situation and my birth mother became present in my life too. All she had ever told me was that she had gotten pregnant and that the father was someone she had known in college."

"Then you didn't know about Ben until the trial?"

"Nope—never knew about a biological dad. My birth mother told me she hadn't told the father that she was pregnant. She is very modern and independent."

"So Ben didn't know about you until then either?" I was struggling to absorb the information and, out of habit, analyze it too.

"No, and was he surprised."

"I'm sure he was," I thought, recalling the overwhelming series of shocks and surprises associated with the trials. I mused, for the briefest moment, over the thought of someone announcing that I was an unsuspecting daddy.

Ben and Maria came out from the kitchen, carrying platters of food. We passed dishes around until everyone had a full plate. Besides the fish and brats, there was a quick Mexican rice dish that Maria had whipped up, plus potato salad, beans, green salad, and all the fixings. I wondered out loud if Ben and Mike had been expecting company.

"You never know who will come knocking on your door up here. I've had car loads show up with no warning at all."

"Sort of like today?" I asked. Mikey the Sheltie was moving from person to person hoping for someone to be a little sloppy.

"Today is a good example. I would have thought you would be out chasing down leads on those shootings you've been trying to solve all summer."

Well, he had opened the subject. "As a matter of fact we were. All these people have spent all day today and many previous days trying to figure out who could have been taking out bad guys and cleaning up our judicial system. Any ideas?"

"Not a one. How about you, Mike?"

Mike answered, "Nope, but if I think of anything, I'll call you right away" he said, his face as blank as a character in a Grant Wood painting

"Well, thank you. I'm sure you will. Fact is we've been trying to reach you for about a month. Where've you been?"

Mike was ready for the question. "Susan and I decided that I should take some time off. I'd just gotten back before the trial and she was all recovered, physically anyway. So I went camping."

"That's it? Just camping? Any itinerary we could check out?"

"Nope—Boundary Waters. I checked in with the rangers when I got there and checked out with them when I left. You'll find about a month in between missing."

The Boundary Waters Canoe Area is 150 miles from end to end and covers about 1.3 million acres along the border between Canada and Minnesota. It would be easy for someone to disappear into it for a long period of unobserved activity, which could include leaving the area. It was a good, hard-to-dispute alibi. I wish I'd thought of it.

"It's that missing month that's troubling me, Mike"—I'd slipped into friendly cop mode right in the middle of my beans—"You have what's called a *motive* in these killings. You have a very good reason to have wanted these people dead, and no way to show where you were when they were killed."

"Yes, that's true. Thank goodness I don't have to prove a negative. I don't have to produce proof that I was camping—someone has to prove that I wasn't. It's a beautiful system, isn't it?"

He was having a bit of fun at my expense, and I didn't mind. His wits were clearly as sharp as his father's. If I wanted to engage him mentally, I'd have to be very careful.

"Let's go over what happened today. You say you were fishing, right?"

"—And we just ate the proof."

"Did anyone see you on the lake?"

"I don't know. You'll have to check around I guess."

He knew that could go tough. Ben's Alumacraft was one of the most popular brands on the lake. Someone will have seen that kind of boat fishing out here every day of the fishing season.

I looked around the room at the other cops and I got the vibe that they understood we weren't going to get this one, at least not today. But I was not ready to forfeit the game. I decided to go all in—just lay it out for them and see if they could add anything that might result in a slip up on their part. I started at the beginning. I looked at my colleagues as if to say, "Hang on,—here we go."

"Mike, you were overseas when the bank robbery occurred, weren't you?'

"Yes, I was overseas when the murders happened."

"You said murders, as in more than one?"

"What would you call the unlawful ending of two human lives?"

I really didn't want to get into a medical or philosophical discussion of when life began, so I let that go.

"Two lives, then. When did you get back to the States?"

"I got emergency leave right away and came back for three weeks. Then I went back to finish my tour. I went Active Reserve just before the trial started."

"And you attended the trial?"

"Only for a couple of days. I wanted to see the guys who had killed my baby and nearly killed the woman I'm going to marry."

"And that was the first time you met Ben?"

"Yeah, and ain't that a hoot. I had never known if I had a dad or not and he turns up in this mess."

"How did you two discover each other?"

"Come on, Detective. Take a look at us—how hard do you think it was?"

"So—you two just looked at each other and knew?"

"Well, no. He didn't know, but I did. That's no surprise. He didn't know anyone was out there, but I did. So when I saw him, I just said to myself, 'There's my dad.'"

"So you said to yourself, 'There's my dad,' and you went over and introduced yourself and said, 'How about we get these guys?' Is that about it?"

"Come on, Dan. You're going to have to do better than that."

"Yes, I am. Let me tell you about my day. I started by having a meeting with these fine people here. These two gentlemen flew here from Atlanta just to talk about you two. This wonderful and otherwise occupied lady flew up here from Arizona. All five of us got together just to talk about you. And do you know what we've put together?" Ben and Mike shook their heads. "I thought not. Here's what we know."

Now, in my world of criminal investigation, you never sit down and tell the suspects what you really know. You tell them what you want them to think you know. You lead them along and try to get them to fill in the blanks in your information. The idea is to get them to believe that you have an airtight case against them and it would be in their best interest to just fess up and take a plea bargain, thus saving themselves and their fellow taxpayers a lot of time and money. You want them to cooperate in hopes of leniency. With the typical street hood, this approach worked very well. They weren't smart enough to know when they were being led along.

These two, on the other hand, were very savvy and, I suspected, wouldn't go along with anything. They hadn't asked for an attorney and I hadn't arrested them yet. So, it was dicey—even if they copped to something right here, I hadn't Mirandized them and anything up to this point would be an argument in court. I'd have to play this carefully with these two, but it was play now—or go home. This would have to be my Oscar nomination scene.

"We know that four people are dead—"

"Six people." Ben interrupted.

"I started the count after the trial. Four people were murdered by very well-placed rifle shots. The first was Tyrone Hill, arguably responsible for the death of your wife, Ben. He was shot in front of a home in North Minneapolis. He was shot by someone using an AR-15 type rifle loaded with frangible ammunition. The shooter was firing from inside a moving vehicle at a range of about 30 yards. Three rounds, center mass. All three rounds were within a one 1-inch circle. That was very precise shooting.

"The next three victims were shot by a prototype rifle using some sort of experimental ammunition. All were shot at extremely long range—in one case, over 1,400 yards. All the shots had some ballistic complication that the shooter was able to solve. All three shots were one shot, one kill. There was one difference in the first two shots though—they were center mass. The last was a head shot at nearly 900 yards. This shot is the most impressive to me. It was taken from an elevated position in a hot and windy city. At that distance the wind and temperature changes could have easily moved the round half a foot off the target. The shooter was skilled and lucky.

"Each targeted victim was involved in the case that included the murder of your wife, Ben, and the injury to your fiancé and the loss of the baby, Mike. Yet, both of you had perfect alibis for the times the shootings took place. And there seems to be another person involved—our mysterious Mr. Cederstrom, who we have recently learned is also a private pilot. You're a pilot too, I understand?"

Ben nodded. "Correct. I've been flying for about 15 years. Why is that relevant?"

"Well, let me tell you about Mr. Cederstrom. It seems that he flew from either Minneapolis or Seattle—in the case of the O'Leary kid—to places that are near the shooting sites, and at times to be on site when the murders occurred. We have no idea of where he was for the first one, but we'll find that out too." I was trying to sound resolute about information I didn't really have—bluffing.

"We know from airport security tapes that our Mr. Cederstrom could have been played by either of you. We know that he's a phantom—there is not and never was a Mr. Cederstrom. He was a false identity made up by you two for the purpose of having someone to take the fall—quite literally, as it turns out—for these murders.

"There certainly won't be any more murders by Mr. Cederstrom in the future because he rented a light airplane from an airport in Duluth today and then, for no known reason, crashed it into Lake Superior. This may have been because he doesn't know how to fly. In fact, the FAA has no record of a pilot's license for Gil Cederstrom. That means that someone was able to get a phony that was good enough to fool the airport guy, Dave—a guy who's seen a lot of licenses. We also know that you, Mike, are an expert in remote control flying, which kind of makes me think that there was no one in that airplane."

I looked at the two of them and they were just watching, fascinated by my deductive skills, or at least wondering where I was going with this. I wasn't sure either—you have to play these interviews by ear and hope for a break.

"That's all stuff we know. Here's what we think—you two planned and executed those killings and made up Cederstrom as a red herring. You found a way to get the rifle barrel and the ammo from BFG and built the rifle. You have the training and experience to do that—don't you, Ben? I also think there is a big field around here that a local let you use for practice. Then you somehow transported the rifle and hid it when you were on your 'Tour of America' vacation you told us about. One of you has the ability to shoot from a moving vehicle and hit a target the size of a quarter with three shots. I think you used the frangible ammo because you have a conscience and were concerned about a miss or a through shot and didn't want any collateral damage. But you didn't miss.

"That's what we know and what we think. Here's what we're going to find out—I'm going to place one of you at each of the shootings. I'm going to prove that you have the skills necessary to have done this. I'm going to prove that you got that barrel and ammo from BFG and built the rifle. I'm going to prove that you knew Davis was paying off Mitchell. And I'm going to prove that this was all about revenge and nothing else. What do you think about that?"

Mike looked puzzled. "Davis was paying off Mitchell?" Maybe he hadn't known. Ben remained stoic. Whoops—sometimes there are things you need to keep to yourself. I'd played a card unnecessarily and that was a mistake.

"Yeah, Davis had Mitchell in his pocket. You knew that and that's why she died."

Ben looked at Mike and slowly shook his head. "That's the first I've heard of that, Detective." Mike said.

I figured that it was the first Mike had heard of it, but I couldn't tell about Ben. Anyway, it didn't matter. I knew that I had the information right. I also knew that there'd never be a trial with what I had. I didn't have anything but conjecture, and a good defense attorney would shoot that down in pre-trial hearings. Nope, there would never be a trial unless these guys just came across and said, "We did it." But I could also see no reason for that ever happening.

Maria could infer this too, and she could see that we weren't getting anywhere with the questioning. I guessed the Atlanta contingent realized it too—they hadn't jumped in with anything from their perspective. They were sensing and sharing my feelings of frustration and resignation. We all knew I had drawn to an inside straight, and now my best move was to fold.

Ben and Mike knew it too. They had recognized my bluffing and posing, and just sat there sipping their beers. Neither offered any comment on or embellishment of my version of the story. There would be no trial based on what I had. And they knew that the only way to prove all the things I said I'd prove was to get one of them to talk. Neither of these two—a father and son who just found each other—were going to rat the other out. Nope—might as well enjoy the view, the beer, and the company. I had to let it go.

Ben smiled sympathetically and summed it up for us all, "Dan, I hope you find what you're looking for."

I think I had, but I didn't feel very satisfied. I was looking for justice, as were Ben and Mike and every cop everywhere. As a police officer and as a citizen of the country with the most equitable justice system on the planet—I felt like hadn't done my job. But I'm not willing to decide that what I believed Ben and Mike had done was unjustifiable. It was certainly as justifiable as what I'd done in that vacant warehouse years ago. Maybe I was feeling what Ben had referred to as "the compromise" of the verdict. He'd said that all verdicts left both sides unsatisfied. Maybe that's what I was feeling and I should just let it be.

I sensed unspoken consensus spreading around the table. We all knew that, as good as our system of justice is, it is not precise. It may or may not be blind, but it is definitely messy. And when it goes astray, it almost always errs in favor of the guilty—to protect the innocent. That doesn't justify murder for revenge but, as a cop, I can understand it without agreeing with it.

What I was looking for was closure, to use that over-used term. For me, closure is about knowing the answers and being okay with them. It's not the same as closing a case—it's more about peace of mind. I knew that I was not going to be okay with what I was convinced Ben and Mike had done, but I understood why they would have done it. They had regarded their motives as pure and temporary—they simply couldn't live with Mitchell's verdict. And I knew they wouldn't be continuing this compromise of their own beliefs. Their private little war was over—they had their closure. I could live with that, and I knew that everyone else in the room could too. These cases would stay open, but would be closed in the minds of the investigators. I let it go. I let them go. The game was over.

Mike got up and said "I have a sweet tooth. Anyone else need a little desert?"

I can always go for something sweet after a meal, so my hand went up. Maria said, "I'm in, what do you have?"

Bushard and Pritchett grinned and chimed in. Mike went into the kitchen and we heard a cupboard door open and close. He returned to the table, carrying a red and green box. He slowly lifted the top, and then tossed one of the Nut Goodie bars to each of us.

"Bon appetite!" he grinned.

I groaned—"Oh, man—" and then we all laughed.

And the little dog laughed too.

# Author's Note

This is a story. I don't fancy myself a creator of literature. I am a story teller and have been for most of my life. I am proud of that. The ability to tell a good story is something I've always loved. I enjoy the great story tellers of our past—Aesop, Samuel Clemmons, and Richard Pryor, to name just a few. They had the ability to make us laugh and cry and enjoy our humanity. They are peerless, but it's something to aspire to.

While this book is fiction, it could be fact. Certainly the American system of justice is the finest and most even-handed in concept. It contains guarantees and double-checks to provide the best protection for the innocent, at the risk of erring on the side of the criminal. That's the way most of us like it and that's the way it should be. Lately, there have been obvious miscarriages of justice in well-publicized celebrity cases, in which it seemed to the average person on the street that money talks when it comes to justice. It has seemed that anyone can commit a heinous crime and get away with it if they have enough money or celebrity. Under our otherwise venerable system, these things will happen. But I don't think we should trade our system for one that is less flexible—that saddles the accused, with some middle-ages burden to prove innocence, rather than the state to prove guilt.

In this story, I have included the use of a weapon that may or may not really exist. Certainly, sabot-type projectiles have existed since the Chinese started launching rocks out of cannons millennia ago. The first were clusters of spears. Later, mortar and flechette rounds were used to great effect through the American Civil War and, in the 20th century, more advanced types were developed. Perhaps the best known in modern time is the APFSDS round used by many modern armies as an anti-armor weapon. The U.S. Army's M1 Abrams Tank fields a 120-mm smoothbore cannon that fires what is basically a big heavy dart. The projectile is made from non-radioactive depleted uranium. It is so heavy it breaches the protective armor of anything currently on the battlefield, without the benefit of any explosive charge. High kinetic energy comes from high mass times high velocity and that makes it practically unstoppable. The projectile itself is only about 1.5 inches in diameter and about 20 inches long, with a set of fins on the rear to stabilize its flight. Hence the name: Armor Piercing Fin Stabilized Discarding Sabot (APFSDS). It is accurate within a 2-mile range, can be fired on the move by the M1 Tank, and flies too fast to be heard. The poor souls in the target vehicle have no warning that it's coming—their tank just blows up. This seems horrific, but war is brutal and extreme, and the United States is not the only world power seeking superiority in this area of weaponry. As General Patton reportedly said, "No poor dumb bastard ever won a war by dying for his country. He won the war by making the other poor dumb bastard die for his."

There is some literature available that suggests that the type of weapon I describe in this story currently exists. There is a .50-caliber round, the M903, which I found while researching details for this book. It's a prized moment, when you find that something you thought you were dreaming up actually exists. At one time, the U.S. Advanced Combat Rifle (ACR) program developed smoothbore "rifles" that fired a single dart or multiple tiny darts (flechettes). This program was officially reported as abandoned due to problems with reliability and terminal ballistics, but who knows? I have no proof and no inside access to what's going on at the U.S. Army's Special Warfare School to support this idea. If our military is working on this, Fort Bragg or the Army Sniper School at Fort Benning is where I'd go to look for it.

Regarding Lake Superior—while there is bathymetry of the lake that shows spots in the 600-foot-deep range, these were too far away from Duluth for this story. There are very deep places along the North Shore, and I've taken a little liberty in making one of them deeper than it actually is, but not too much.

There are many people I'd like to thank for their help in writing this. Mostly, for the encouragement they've given me in the process. A few of great names don't know of their influence on me in particular, but must have helped an untold number of students of their craft. Prior to 1990, I was not a reader in the sense that I now regard the term. I thank Tom Clancy for writing *The Hunt for Red October*, a book I picked up in the Milwaukee airport while on a business trip so many years ago. This was before the movie or any of Clancy's ensuing fame so all I had to go on was the cover and the teaser on the back. I was hooked. It was the first of hundreds of books I've read since. I thank Stephen King and James Michener for their books on how to write books. Mr. Michener's advice to get up and write every morning as soon as you are awake—even if it's crap and you throw it away—was right on the money. Mr. King's point that writing is like digging up a dinosaur—you don't know what it is until it reveals itself to you—could not be more true. Getting up early—right after that 5:00 a.m. bathroom call—and writing for two hours, while not really knowing where the story was going, yielded results. Many parts of this story seemed to write themselves.

No one who has never written—a group that included me—can truly appreciate the work of an editor. While I knew I wasn't particularly literate, I had no idea what a good editor would do for my work. I sent my editor what I thought was a pretty well gone over, corrected and cleaned up manuscript and he changed it from an ugly duckling into a swan. I thank my friend and fellow shooter D.W. for referring me to Keith Hanson of Thatwhich Communications who took my rough ideas and made them sound good even to my wife.

I thank my father and brother for nagging me to keep going, J.A. for her help on the legal system, T.M. and J.M. for theirs on firearms, and D.A. for help on law enforcement procedures. My daughter, who teaches German, proved surprisingly astute with English grammar, punctuation, and general editorial help. She caught a lot of mistakes that were simply invisible to me. Finally, I must thank my wife, Cindy, for putting up with me as I wrote this. She also read and worked on the early drafts of this tale. I only wish my Mother had lived to see this. She knew years ago that I had it in me and she told me so. I wish I had listened.

Finally, this is a work of fiction. It is an invention of my own occasionally paranoid imagination. No person in this work is real and any similarity to any real-life person is pure coincidence, more or less. Except for you Doug—you know who you are.

# *Alamo, North Dakota*

## Minnetonka, Minnesota

For the third time in 6 days he turned the plain white contractor type van off County Rd 19 toward Pete Anderson's house. Before he'd first been down this road he studied the maps and over head photos and had concluded that the road was basically a very long dead end. Once he made from Wilshire onto Tuxedo he was on the cul de sac. The road connected a chain of islands and terminates on Shady Island, one hop past Enchanted Island where the Anderson house was situated. He drove carefully, not wishing to attract the attention of either law enforcement or watchful citizens. Once on the island he turned onto Enchanted Point—the last street he'd need.

His reconnoitering had not only prepared him for the lay of the land and water—such as it is, it had revealed some other interesting information. The main kernel resulted from an electronic sweep of the neighborhood.

As he drove he reviewed the plan is his mind. Park in the drive like any other repairman, remove the tool box from the rear of the van. Walk to the front door and knock to see if anyone might be home. His research had revealed a neighbors Wi-Fi system that included a security camera that was directed on the homes driveway. Fortunately, from the businessman/burglar's point of view it also showed Pete's driveway. He'd been able to hack into the local server through the camera feed and had downloaded a week's worth of that view. The recording revealed that Pete left nearly every day by 9:00 and went—who knows where—until at least lunch time. Two days he'd come home at noon, four he had not. Either way was fine with him, he'd be long gone by then.

After verifying that the house was vacant he would walk around to the left side of the house where he surmised the phone line came in. There he would neuter the security system. Continuing to the lake side of the house, which appeared secluded in the overhead imagery, he would make his entry, find the paper, and leave. This time he'd be sure to take the device off the phone line when he left.

He pulled boldly into the drive and parked the van. Getting out of the truck, he went around to the back and pulled out a tool box, looking for all the world and any interested neighbors like some kind of repairman. The front walk was a wide sweeping curve set with paving stones and lined with a variety of northern perennials. He knocked loudly on the door and waited.

Inside the house was Pete's study—a dark heavily paneled office with two of the three interior walls covered with bookshelves. There was a large desk with attached computer stand, a 40" inch plasma screen on the remaining interior and the final wall facing the lake. The lake view was made possible through a set of windows relocated from a home built on Minneapolis's Lake of the Isles in the 1910's. They stretched from about 2' above the floor all the way up to the 10' ceiling and were glazed with the original poured plate glass. Variances in the glass gave the lake a wavy appearance whether the wind was blowing or not. Behind Pete's desk a dark shadow moved at the sound of the pounding.

The would-be burglar satisfied himself that there was indeed no one home. He would have been surprised if someone had been—he'd seen Pete drive away that morning as he drank a cup of coffee in the Caribou parking lot in Spring Park. But he was prepared just in case. He had donned a false beard and wig obtained from a local theatrical costume supplier. He also had a phony work order for a house with the same address number but located on Enchanted Drive, not Point. He was happy—the event was going as planned.

He walked around to the phone box and bypassed the line. Then he finished the walk around to the lower level walk out on the lake side. He scanned the lake just in case there were any late season boaters out and seeing none he tried the door. As with the Edina house, it was unlocked.

The dark shadow in Pete's office had followed the burglar's progress around the house. The shadow had much better hearing than a normal person and he knew exactly where the man was all the way around. As the man circled the house the shadow moved with him until he was at the top of the stairs when the man entered. The shadow slipped behind a couch as the man came up the stairs. When the man reached the top, stopped and looked around, the shadow pounced.

Sinbad was a 68 pound Flat Coated Retriever. He was 9 years old, jet black and in great shape in spite of his age and spending most of his time indoors. When Pete walked him he went out the side door—unobserved by the neighbor's security camera. And they went for a walk/run (depending on how Pete's knees were doing) of at least 5 miles every day. While he was normally a friendly happy very social dog—typical of the breed—this was an unusual situation. Like many dogs of any breed he was territorial and had a very different personality when someone entered his personal space with no master at home. He was defensive.

Sinbad leapt from the shadow of the couch with a roaring bark and caught the burglar full in the chest. The burglar's instincts had kicked in as he detected the motion and he brought his left arm up just in time to protect his face. The pair toppled over tumbling down the stairs and coming to a crashing pile against the wall at the turn of the bottom step. Sinbad rolled off to the side and the burglar made his escape. He jumped to his feet and dashed for the door—never looking back. He slammed the door behind himself and ran for the drive. As he rounded the side of the house he remembered the phone gizmo and stopped long enough to pop the box open and rip it off the wires. He slammed the box shut and ran for the truck.

# Look for *Alamo, North Dakota* early in 2010
## at
## PhilRustad.com